Books by Madison Night

Single Titles

Little White Lie

I0607494

Little White Lie

ISBN # 978-1-78686-159-7

©Copyright Madison Night 2017

Cover Art by Posh Gosh ©Copyright 2017

Interior text design by Claire Siemaszkiewicz

Totally Bound Publishing

Published in 2017 by Totally Bound Publishing, Think Tank, Ruston Way, Lincoln, LN6 7FL, United Kingdom.

Totally Bound Publishing is a subsidiary of Totally Entwined Group Limited.

LITTLE WHITE LIE

MADISON NIGHT

Dedication

Because you believed in me, pushed me, and never let me give up. Because, no matter what, I never let you down and I always made you proud.
Thank you.

Chapter One

Nikoleta Sydney Bennett navigated the dark, icy roads with care as she cradled the cell phone between her chin and shoulder.

"Yeah, Papa. I know. I'll talk to you tomorrow. I love you, too," she said, then hit *end* and tossed the cell into the open purse on the seat beside her.

"Damn Alberta weather," Sydney cursed. It figured that the one weekend in March she'd have to travel to Banff for work would be the last *real* winter weekend according to the radio's weatherman. There was no enjoying it either, she reflected miserably. She had several meetings at the restaurant the following day, so it looked as if there was no skiing in the books for her.

She let out a loud yawn and fantasized about curling up in her bed back at the Fairmont Hotel. Syd was tense from the meetings she'd just finished at the Banff location of her family's restaurant, Christou's. The franchise hadn't been doing as well as they had hoped and she'd spent the last few hours discussing options on how to cut costs and boost revenue. She had one more series of meetings tomorrow, as well—strategic sessions on how to get more patrons to come in and how to create more of a point of difference in the Greek restaurant market.

She tucked back a strand of dark hair that had come loose from her haphazard bun and sighed, weary, as she rounded a bend in the road. Blinking lights shone directly ahead of her and she squinted, the brightness stabbing at her eyes.

"What the...?" She hit the brakes, slowing the car.

But that did anything *but* slow her down, and Syd's Ford

Escape kept skating along the black ice, straight toward the big vehicle that loomed ahead.

"Oh, shit," she yelled, pumping the brakes, knowing full well it was an exercise in futility at this point.

With a loud bang, her SUV crashed into the other vehicle and Syd's body first jerked forward then was thrown back against the seat. She shook her head at the nice steady stream of smoke that was coming out from under her hood, watching it rise into the air and dissipate.

"Well, that's fucking fantastic," she groaned.

Annoyed, she grabbed her purse and pulled on her black leather gloves. She opened her door, stepping out onto the road and nearly falling flat on her face. Syd latched onto her car for dear life as her high-heeled boots slipped and slid on the icy road. "Fuck," she swore, dangling off the door, trying to regain her footing.

A strong arm wrapped tightly around her waist, steadying her.

"Here, come stand over in the grass," he said. "I almost died when I got out, too."

After a couple of steps, she shook off the stranger. "This is precisely what I needed," she mumbled.

"Are you okay? You're not hurt, are you?" he asked, his voice filled with worry.

"No, I think I'm okay. What happened to your car? Why didn't you pull over instead of stopping in the middle of the damn road?" She carefully navigated her way to the snow-covered shoulder.

"I wish I had time to pull over. All of a sudden the lights started flickering, and the damn thing sputtered to a stop. I tried to get it to restart, but it refused," he said, his voice full of apology. He glanced at her car. "Looks like your radiator got trashed."

"You think?" Syd said, rummaging through her purse for her cell phone.

"I already called roadside assistance for myself. It must have been my battery that pooched out, so while the truck is here, he can take care of your Escape at the same time. I'll pay for the tow to the garage to get it fixed. And whatever damage is done to your car, I'll gladly pay for the repair and the bodywork, too," he offered. "I should've tried steering over toward the shoulder, damn it. Especially knowing there's nothing but ice on the roads. I'm so sorry."

"It's not your fault," Syd muttered, her anger dissolving. His kindness was making it very difficult to be mad.

She glanced up at the stranger, whose back was turned to her while he inspected her car.

"Lucky you managed to slow at least," he commented. "There's not too much damage to the body. It's mainly the bumper and that's more often than not an easy fix."

"Mhmm," she murmured, continuing her silent assessment of him.

He was tall, six feet for sure. He was wearing a gray wool coat that ended mid-thigh on his long black-clad legs. Thick blond hair teased the collar of the coat and he had his hands stuffed into his pockets.

He walked over to the passenger side and peeked in the window. "How come your airbag didn't release?"

Syd huffed. "Because that hunk of metal is an ancient piece of shit, that's why."

He turned around and Syd was finally able to get a good look at his face.

Well, fuck me sideways.

A giggle bubbled up inside her and, although she worked to contain it, a soft snort escaped, making her want to laugh even more.

Brow creased over piercing blue eyes, he smirked at her. "What was that?"

She quickly shook her head.

A moment later, the flashing amber lights of the roadside assistance vehicle came into view. He walked over to the truck as the technician got out. He thumbed back toward Syd's car and the tech nodded.

He returned to her side. "So he can take your Escape to

his garage if you want, and take care of the rad and get the body work done. He won't have it ready for tomorrow, but the morning after, bright and early, it's all yours. Does that work?" he asked.

She nodded. "Yeah, thanks for organizing all that for me."

He smiled at her and walked back to his Cadillac Escalade. He was chatting up the technician while he worked to replace the big SUV's battery.

Syd turned her back on the pair and made her way to a tree, one cautious step at a time. She leaned against it, crossing her ankles and folding her arms across her chest. It was unbelievable how out-of-the-blue, never-in-a-million-years things…could happen.

She could have hit anyone's vehicle—anyone at all in Banff—and whose truck did she hit? Oh, no one but the killer band Divine Intervention's lead guitarist and co-vocalist…that was who. *He doesn't even live here for God's sake!* She chuckled at her fortune.

"What's so funny?" he asked as he approached her, one corner of his mouth hitched in a half smile.

"It's nothing." She nodded toward the tow truck driver. "Is he ready for me?"

He cocked his head at her. "Well, see, you have two choices now. You can either squeeze into the cab of that tow truck with Burly Barney over there, or, now that my truck's functional, you can let me take you to dinner."

She raised an eyebrow.

"As an apology," he continued.

"An apology? I was the one who crashed into *you*, remember?"

He smirked. "I didn't pull over."

"Because your car died, something that was kind of beyond your control…"

"And if I *had* pulled over, you wouldn't have crashed into me to begin with." When she opened her mouth to counter him again he held a hand up in front of her face. "Don't argue, you won't win. So, dinner?"

8

"Um…"

"That is, if you haven't already eaten."

"I don't even know you," Syd said, trying her best to look serious. "What if you're some kind of psychopath?"

He laughed, tossing back his head and exposing a nice, long, lick-inspiring neck.

She blocked the image from of her mind. Those thoughts would lead to nowhere good.

"Well," he said slowly, "My name is Caleb Jones. But you already knew that, didn't you?"

Syd was almost unable to contain a smirk and she feigned shock. "What? Why would you say that?"

He laughed again. "It's written all over your face, darlin'."

She blushed and tittered. "I was trying to be polite."

"I realize that, and I truly do appreciate it."

"I mean, I'm sure you have tons of women vying for even a second of your attention, flirting shamelessly, flinging themselves upon you…"

I'm babbling. Why am I babbling? I mean, he's gorgeous and all, and the way his hair flops to the side and covers his eye like that is beyond sexy, and…

"You're staring."

"I…uh… Sorry," Syd said, turning away, embarrassed. "I didn't want to make you uncomfortable and get gushy," she explained, glancing over her shoulder at him. "Not that I'm the gushy type or anything."

"Again, I appreciate it. Although coming from a pretty lady like you—I might not mind the gush so much," he said, winking at her. "Come on, let me take you to dinner."

She rolled her eyes. "All right, but *only* because I don't have the energy to argue with you. And I'm hungry. You're famous, but that doesn't mean you aren't some kind of psychopathic murderer," she teased.

"You just never know these days, do you?" Caleb remarked, holding out his hand to her.

She placed her hand in his and allowed him to lead her to the Cadillac. The tow truck was waiting behind them, her car already hooked up. Caleb opened the passenger door for her and helped her in.

"I'm gonna need your car keys, ma'am," the tow truck driver called out as he came toward them. "And some information, if you could."

"Oh, right," she answered, drawing her keys from her purse. She handed her business card to the driver. "Everything you need should be on there, but give me a call if there's anything else you require." She worked to wiggle her key off the ring, and added, "Would you mind telling the shop to call the Fairmont's front desk when they're done? You can tell them it's for Sydney. They'll recognize the name."

The driver nodded and shuffled back into his truck.

"Sydney, huh?" Caleb said, flashing a smile in her direction before rounding the big truck to the driver's side. *What are you doing, Syd?*

"So, Sydney," he drawled as he got into the car. "You have a last name?"

"Bennett," she replied, retuning his smile.

He started the car, and, as he began driving along the dark road, he asked, "Well, Sydney Bennett, is there a man waiting for you back at the hotel who would get jealous if I took you to dinner?"

Hands folded in her lap, she fiddled with the bulge of her engagement ring through her glove before answering. "No," she said quietly. "There's no one."

Chapter Two

"So, tell me, Sydney, what brought you to Banff?" he asked, making small talk.

"Work," she said. "And you? What brings a native Floridian to cold and snowy Banff?"

"Pleasure." *Not that there's been much of it,* he thought. Caleb had gotten in some skiing and relaxed, but hadn't really interacted with anyone. It was a personal choice — he'd wanted a bit of a vacation, chill time away from everything and everyone. There was no denying he was flat-out bored, and even though he hated the circumstances in which he'd met Sydney, he had to admit he was pleased to have a beautiful woman join him for dinner and conversation, keeping the loneliness at bay. "I noticed you had B.C. plates. Where in British Columbia do you hail from?"

"Vancouver." She twisted to face him. "And please, call me Syd."

He glanced at her and grinned. "All right...Syd."

"So, where are we headed, Mr. Jones?"

"A little place called Fuze. Ever been there?"

She nodded. "Many times. It's a great place. Good food, good wine, good atmosphere."

A few minutes of comfortable silence and they arrived at the restaurant. Caleb parked and hurried out of the car, making his way over to Syd's side to open the door for her. "Madam."

She smirked. "Thanks."

They walked to the entrance and she pulled the door open and stood to the side. "Monsieur," she said, winking at him.

I like this chick.

"Thanks," he laughed, stepping into the warmth of the restaurant.

A short man wearing a navy sweater vest and a colorful plaid shirt came running to the front. "Mr. Jones, your table is ready." He flicked his eyes from Caleb to Syd and back again. "You brought a guest. How delightful! We'll set up a second place right away. Follow me," the small man said, leading them to a spot near the back of the restaurant, away from the windows.

"Thank you, Jerry." Caleb stood behind Syd. "Can I take your coat?" She hesitated a brief moment and nodded, shrugging the long black coat off her shoulders and into his waiting hands.

He nodded toward her gloves. "Want to stuff those in your pocket?"

"Oh, uh no, I'll keep them in my purse, thanks," she said, struggling to get the gloves off.

After Caleb draped their coats over a spare chair, he turned his attention to Sydney. Her back was to him as she zipped up her purse. It had been easy to tell she had a nice figure hiding underneath her coat—it had pulled in all the right places. But looking at her now... Shit. She had a rockin' body.

She turned to face him and he continued his silent appraisal of her. She was tall for a woman—five-nine or five-ten maybe. Her never-ending legs were covered in a pair of black high-waist dress pants and a silver-gray wrap top hugged her curves. She reached up and pulled a pin from her hair and the glossy black waves tumbled around her shoulders. He took in her face—high cheekbones, soft skin, full lips that begged to be kissed. But it was the impossibly gray-green eyes dancing with amusement that just finished him off.

"So it's your turn to stare?" she joked.

"It most certainly is," he admitted, his gaze unwavering.

"Enjoying yourself?" she asked, planting her hands on

her hips.

Caleb smirked. "I most certainly am." He moved around the table and pulled a chair out for her. When she sat, her long hair brushed the back of his hands and his heart rate quickened.

Behave, Caleb.

"Ah, good. I wouldn't want to disappoint." She didn't give him another glance, just sat and began perusing the menu.

Christ, the woman was lean, sexy and confident. It was a refreshing change from his norm.

Jerry returned to the table. "What can I get you this evening?"

Caleb motioned for Syd to go ahead.

"I'll have the roasted tomato soup." She glanced up at Caleb. "I'm dying to try these chili-rubbed espresso ribs, but there's no way I'll be able to finish them on my own. Wanna share?"

"Sounds great." He looked up at Jerry. "If you get me the *Insalata Caprese*, and bring out an order of those ribs, that'd be great." He glanced at Syd. "Wine?"

She nodded. "Only a glass, though. I'm too tired for much more than that."

He smiled up at their waiter. "Your choice, Jerry, and bring us two glasses if you could."

"Right away, Mr. Jones," the waiter said, scuttling away.

Syd leaned back and sighed. "I love this place."

He smiled as she took in the dark leathers, rich woods and crisp white linens of Fuze, delight evident on her face. "So what is it that you do for a living, Syd?"

Peeling her gaze away from the décor, she looked at him and beamed proudly. "I help manage a small chain of restaurants. We have a location here in Banff, and I've been meeting with the manager and head chef these last few days."

He nodded. "What's the name? I wonder if I've been there."

"Christou's."

"Never heard of it."

She waved her hands in the air as she spoke. "It's a Greek restaurant. You do like Greek, don't you?" When he nodded, she continued, jokingly. "Good, I was afraid we'd have to stop talking. Christou's is a little more upscale, but upscale in the food and quality, not in the price tag. The food is fantastic, and the atmosphere is casual and welcoming. Warm." She smiled as she described her favorite items on Christou's menu and the venue's décor, her voice animated and passionate.

The food arrived a few moments later, and they continued their idle chatter while eating and sipping on wine.

"Oh my God, these ribs are divine," she mumbled, grabbing a second piece and bringing it to her lips.

"I'm surprised you're not using a fork and knife with those," Caleb teased.

She furrowed her brow and scrunched up her face. "A fork and knife? For ribs? You're kidding me," she guffawed. "Listen, I may be a chick, but that doesn't mean I'm one of those who only talks about makeup and shoes, and who's afraid to get food on her fingers. This," she said, waving the meat at him, "is good food, and it should be eaten with your hands. Period." She brought the meat to her mouth and tore off a piece. She sat back as she chewed. "Mmm, so good," she mumbled, eyes closed.

My God, does she even realize how much of a turn-on that is?

He had a feeling it was natural for her, part of who she was, but the little things she did and said, the moans of satisfaction as she ate the juicy meat and licked the rub off her fingers, affected him in a very big way. He shifted in his seat, growing more and more uncomfortable as he studied her.

Caleb reached for another piece of meat and bit into it, hoping that would derail his current train of thought.

Their easy conversation continued until Syd glanced at him and suddenly began to giggle.

He frowned. "What?"

"Your face was hungry, too."

"Oh, shit," he laughed. He wiped at his face. "Gone?" She shook her head no. He blotted his face again. "Now?"

"No, here," she said, reaching across the table and gently swiping her thumb at the corner of his mouth. She held up her hand in front of his face and on the pad of her thumb was a glob of the rub. "Go on."

He raised an eyebrow. "Go on, what?"

She nodded toward her thumb. "Eat it."

"What, the rub? Off your finger?"

"I don't have cooties, for heaven's sake," she said rolling her eyes. "It's fucking delicious—you can't let it go to waste." She eyed him. "If you don't eat it, I will," she warned.

He paused a fraction of a second before responding. "I don't think so," he said, his voice just a whisper, grabbing her hand and bringing it toward his lips. He carefully bit the chunk of rub off her thumb.

She laughed. "Okay, you got it, you can let me go now."

He grinned. "Naw, darlin', there's still one little bit on there." He nipped at her lightly and met her stare. "All done."

A rosy flush crept up her neck and into her cheeks. She reeled her arm back in and concentrated—perhaps a bit too hard—on wiping her thumb with her napkin. She peeked up at him through her eyelashes and smirked. "Was it good?" she joked.

"Baby, it was amazing."

After finishing the ribs, they shared a white chocolate cheesecake and called it a night. Caleb thanked Jerry for everything and gave him a big hug. He led the way back to the Cadillac and helped Sydney climb inside.

Driving her back to the hotel, Caleb reflected on the happenings that night. He really enjoyed Sydney's company. He was unusually relaxed and comfortable around her and he loved the subtle teasing that went back and forth. It was a true treat, feeling as if he was able to be one-hundred percent himself. She didn't treat him like a rock star, even though she clearly recognized him. To her, it seemed, he was an average, ordinary man.

He didn't want his time with her to come to an end.

Caleb pulled the Escalade in front of the Fairmont and turned to face her. "What are you doing tomorrow?"

She pulled her purse into her lap. "I've got a couple meetings."

"Reschedule them."

She stared at him, green eyes wide. "Why?"

"I want to take you skiing tomorrow."

"So I'm supposed to rework my day simply because you want to take me skiing?" she chuffed.

"No, you're supposed to reschedule your meetings because you want to spend more time with me, too."

She burst out laughing. "Ego?"

He chuckled. "Aw, come on, Syd. It's the last good ski weekend of the season. I've had a great time with you this evening, and I'd like to extend it till tomorrow, too. Consider it the balance of my apology to you, darlin'. After all, if I'd pulled my car to the side of the road, even a little bit, yours wouldn't be in the shop right now." *And I wouldn't have met you.*

She sat there studying him for a moment, gnawing on her lower lip. She waved a hand in the air. "Okay, fine, you're on, even though the accident wasn't really your fault. I can cab it and meet you at the rentals. What time were you planning on going?"

"Ten o'clock work for you?"

"Ten o'clock works perfectly." She leaned across and gave him a light kiss on the cheek. "Thanks for dinner and the lift back here, Caleb. See you tomorrow."

"Yeah, tomorrow," he answered, his voice soft.

She got out of the car and walked into the hotel. Standing in the doorway, she then turned back to wave at him and smiled brightly.

And Caleb was a goner.

Chapter Three

Syd, having slept through the alarm, was running around the hotel room in a frantic rush to get ready when her cell phone rang, startling her. She grabbed her sky-blue ski jacket and glanced at the cell, which rested on the ornate wooden dresser.

It was Brett.

She picked up the phone and held it while it rang, letting the call go to voicemail, knowing full well he'd call again in less than five minutes. She sat on the edge of the bed, staring at the phone, waiting for it to ring, hoping it didn't.

Sydney sighed and glanced at her left hand.

Looks so much better without that big honkin' ring on my finger, she thought miserably. She had managed to wiggle the ring off as she'd removed her gloves at Fuze last night, and it was now tucked away in her suitcase, safe and sound.

She pushed Brett out of her mind, refusing to mull over her situation. If she did, she was sure she'd fall to pieces and burst into a salty ocean of tears. After the great time she'd had with Caleb, she was eager to escape the reality of her life for a few more hours. There was so much bad happening right now — she needed the good to help balance it and pull her through.

As predicted, the cell rang a second time in her hands.

"Fuck it," she whispered, tossing the phone back on the dresser and heading downstairs to the waiting cab.

* * * *

Caleb had already arrived at the rental office and was

waiting for her, looking handsome as ever. He was leaning against the small building, wearing a pair of blue jeans, a black bomber jacket and sunglasses. He smiled as soon as he saw her coming and stood up straight.

"Good morning, pretty lady," he said, reeling her in for a big hug.

Syd wrapped her arms around him and hugged him back. The warmth of genuinely being wanted around felt amazing. Sure, Brett acted happy when he was with her, but there was always a stiffness about it. It never appeared authentic. She took a deep breath and pushed him out of her thoughts. "Hey, Caleb."

"Call me CJ, please," He grinned. "All my friends do. I've got my skis already, darlin'," he said, pointing behind him. "Let's grab yours and get going."

Syd glanced at his equipment and frowned. "Those," she said, pointing a white mitten-covered hand at them, "are cross-country skis."

"Very observant," he said, a twinkle in his eye.

"Um, I don't know how to cross-country. I've never done it!"

"Well, you'll learn today."

"Oh God, CJ, are you serious?"

"I'll teach you, you'll be fine. I promise."

She was skeptical. "Okay, but if I break something... Well, *that* accident will be your fault," she said, whapping his shoulder before turning to get her skis.

She was surprised at how fast she got the hang of it, she mused a while later. Caleb had said it was much the same as walking, and she had mastered the flat stretches and small downward slopes easily.

They approached another hill, but this one she'd have to climb *up*. "Oh, good Lord," she mumbled.

"It's easy, darlin'. Just do what I do," Caleb remarked, expertly maneuvering the small hill.

Syd stared at him from the base of the hill and laughed. "It's easy, darlin'. Just do what I do," she mimicked,

19

deepening her voice.

"Come on, what's taking you so long?" he teased.

"Mr. Jones, you come here this instant and save me," she demanded.

With one push of his ski poles, Caleb slid down the hill and stopped at her side.

"You just go up it, darlin'," he explained, hardly containing a laugh.

She scowled at him. "Knock it off and show me what to do, stud."

He chuckled. "All right, you've got two choices here. Watch my feet. You can go up by sidestepping." He turned his body so he was aligned with the slope and began climbing up, digging his skis into the snow.

He hopped down. "Or, you can do like this." He faced the hill and began walking up, turning his ankles in, again digging the skis into the snow.

He glided back to her and grinned. "Your turn."

"I am going to die," Syd announced, her voice dripping with drama, turning her body to the hill. "I'm gonna try the sidestepping. God help me."

Caleb laughed, and in an instant Syd decided it was a sound she could easily get used to hearing on the daily.

Careful, Syd.

"Look, I'll stand right here," he said, putting his poles on the ground. "I'll catch you if you fall. Go on, you'll be fine."

She made a face at him and returned her focus to the task at hand. She began to her skis into the snow as he had shown her. After about three steps she lost her balance and began falling to the side.

"Gotcha," Caleb said, reaching out to catch her. Their faces mere inches apart, he smelled like hot chocolate and Syd's stomach did a little flip. "You okay?"

The feel of his arms wrapped tightly around her caused her heart to thump wildly. Rendered unable to speak, all she managed was a nod.

He helped her to her feet. "Why don't you try the other

way," he suggested.

Syd nodded again. She walked up the hill, making sure to turn her ankles in and dig the skis into the snow. She made it about halfway with ease and, overconfident, she upped her speed, only to lose her balance and teeter backward. "Oh, shit!" she cried out.

Two strong hands planted on her ass, steadying her.

"Easy there, Syd," Caleb said, helping Syd straighten up again. He followed her the rest of the way, snickering.

At the top and at last on level ground, Syd bent over, resting her hands on her knees. "Oh God, I'm alive, I'm alive!" she exaggerated, taking deep breaths.

Caleb chuckled. "So, how was that for ya?"

She stood and met his gaze, smirking. "I don't know about you, but I think I need a cigarette after all that intimacy," she joked.

She noticed the usually unflappable Caleb's face flush. "Well, as nice as it was to grab your ass, darlin', that's not what I meant. I was asking about the way you clambered up the hill."

Syd skied past him and whacked his butt with her pole. "I survived, so I can't complain too much."

They continued along the snowy path for a few more minutes, until the rumbling of Syd's stomach broke the silence. It was so loud she was certain she startled a few birds out of the trees. She paused and glanced at her watch to find it was already closing in on noon.

She caught up with him again. "Caleb," she whined. "I'm tired and hungry. How much longer is this trail?"

"We're about halfway on it."

She whipped around to face him. "We're what? You're kidding me?" She groaned. "Just grab my collar and drag me. I don't have the energy for this. I need sustenance. And a nap. And did I mention sustenance?"

He winked and nodded. "There's a shortcut. Follow me."

After about ten minutes, Caleb deviated from the path and moved between the tangles of trees that surrounded them.

"Um, where're you going?"

He turned back to her. "Trust me."

She sighed. "Well, you've already felt me up, and I believe we've established you're not a *total* psychopath, so what's the worst that can happen?" she mumbled, stepping off the trail after him.

A few minutes later they came to a clearing that overlooked the snow-capped Rocky Mountains.

And about a hundred feet ahead, underneath a small gathering of larch trees, was a wicker picnic basket and couple of fuzzy red and white blankets folded neatly on top.

Syd turned to him, mouth agape. "What's this?"

"Lunch," he said, leading the way to the tree.

She hurried after him. "But... But how did you get all this up here?"

He set his poles on the snow-covered ground and grabbed a blanket, spreading it out on the powdery snow. "I'm pure magic, baby," he said, winking at her.

She groaned. "You didn't just say that."

"Afraid I did." He chuckled, turning his attention back to creating a place for them to sit.

Syd stared at him. This was one of the most romantic things that had ever happened to her, and it came from a guy she'd known for less than twenty-four hours. She blinked back tears.

"Come," Caleb said, taking her elbow and leading her toward the trees. "Let's eat." He took the poles from her and placed them on the ground next to his.

They unsnapped their skis and settled beneath the largest of the big trees. Syd leaned back as Caleb opened the picnic basket, admiring the beautiful scenery and trying to take everything in. She'd never get over how bizarre and sweet this was.

"I hope this is okay," he said, pulling out items and placing them on the blanket in front of her. "I get how much you love your food after our conversation last night, and it's not my first choice, but everything else would've gotten cold and gross."

Syd inspected all the goodies spread out before her — chicken salad, tuna, and cold-cut sandwiches, a container of potato salad and a small tray of cut vegetables. "Oh my God, CJ, don't even worry about it. This looks delicious!"

"Good," he said. He twisted open a bottle of soda and poured them each a glass. He handed her a plastic cup and raised his own in the air. "To surviving the trek home," he joked.

She grinned and tapped her glass to his. Syd leaned forward to kiss his cheek, feather-soft. "Thanks for this, Caleb," she whispered.

He turned to her and smiled, his eyes unreadable behind the dark sunglasses. "You're welcome, darlin'."

They ate in amiable silence, each of them enjoying the view and recovering some spent energy.

"My chalet," he said all of a sudden, raising his arm, "is somewhere over there."

Syd set her sights on the direction he was pointing and laughed. "Where? All I see is snow, trees and mountains."

He put an arm around her shoulders and adjusted her position. "There."

She nodded emphatically. "Yeah. I can totally see it. In detail, too. It's gorgeous."

He scowled at her.

"No, really. It's stunning. That is the most breathtaking pinprick of a chalet, miles away from us, amongst all these trees, that I've ever seen."

He chuckled. "Silly girl."

"Pot, meet kettle," she said, rested against his shoulder.

She was in amazing spirits. Her life back in Vancouver was lost to her when she was with CJ. She felt weightless, relaxed, happy. She closed her eyes, enjoying the wash of emotions running through her, the strong arm around her, the hard chest, his steady breathing, and she drifted off into slumber.

Caleb sensed the instant Syd fell asleep.

He thought back on the past few hours. Syd was a total sweetheart, full of life and spunk and charisma. She was quick to smile and quicker to try to make *him* smile, and that alone told him volumes about her.

But beneath her cheerful exterior he detected sadness. Loneliness, even.

And the fact she so obviously worked so hard to hide that sadness got to him. He wasn't sure what compelled him, but he wanted to uncover what was hurting her so much. He wanted to try to fix it.

I barely know her.

There was something about her that drew him in and he needed to uncover where it led them. He didn't love her— he'd been around the block more than once, and wasn't that foolish. However, there *was* a definite connection, a spark—he'd felt it both times she'd kissed his cheek—and he wanted more.

Much more.

He wanted her lips on his.

He tipped down to the top of her head and inhaled. She smelled like plums. Careful not to disturb her, he nuzzled her hair, its softness making his fingers itch to run through it.

Shit.

His body immediately reacted to her and he shifted his position. She stirred in his arms and rested her cheek against his chest.

Fuck. He didn't remember the last time he'd held a woman like this. Maybe after a roll in the hay, sure, but not random cuddling or anything as intimate as this. Nothing sexual had even happened between them—well, besides the ass grab, he recalled, hardly containing a quiet laugh.

Sydney adjusted him again and let out a soft moan.

Caleb closed his eyes and sighed. *Man, am I ever screwed.*

Chapter Four

Syd's eyes fluttered open and the sleep-induced fog cleared from her mind. A cold breeze wisped across her cheek, and, as her vision focused, her heart began pounding. *Uh-oh.*

She shifted to look to her left and her fear was instantly verified — she had fallen asleep in Caleb's embrace, his arm wrapped tightly around her shoulders. She closed her eyes again briefly, reveling in his warmth. She tilted her head to get a look at him. His eyes were shut and a soft smile played on his delicious lips.

Beginning to cramp in her awkward position, Syd was desperate to sit up straight, though she didn't want to wake Caleb. She began to gently twist and slide out of his grasp when he tightened his grip, startling her.

She met his gaze, his blue eyes clear, bright and full of amusement.

"I fell asleep?" she asked.

"Yup."

"Was I out a long time?"

"Yup."

"Did I drool?" she joked.

He chuckled. "I sure hope not, darlin'. I like this coat."

Syd smirked at him. "It's your fault if I did. You make a great pillow."

He arched an eyebrow and grinned. "I make an even better mattress," he whispered in her ear.

Goosebumps spread across her skin. They had nothing to do with the chilled wind that was blowing on her and everything to do with the not-so-subtle innuendo. She tittered like a shy teenager and struggled to her feet. "Yeah, I'll bet you are."

"I am, really. You should try me out," Caleb said playfully, wiggling himself on the blanket so that he was flat on his back.

She laughed. "What on earth are you doing?"

He waved at her. "Come on. Come try out the CJ Extra Firm Mattress, darlin'."

Syd shook her head and held out her hands to him. "Up you go, stud. We have a long trek back."

"Which is why," he answered, taking hold of her and pulling her toward him, "you need to rest on the CJ Extra Firm Mattress for a moment before we continue."

Syd landed on top of him with an *oof*. Their noses were inches apart and the weight of her body pressing on his told her just how hard he was. Everywhere.

"Comfy?" he murmured.

She gazed at him. "For now. But why do I have a feeling the CJ Extra Firm Mattress might be getting a bit lumpy soon? Right around here," she said, putting her hands on his hips.

The smile quickly left his lips. "You might be right, there, Syd." He reached a gloved hand behind her head and brought her mouth to his. He kissed her softly, lightly, before letting her go.

Syd was stunned. She hadn't at all expected Caleb to kiss her. Sure, they'd been flirting shamelessly with each other, but to have him kiss her? She was hardly able to think. She was dumbfounded. All she knew for certain was she wasn't in the slightest upset about it.

Even though she should be.

Shouldn't I be?

She resisted the urge to kiss him and rolled off, getting to her feet. "Care to try this again?" she asked, holding her hands out to him.

"Which part?" he kidded, letting her help hoist him up.

"It's already close to three," she said, glancing at her

watch. "We should get back. But what do we do with all this stuff?" She waved at the blankets and leftover food.

"Nothing. My friend should be back here in an hour or so, he'll take care of it."

She nodded and began tidying up, stacking the remaining food and dirty plates into the wicker basket. They snapped their skis back on and headed out to the trail once more.

* * * *

Nearly two hours later they reached the end of the cross-country trail. Syd wasn't very talkative — she was both exhausted from the day's exertion and sad that her time with Caleb was coming to a close.

After returning their skis, he faced her. "Can I drive you back to the hotel, darlin'?"

"That would be freaking amazing," she answered, grateful for the chance to rest her weary legs.

On the short drive back, Sydney reflected on all that had transpired since she and Caleb had quite literally crashed into each other. Things would be back to normal tomorrow, with a steady flow of meetings then the long trip home to her family. During her time with Caleb, all the stresses and worries of the past few months melted away and for the first time in too long, Syd was carefree and content.

But always deep in the back of her mind was Brett.

Caleb slowed to a stop in front of the Fairmont. She turned to face him. "Well, thanks again for everything today." Her smile genuine, she added, "It was a lot of fun, Caleb... I had a fantastic time."

He didn't say anything. He seemed focused, staring out the windshield.

"Caleb?"

He twisted to face her. Voice barely audible, he asked, "Can I cook you dinner?"

Her heart thumped. "What? When? Tonight? Like now?"

He nodded. "Yeah. Yeah, now."

Oh my God.

She grinned. "Do I at least get to go upstairs and freshen up first?"

He sniffed the air and made a face. "I'm really hoping you will," he laughed, wrinkling his nose.

She flicked the side of his head. "I do *not* stink. I'll be back in ten minutes."

"If you say so, darlin'," he retorted, chuckling. He added, "I'll wait over there." He pointed to a couple of guest parking spots to the hotel's right.

Syd hopped out of the SUV and raced inside. She stabbed at the elevator call button, impatient, nervously gnawing on her thumbnail as she waited for the doors to slide open.

When she got back to her room, she threw her jacket onto the back of a chair and stripped off her damp jeans and sweatshirt. "All right, so Caleb Jones is cooking me dinner. I didn't exactly plan for this. What the hell am I going to wear?" she mumbled, rummaging in the closet.

Dark green pantsuit? No, too businesslike. Black gauze shirt and wide-legged pants? Nope, too dressy.

"Shit, shit, shit," she cursed. "Aw, fuck it." She grabbed the one casual outfit she had brought with her, which she had intended to wear on the drive home. She pulled on a pair of black leggings and slipped her feet into her black leather boots. After changing into a strapless bra, she tossed an oversized burgundy off-the-shoulder sweater over her head.

She stopped to assess herself in the mirror and groaned.

She hurried into the bathroom and quickly ran a brush through her hair, gathered it into a ponytail and swept it around her right shoulder. A touch of much needed makeup and a spray of perfume and she was ready.

A steady red flashing from the dresser caught her eye as she slipped her arms into her wool coat.

Any bets on how many messages from Brett are waiting on there for me? Any bets on how pissed off he is right about now?

She sighed and, as she buttoned up her coat, her phone

started ringing yet again.

I should answer it.

Sydney closed her eyes and took a deep breath. "No," she whispered.

She grabbed her purse and left the room, the cell ringing in the dark behind her.

Chapter Five

It had been a long time since Caleb had spent an entire day with a woman he barely knew...*without* copious amounts of sex being involved. He'd only known Sydney for about twenty-four hours, but it seemed as if he'd known her for years. They just *connected*.

There was a definite sexual tension there, too—it was there in her eyes, on her lips when he kissed her and in the way her body responded to his touch.

A light tap on the passenger-side window startled him out of his thoughts. Syd stood outside, waiting for him to unlock the doors, smiling brightly. He hit the button and grinned as she got in beside him.

He glanced at the dashboard clock. "Hmm. Eleven minutes. Not bad for a chick."

"The boy think he's a comedian." She laughed, shaking her head. "Now feed me. I'm starving. Someone thought it'd be a good idea to go skiing for hours and hours and hours," she said, feigning annoyance and rolling her eyes.

He wanted to kiss her again.

Instead he waited till she buckled up then pulled out of the hotel lot. They rode in comfortable silence to his rental chalet, neither needing idle chit-chat. He took a chance and moved his right hand from the steering wheel, placing it gently on her knee. She jerked at the contact at first, but then relaxed beneath his hand. She didn't push him away and instead placed hers atop his.

Booyah.

As they approached the chalet, Syd burst out laughing. "Wow. Don't you think this place is a bit small, CJ?"

He chuckled as she continued. "How could you live in something this puny, even for a day? I mean, it's a micro-house! It looks like it'd be a tight fit to get all your stuff in here."

"What can I say, I like it tight," he quipped.

She raised her eyebrows and turned to him as he put the SUV in park. "Is that so?"

He twisted to look at her. His gaze wandered over her face, down her body and back up again. He whispered, "It sure is," and leaned in to kiss her.

Syd was shocked once again when Caleb kissed her, but the shock rapidly gave way to intense desire. His mouth felt amazing and she didn't want him to stop.

When he pulled away Syd took a deep breath and announced, "Well, this is shaping up to be an interesting evening, Mr. Jones."

He gave a little smile and shrugged, winking at her.

She grinned back at him, enjoying how he was naughty and funny at the same time. It was refreshing, especially compared to Brett's uptight nature. That was one guy who had no idea how to have a stitch of fun.

He used to, though…

She took a deep breath, trying to calm herself. She refused to let her mind wander into dangerous territory. She was blessed to have a few more hours of freedom and she intended to enjoy every minute.

Syd got out of the car and headed toward the front door, taking in her surroundings. The two-story chalet was set amidst snow-covered pines, the big trees flanking the house and creating a breathtaking backdrop. The rustic-stone facing was complemented by wooden accents—it looked like the quintessential chalet. In the distance one could even see the ski hills and the Rockies. Syd understood why Caleb had chosen this place to rent, even though it was much bigger than he needed. The place exuded peace.

He unlocked the dark wooden door and opened it,

standing aside to let her in first. She stepped over the threshold and smiled. "Very nice," she said, kicking off her boots and making her way into the big family room. She ran her fingertips along the back of the tan leather couches as she passed.

Caleb moved ahead of her and flicked a switch, turning on the gas fireplace. "Let me grab your coat."

He reached for her collar and pulled off the coat, fingers grazing the bare skin of her shoulder. A sizzle immediately coursed through her and she momentarily daydreamed about the feel of his fingers on other parts of her body. She quickly shook out of her reverie and worked on calming her thumping heart.

Caleb came back into the family room, moved one of the couches out, and pushed the coffee table to the side, making a place for her to sit on the floor in front of the fire. "Have a seat and get toasty," he offered. "I'll grab us some wine."

She sat, enjoying the warmth of the fire, and a moment later he reappeared, bottle of Shiraz and wine glasses in hand. He poured each of them a glass and settled beside her.

"To new acquaintances," Caleb said, beaming.

Instead of clinking her glass to his, she snorted. "I think I'm offended," she joked. "Is that all I am to you? An acquaintance? Even after you grabbed my ass?"

He furrowed his brow. "Hmm, that would add a twist on the whole acquaintance thing, wouldn't it?"

"And don't forget, you were, at one point, both my pillow *and* my mattress." Syd swirled the ruby liquid in her glass. "I don't go around sleeping on every guy I meet, you know?"

"Still, I'm not too sure what I should call us?" He rubbed his chin, trying his best to appear serious.

"And what about that kiss, Mr. Jones, hmm? Actually, what about both of them? Do you kiss all your acquaintances?"

"Most of them, yeah," he answered, chuckling.

"On the mouth? Like this?" Syd asked, leaning forward and kissing him softly. She let her lips linger a moment before pulling back.

Caleb smiled at her. "No, darlin'. None quite like that."

She leaned her back against the sofa. "Good. I was starting to wonder about you."

"Oh, no. You don't have to wonder about me at all." He cocked his head to the left. "So, to new..." — he hesitated — "friends?" He raised his glass in the air.

"Friends could work," she said, touching her glass to his.

They both sipped their wine for a few minutes without saying a word, simply studying each other in the flickering light. A heat spread throughout her that had nothing at all do with the flames. Caleb Jones was one incredibly handsome man–chiseled features, a jaw line to die for, bright blue eyes that twinkled in the firelight, capped off with a head of blond hair she wanted to thread her fingers into and grab while he...

Whoa there!

"All right," Caleb said, breaking the silence. He let out a puff of air and shook a lock of sunny hair from his eyes. "I'm going to run upstairs and change before I start on dinner."

As he walked away, Syd called out. "Call me if you need any help."

"With getting changed or with dinner, darlin'?"

Not bothering to face him, she answered, "Either. Or both."

Chapter Six

Either or both? God damn.

He took the stairs two at a time before he changed his mind and accepted her soft-spoken offer.

That sassy attitude of hers was going to get him into some serious trouble if he wasn't careful. He was barely able to control himself around her as it was — those little comments of hers weren't making it any easier. Her kisses certainly didn't help either.

He peeled off his clothes in a hurry and pulled on a pair of snug blue jeans and a navy V-neck cashmere sweater. A quick run of his fingers to sweep his hair out of his eyes and he was ready to head back down to work on dinner.

When Caleb got to the bottom of the stairs he peeked into the family room prior to immersing himself in chef duties. He studied her profile, from the slope of her nose to her full lips, and along her neck. The glass of wine she was holding dangled from her long, elegant fingertips, her arm resting atop one bent knee. Her skin was golden and her eyes shimmered in the glow of the firelight.

She was beautiful.

He stepped into the kitchen and started pulling food out of the fridge, thankful he had stocked up and had enough in there to make a meal fit for two. He sighed, unsure of how in the hell he was going to keep his hands off her for the rest of the evening. Not that he *wanted* to keep his hands off her, he admitted to himself. He was tired of his typical sexually driven, 'meet girl, fuck girl' so-called relationships. He'd had his fill of those after he'd broken up with his ex, Mel, and it was time for something more.

Even if things with Syd never got the chance to be explored to their full potential, he just didn't want to be that guy anymore. When he was younger he had looked to his parents for an example of what a lasting relationship should be like, and they had raised the bar high, setting a gold standard in his books. He was finally at the point in his life where he was not only ready, but eager to reach for that bar. Besides, he liked Sydney way too much so far to fuck 'n' chuck her, and he'd be damned if he'd add to the sadness that lingered in her eyes.

He frowned and concentrated on wrapping the salmon fillets, sliced lemon and dill in foil, and placing them in the oven. He heard movement behind him and he turned.

Wine glass in hand, Syd smiled up at him. "And he cooks, too," she said, trying to peek over his shoulder.

"You should see me chop, darlin'. It is a sight to behold."

"Ooo, an exhibitionist. I like." She set her glass on the counter. "Let me help," she offered, reaching for a knife with one hand and grabbing a tomato with the other.

"No, no. It's okay, Syd, you're my guest. I got this," he said, carefully taking the knife away from her.

"Hey!" Syd cried. When Caleb reached to take the tomato back, Syd pulled away, giggling. "No! My tomato!"

She whirled away from him, holding the vegetable close to her. He reached out, trying to snatch it.

"Syd, come on, darlin', give up the tomato."

"No!" she squealed as he looped his arms about her waist, trying to steal it from her.

Arms still wrapped around her, Caleb rested his chin on her bare shoulder. "Please?" he whispered at the curve of her neck.

Her body went rigid then at once relaxed against him. She turned her face to his, their nose now inches apart. "You want it back that bad, eh?"

He nodded and brushed his lips lightly on hers. "Yeah, I do. Can I have it now, darlin'?"

She pulled away to get a better look at him, and took her

35

time licking her bottom lip. She glanced up at him beneath long lashes and whispered, "No."

Caleb burst out laughing. "Okay, Syd. Fine. You win, you can slice the damn tomato."

She held up the juicy red sphere triumphantly. "Woo hoo!" she cried.

He plucked it from her fingers.

"Hey!" she laughed. "You cheated!"

"So did you," he chuckled. "Bad girl, distracting me by licking your lip like that."

She picked up her wine glass. "Oh, you noticed that, did you?" she asked, teasing him.

"Darlin', a blind man on another continent would've noticed."

She flushed and reached for the wine, refilling her glass. She tipped the bottle in his direction. "More?"

"Naw, I'm good, thanks."

She chuffed. "*That* I'll have to see for myself, Mr. Jones," she muttered, leaning against the black granite counter, jutting her hip to the side.

Caleb nearly chopped off his finger.

Concentrating was out of the question with her standing there like that, observing him. "So," he said, desperate to take his mind off her curves. "Yesterday you told me all about Christou's, but not too much about what it is that you do there exactly, besides that you help manage the restaurants. Are you an owner?"

"Mmm," she mumbled, taking a sip of her wine and wagging a finger at him. "No. No, they're not my restaurants, they're my father's. Managing them keeps me busy enough as it is. I'm forever flitting from city to city, making sure each location is running smoothly and turning a profit, or at least trying to *get* them to turn a damn profit. I'm involved in working with the head chef—who happens to be my brother, by the way—to create new menus and dishes to entice more patrons to come to the venue. I do hiring and, unfortunately, firing of staff." She frowned.

"As of late, I've been letting people go much too often. The restaurants aren't doing so hot. Not sure why just yet, but we're working on figuring it out."

"Aw, I'm sorry, Syd."

She shook her head. "If everything goes as planned, we'll be opening a new location in Toronto sometime in August. Things should pick up. I'm cautiously optimistic."

He set the green beans to steam. "What other locations do you guys have besides Banff? I'm assuming you have one in your hometown, too?"

"Yeah, we've got one in Vancouver, Banff and Seattle. One in Toronto, as I mentioned, but also exploring opening one in Montreal, maybe next spring or toward the end of next year. I closed the Ottawa location about two months ago."

"So you really do travel all over the place," he commented.

Syd nodded, taking another sip of wine. She licked a drop from the rim of the glass, probably not realizing how sexy the innocent action was. "I'm on the road two weeks out of a month, more or less."

"Your friends must miss you." Caleb took the salmon out of the oven and carefully opened the little foil packets, mindful of the steam escaping them.

She shrugged. "Not so much. I've really only got one good friend. The rest I'm kinda distant from." She pursed her lips. "Life takes you in opposite directions, you know? You end up on different ships. Mine seems to be sailing an empty sea at the moment." She frowned again and stared into the depths of her near empty glass. "All good, though."

He plated the food and brought it to the table. "Your boyfriend must miss you something fierce."

She sat across from him and raised an eyebrow. "We already established this. There is no boyfriend."

"I just can't believe there's no man in your life, Syd, I'm sorry."

She sighed and drained her glass. "Do I have male friends? Yes, a couple acquaintances. But do I have a man in my life, a partner who loves me and who I love with all of my being? A soulmate, so to speak? That," she said, jaw clenching almost imperceptibly, "that doesn't exist."

Chapter Seven

After dinner, they retired with their drinks to the roaring fireplace in the living room and continued their conversation.

They had touched upon the topic of Caleb's youth and all the trouble he had managed to get into. He jutted his chin toward her. "So, now that you've heard my closetful of dirty secrets, it's your turn to fess up."

"Oh, CJ, I'm not quite sure anything I say could top that story you told me about you and your brother losing a drinking bet in high school and having to go in the next day wearing skin-tight pink tanks and tutus," she admitted, laughing hard. "That's a gem."

He groaned. "The scary thing is, I'd bet anything that Pat has a picture of us in those damn poofy pink things. He's probably waiting for the opportune moment to bring up the fiasco in an interview or something, and he'll just happen to have a snapshot handy. New topic, before you ask us to dig up that dreadful image for you to poke fun at. What about you, Syd? What were you like as a kid?" he inquired. "I see you as being a bit of a wild child."

Syd chuckled. "Yeah, eh?"

He snorted.

"What?" she asked, perplexed.

"You are *so* Canadian," he teased.

"What do you mean?"

"That's about the third or fourth time today you've said 'eh'."

She stared at him, her expression flat. "I have not."

Have I?

"Yes, darlin'. You have."

"No. It wasn't me," she said, beginning to giggle.

"Then don't say it for the next half hour."

Her eyes widened. "Oh no. I can't promise that."

"Well, you claim you don't say it, so it should be a breeze," he retorted.

"This was supposed to be a fun night, and you're going to make me work and use my brain. That's not fair, damn it."

"You're a chicken. A pretty chicken, but one nonetheless. You're afraid you're going to lose."

She shrugged. "Lose what? Give me an incentive, then. What's at stake?"

He pursed his lips. "If you win, you can ask anything of me—within reason—and I can't refuse. Vice versa if you lose." Syd squinted, skeptical, and he smirked back at her, egging her on. "And you *will* lose."

"Oh! Oh, there, Mr. Jones! Game on."

He smiled and nodded. "We'll start from…now." He pressed a button—setting a timer on his watch, she assumed. "So, answer the question. Wild child?"

She smiled back, taking off her chandelier earrings and placing them on the coffee table. She rubbed at her ears. "Yeah, I was a wild child. Man, I got into more trouble than my parents would care to remember," she laughed. "In my teens I was just plain rebellious. It didn't matter who, it didn't matter why, I wanted to do the opposite of what was expected of me. I never did as I was told. I was good in school, but only because *I* wanted to do well. Anything else I was told to do, I never did."

Syd leaned back and sighed, content. She loved talking to him, and she appreciated that he seemed to take a real interest in her. "They'd ground me, for example," she continued, "and I'd sneak out a window. They didn't want me to date someone, and I would find a way to make it happen, whether I was into the guy or not. It didn't matter. My mom refused to let me color my hair, so one day I came home with platinum-blonde locks."

"You, as a blonde?" he asked, raising his eyebrows. "Really?"

"Yeah. Suffice it to say it was not a good look for me, and it was *very* short-lived. And no, I don't have any pictures. I hope," she laughed. "Anyways, I gave them a lot of back talk, too. Disrespectful at times, downright bitchy at others. I'm lucky they loved me as much as they did," she reflected.

She took a sip of wine before going on. She glanced up at Caleb, who was smiling softly, waiting for more.

"In my university days and a few years thereafter, I was insane. Capital 'I'. Lots of drinking. Lots of men. Too much *fun*, half of which wasn't actually all that fun, thinking back on it now. I met a guy at school," she continued, her voice tight. "We were pretty serious, but it didn't work out. It turned me off guys for a while, to be honest, but then I went back to my old ways." Syd carefully placed her wine glass on the floor beside her and reached up to pull the elastic from her hair. Her long tresses fell across her shoulders and she used her fingers to fluff it a bit, fully aware that Caleb was staring at her, jaw clicking.

She paused a moment and stared into the fire, working to rein in her emotions. She sighed, recalling painful memories. "Then things...changed." Her eyes began to water, and she shook her head. "Ah, damn it, I'm sorry." She closed her lids tight, willing the tears to go away.

"Baby, it's okay," he said, his voice gentle.

Syd dropped her chin to her chest and shook her head again.

Caleb scooted closer and wrapped an arm around her shoulders, pulling her to him. She relished being in the comfort of his arms, how the concern was genuine. He was strong and reassuring and the sensation of him all around her made her feel like a woman again, instead of a fucking business deal.

They sat in silence for several minutes as Syd composed herself. She appreciated he didn't press her to continue until she was ready. He let her take whatever time she needed.

This was hard to talk about, but she believed she owed him an explanation for her sudden tears.

She took a deep breath. "Nine years ago," she whispered, "my mom was diagnosed with lung cancer and passed away." It was as if her heart were in a vise, the pain gripping her as it did every time she thought about her mother. "She was everything to me, Caleb. She was my rock, my solace, my laughter." She swiped at a fresh tear that had escaped. "My father — my real father — passed away when I was six."

"Shit, Sydney. I'm so sorry," he said quietly, smoothing her hair.

"It's been a long time. It is what it is, right?" She sighed sadly. "When Mom passed on, I kind of changed my life. That's why almost none of my old friends care too much for me. I'm much more reserved now. I don't need to go out to bars or clubs, trolling for fresh meat." She shook her head. "I can live without that, trust me. I don't need to be bouncing from man to man. I did my time."

She picked up her wine and took a swallow, leaning back against Caleb's shoulder. "It sucks, you know. I miss her, and could really use her strength and optimism these days."

"I know what you mean," he agreed. "It's how I think about my dad, too."

"Oh crap, that's right." She frowned, recalling something she'd read months ago in a celebrity magazine about Caleb's father passing. "I'm sorry, CJ."

He rested his cheek on the top of her head. "It's okay. We were super close, and sometimes it still hurts like a bitch, but we've got our memories, right? Those we'll cherish forever. I was blessed to have him in my life as long as I did and Pat and I need to stay strong for our mother. And," he added, giving her a squeeze, "I'm betting you have more strength than you give yourself credit for, Sydney."

She shook her head. "I highly doubt that."

His watch beeped, snapping them out of their somber moment. "Well, good job, my dear! Half an hour and no 'eh'."

"I did it! I did it!" She sat up straight and grinned, trying to infuse laughter back into the evening. "I told you I could do it."

"Sure you did, Syd. You were so thrilled at the prospect of the challenge." He rolled his eyes and chuckled with delight when she stuck out her tongue at him. "So, you won. What do you want your prize to be, darlin'?"

She turned and studied him. There was a slight five o'clock shadow on his baby face. His full lips were curved into a soft smile. His big, blue, soul-searching eyes danced in the glow of the fire. The planes of his face made her ache to touch him. She reached up and pushed a chunk of blond hair away from his eyes.

All she wanted was, for the first time in forever, to feel loved.

Thank you, liquid courage.

"I want you to kiss me. And not some sissy kiss like before."

He appeared taken aback. "What? Syd, I mean, not that I have any problem with kissing you, believe me, but I have a feeling that's the wine talking," he said, voice wavering.

"I'm not drunk, CJ. I may be a bit buzzed, but I can think clear enough."

"Yeah, but..." he began.

"Look, I thought you said whoever won gets what they ask for, and the loser can't refuse. Now kiss me."

He nodded. "Yeah, I did say that. But, Syd, look, I don't want to do anything that tomorrow morning you'll regret. So maybe—"

"Oh, shut up and kiss me already," she whispered, pulling his face toward hers.

Chapter Eight

The moment their lips met, a jolt ran its course through Caleb's system from top to bottom. This wasn't an innocent, almost chaste kiss like the one they'd shared earlier. Far from it. This was different. It was deep and longing, tender and brimming with passion waiting to be unleashed.

Syd looped an arm around his neck and brought him closer, kissing him fervently. She traced the seam of his lips with her tongue, featherlight, begging for entry. More than happy to oblige, he parted them, his tongue meeting hers in a slow swirl that made his pulse quicken and his groin tighten.

He broke away and scanned her face. Her eyes, now the shade of dark jade, were shiny with want. Whether she admitted the wine had skewed her judgment or not was irrelevant. It was clear the alcohol had affected her, and he didn't want this to happen. Not like this.

He brought his hand to her cheek and caressed her soft skin lightly. "It's late."

"I know."

"What time is your first meeting tomorrow?"

Her eyes focused a bit. "Eleven."

He nodded. "Why don't you just sleep here? There's plenty of room and I'll drive you back to the hotel tomorrow morning."

She raised a corner of her mouth in resignation. "Sounds like a good plan, Mr. Jones."

He kissed her forehead. "Come on, darlin'. Let's hit the sack." He helped her to her feet and hit the switch, turning off the gas fireplace. He took her hand and led her up the stairs to one of the bedrooms.

He opened the door and as she crossed the threshold he said, "Sweet dreams, darlin'."

She turned to look at him, her face going through a medley of changes — a stunned expression turned to disappointment, and that in turn morphed into embarrassment, and finally a small smile touched her lips. "You, too. See you in the morning," she whispered, shutting the door.

He turned away from her room, froze a moment and pivoted back to knock at her door. She opened it and smirked. "Can I get you a T-shirt or something to sleep in?" he asked quickly, willing himself not to focus on the curve of her lips as she smiled up at him.

The sexy smirk stayed on her lips a moment before she answered him. "No, that's okay. I'll sleep in the nude tonight." She winked at him. "Sweet dreams."

Syd closed the door, leaving Caleb to groan quietly in the hallway. "Aw, man," he wailed, heading to his room for the night.

* * * *

His alarm went off at eight a.m. and Caleb slapped at the small white clock radio, nearly knocking it to the floor. He was awake anyhow, as he had been for the better part of the night. The thought of Sydney down the hall from him naked beneath her blankets had him restless and had made him toss and turn all night. He wasn't sure if she was serious or teasing, but the thought alone nearly did him in. There was no denying he wanted her — and bad.

He rolled out of bed and put on a T-shirt and a pair of sweatpants, adjusting himself so that the bulge wasn't quite as noticeable. They had to get out of the house at ten in order to get Syd back to her hotel in time to change and make it to her meeting. He stepped into the hall and, greeted with silence, went to wake her.

He padded to her room and tapped on the door. There

was no response.

He knocked again, louder this time. Still nothing.

He sighed, standing outside her door, unsure what he should do. She needed to get up, shower and eat breakfast before they left. He didn't want her to be late for her meetings. He shrugged, opened her door a crack and peeked in to find her sleeping soundly with one arm tossed over her head.

He tiptoed over to the bed and his breath caught in his throat. She *wasn't* kidding. There was no denying she was, indeed, bare under the blankets. She was lying on her back, tilted slightly to the right. The cream-colored blankets skimming along her breast, exposing its soft curve.

Caleb clenched and unclenched his fists, almost unable to resist the urge to touch her skin. Instead he took a deep breath and gingerly plucked the linen between thumb and forefinger, gently pulling it over her, covering her. His heart thumped when his fingers inadvertently grazed her soft skin as he tugged it over.

Composing his raging hormones, or at least trying to, Caleb gently shook Syd's shoulder. "Hey, sleepyhead, wake up." He shook her again.

"Muh, go away," she muttered, grabbing the blanket and rolling onto her right side.

And just his fucking luck, when she rolled over, her back was left completely visible. Not only a small bit of it, no, but her entire back, including the dip and curve at the start of her ass. There was the small ridge of her spine, the sharp angles of her shoulder blades and skin so golden and smooth it just had to have the texture of freshly spun silk.

He twitched.

"Shit," he whispered, his body reacting to the sight of her. He was barely able to manage the surge of carnal desire that washed over him and he had to close his eyes and take a few deep breaths to get hold of himself. He moved around to the other side of the bed and knelt beside her. He swept a strand of raven hair off her forehead and ran his thumb lightly across her lips. "Hey," he whispered. "Syd, you gotta get up, darlin'."

"No," she whined.

He chuckled. "Yeah, babe, you've got to get going. It's almost eight-thirty, we have to get you out of here in an hour and a half."

Her eyes popped open. He stared into them. The impossibly pale green eyes were filled with shock. "An hour and a half?" she repeated.

He nodded.

"Oh crap. Okay. I'm up. I'm up," she said.

"Good girl. Come down for breakfast after you shower, okay?"

She nodded. "Thanks, CJ."

He bent over and kissed her nose. "Not a problem. Don't fall back asleep," he warned as he went back into the hall.

He peeked over his shoulder as he closed the door behind him and witnessed Syd stretching languidly in bed, the thin linen sheet clinging to all her curves and making his heart race. He shook his head as the door clicked behind him.

That woman is going to be the death of me.

Chapter Nine

Syd popped to her feet as soon as she heard the door close behind Caleb. She stretched on the way into the bathroom and tipped her head from side to side.

"Damn it," she grumbled. Her neck was absolutely killing her this morning, likely from a Caleb-inspired restless quasi-slumber and being in an unfamiliar bed. It had been pure torture knowing he was only a few rooms away, and she had pictured him naked in his bed numerous times as she lay in hers. She had to stop herself — on more than one occasion — from getting up to go look. It was a miracle only her neck was damaged from all the tossing and turning she'd done.

She rummaged around under the sink, finding soap, shampoo and conditioner, a toothbrush and toothpaste — all the amenities a guest could hope for. As she stood back up she cursed again at the pain.

She turned on the shower and stepped inside, reflecting on the previous night's events — the way he looked, the way he'd looked *at* her, that kiss... She let out a whoosh of air, not sure whether she should frown or smile, and glanced at her left hand guiltily.

Syd shook her head and leaned forward under the showerhead, letting the hot water rain down on her. "Why the hell should I feel guilty?" she asked herself out loud.

Because, a small and rather annoying voice in her mind whispered, *no matter the how and why, you're still engaged.*

"To a man I despise. Yay, me."

That didn't stop me last night, she reflected, trying to work through the muddle of confusion in her mind. Man, if Caleb had wanted her, she would have slept with him in a second. It had nothing to do with the fact he was in a rock band. Sure, she liked Divine Intervention's music, but she was one of those who liked them *only* for their music. She knew almost nothing about the guys themselves. So it wasn't that she was infatuated with him because of his celebrity status.

More than anything, it was because he treated her like a woman, like someone whose worth mattered, whose emotions mattered. He talked to her, valued her opinion and made her laugh. He was gentle with her and was genuinely interested in her life, the restaurant and her family.

In a brief amount of time, he made her somehow believe she *meant* something to him.

Then there was Brett.

She wrote out the words *Fuck you Brett* on the misty glass shower door, then quickly swiped it away.

She rubbed her face and rolled her shoulders. *I still have an hour or so of happiness,* she thought sternly, *no Brett allowed.*

She furrowed her brow as she worked the shampoo then the conditioner into her hair, her thoughts flitting back to CJ. He was going to make some woman very happy one day, she mused. Too bad it'd never be her.

She turned off the shower, reached out to grab something to dry off with and stared in disbelief at the scrap of a towel she had in her hand. She was hardly able to wrap it around her. She peeked around the shower door to see if there were more. "You've got to be kidding me," she groaned. There was nothing on the towel rack and the open shelves of the vanity yielded no towels either. *There has to be a linen closet or something in a place like this,* she thought. This one little towel simply wouldn't cut it.

She stepped out and dried her legs and hair as much as the small towel would allow to prevent her from dripping everywhere, then wrapped it around her as best she could. She glanced in the mirror and snorted. It barely covered her ass.

She chuckled as she padded out of the room and into the

hall, beginning her search for more and hopefully bigger towels. She tiptoed along the hall, not wanting to attract Caleb's attention in her half-naked state. She opened and closed doors, finding another two bedrooms and a bathroom that had no more than a face towel in it. At last she opened a door to find a treasure of plush white fluffiness.

"Finally," she muttered, reaching in to grab a couple of them, as well as a cozy, fluffy robe.

"Looking for me?"

She pivoted, startled by Caleb's voice, and in doing so her long, wet hair whipped her cheeks. He was wearing nothing but a pair of light gray sweatpants, which fit him *very* nicely. His hair was dripping and his hard chest had beads of water rolling down his bronzed skin.

She raised an eyebrow and boldly asked, "If I said yes?"

She observed him as he took her in, her cheeks flushing as his gaze wandered up her legs, along the tiny towel, across her shoulders, finally settling on her face.

"I'd say I was one lucky man," he whispered, coming toward her. He moved against her, backing her to the shelves, and leaned forward to grab a towel of his own, all the while keeping his eyes locked on hers. "Though I have a feeling you were looking for something to dry you off, not make you any wetter."

She smiled up at him and tried to remain standing despite her weakened knees. "God, you're good, detective."

He dipped his head and whispered against her lips, "Baby, you have no idea."

Through the thin fabric of his sweatpants, Syd could feel his arousal and she responded, pressing her hips to his.

His eyes went storm-blue momentarily and he pulled away. "See you downstairs, darlin'," he whispered before turning and heading back into his room.

Syd stood there a moment more, willing her heart rate to calm.

What. Just. Happened?

She hurried back to the guest room and finished drying

herself. Fuck, he got her riled up so easily. Simply being close to him, or a whisper of his hot breath on her skin, made her clench with need.

"Chill, Syd," she chastised herself as she paced the room, trying to work off some hormonal energy. "Just relax and stop being a freaking teenager."

She dried her hair and finished putting on a touch of makeup when the savory scent of onions and peppers assaulted her. Her stomach rumbled in response and she quickly threw on the robe, needing food in her belly pronto. She'd finish getting dressed after breakfast.

She cinched the belt around her waist as she hopped barefoot down the stairs. She bounded happily into the kitchen. Caleb, now wearing a pair of worn blue jeans and a light blue sweatshirt, was busy in front of the stove.

No one should look that good in jeans and a sweatshirt. No one.

"Oh my God, that smells amazing," she moaned.

He chuckled and turned around to face her. "Omelet okay for you?"

She nodded. "Oh yeah. That would be perfect."

He smiled at her, and shook his still wet blonde locks out of his eyes. "Great. Have a seat. It'll be ready in a minute," he said, nodding in the direction of the chairs before turning his attention back to the stove.

Syd bit her lip and, against her better judgment, walked up behind him and wrapped her arms around his midriff, hugging him. "You've cooked for me twice in a row. Thank you." She released her hold and plopped into a chair. "You already made coffee, too? And it's sitting in a mug waiting for me? You *are* a miracle, Mr. Jones."

"Some would beg to differ," he laughed.

She leaned back in the chair and crossed her legs at the ankles, sipping on the strong black beverage. "Mmm, so good."

She turned to glance up at him. His gaze was focused on her, his nostrils flared and eyes hooded, and Syd's breath caught in her throat.

He wanted her. It was written all over his face.
And the truth was, she wanted him, too.

Chapter Ten

He was staring at the long, smooth legs that peeked out from beneath Syd's robe and had to work to tear his eyes away from her.

Snap out of it, CJ.

Mentally slapping himself upside the head, he carefully plated omelets and toast and brought his bounty to the table.

"Yum," she said, immediately picking up a piece of toast and biting into it. Mouth full, she looked up at him with wide eyes. "I'm sorry," she said, chewing, "that was rude." She swallowed her bite and grinned sheepishly, her gray-green gaze following him as he sat opposite her. "I'm kinda hungry."

He chuckled. "It's okay, darlin'. Eat up."

After she took a couple of bites, Caleb asked, "So, how's the omelet?"

She winked at him. "Meh, I've had better."

His raised his eyebrows, delighted at her candidness. He wasn't in the slightest bit offended, and he sat there quietly smiling at her.

Evidently taking his expression and silence as a bad sign, she quickly corrected. "I mean, not that it's bad. It's very good."

He continued staring and smiling, now fully amused.

"It's exceptionally good, in fact. There's nothing wrong with it at all."

"Syd, you can stop now."

She stared blankly. "Stop what?"

"Stop trying to make me feel better. You didn't bruise my

ego, baby."

"I didn't? Really? You're sure?" she asked, worried. "Because, see, I have this really bad habit of forgetting I work for a restaurant. I'm constantly sampling foods that are created by these amazing chefs, and I compare what the chefs give me versus what friends and such make. I can be a bit of a food snob, and I would hate to ever make anyone think that—"

"You're babbling again, Syd."

Her cheeks went crimson. "Shit, sorry."

He laughed. "It's kind of cute when you babble."

She shrugged, and her eyes twinkled. "Well then let me add that *my* omelets kick ass. So it's hard for anything to compare, really." She popped the last piece into her mouth and smirked at him.

"They do, huh?" he asked, lifting an eyebrow.

Sydney nodded. "Mmm-hmm. Secret ingredient."

"And what would that be?"

She snorted softly. "Pfft, please. If I told you it wouldn't be a secret anymore, now would it, stud?"

"Oh, come on. You can tell CJ."

"Not telling. Nope, no way, no how."

He laughed. "Fine. Then it's your turn to make breakfast next time."

She nearly choked on her coffee.

He grinned. "You okay there, Syd?"

She nodded and blushed furiously, wiping at the dribble of coffee that escaped her lips. "Yup, I'm a slob, that's all," she fibbed, not about to verbalize the effect he had on her. "Do you have any napkins?"

He nodded and tried not to chuckle at how his words affected her. "Right behind you, there's a stack."

She twisted around and reached for one, but suddenly froze in place, grimacing. "Oh, ow. Shit."

"Hey, you okay?"

She slowly turned to face him and nodded with obvious difficulty. "I slept all fucked up. My neck's been killing since you woke me. It's no biggie. It'll go away eventually."

He stood and moved behind her, taking his empty plate with him. "Maybe it was the pillow?"

"Naw, I think I slept in a funky position."

Caleb put his dishes on the counter and glanced at Syd. She was tilting her head from side to side, trying to stretch and loosen the muscles. *I shouldn't do this*, he thought, as he swept her hair off to the side. She gasped when he placed his hands on her neck.

"Here, let me see if I can help," he said, his voice gentle.

She stiffened for a brief moment before relaxing and going limp beneath his touch.

"Can we move this to the side a little bit so I can get in there? Pretty sure your neck needs this massage more than your robe does."

"Sure." She took hold of the lapels and pulled them apart slightly, exposing the tender curvature where neck meets shoulder, as well as the swell of her breasts and a fair bit of cleavage. She sighed and stretched her legs out in front of her, crossing them at the ankle.

Caleb took a deep breath and willed himself to behave.

Fat chance.

He kneaded the soft skin gingerly at first, not wanting to hurt her even more. There was tension beneath the surface, and he gently began working out the knot. He continued his tender manipulation for several minutes before asking if it felt all right.

"Yeah," she answered. "It's amazing."

Aw, fuck it.

He bent and ran his lips along the curve of her neck. Syd audibly sucked in a sharp breath and tipped her head back to allow better access. He accepted her unspoken invitation and parted his lips, lightly tracing along her skin with his tongue, tasting her.

"Caleb," she whispered.

It was as if his whole body had coiled at the sound of his name on her lips. He growled and slid his hands along her shoulders as he continued sampling with his tongue and lips. Syd arched her back and moaned the moment his hands made contact with hers. He bit her just below the ear and she purred, threading her fingers into his, gripping tightly.

Don't rush it, he thought suddenly. *She's special – don't ruin whatever this might be.*

He quickly righted himself and looked at Syd. She opened her eyes to gaze up at him, her head still tilted back. Her lips were slightly parted, her breathing was visibly heavier and her eyes shone with desire.

"Well, that escalated quickly," he joked.

"You could say that."

"Um, so I guess you should get dressed," he stated, backing away. "We've got to get you back in time for your meetings."

Her shoulders sank for a moment, then she abruptly sat up rod-straight. "Yeah, the meetings." She turned to face him, clearing her throat. "Thanks for the, uh, massage. My neck feels a bit better."

"Yeah, no problem."

She stood, awkwardly staring at her feet for a moment, until finally she glanced at the staircase. "Yeah, um, so I should get going," she muttered, hurrying off.

"God damn it," Caleb whispered, combing his fingers through his hair. "Fuck, I screwed this up but good, didn't I?"

He had cleared the dishes and was getting his shoes on when Syd bounded down the stairs and into the foyer. She smiled brightly, but he swore there was sadness in her eyes again and prayed that what had happened earlier wasn't the cause of it.

"Ready?" she asked all too cheerily, sitting and pulling her boots on over her leggings.

"Yeah, ready."

He helped her with her coat and followed her out of the chalet to the Cadillac.

The drive to the hotel was deafeningly silent. *Too silent*, Caleb thought, considering how much they had chattered away the previous evening. Something was bugging Syd and he wished he could figure out what it was. She stared out the window, silently watching the scenery fly by.

He quickly glanced at her again before directing his attention back to the road, and sighed. She was definitely a looker, he mused, but there was so much more to her than that. Her personality, attitude, style, confidence, even her story…the combination of *everything* made her beautiful. And something told him that was the just the tip of the iceberg with Syd.

Which was why he liked her so damn much. To think he'd only known her for less than two days — there was still so much more he wanted to discover about her.

He pulled in front of the hotel and shifted into park, fiddling with the heating controls and procrastinating getting out of the car. He didn't want her to leave. After a couple of moments of silence, he relented and stepped out, moving around to the passenger side. He opened the door with a flourish and she chuckled.

"You don't have to do that for me, you know?"

He shrugged. "I know. I wanted to be a gentleman."

"Well," she said, stepping out and grabbing her purse, "you've been a perfect one. Thanks for everything, CJ. The ride back here, the food, the skiing, the company — everything."

"Sorry again about your car, Syd."

"You're kidding me. Caleb, stop — it wasn't your fault. You were kind enough to cover the cost of the repairs. You certainly didn't have to do anything else."

He nodded. "Well, I'm certainly glad I did. You've made the last couple days exceptionally enjoyable."

They stood there for a moment, Syd's gaze to the ground, Caleb shifting from foot to foot. He couldn't do this. He couldn't say goodbye. Not without knowing if she felt something too.

He hooked a finger under her chin and lifted her face up to his. Caleb leaned in and kissed her lightly, the same way he had on the trail and in front of his chalet. She responded to him, her body tilting toward his. He let his lips linger on hers, hoping that his kiss told her he wasn't ready to part ways.

But when he pulled away from her, Syd's only response was a frown. A cold stone formed in the pit of his stomach.

"Stay," he said softly. "Just one more day."

"I... I can't."

"I'd like to see you again," he whispered.

Her lower lip trembled.

"Will I *ever* see you again, Syd?" he asked quietly, his stomach in knots.

Her green eyes flooded with tears. She drew in a shuddery breath and shook her head. "Goodbye, Caleb," she whispered, her voice hitching, as she turned from him and ran into the hotel and out of his life.

Chapter Eleven

Syd barely made it into her room before breaking into tears. She sank to the floor in front of the bed and covered her face as she sobbed. She was miserable from saying goodbye to Caleb and angry with herself for spending time with him in the first place. It only made everything impossibly worse.

These last two days reminded her of what it was like to be truly needed and wanted by a man. It showed her that she had a right to be treated respectfully, that she had a right to laugh and that she had a right to be happy. Yet even though she *had* those rights, they didn't matter. Her father, her family, came first and always would—and that meant she was stuck with Brett. To spend any measure of time with Caleb risked it all, but she did so anyway. And showing herself that she deserved better? That was dangerous.

"Stupid," she spat out. "I'm so stupid!"

I don't need to be reminded of what I can't have, what I'll never have if I marry Brett, she thought bitterly, shoulders sinking.

But there was no way out of it, not yet. If they found a means to make the restaurants profitable again, they could sell the chain, take the money, and use it to find a solution for their family woes—if such a solution even existed. Until then, though, they were at Brett's mercy. If he told the world what he'd uncovered…

She shook the thought out of her head and reached for a tissue to blot her tear-stained cheeks. Her family was everything to her, and there was no way she'd risk it. Her father, and how frail he'd been looking as of late with all this stress on his shoulders—nothing was worth the risk of losing him.

She stood and moved to the dresser to retrieve her cell phone. She plugged it in, turned it on, and was greeted by the little red message light, blinking away incessantly, urging her to call her voicemail and have a listen if she dared. She stared at the screen and wasn't sure if she should laugh or start crying all over again.

There were thirty-seven messages. Thirty-seven. In the span of thirty-six hours.

Syd rolled her eyes and sighed, hitting the voicemail button and entering her password.

The first two messages were from Brett.

"Nikoleta, where are you? I need to speak with you. Call me."

"Nikoleta, why aren't you answering your phone!"

She groaned. All these years, and still only he, her father, and occasionally her step-brother when he was really worried about her, ever called her by her first name. According to Brett, going by her middle name was 'silly, improper and unrefined'.

Her father, well, he had been born in Greece. And he was her *father*. He had an excuse.

The next message was from her step-brother, Theo, and she smiled.

"Hey, Syd! When you get back in town, call me. I want to hook up for lunch or something. Love you!"

Roughly a dozen hang-ups came next, followed by a message from her father.

"Nikki, it's Papa, honey. I need to talk to you. Brett is very upset because he can't reach you. You cannot do this." A pause, a sigh. "I'm sorry. I'm so sorry. Just...just call me when you get this, okay, Nikki? Okay."

Syd sighed and deleted the message. Her father knew she was hurting, but he was frightened. And he was right to be—she was scared, too.

Still going through her messages, she deleted a few more hang-ups, then she was blessed by another message from

Brett, this one showing the Brett she despised.

"Nikki, where the fuck are you and why the fuck aren't you answering your phone? It's past midnight! You call me as soon as you get this!"

The next message was from Cara—the best friend and sista' from another mista' who never ceased to make Syd smile.

"Syd, I've got this great idea, ya know? You, me, wine. Sound good? Yeah, I thought you'd like it. Call me!"

Finally, Syd made it to the last of the thirty-seven messages, and of course, it was another from dear Brett, less than half an hour ago.

"Nikki, you better have a good fucking explanation for this! I've been calling you since yesterday morning—where in the hell are you? If you don't call me before noon I'm going to have to have a little discussion with your father. And we all know what that means, don't we?" he said before disconnecting.

Syd was nearly unable to resist the urge to throw the cell against the wall. "Asshole," she grunted, tossing the phone onto the bed instead. She stripped out of her clothes and quickly donned a dark green pantsuit and cream-colored silk blouse. She wrapped a gold lariat chain around her neck and began rummaging through her purse and suitcase.

"Where the fuck are my earrings?" she muttered impatiently.

She stood straight, eyes widening as it came to her. She had taken the gold chandelier earrings off after dinner last night while they were sitting in front of the fire. She had put them on the coffee table, but didn't recall picking them up.

"Damn, I liked those," Syd grumbled, opting for a pair of gold and diamond studs instead.

She surveyed the room quickly. "Okay…purse, laptop, cell. Ready to go." She snatched up her coat and swung it on when her purse starting buzzing.

She groaned and glanced at the clock. She had fifteen minutes to make it to the restaurant. She pulled the phone out of her purse and checked the call display.

"Brett," she said flatly, answering the call.

"Nikoleta! Where the hell have you been? I've been worried sick about you! I thought something was wrong!"

She sighed. "No, Brett. You weren't worried about me. You were checking up on me and you got upset when you didn't know exactly where I was or what I was doing." *Fuck*, she mouthed, angry with herself. Why the hell did she have to say that? It would only piss him off even more. When would she learn that giving Brett grief was never a good idea?

"Well, my beloved, you're in a dangerous mood this morning, aren't you? You were supposed to be heading back home today — you're still in Banff?"

"Yes, and look, Brett, I'm sorry, but I need to get to the restaurant. I pushed my meetings to today and I have one to be at in ten minutes. If I don't get out of here now I'm going to be late."

"I called the restaurant and found out you rescheduled your meetings, Nikoleta. You had to realize I'd find out what you were up to, one way or another."

Oh God, he knows.

"Now tell me, *why* did you move them? What reason could you have possibly had?"

A rush of relief washed over her and she sighed. There was no way he knew. Brett was a lot of things, but he certainly wasn't one to play dumb. "I was tired, Brett, that's it. I've been running myself ragged lately and I needed a recharge."

"And I need you back home where I can keep an eye on you! We have a deal, Nikki. Don't forget that."

How can I?

"What were you doing yesterday?" he persisted in his interrogation.

"Relaxing, as I said. Listen, I really do have to go or I'm going to be late."

He huffed. "Fine, go. But I'm not done with you, Nikki.

We'll finish talking about this when you get home!"

"No, Brett. We won't," Syd said wearily as she broke the connection and left the room.

* * * *

The day went agonizingly slowly, but eventually her meetings ended. In a rush, Syd hadn't picked up her Escape from the mechanic prior to her appointments and she had to swing by the shop before heading back to the hotel.

Finished with errands, finished with meetings, Syd wearily dragged herself into her room and packed up her stuff. In the morning, she'd make the ten-hour drive back home.

Syd buried herself in the thick down comforter and rubbed her grainy eyes, yawning. She reached to turn off the bedside lamp and froze, catching a glance of her hand.

She'd forgotten that she hadn't put Brett's ring back on.

She didn't love him. She didn't want to marry him. But it was either that or fail her father, and she couldn't lose another parent—it would be unbearable.

She flicked the lamp off and rolled onto her side, curling her knees up to her chest.

Alone in the dark with her thoughts, Syd began to cry.

Chapter Twelve

Syd woke up somewhat rested, at last able to have had a good night's sleep now that she was back at home in her own bed. She had survived the long drive back to Vancouver and had turned off her cell as soon as she stepped in the door, wanting nothing more than to shut out the world and sleep for a while. *That quick nap turned into a whole night of slumber and then some,* she mused, rubbing at her eyes. She glanced at the clock—it was closing in on eleven in the morning. She plucked her cell phone from the nightstand beside her, unplugged it and turned it on.

"Huh, what do you know, only one message this time," she snorted.

She listened to the voicemail, and was unbelievably relieved to discover Brett had been called away on business to Montreal for a couple of days, trying to close a big real estate deal. Between his appointments and travel, Syd had some breathing room before she had to worry about seeing him again.

However, she still had her father to answer to.

She grunted as she got out of bed and padded down the stairs to the kitchen. Syd's Pomeranian, Puff, followed her, hopping about, eager for some morning love.

"Give Mommy a minute, baby. She needs coffee," Syd cooed, bending and scratching the fuzzy beast behind her ears. "And you," she continued, opening the French doors that led to the back yard, "you need to do your business."

She set the coffee to brew and popped an English muffin into the toaster. Dog treat in hand, ready for Puff when she came back inside, Syd walked over to her CD player in the family room, turned it on and hit shuffle. She was hoping a bit of music would help soothe her battered nerves before she called her dad. Spirits momentarily lifted by the music, she danced her way back into the kitchen to the tune of the Beatles classic *A Hard Day's Night*.

A few moments later, Syd sat on the floor in front of the sink, buttery English muffin in one hand, wrestling Puff with the other. The song ended, the CD changed and suddenly Caleb's voice drifted out of the speakers. She had completely forgotten she had a Divine Intervention CD in the rotation. Stomach now roiling, Syd groaned and tossed the remainder of her breakfast over her head and into the sink behind her, knowing there was no way she was going to eat another bite.

Puff curled into her lap as she sat there listening to the music. Head leaning back against the cabinets, eyes closed, she focused on the soothing lilt in his voice. Goosebumps spread across her skin as she recalled what his lips and teeth had felt like on her neck, his hands on hers, and the unspoken promises of pleasure when his body pressed against hers...

'Baby, you have no idea...'

She jumped up, ran into the family room and turned off the stereo. "No, no, no," she whispered. She needed to get him out of her head, not fantasize even more. She took out the CD and returned it to its case. She wouldn't be listening to that one again any time soon.

She moved back into the kitchen, poured coffee into her mug and was about to take a sip when her phone rang. She glanced at the call display, and picked up quickly.

"Hi, Papa."

"Nikki! I hadn't heard back from you and I was getting worried. Is everything okay?"

"No need to worry, Papa. I'm fine. I meant to call you last night, but I was pooped from the drive and collapsed in bed with Puffy as soon as I got home. How are you feeling?"

"Okay, good, that's good. And me, I'm okay, Nikki, you

know how I am. Listen, can you come visit me today? We need to talk."

She sighed. "Sure, Papa. Lunchtime work for you?"

"Yes, that's perfect." He paused briefly. "I love you, Nikoleta."

"I love you too, Papa. I'll be there soon." She put the phone back in its cradle and frowned. Her father would undoubtedly talk to her about Brett—again. She didn't need him to review what was at stake, she understood quite clearly. After all, she was the one who had convinced her father and Theo that accepting Brett's proposal made sense, at least for the moment.

The thought of coffee now making her sick, she left it steaming on the counter and went back upstairs to shower and start her day.

* * * *

An hour later, as Syd was throwing her hair up into a haphazard ponytail, her cell rang.

Without checking to see who it was, she answered the call.

"Hello?"

"Oh well, fuck, there you are!" Cara squeaked.

"Hey, girl. What's up?"

"Um, you never called me back, *that's* what's up. I was heading over to your place to check in on you and make sure you weren't, ya know, *dead* before I headed to a meeting."

"Oh crap, I'm so sorry, Car. It's been a hell of a few days."

"Don't worry about it, Syddie. I figured you were busy with something or other, but it's very unlike you to ignore me for that long. I got worried."

"It's impossible to ignore you, darling," Syd chuckled. "So, you mentioned wine in your voice mail. I'm ready for it. Lots of it. Does tonight work for you?"

"Hell yeah! Wait…no. Something's not right. You don't usually give in that easily to an offer of wine, madam. I hardly ever drink. What's going on?"

"What? Nothing, why?"

"Hmm," Cara said, hesitating before continuing. "You sound different, too."

"I do not."

"You do. You sound…I don't know…extra tense. Kind of like you're about to cry. I'm coming there right now."

"No, Cara, come on. You said yourself you have an appointment to get to, and I've proven I'm still alive and well. We'll talk tonight."

"Alive, yes. Well — I'm not so sure on that one. I can spare a few minutes, Syd, and like I said, I was already on my way over to your place. I'll be there in," she paused, "two."

"No," Syd laughed. "Cara, seriously, I'm fine!" Was she though? Ever since her rendezvous with Caleb, even *she* noticed she wasn't acting herself. She was short on patience with Brett and her anxiety over the situation had increased tenfold. Tack on that normally Cara had to work to convince her to share a bottle of wine, let alone have a single glass — of course her friend would think something was up.

"Yeah, no, seriously, you're not fine."

The doorbell rang and Syd began to laugh. Still on the phone with her friend, she replied, "No, really. I'm fine," as she opened the door.

Cara shoved her out of the way, hit *end* on the cell and slipped it into her purse. "No. You are *not*. I can tell. I've known you for far too many years. Like I said, I've got five minutes. So spill it," the leggy blonde said, tapping her high-heeled foot on the slate-gray ceramic-tiled floor. Her bright blue eyes shone with intelligence, and a perfectly manicured eyebrow was arched knowingly.

"Damn it," Syd said, leaning against the wall in resignation.

Puff ran into the room and bounced around at Cara's feet. She bent to scratch the pup. "Hi, little baby girl. Auntie Cara has to talk to Mommy, okay? But I'll be back tonight, sweetie," she cooed. She straightened up again and met

Syd's eyes. "I'm waiting. Clock's a-ticking. Tickety-tock."

"What do you want me to say, Cara?" Syd asked, shrugging.

"Tell me why you're acting all different? Did you finally break up with that twit?"

Syd felt like crying as she shook her head.

Cara's eyes widened. "Oh my God. Tell me you didn't get that from the slug."

"Get what?"

"That!" her friend squealed, turning Syd around to face the mirror that hung in the foyer and pointing to her neck, just below her left ear. "That! There!"

"Oh no." Syd raised a hand and gently traced the tiny bite mark on her neck. "Caleb," she whispered.

"Caleb?" Cara said, perking up. "What Caleb? Who's Caleb? Oh my God, Syd, what's going on?" She checked her watch and cursed. "Right when this gets good! Fuck! Okay, I'm coming here later, around sixish, and I'm bringing Chinese food, and two—yes you heard me—two bottles of wine. And so help me God, if you don't tell me absolutely everything, I *will* kill you. And then bring you back because I'd still want those details."

"Go to your meeting, Cara. I'll catch you later," Syd said sadly.

"Oh my God!" her friend squealed again, mouth agape. "You *like* this Caleb dude!"

Syd turned her friend toward the front door and put her hands on her back, gently pushing her out. "Later, Cara. Please."

She spun around. "Okay. But word of caution, babes. Cover up that neck of yours before you see your dad or Brett, okay?"

Syd nodded and watched Cara get into her car and back out of the driveway. She waved goodbye and closed the door.

She stood in front of the mirror, pulling her hair out of the way to better examine the bruise left by Caleb's teeth.

Touching it, she closed her eyes and visualized every detail of the when, where and how. Her heart rate quickened and hot tears stung her eyes.

She didn't have a right to miss CJ. Not this badly. Not when she barely knew him.

But she did.

Chapter Thirteen

"Wow, Papa! That's great! You're getting better and better every day!"

"Not like you, Nikki. You have that special talent. I'm a simple cartoonist compared to you," Stefanos Christou said, affectionately touching her hand.

"No, Papa, really. You've improved so much over the past few months," Syd encouraged, sitting beside her father.

"Meh," he laughed, waving at the canvas. "I do still life... pottery, fruit, flowers. That's not a big deal. But you...you do people. You're able to capture their essence on that canvas. The sorrow, the love, the happiness — you can see it in their eyes and on their faces and in their posture. It's as if they were standing right there in front of you."

Syd smiled gently. "Whatever talent I do have I got from Mom."

Stefanos gazed at his daughter, his brown eyes seemingly filled with love. "You look so much like her, Nikki." He reached up and stroked her cheek lightly, a reminiscent smile on his lips. He pushed his glasses up his nose and returned his attention to the painting before him, dabbing at the canvas.

She sat with him in silence for a few minutes. Even though Stefanos wasn't her father by birth, they were alike in so many ways. It was no wonder — Stefanos had been in her life since she was ten years old. Her real father, Jeffrey Bennett, had passed away when she was six, from hereditary heart failure. Every time she looked in the mirror she was reminded of her biological father — she had his height and the same pale green eyes that had made her mother fall in love with him. Her mother, Thalia, had been of Greek heritage and Syd was blessed with her long, thick black hair, high cheekbones and lithe figure.

Her mom had been beautiful, Syd reflected, as her father carefully worked the canvas with a small angled brush. She'd never had a problem meeting men. But it was the handsome and kind Stefanos who had stolen her heart and swept her off her feet.

Stefanos, also a widower at the time, had a son, Theodore, who was one year Syd's senior. They had moved to Canada from Greece two years prior to meeting her mom and from the start the two had clicked, each fitting easily inside the gaps in the other's hearts, filling them and making them whole again. When Syd had been eleven years old, the two families had become one.

Sydney sighed and took her father's free hand in her own, stroking the weathered skin. "What did you want to talk to me about, Papa?" she asked.

He turned to her and took off his glasses. "Brett."

"Well, I figured as much. But what about him?"

"He was very upset when he wasn't able to find you, Nikki."

"He's not my keeper." She scowled.

He sighed and cupped her cheek. "But we shouldn't upset him. Not when things are so unstable."

Syd jerked away from his touch, instantly feeling awful for having done so. "I understand what's at risk, but I won't have him keeping tabs on me like I'm some kind of dog, Papa," she explained, standing and starting to pace.

"Sydney, look at me."

He *only* used that name when she was very upset, as it would gain her one hundred percent attention. She turned to face her father. He appeared so incredibly frail for only being sixty-seven.

"Sydney," he continued. "I... I know this is hard. This situation... I wish you and Theo never had to find out about what happened all those years ago." His voice wavered.

"But Brett found out and now he's hurting our family." His sigh was heavy. "I wish you weren't put in a situation of sacrifice. I don't want you to marry that heathen, my sweet, sweet child. But your hand is the price for his silence, and I am scared for all of us. What other option do we have right now?"

"I know."

"I wish the choices I made when I was young and stupid didn't come back to haunt us now, didn't have to make you do this." He paused and turned away as she sat beside him once again. "Maybe, maybe we should call it off, and let things unfold as they will. He can tell whomever he wants to, and then…"

"No!" Syd cried out. "No, that is not going to happen!" She rested her head on her father's shoulder for a moment. "We'll find a way to fix this, Papa, I swear."

Stefanos rubbed the bridge of his nose wearily. "This is our only hope of saving our family, Sydney." He frowned. "The only chance I have of being a part of your future, Theo's future. I just hate what has to be done."

She reached out and held his hand.

"Nikki, I'm serious. If you want to back out, call it off, please do it. I understand and love you no matter what, and your happiness means so much more. I won't stop you. I can go back to Greece. I can fight."

"No, Papa, you can't. If you go back, they'll find you," she whispered, terrified at the thought of losing her father all over again. "This is just till we can figure out a different plan. If marrying Brett is the price to be paid for keeping his big mouth shut for now, so be it." She drew in a shuddery breath. "I can handle it."

"My sweet, strong girl," he whispered, leaning forward to kiss her forehead.

"Is, um, is Theo around?" she asked, swallowing hard. She needed to step away before she cried and her father saw the truth—that she wasn't very strong at all.

"No, Nikki, he's not here."

"Tell him I was looking for him, okay? I have to go."

"Nikki?" he said tenderly, tears in his tired eyes.

Syd walked over to her father and gave him a hug.

Hugging her back tightly, he whispered, "Thank you."

* * * *

Caleb cursed, tossing his pick onto the small table beside him. "Damn it."

"What's wrong, bro?" Pat asked, putting down his guitar.

He sighed and turned to his brother and bandmate. "I don't know. I can't concentrate."

"Yeah, you've been saying that since you got home yesterday. You need a new line. Your creativity is lacking."

Caleb chuckled. "You make it sound like I've been saying it for weeks. I've only been back in Florida since yesterday, PJ."

"Well, it certainly feels like that's all I've been hearing from you, man," Pat laughed. "Fess up. What's gotten into you?"

"Nothing," he answered, immediately realizing the one-word response was fooling no one.

Pat leaned back in the dark brown leather chair and crossed his feet at the ankles. "Bullshit, CJ. Who is she?"

"Who's who?"

Pat raised an eyebrow, his blue eyes sparkling. "Dude, don't forget I *am* your older brother. And I'm an incredibly smart big bro. What's her name?"

Caleb's shoulders drooped and he laid his guitar across his lap. "Sydney."

His sibling nodded knowingly. "How'd you meet her? Is she a fan? Did she throw herself at you? What does she look like? Did you—?"

Caleb laughed. "Holy Jesus, man, hang on a minute!" He smoothed his fingers over the gleaming instrument as he spoke. "My rental stalled and I couldn't manage to get the car over to the shoulder. The road was nothing but black ice and she came around the bend and was able to slow down, but not stop. She bumped right into the back of the Caddy." He smiled softly. "Total fluke our paths even crossed."

"You're kidding." Pat chuckled. "Man, you've taken picking up chicks to a new level. You stop in the middle of the road and wait for them to smash into you."

"See, you can learn new tricks from your younger brother now and then, Pat. I'm full of awesome ideas." Caleb winked.

"Not exactly my style, but it may come in handy one day," he teased. "So she smashed into you. Then what?"

"Her rad blew, so roadside assistance took her SUV to the shop and I took her to dinner."

"And then she realized who you were and jumped your bones," Pat stated, standing and stretching. "All becomes clear."

"No, you asshole. Fuck, PJ, I don't even really know if she's a super avid fan or not. I mean she recognized me, but the only thing she alluded to knowing was the fact Dad passed away."

Pat glared at Caleb, his lips pressed tightly together. "Okay," he said slowly. "And why in God's name would she even mention anything about Dad? That's way too personal for my liking."

He scratched his head. "She was telling me about her mom passing away nine years ago."

"You spoke about *that*? On a first date?"

"It wasn't exactly the first date," Caleb explained. "This didn't happen during our dinner together the night of the accident. I took her skiing the next day. We spent the better part of the day on the trails, and then I made her dinner back at the chalet," he said quietly. "We were talking while sitting in front of the fireplace. The conversation was amazing. She's fun and challenging, intelligent and sassy, and fuck, PJ," he said glancing at him, "Fuck, is she ever gorgeous."

Pat squinted at his brother and ran a hand through his

short dirty blond hair before asking, "So? Didja?" He wiggled his eyebrows and dry humped the arm of the sofa.

Caleb groaned. "Oh my God, how are we actually related?"

"You did, you little bugger! You banged her!" Pat laughed.

"No, bro. That's the thing—I didn't. We kissed a couple times, and that's it." He briefly recalled the feel of her on his lips, the taste of her skin, and he was suddenly grateful the guitar was lying on his lap.

"And?"

"And it got really late, and she had meetings in the morning, so she slept over. In a separate room," he added quickly, before his brother asked. "And in the morning, when I dropped her off at the hotel, I asked if I could see her again." He let out a puff of air. "She basically said no. She said goodbye and walked away."

Pat appeared as taken aback as Caleb felt. "She just said goodbye?" he asked incredulously. "That must be a first for you, CJ."

Caleb tossed his brother a dirty look. "She was different, Pat. It wasn't about a conquest with her. I'm tired of that game."

"Well, did she at least give you her number or something?"

He frowned. "Nothing. Fuck, I don't even remember her last name. All I have is a pair of earrings she left on the coffee table at the chalet."

Pat walked behind him and whacked the back of his head.

"Ow! What the fuck was that for?"

"Hello, genius?" Pat said, rolling his eyes. "Call the hotel she was staying at and work on getting any information you can on her. Use your magical sweet-talking ways. Charm the pants off the concierge, use the band's name to your advantage. And if they won't give you any information, then get them to send the earrings back and include a little love note."

"I don't know, PJ. She didn't really seem like she wanted to continue…whatever it was."

"Try, would you? Could it hurt? You're acting like you lost your puppy, so just fucking do it."

Caleb shrugged. "I guess."

"Good boy," Pat said, ruffling his kid brother's hair. He glanced at the clock. "Okay, man, I'm out of here. We'll speak tomorrow. I have a few song ideas I want to run by you, but on this particular topic—I'm going to want a *full* update." Pat gathered his things and let himself out, leaving Caleb alone in the sitting room, with his thoughts of Syd.

He stood and wearily made his way up the staircase to his bedroom, bone-tired. He hadn't been sleeping well—every time he closed his eyes he imagined Syd smiling at him, then there were tears in her eyes as she turned away. He didn't understand what had gone wrong. *They had gotten on so well, and suddenly she turns and says goodbye?*

Caleb stripped off his T-shirt and tossed it to the floor as he approached his dresser. He picked up the delicately woven gold chandelier earrings and admired the way the light glinted off them.

He shook his head. He wasn't going to do it. He wasn't going to try to contact her only to get shot down. He'd send the earrings back to the hotel and ask for them to return the jewelry to Syd, and that was it. No letter. No communication.

He gently put them back and rubbed at his face.

She'd made it pretty clear that she didn't want to see him again.

So what was the use?

Chapter Fourteen

"All right, are you going to dish out the details yet, young lady? I've been here for, what, fifteen minutes already and you haven't said a thing about this Caleb guy!" Cara huffed impatiently, sitting cross-legged on Syd's cream-colored leather couch.

"I haven't?"

"Syddie! Come on, you can't do this to me!"

"Mmm." Syd nodded, taking a sip of her Chardonnay. "Yes, I can."

"Tell me," Cara laughed, grabbing Puff, who was sitting on her lap, and raising her front paws in the air, "or the Puffmeister here is going to fight you for the details! Now, what's he like?"

Syd sighed. "He's amazing. He's handsome and so much fun to be with. He's flirty and sexy and interesting and sympathetic and caring."

Cara snorted and grabbed her glass of wine. "So you didn't like him much, then."

Syd groaned miserably.

"Did you...ya know?"

"No we did not 'ya know'. But God, I wanted to. It was more than a superficial attraction, Cara. He treated me like a woman, not some piece of property. He made me feel desired and happy and tingly. I haven't felt like that in so damn long."

"And what did this mystery man look like, pray tell?"

Syd nervously played with a loose strand of hair. Cara was going to absolutely freak when she figured it out. "Oh, um, well," she began. "He's tall, over six feet for sure. He has blond hair, short at the back, longer in the front. He has the bluest eyes I've ever seen and a killer smile."

"Sounds yummy. Go on."

"He's, uh, muscular, tanned and has these long fingers that kinda put your imagination into overdrive," she continued, reaching over and plucking Cara's wine glass away from her.

"Hey, give that back!"

Syd ignored her friend and continued. "He's also a guitarist. And a vocalist."

Cara narrowed her eyes, calculating and absorbing what Syd was saying. Finally, she whispered, "Shut up."

Syd nodded. "Yeah, he plays in, oh, just your favorite band."

"Shut up!" Cara squealed. She rattled off the facts, counting on her fingers for emphasis. "Guitarist, tall, blond, and good-looking, his name is Caleb... Holy shit! You hooked up with Caleb Jones," her friend exclaimed, excited hands flying everywhere.

Syd leaned back and grinned.

"Oh my God, I am so jealous," Cara shrieked one last time. She took a deep breath and laughed. "Okay, I'm calm. I won't go flapping my hands anymore. Can I have my wine back now?" She adjusted her position on the couch and urged Syd to continue. "So how did you two meet?"

Syd smiled as she offered the glass back to her friend, and began recounting the series of events that had led to her chance meeting with the rock star, and the evening they'd shared.

"Okay, so let me get this straight," Cara said, holding up a hand to stop Syd from going further. "You met from a mini car accident, and even though *you* bumped *his* car, he takes you to dinner and treats you to an amazingly romantic day on the slopes. Then he takes you back to his glorious chalet, where he cooks you dinner and you have an intimate conversation in front of the fire." She shrugged and scratched Puff behind the ears, making her whine happily and her tail wiggle back and forth with excitement. "Not to mention that you guys kissed a couple times. Now, what you failed to mention, was exactly how you got that bite mark of yours."

"Oh, that. Um, well, that happened when he gave me a neck massage," Syd mumbled.

"Of course, right, that makes perfect sense. He was obviously massaging you with *his teeth*."

Syd almost spit out her wine. "No! My neck was cramped and he tried massaging the knot out after breakfast. It was the way I slept."

"Oh, I get it now." Her eyes widened. "Wait a sec. No, I don't. You slept there? But I thought you said you didn't...?"

"We didn't! He was too much of a gentleman, damn it," she laughed. "It was actually really refreshing. He led me upstairs, dropped me off in a guest room and said goodnight."

"Sure, sure, whatever." Cara waved her hand in the air. "Details on this so-called massage, please."

"Well, he was just rubbing my neck and then all of a sudden his mouth was there instead of his hands." Her cheeks grew warm. "And that's it."

"How did his hands feel?" Cara probed, tucking a chunk of blonde hair behind her ear.

Syd smiled softly. "Strong and calloused," she whispered. "But so soft and reassuring at the same time." She furrowed her brow.

"Are you going to meet up with him again, Syd?"

She whispered no and bit her lip, trying to avoid the rush of tears that always accompanied thoughts of Caleb.

"Is that your choice or his?" Cara asked.

"Mine."

"He *wants* to see you again! So why not?"

"Car, I can't. I want to so bad, but I can't. I'm engaged, remember?"

Cara pouted in anger. "Syddie, why don't you just break things off with Brett, honey? You don't love him at all—that much I know."

"I... I can't."

Cara put the pooch on the floor and sidled up beside her Syd, enveloping Syd's hand in her own. "You know how much I love you, right, Syddie?" Syd nodded. "Then don't be mad at me for saying this. This morning, and all evening, I've noticed something in you that I haven't seen in years. There's a light in your eyes again, Syd, a flush in your cheeks. Genuine happiness in your laughter when you talk about Caleb. I'm certainly not one to tell you what to do." Cara snorted. "Hell, look at my track record. I'm still single."

Syd eyed their clasped hands and frowned. "You're my best friend, Cara."

"Well, if I *am* your best friend it's high time we had a talk. Listen, Syd, you never told me why you even agreed to marry someone you essentially despise. You need to come clean with me and tell me what's going on. I can't help you get through this if I don't know."

"I made a deal," she whispered harshly. "A fucking deal. If I married him, my father—" she paused, trying to rein in the tears.

"What? A deal? No. No, no, no, Syddie. Break the deal!"

"It's too late," she said, covering her face and letting the tears that flooded her eyes flow freely.

"Talk to me, Sydney," Cara said softly.

She took a deep breath and sniffled. "It's been so hard keeping this from you, Car. It's a long story and you have to promise not to say a word of this to anyone, ever. Okay?"

"I swear, Syd."

"When Papa lived in Greece, years before he came here, he was married, as you know. Her name was Nalla. Nalla Papandrea. And Papa, his name was Stefanos Papandrea."

Cara interrupted. "Wait a sec, but...isn't your family's last name Christou?"

Syd nodded. "I'm getting to that." She folded her hands in her lap and continued. "They both came from poor families and didn't have a lot when they set out on their own. Papa cooked in a tiny restaurant and took on other odd jobs when he could to help make ends meet. Nalla worked in a factory, packaging food. They were okay until Nalla got pregnant. Later in the pregnancy, Nalla was finding it harder and harder to spend those long days on her feet, and Papa finally forbade her to work any longer, worried for her health and that of the baby."

She stood and paced as she spoke, a confused Puff shadowing her every step.

"There was no way they could survive on one salary, especially when the baby came, so Papa...well..." She paused, trying to find the words. "Cara, he joined this gang, worked for a crime boss, a 'godfather of the night' as they're called apparently."

"Oh no," Cara whispered.

"He was running small, nondescript errands for them at first and he was making enough extra money so that Nalla didn't have to go back to work right away after Theo was born. She had no idea what he was doing to make the extra money. He said that he told her he had gotten another restaurant job and she never questioned him, happy to have the extra time with Theo, I guess. Eventually Nalla went back to work when Theo was a couple years old and in school. But Papa...well, he couldn't quite give up working with the gang. It was easy money for an easy job, mainly delivering packages and whatnot."

"What was he delivering?"

Sydney shrugged. "He never asked. He liked the quick cash, and the praise he'd get from being so reliable over the years made him believe he had succeeded at something big in life. There were rumors of him moving up the gang's ranks, and that enticed Papa to work harder. He brought more and more money home and eventually convinced Nalla to be a stay-at-home mom. One night when Theo was eight or nine, Nalla sent him over to a friend's house for a sleepover. Papa had been spending time at one of the crime boss's homes and was coming home late almost every night."

Syd sat and pulled a panting Puff onto her lap. She buried her face in the soft golden fur and closed her eyes. This wasn't even her story to tell, and yet still...in recounting the details she felt the pain of the coming events herself.

"There were prostitutes there, Cara. A lot of them. Papa, he swears left and right he never touched a single one, and I believe him—he loved Nalla with everything, it's how Papa loves. But these ladies knew he was a boss favorite, so they clung to him. He'd come home with the stench of their perfume all over him time after time. He lied to Nalla, trying to explain it away, but she must have gotten suspicious and, Papa thinks, she wanted to confront him without Theo present.

"There was this other gang member, Bacchus I believe his name was." She turned away from her friend and leaned her head back on the sofa, staring at the ceiling as she forged on. "He was jealous of Papa, how likeable he was and how successful he was becoming. He wanted Papa's rank in the gang, and was willing to do whatever he could to secure it. Papa..." She paused, working to hold back a sob. "Papa said that Bacchus must have been waiting outside the house for an opportune moment, and when he saw Nalla was alone that night, he snuck in..."

"Oh no."

"And he... He killed her, sliced her throat." A tear rolled down her cheek as her heart broke all over again for her father and Theo. "He killed her, Cara, and planted tons of drugs all over the place." She turned to her friend. "Papa came home and found her—blood everywhere. The knife was on the ground beside her and Papa, in shock, picked it up. He was about to call the police when Bacchus walked in. He... He threatened to kill Theo next if Papa didn't leave. He had to take the blame for killing his wife, for the drugs in the house—for everything—and run. After all, his prints were on the murder weapon and her blood was on his hands. He was scared for Theo's safety so that's exactly what he did. He fully understood what these people were capable of and he grabbed what he could, whatever money he could, picked up Theo and ran."

"Oh Jesus, Sydney!" Cara reached out to hold one of her friend's shaky hands.

"Papa got fake IDs, changed their last names and fled to Canada. They kept a very low profile. Back in Greece, he was a wanted man. He still is. The police hunted him for the murder of Nalla and for the possession of contraband, and his old gang was looking for him because they thought he was a traitor and stole from them."

"Was your mom aware of any of this?"

She shook her head. "No, Papa worked very hard to keep it a secret. Theo wasn't even told all the details surrounding their departure from Greece and the death of his mom until recently."

"Syddie, this… This is a terrible story. My heart absolutely breaks for your family… Poor Theo," Cara whispered. "But, honey, how does Brett fit into this?"

"Fuck," Syd ground out, "I've known Brett since university, right. We dated for a while, and honestly things were amazing. I was positive he was my happily ever after, even though I was only twenty-one. But then something changed in him—he became a total stranger with the way he treated me—and I ended it. Even back then I could see he had become possessive and controlling, and a little unstable. He was furious when I broke it off with him, furious because *I* was the one to call it quits. He felt that it somehow undermined him, that he wasn't in control of the relationship. How dare *I* shun *him*? He's never been able to let it go, you get how he is. Eleven years and he can't let it go. He'd call me now and then, show up on my doorstep unannounced, and has tried to force me to get back together with him. He told me years ago he'd find a way to not only get back together with me, but also to get back at me for what I did."

Cara drained her glass. "Okay, so we've established Brett is a freak of nature, but how does this tie in with your dad's story?"

"Brett comes from a highly affluent, highly influential family. I don't know how, but he managed to do some digging — very deep digging by the looks of it — and found out about Papa's history. He knows *everything*, all the gory details, and is threatening to tell the government and have Papa extradited." She twisted her hands in her lap.

"Oh, shit."

"My father is still a wanted man in Greece, Cara. And Bacchus, well, Theo and I did a bit of our own digging. He's the godfather, or whatever they call it, of a mafia household now, and has a great deal of power. Papa can't go back to Greece — Bacchus would hunt him and have him killed. It's not like Papa is a real threat to him at this point, but Theo and I are positive he'd hurt him just for the sport of it. We're stuck, and Brett is well aware of that and is making the most of it. He finally has the leverage he needed to regain the control over me he'd lost a decade ago. He could, at last, get what he always wanted — me, groveling to him, doing anything and everything he asked of me. He said he would keep quiet about it, and that, I quote, 'my drug-dealer, wife-killing father' can stay free in Canada, but only if I agreed to marry him."

"That bastard," Cara spat, standing suddenly, her face furious.

"Papa said he'd never ask me to agree to Brett's terms. But it's the only way. Forget about the fact the legal costs would cripple us right now, more importantly I am so terrified of this coming to light — Cara, Papa doesn't seem well lately. He's been getting progressively worse, and I don't think he'd survive it."

Her breath shuddered and tears traced along her cheeks. Cara sat again and reached an arm around her, hugging her tightly. "Syd, honey, I'm stunned by all this. I don't know what to say. I can only imagine how trapped the lot of you feel."

"I've already lost two parents, Car. I can't lose Papa, too," Syd sobbed. "I just can't."

Chapter Fifteen

Syd had opened her front door and was about to head out to the restaurant when her phone rang. She groaned and moved back into the foyer, dropping her purse on the floor with a *thunk* and muttering under her breath. She ran into the kitchen and snatched up the receiver.

"Hello?"

"I'm coming over tonight, Nikoleta," Brett said flatly.

"Is that right?" she asked, her voice unintentionally thick with impatience.

He huffed. "I'll be there at seven."

"That's fine, but you can't stay long. I'm meeting Cara for dinner," she lied.

"I'll stay as long as I want to," he snapped and abruptly hung up.

Syd put the receiver back in the cradle and stuck her tongue out at the phone. She kneeled and scratched her little dog, taking the small face in her hands. She nuzzled Puff nose to nose and sighed. "Aw, Puffy, what am I gonna do?"

Puff wagged her fluffy tail and licked Syd's face happily.

She laughed and got to her feet. "Now, now. Don't mess with the makeup."

Syd picked up her purse. She let out a big sigh and headed out to Christou's in the balmy March weather.

* * * *

"Theo!"

"I'm sorry I'm late, sis. I don't just wake up this beautiful, you know." He struck a pose and pretended to flip hair over his shoulder, all diva-like.

"Aw, I appreciate how much time you spend getting pretty for me," she laughed. "Now come here and give me some sugar." Syd spread her arms out wide, inviting him in for a hug.

He marched straight for her and picked her up, twirling her around in his strong arms, before gently setting her on solid ground again.

"Are you ever going to stop doing that?" she asked, laughing.

His brown eyes twinkled as he grinned at her. He planted a kiss on her forehead. "Nope. Never. It's an honor reserved especially for you."

"Thank God for that. I wouldn't wish being swung around in mid-air like that on anyone else."

He winked at her. "Being my little sister has its perks."

"So does having you for a big brother," she commented, smiling softly. "I need some sort of happy in my life right about now, and I knew I could always count on you."

Theo glimpsed at her, a deep frown creasing his brow. "Brett," he simply stated, knowing that was the cause for her misery. He nodded at her hand. "Not wearing the engagement ring, I see."

"Oh, shit," she whispered. She had totally forgotten to put the ring back on after her time with Caleb.

"Aw, Syd, just break things off." When she gaped at her brother, he continued. "Papa won't die, I promise you. He's much stronger than you think. If Brett chirps after you break it off we'll close Seattle. Banff, too, if we need, take the money and get some legal help. We'll go with Papa to Greece and…"

"Are you *kidding* me?" Syd asked, stunned that her brother even suggested what he did. "If we go to Greece, if this story comes out, Bacchus and his goons will be right there to kill Papa!"

Theo's face went stony. "So let that bastard come."

"Theo!"

"What? I'll kill that son of a bitch with my bare hands before he has a chance to get to Papa. He'll pay for what he's done."

Heart racing, Syd gazed at her brother in a whole new light. She had been so busy moaning and groaning over what this situation had done to *her* life—and yet, Theo had found out only three months ago that his biological mother had been brutally and senselessly murdered. Papa, he'd had to relive the horror of the day he had found his wife. What *she* had to do to protect her family… That was *nothing*.

"Come," she said softly, taking Theo by the hand and leading him to one of the darkened corner booths in the restaurant. It was only eleven in the morning and the venue wasn't open yet. Syd heard the cooks busily moving in the back, banging pots and pans, chatting and getting prepared for the evening ahead, but they weren't within earshot so she and her brother could speak freely.

"Theo, please, *please* don't let this knowledge change who you are. Don't think those thoughts. We need to protect Papa—*here*. Not in Greece. What you were thinking, you have to get that out of your head."

"But…"

"Do you believe for a moment if Papa heard what you said that he would be proud? That it would make him feel better? That it would be helping the situation at all?"

"No," he mumbled, dropping his chin to his chest in resignation.

"What *does* help Papa is your boundless positivity. You're always sure things will turn out right. You've always been like that, no matter what this world has thrown your way. Don't lose that, Theo. Don't lose yourself in the hate and anger." She reached over and took her brother's hand. "We need our goofball, ray of sunshine, happy-go-lucky, nice-guy Theo back. Can you please bring him back?"

His face a mask of pain, he answered, "It's hard. I have to protect you and Papa, Syd."

"It's not your responsibility, Theo. And I know… I know it's hard for all of us, in a whole lot of different ways. I'm marrying Brett — that is a burden I'm willing to take on for now. But I'll only have the strength to do it and make it through if I have my brother back."

He sighed. "He's an ass for even suggesting this, you know."

"He's more of an ass for thinking he can somehow make me fall in love with him again."

"Oh my God. What if you *do* fall in love with Brett?" Theo asked, horrified.

Syd chuckled. "Not a chance. If the way he's acting now is indicative of what he perceives romance to be all about, it's a wonder he doesn't have women lined up on his doorstep, armed with guns. No," she said, clenching her jaw. "I'll never be his trophy wife, I'll never let him control me like that and I'll never fall in love with him, that's for sure."

"All right, Syd, I hear you loud and clear." He smiled softly at his sister and squeezed her hand. "Thanks for the pep talk, mom, slash sister, slash motivational speaker, slash therapist, slash dork."

She grinned back at him. "You're welcome, brother, slash fellow dork, slash he who is not-so-secretly in love with Cara…"

His eyes widened briefly. "And, new topic!"

"New topic," Syd laughed.

"Let's talk food. It *is* the reason you're here after all." He popped out of his chair and headed toward the back of the restaurant. A moment later he was on his way back, two menus and two pads of paper in hand.

Syd pulled a couple of pens out of her purse as her brother navigated the empty tables. This was one part of her work she enjoyed — discussing a menu revision, coming up with modern twists on classic recipes, trying to spice things up a bit. Theo had graduated from George Brown's culinary program in Toronto, and his vision and creativity were renowned in the Canadian marketplace. He'd been offered position after position at various hotels and resorts, and yet he remained Christou's top chef, earning less than half of what he might elsewhere.

"Okay," he said, sitting opposite Sydney once again. "Let's do this. I was thinking for appetizers—getting rid of the humus. It hasn't been the greatest seller, and to be honest it's *so* boring. What about adding something different and fun like...like Greek salad tacos, or tzatziki flatbread pizza somethings?" he suggested, his voice bubbling with culinary excitement.

"You know," Syd said, wiggling her pen at him, "with all the health kicks going on, what about getting rid of the deep-fried calamari and replacing it with a marinated, grilled version?"

The front door opened and a courier rushed in. "Where can I find a..." He paused and consulted the thick padded envelope in his hands. "A Sydney Bennett?"

"That's me," Syd said, waving the courier over. She signed for the package and thanked him as he ran back out to his truck.

"What's that?" Theo asked, peering across the table.

She shrugged. "Not a clue. I wasn't expecting anything." She ripped open the envelope and pulled out a small gold box with a business card tucked under a red velvet ribbon. She plucked the card out and eyed it. It was from the Fairmont in Banff.

"What is it, Syd?"

"Something from the Fairmont," she said, shrugging again. "Since when do they send out gifts?"

She lifted the lid off the box and peered inside. Her heart began pumping furiously. Nestled in rose-colored tissue paper was one of the chandelier earrings she had left at Caleb's chalet. A wash of emotion overtook her and she immediately tried to rein it in.

"What, what, what?" Theo asked. "What'd you get?"

She held up the earring, dangling it in mid-air.

"Someone sent you earrings?"

"Just one."

He winged an eyebrow. "*One* earring? Isn't that kind of, oh, you know, useless?"

She grinned. "What can I say? I'm special."

"Yes, Syd. Yes, you are." He crossed his eyes and tapped his temple, tongue lolling out the side of his mouth.

Syd threw back her head and laughed. "Jerk. I lost a pair of earrings at the hotel," she fibbed. "I guess they only found one, so sent it back."

He waved his hand in the air. "Congrats on getting an earring back, then. This is cause for celebration, and I'm hungry. Let me grab some food from the kitchen." He kissed the top of Syd's head as he walked past her on the way to the back.

As soon as Theo was out of sight, Sydney opened the box again and picked up the second business card that was hidden inside, tucked under the jewelry. She took a deep breath and flipped it over, her heart thundering in her ears. There was a phone number and, beneath that, a simple line.

I'm holding the other one ransom till you call me.

Chapter Sixteen

Syd had been home and settled for less than five minutes when the doorbell rang.

"Fuck," she muttered, intuitively knowing exactly who was waiting for her on the other side of that white door. She tucked a barking Puff under her arm and moved into the foyer.

She opened the door and frowned. "It's not even six o'clock, Brett," she said, exasperated. "You're not supposed to be here till—"

"Yes, well, my schedule changed," he interrupted.

"And you couldn't have at least called?"

"Why should I?" He pushed his way past her into the house.

"Well, gee, come right on in," Syd said, dramatically rolling her eyes. She closed the door behind him then bent to put Puff back on the floor. The minute her tiny paws touched the tile she shot off after Brett, barking and yapping up at him, trying to nip at his toes.

"Nikoleta, when are you going to get rid of this stupid thing?" Brett asked angrily, trying to get away from the frisky little Pomeranian.

"Never," Syd answered, her voice matter-of-fact.

"Let's see if I can speed that up," Brett said, bringing his foot back, threatening to kick Puff.

Syd scooped her up and cradled her protectively. "Don't even think about it, Hudson," she ground out through gritted teeth.

He kept his eyes on her, his face set in stone. Silence echoed through the foyer as they stared at each other.

Syd studied Brett. There had been a time, many years ago, when she'd considered him handsome, and technically speaking he still was in the physical sense. Back in their university years Brett Hudson was self-assured and exciting, rich and eager to flaunt it. Sydney had easily fallen for Brett's bright blue eyes and confident smile. He had been sweet, funny, romantic and she was sure she'd been in love with him. Brett's mother and sister loved her dearly and everyone was certain they would end up getting married one day. Nearly a year into their courtship, though, Brett had changed. She was never really sure what had happened or what had triggered such a sudden change, but he had, seemingly overnight, become someone she couldn't allow herself to be with, no matter how strongly she felt for him. A controlling, nearly abusive nature had surfaced, and Syd's emotions had done an about-face. She'd gotten the hell out of their relationship and away from him.

Funny how things work out.

"Where's your engagement ring?" he demanded, startling her out of her reverie.

"I took it in to get cleaned." She prayed he'd accept the lie without question.

He grunted in response. "We need to talk about last week and your business trip to Banff. All those times I called and you didn't answer — where were you, really?"

"I told you this already, Brett. I was getting some R and R in. I was wiped out and I took a chill day, which meant not only tearing myself away from the restaurants, but also tearing myself away from my phone." Syd bent and put the little dog back on the floor, who immediately ran to Brett and resumed her barking. "Puff, no," Sydney whispered.

The dog glanced at her owner and ceased immediately. Puff padded over to Syd and sat beside her, guarding her and glaring at Brett menacingly, letting out a soft chuff now and then. Once false move and she'd be set right off again. "Good girl," Syd murmured as she leaned to stroke Puff's back.

Brett gawked at her, eyes slightly bugged out. "You mean you could've controlled that fluffy rat every time I've been here?"

She nodded. "Of course."

"And you didn't? You just let her try to bite me?" he asked incredulously.

Syd smirked. "Of course."

"Let's get something straight here, Nikki," Brett said through clenched teeth, taking a step toward her. "You *belong* to me. You do what I say, when I say."

As he approached her she backed up, matching his pace. "You go where I tell you to go."

Her back hit the wall and she froze, realizing she had nowhere else to escape.

Puff let out a low warning growl.

"You're going to be my wife, and you will act as such. No more of this bullshit. You're mine, Nikki," he said, pressing up against her. "Mine." He lowered his mouth to hers, kissing her and thrusting his tongue inside.

Syd bit down...hard.

Brett pulled away, shocked at the pain.

"Get your fucking hands off me, Brett. I'm not your wife yet and I'm most certainly *not* your property. I don't want you touching me, kissing me, or making any type of advance on me until I say *I do*." She took a step forward, making Brett back up this time. Puff blew air out of her nostrils, seemingly in support of Syd's words.

Syd stood straighter and held her head high. "Get out."

He leered at her angrily. "You're lucky I've always loved the fire in you, Nikki. Otherwise, right about now, I'd be going to your dear father to tell him to start packing for Greece and pull the plug on the whole thing." He spat blood from his bitten tongue onto the floor. "And you know what that means, don't you?"

Her shoulders sagged. "Yes, Brett, I do, believe me." She shook her head and sighed in resignation. "Look, I'm trying here, I really am. You have to admit the situation isn't exactly...orthodox. What you're doing, Brett, deep inside somewhere you have to understand this isn't right."

"The only thing that matters is I get what I want. Learn to control that attitude of yours, or it *will* be your undoing—and your family's."

"Well, if you want me, all of me, my heart and soul, you can't be like this. I see how you are, Brett. I understand you like to be in control. You're in charge, I get it. But you forcing yourself on me like you did, it doesn't make things better or easier. It pushes me even further away."

"And when we're married?" he asked stiffly.

"When we're husband and wife, we'll act like husband and wife," she answered, her stomach roiling at the thought. "Maybe, by that point, things will have changed."

That placated him for the moment, and his boiling anger was reduced to a mere simmer. "I still have a right to keep tabs on where you are."

Syd winced. "I'm sorry, but not really. I don't need to report in to you, as fiancée or wife."

"But—"

"For God's sake, Brett, I'm incredibly aware of what's going on here and what's at stake. I'm not stupid and I won't mess it up. You have to see that." She moved closer to him and placed her palm on his chest, fighting the urge to vomit. "And," she continued, "how can you ever expect to really win my heart back if you keep acting like a caveman?"

His face softened and for a fleeting moment he reminded her of the old Brett from days gone by. Now would be an opportune time to get him off her back.

"Brett, you really don't need to keep tabs on me. I'm not a child. You can trust me." She looked at her feet, frowning.

"Yeah, well, it's easy for you to tell me I don't need to, but you're my property and I do need to keep tabs on you at all times." His voice held little conviction—it was as if his old self and his controlling nature were warring within him.

She peeked up at him through her thick lashes and

whispered, "But that's exactly it, Brett. I'm not your property — I'm a woman."

He covered her hand with his and genuine affection shone in his eyes for a brief moment. "Yes, that you are."

"Then respect me as a woman, Brett. Treat me like one, like you *used* to. Don't treat me like I'm some sort of prize." That would be a tall order. For the past decade, respect for anyone other than himself had been a concept foreign to Brett.

He nodded slowly. "I'm going to visit my parents in Florida this weekend."

"Should I be expecting calls from you every two minutes?" It was apparent it took everything he had to shake his head. "Thank you. I won't see you for a bit — I'm in Seattle on Monday for the majority of the week. I'll call you next week and update you on how things are going, okay?"

He nodded and headed to the front door, ready to leave. Syd bent to pick up Puff, lest she escape and chase Brett down the driveway once he opened the door. When Brett leaned in to try to kiss Sydney goodbye, the dog warned him off.

"I'll be in touch," he said stiffly, opening the door.

"Brett, wait!" Syd put the dog back on the floor and moved closer to Brett, giving him a light kiss on the cheek.

He blinked at her. "Um. Right. Speak with you next week then."

As soon as the door was shut behind him, Syd's body went weary from the stress of the past ten minutes. She went into the living room and collapsed onto the sofa. Puff jumped into her lap and Syd began to scratch her behind the ears.

"You're such a good girl," she cooed. "Protecting Mommy. Trying to keep the bad man away." She reached for her purse and pulled out the small gold box from the Fairmont, and the card within it. "Now *this*," she said, waving the card at the dog, "This is a man you'd never have to growl at. He's a gentleman. He's sweet and kind and gentle."

There was the familiar sting of tears. "He knows how to treat a woman. He made me forget all this bad stuff. He made Mommy happy, if only for a day."

Puff sniffed the card and gave the edge a quick lick, grinning up at Syd.

Syd laughed and hugged the little dog. "You like him, eh?" she asked. "Yeah, me, too."

She leaned back against the sofa and reflected on what had transpired with Brett. Pretending to be interested in rekindling a romantic relationship with Brett had appeared to calm him a bit and get him off her back. She was sick to her stomach at the thought of touching him, let alone anything else, but it seemed to be what he wanted to hear. The illusion she'd ever love him again was something he wanted to hold on to desperately, and if pretending she could regain those feelings bought her time and made him ease up on her, then she had to do what she had to do.

She thought back on what she'd said to him.

'How can you win my heart back?'

'You can trust me.'

She picked up Puff, turned the little face to her own and whispered, "And the Oscar goes to..."

Chapter Seventeen

"Caleb, I'm at your place and you're not answering the door, dude. We had a date, remember? You're not standing me up, are you, because, if you are, I swear, I'm going to have to break up with you. I will not be treated with such disrespect."

Caleb cursed under his breath. "Fuck, PJ, I totally forgot you were coming over. I'm sorry, bro."

"Well, stop being sorry and get your ass back here. We have a shit-ton of writing to do for the next album. I'll wait for you on the back deck. If you're lucky I might even put on that frilly little pink piece you like so much, baby," Pat added, in a mock-seductive tone.

"Um, yeah, as appealing as that sounds coming from my *brother*," Caleb began, taking one hand off the steering wheel and scratching his head. "I, um... I'm kind of not in the country at the moment."

"You're what? Where the hell are you, man?"

"Vancouver."

"You are *not!*" Pat laughed. "You sly bastard, you're going to try to find little Miss Sydney after all."

Caleb's face burned. "I sort of...already found her. I took your advice and spoke to someone at the Fairmont."

"Wow, you work fast. I knew you couldn't resist—your boner for her hasn't let up since you got back from Banff," PJ joked.

"Yes, yes, you can rub this whole situation in my face when I'm back in town."

"Which will be when, exactly?"

"It depends on how things go, PJ. I could be on my way

home tomorrow, or...who knows." With the way things had been left last time he'd seen Sydney, she may not even open the door a crack, let alone spend any measure of time with him. He sighed. "Okay, I turned onto her street so I've got to get going."

"All right, good luck, man. And remember," Pat said, snickering, "If you get laid you have me to thank."

"If you say so, asshole," Caleb laughed as he hit the disconnect button on the dash console.

A minute more and the car rolled to a stop in front of Syd's house. It looked as if she was home—her Escape was parked out front and the foyer light was on. He got out of his rental car and stood on the sidewalk for a moment, pausing to examine the small house in front of him. It was a simple two-story brick structure, nothing special, nothing out of the ordinary. But for some reason Caleb couldn't pinpoint, he was certain that the house, although unexceptional on the outside, was filled with a special brand of warmth that he felt only Sydney possessed.

He couldn't wait to see her.

He took a deep breath and walked up the few steps that led to her porch and front door. He raised his finger to ring the doorbell and brought it back down to his side, unaccustomed to being this nervous about a girl.

He stretched the muscles in his neck, held his breath and hit the button.

The doorbell sounded, followed by sharp barking. He heard Syd's voice on the other side of the door.

"Come here, you little monster," she laughed.

A moment later, the door opened and Syd stood staring up at him, her pale green eyes wide.

Caleb smiled.

She remained rooted to the spot, not saying a word. A small gold and white fuzzy dog wiggled under her arm, trying to get loose.

He reached his hand into his pocket and pulled out the chandelier earring he had kept, showing it to her. "Can I come in?"

She shook her head and blinked repeatedly. "Oh, yes, of course," she murmured, stepping aside. "I'm sorry. I'm just shocked to see you. Here. At my house." She locked the door behind him and turned around.

"I could tell."

She smiled and tilted her head to the side. Her eyes flashed to the earring he was still dangling like a carrot in front of a racehorse, then met his. "I thought you were holding that ransom till I called you?"

He shrugged and placed it on the small table that decorated the foyer. "I lost patience."

"It's only been two days," she chuckled. "How did you even find my address? I'm unlisted."

He grinned. "I charmed the pants off the concierge at the Fairmont."

Her jaw dropped. "And she just *gave* you my information?"

Laughing, he answered, "Well, it took a bit of work and persistence, but you should know firsthand what an expert charmer I am. After all, I did manage to get you to agree to dinner. And skiing. And dinner again."

"Oh boy…"

"And breakfast the next morning," he whispered.

Caleb's gaze never wavered as he tried to assess what was going through her mind. He had no idea if she was happy he was there or not. No clue if his visit was welcomed, and no clue if she would send him on his way. He took her in, memorizing each detail, afraid he'd never set eyes on her again.

Damn, there wasn't a single curve that was hidden beneath the high-waisted black pencil skirt and gauzy periwinkle blouse, fitted snug and pulled taut across her breasts. The first few buttons were undone and a sweet little black satin bra peeked out from beneath it.

It had only been about a week since he'd seen Syd, but he felt as if it had been months.

It had only been a week and a half since he'd first met

Syd, but it seemed like years.

And that scared the crap out of him.

She put the dog down and it ran to him, yipping and yapping and jumping all over the place, as if it had tiny springs attached to its feet.

He snorted. "What *is* that thing?"

She made a face at him. "That's my dog, genius," she answered, walking past him. "Come on in."

He followed her deeper into her home and into the kitchen, the dog tailing him the entire way.

"Do you want a drink?" she asked. He nodded in response and she opened the fridge. "Okay, I've got beer, wine, coffee, water and some kind of fruit punch I don't remember making." She pulled the container out of the fridge and examined it. "Scrap the fruit punch, it's alive," she laughed, pouring it down the drain.

"A beer is great, thanks."

She grabbed one and tossed it to him, then snatched an apple out of the crisper and rinsed it off. "So," she said before biting a chunk out of the fruit and leaning her hip against the counter.

He opened the bottle and glanced at the dog that wouldn't quit its barking. He grinned at Syd. "Hey, Syd, you should make sure your little pup here doesn't plug its tail into one of the electrical outlets again, huh."

She rolled her eyes. "Because anyone that's ever owned a Pomeranian has never heard *that* one before." She elbowed him as she walked by and into the next room. "No matter what you do, don't pet her," she advised.

He followed her into the family room. He smiled, realizing that his impression of Syd's house being filled with warmth was indeed correct. He was surrounded by overstuffed cream-colored leather sofas and dark rich woods, a fireplace and a small black baby grand piano tucked away in the corner.

He nodded toward it. "You play?"

She raised a corner of her mouth in response. "Yeah, a

bit."

He set his beer on the wood and glass coffee table. "Gonna have to play a bit for me one of these days."

Syd chuffed. "Let me think about that. Wait... The answer's coming to me... No."

Caleb laughed and shrugged. "We'll see about that." He bent in front of the growling dog. "Aw, come here, little guy. Give Caleb a kiss."

"First off, the dog's a *she*," Syd snorted. "Second, I was serious with the warning. If you want those glorious strumming fingers of yours intact, don't be doing that. She seems to believe I need her protection, and lately, she's got this thing against men." She sighed. "Not that I can blame her."

He dismissed the words of caution and continued trying to win the dog's friendship, motioning with his hand and making kissy sounds. "Come here. Come on."

The dog eyed him suspiciously, ceased her growling, cocked her head to the side and approached him slowly. Caleb wiggled his fingers at her and a low growl sounded in her throat as she lunged at him, nipping said fingers.

"Aw, shit!" he swore, pulling away and immediately standing.

"Puff!" Syd cried, running to Caleb's side. "Bad girl!"

The dog's tail tucked between her hind legs and her ears flicked back as she ran to hide under the coffee table.

"No biting him," Syd chastised. "We like him."

"We do, do we?" Caleb asked, grinning.

"Don't let it get to your head, Mr. Jones," she said, rolling her eyes. "You okay?" She took his hand in hers to examine his fingers. "Aw crap, she broke skin on this one, the little monster. You're bleeding."

"Syd, it's okay, it's a drop. A papercut would have done more damage."

She led him into the brightly lit kitchen. She gathered her hair and twisted it into a knot, exposing her neck and the remnants of a small bite mark just below the ear. He remained fixated on the slight yellowish-green bruise, knowing precisely how she'd gotten it. His groin tightened at the memory and he let out a weak groan.

"Let me clean it up a bit," she said.

She stood in front of him and wrapped a wet tea towel around his bleeding index finger, applying slight pressure.

Fuck, he thought miserably, being this close to her was pure torture. She wasn't even looking at him—instead she was concentrating all too hard on holding the towel tightly around his finger. Was she having as much trouble staying composed as he was?

"You named your dog *Puff*?" he asked, smirking.

"Yes, I did. Laugh all you want," she retorted, finally meeting his gaze and giggling. "Well, look at her! What would you name her?"

"It *does* fit," he admitted, laughter bubbling up in him, as well.

Hearing laughter, Puff dared to poke her head out from under the coffee table and snuck a glance at them. Sensing Sydney was no longer ready to roast her, she came out and moved to Caleb, sniffing his pants.

"Well," Syd said, nodding toward the Pomeranian. "Looks like she showed you who the boss is, and now she's ready to be friends. She's such a dominant little—"

"Syd," Caleb whispered low, wrapping his free hand behind her head and pulling her lips to his.

Chapter Eighteen

Syd's body jolted as soon as their lips met. She let go of Caleb's hand, the towel she was holding around his finger dropping to the floor.

He pulled his lips from hers and gazed at her. She was undeniably more beautiful in the dim light filtering in from the kitchen than he recalled. Her eyes were completely unreadable as she stared wordlessly back up at him.

Shit. Shit, shit, shit. I shouldn't have done that.

He hadn't even been in the house for ten minutes and already he'd been unable to keep his hands to himself and had planted one on her. He was rushing things again, unsure if she was okay with him even being there, and he felt like a world-class idiot. He put some distance between them and scratched his head. "Um, listen. I'm really sorry about that. I should probably leave." He turned away and started toward the foyer.

"So basically, you came all the way to Vancouver to give me my earring, kiss me and then run away? I don't think so."

Syd grabbed Caleb's arm and whirled him around to face her. In one swift motion, she threaded her fingers into his hair and pulled his lips down to hers, kissing him fiercely.

He was stunned, rooted to the floor. He certainly hadn't been expecting *that*.

"You're not mad at me?" he whispered when she finally tore her mouth from his.

"I'm livid," Syd answered, breathless, drawing him in for another kiss, leaving no doubt whatsoever as to her desire for him. Her soft body pressed onto his, supple curves molding against his chest. She trailed her fingers south from his head to his neck, tugging his hair gently along the way. She moved to his torso, stopping at the hem of his indigo graphic T-shirt.

Caleb dropped his hands to her waist, encircling her and bringing her flush to him. He deepened the kiss and gently coaxed her lips apart. She met his tongue with equal fervor and purred in the back of her throat, pulling his shirt out from his pants.

He broke the kiss and leaned away from her a few inches. "Are you sure?" he asked, tracing his thumb along her delicate jaw line.

"Am I going to have to tell you to shut up like I did back at the chalet?"

He clenched his jaw in anticipation. "No, darlin'. Not a chance in hell of that."

He raised his arms, allowing her to pull the shirt up and off him with ease. His heartbeat quickened when she whipped it, without care, to the side. Syd met his gaze, dark with desire, and trailed down to his jeans. Her smile was crooked as she feathered her fingers over his chest. His skin felt as if it were on fire as her nails gently scraped along his abdomen, finally hooking into the waistband of his pants. While she concentrated on unbuckling his belt, Caleb tried his best not to tear off all the buttons on her blouse in his eager bid to touch her, get impossibly closer to her. It was all he thought about now. The need consumed him and when he finally undid the last button, he ripped the garment from her body and threw it behind him.

He splayed his fingers over the smooth skin of her back, Caleb tipped down and nuzzled Syd's neck. She remained still for a few seconds, panting shakily, before cursing under her breath and resuming her quest to get his pants off. He moved her unsteady hands away and unclasped his jeans himself, kicking them off onto the floor.

When he looked back up, he was a bit shocked to find that Syd, in her impatience, had hiked the skirt up over her hips and was tearing off her nylons. He took in her smooth, golden, almost endless legs.

She latched onto him and he was hoisted to the couch atop her. He fell between her legs and she immediately cinched her ankles at the small of his back. He groaned in her ear when her heat pressed to him and he shifted his hips, yearning for what was to come. Syd slid her hands down his back and into his underwear, her nails scratching his ass as her fingers moved beneath the thin fabric.

She licked his neck and pressed her hips up against his hard cock, and a soft, sexy sound escaped her lips. "Ready when you are," she breathed.

Caleb balanced carefully above her, bracing himself with one arm on the back of the sofa. He used his free hand to unclasp her bra and strip it from her. Gentle, he drew his fingers along the supple curve of one breast and dipped his head to take its hard nub into his mouth, biting lightly, enjoying the musky taste.

Syd maneuvered a hand between them and snaked it into his briefs, grabbing hold of the length of him and murmuring appreciatively when he throbbed in response to her touch.

"Jesus, Syd," he rasped. He kissed her hard and carefully lifted off her. He stood, wondering at her near-naked body sprawled across the sofa, her skin glowing in the subtle light filtering in from the kitchen. He knelt, slid his hands beneath her bottom and slowly pulled her lace panties down and, finally, completely off her.

She wiggled restlessly. "You have something," she whimpered. "Please tell me you have something."

Caleb grinned at her and reached for his pants, snagging his wallet then pulling out a short strip of foil packets. He ripped one off and tossed the remainder on the floor. He expertly rolled the condom on and was on top of Syd again within seconds. He positioned himself between her legs and exhaled slowly as he gradually entered her.

Syd instantly hooked her heels at the small of his back

and applied pressure, pushing him completely into her, not allowing him the opportunity to take it slow. "Finally," she whispered as she nibbled on his ear.

He rolled his pelvis, quickly learning that soft and easy were two things Syd wasn't interested in at the moment. She dug her nails into his hips, urging him to drive himself into her faster, deeper. The feel of her wrapped around him and her breath in his ear were almost too much for Caleb to bear. He'd wanted Syd from the second he'd laid eyes on her on that icy road in Banff. And now, to have her finally, after nights of restless sleeps and vivid dreams, there was no way he could last.

He began moving within her at a frenzied pace, his strong hands on her for leverage. She gripped his hips hard, guiding him to go faster and push harder up and into her. Within moments, she clenched, vise-like around him, her body rippling with release. The sound she made as she reached orgasm was guttural and it sent Caleb tumbling over the edge. He threw back his head and, doing his best not to scream and alert the entire block, shuddered as he emptied into her.

Gasping for breath, Caleb gently rested his body against Syd's, sweat mingling with sweat. He ran his hands up and down her arms and closed his eyes in contentment when she stroked his head, combing the damp hair off his forehead before kissing it.

"Holy shit."

"I know," Syd giggled.

"That was unexpected, darlin'."

She burst out laughing and pushed him off her. "Right. That's why you came fully equipped," she snorted.

He smirked back at her. "Wishful thinking?"

"Well, in that case, I like the way you think." She leaned over and planted a soft kiss on his lips. Syd glanced at the foil packets in her hand then shifted her gaze to his. "Are these all you have left?"

He nodded in response.

She grinned at him as she swung a leg over his, straddling him. "Not nearly enough," she whispered, her green eyes locked onto his.

Caleb barely resisted the urge to laugh. "Darlin', I'm not twenty anymore."

"Neither am I." She used her nose to nudge his head up and slowly licked his neck, ending right below his ear. She gave the lobe a light bite and got to her feet.

"Oh, that's pure evil."

She smiled sweetly at him and bent to retrieve her bra from the bowl of oranges it had landed in on the coffee table.

Puff, who had escaped the room the moment the moaning and groaning began, now trotted back in and hopped up onto the couch beside Caleb, resting her little head on his thigh.

Caleb, covering his tender bits with one hand lest the dog attack again, admired Syd in the dim light. Her hair was disheveled, her mouth slightly bruised, her breasts set into stiff, bright pink peaks and her pencil skirt remained hiked up around her hips.

God, she's gorgeous.

"I still can't believe you actually brought condoms with you. Not that I'm complaining," she continued, unzipping and pulling the pencil skirt down and off her, leaving her totally nude. "You're a cocky bastard, is all."

His jaw clicked as she navigated the room. "And if you keep flashing that fine ass of yours at me like that, you might end up being right about two more condoms not being nearly enough."

"What? This ass?" she asked, bending over and wiggling it at him.

He jumped to his feet and reached his hand out to grab her. Syd squealed and, escaping him, took off down the hall. He ran after her, Puff following closely behind, yapping playfully. She climbed the stairs and made it to the landing before he caught up and snatched her ankle. Syd landed with a *thud* and began giggling hysterically.

He went to his knees a couple of steps beneath the landing and pulled her to him, so that her bottom was barely resting on solid ground. He leaned over her and swept a rogue lock of hair off her face. He brushed his lips against hers, loving the way her entire body seemed to sigh in response to his touch.

A moment later, Puff was trying to get in on the action, her tongue lavishing them with puppy kisses.

Syd's body trembled as she began giggling again. "Not now, Puffy," she whispered. "Mommy's busy being attacked by a sexy rock star."

Puff gave Syd's nose one last lick before bounding up the rest of the stairs to play with a squeaky toy.

Caleb lifted himself off her, and when Syd tried to sit up, he gently pushed her shoulders back down. He trailed his fingers across her collarbone and over her breasts, stopping and resting on the soft mounds. "Sexy rock star, huh?"

"Nyeh, sometimes anyway," she joked, unable to stop laughing.

He raised his eyebrows. "Is something funny?" he inquired, sliding closer to her and kissing the inside of her thigh.

"Maybe. Just a little."

"How about now?" he asked, his head diving between her legs.

Chapter Nineteen

Oh my dear God in heaven. Syd sucked in a sharp breath.

The things this man did with his mouth made her dizzy and she tried not to pass out from the sheer delight of it all. He slid his tongue slowly along her inner thighs, swirling from left to right and back again, teasing her.

"Not... Not laughing," she stuttered breathlessly.

"Good girl," Caleb mumbled, lifting his head and using his hands to spread her legs even farther.

She arched her hips in silent invitation and he accepted, finally skimming his tongue slowly up and down her oversensitive slit. Syd shuddered and closed her eyes, reveling in the sensation. He flicked that nub between her folds and she cried out.

Syd couldn't remember the last time she'd had this level of intimacy and the connection with Caleb both exhilarated and shocked her. She wanted to watch him, to engrave this moment and the heat they had for each other in her mind forever. She lifted her head to catch a glimpse of him, only seeing shapes and shadows — the faint light that seeped in from the kitchen wasn't enough to reveal much more than silhouettes in the darkened stairwell.

He applied gentle pressure to the tiny knot of skin and she almost jumped to the ceiling. He pressed one palm flat on her stomach to hold her still while, with his free hand, he inserted first one, then two fingers inside her. She gasped and gripped the edge of the landing, trembling.

"Easy there, babe," Caleb whispered below her.

She whimpered beneath him, wiggling her hips impatiently. He moved to her abdomen and kissed and licked the soft skin there, all the while rhythmically moving his fingers in and out of her. She was teetering on the edge, the fuzzy shroud of pleasure about to overtake her completely.

But she didn't want to waste this orgasm on his fingers.

She roughly pushed him away and reached for the two condoms that had escaped her grip when Caleb had snagged her on the landing.

"You. Inside me. Now," she ordered, tearing one off and tossing it to him.

He growled deep in his throat as he rolled it on and plunged inside her.

Jesus.

That was the only word that came to mind as soon as Caleb began gliding in and out of her in long, smooth strokes. He felt better than she had ever imagined, better than she'd ever dreamed he'd feel. She maneuvered so that she was supporting herself on her forearms and elbows, and locked eyes with him. He gripped her harder, fingers digging into her soft flesh, and he closed his eyes. Dots of sweat glistened on his forehead in the murky darkness and his brows were knit together with concentration.

Witnessing Caleb in this state was almost too much for her to bear — it was sexy and passionate and *raw*. He moved one thumb to the sensitive nub between her legs and began circling it lightly, sending jolts shooting through her body. Syd sucked in a sharp breath and cried out his name, throwing her head back and letting go.

When she opened her eyes and recovered from the aftershocks, she could see Caleb in the murky darkness, his face screwed up with desire. In an instant, Syd realized he was holding off his own release and was trying to make it last as long as possible for her. She didn't want him to stop and, gasping for air, bucked her hips, encouraging him to go on.

Caleb leaned over her, bracing himself on the landing with palms flat on the floor on either side of Syd. He crushed his mouth against hers and forced his tongue inside. He drove within her, each stroke harder and wilder than the one before. After but a moment, Syd screamed and clamped around his cock, spiraling into another blissful orgasm. Caleb let out a hiss of breath and shuddered above her, experiencing his own release.

He rested his head on her sweat-slicked stomach for a few moments, his hands hooked around her bottom. He nuzzled her right above her belly button and gave a happy sigh. Syd found his face in the dark and gently stroked his cheek, still trying to catch her breath.

"Shit, woman."

"This," Syd said, sliding out from under him, and trying to maintain her balance as she got to her feet, "is all your fault. If your car hadn't stalled none of this would have ever happened." She extended her hand to him.

He took the hand she offered and joined her up on the landing, and as soon as he was by her side he pulled her roughly into his arms. "Well, I can tell you one thing, darlin'. However it happened, I'm damn happy I met you."

Caleb tipped his head down to hers and kissed her tenderly. She molded herself against him and looped her arms around his neck. He reached behind her and cupped her ass, pressing her into him.

"Someone's starting to get happy again," she quipped.

"Have you looked in the mirror, baby? Most men can't help but get happy around you." He kissed her nose. "Unfortunately, this one's pretty close to passing out at the moment." He waved his hand in the air and explained. "Time difference."

She nodded. "Okay, come on, big guy." Syd went on her tiptoes to nibble on Caleb's chin and reached down to grab hold of his hand. He threaded his fingers into hers and followed her into her bedroom. Syd didn't bother turning on the light and instead walked to the window to open the drapes, leaving the milky moonlight to fend off darkness and shadow.

Syd pulled Caleb toward the unmade bed and they collapsed into it. Caleb lay on his back and Syd cuddled into the crook of his arm, one of her own wrapped around his middle. Puff bounded into the room and hopped up her little stairs to get on the bed, snuggling between their legs.

"Time to recharge," she whispered, giving Caleb a squeeze.

"Sounds good," he murmured into her hair.

Sounds good, she thought sleepily as her eyes closed. His arm around her was strong and loving, sincere and solid.

Forget good, she thought. *This somehow feels right.*

* * * *

Caleb awoke to the feathery sensation of a soft fingertip tracing the contours of his chest and abdomen. Without moving, he opened his eyes and shifted his gaze down and to the left. Syd's head hadn't moved from his shoulder and he smiled.

The room was still bathed in moonlight and Caleb turned to the clock. It was barely even midnight—they'd passed out for less than two hours.

He reached a hand up and combed his fingers through the dark waves of her satiny hair.

"Mmm," she murmured, snuggling closer to him. She threw her leg over his and slid her foot up and down his calf.

"What are you doing up?"

"I don't know," she said, sighing.

"What is it, darlin'?"

"I still can't believe you're here, that you wanted to be here, that *I* wanted you to be here so badly. Good things like you don't happen to me anymore," she whispered.

His brow furrowed. "No one should have those thoughts, Syd, especially not you." He kissed the top of her head. The way she sounded, what she said, reminded him of the sadness he'd seen in her eyes back in Banff, and it troubled him. Again, he had an overwhelming need to reassure her. "Syd, you're smart, fun, beautiful and so much more. There's a whole world of goodness out there for you. You should always be blessed with those things in your life."

She gripped him tighter, and when the warmth of teardrops landed on his chest, his heart broke. "Aw, baby," he whispered, and maneuvered his body so that he was on his side, facing her.

He tenderly caressed her cheek and she buried her head against him, as if embarrassed by the sudden tears. He hooked a finger under her chin and brought her lips to his. This was unlike the kisses of pure passion they'd shared earlier — he wanted this kiss to convey nothing but tenderness, care and hope.

He didn't *love* Syd. Hell, they barely knew each other. Still, he did know there was *something* there and that something scared him a little. He had experienced this once before, and the last time it had blossomed into love. It hadn't happened this quickly, though. One thing was for certain — he sure as hell hoped that whatever was developing between him and Syd didn't result in the same dreadful outcome as the last real relationship he'd had.

He mentally shook memories of his relationship with Meg out of his head and focused his attention on Sydney.

He kissed her again, moving his tongue lightly along the seam of her lips. They parted and their tongues danced languidly along each other. He moved his hand to her body, tracing the gentle dip of her waist and the inviting curve of her hip. Her hands were at first pressed against his chest, and now she slid them along him — one on his hard abdomen, the other wrapped around his back.

They lay there, kissing and caressing each other affectionately, exploring in a way they hadn't bothered with earlier. He had never experienced anything quite like this. He wanted the hands on the clock to remain unmoving when he was with Syd, allowing him the time he needed to unlock all the mysteries of her body and mind. Above all, he ached for her to believe without a doubt he could be both her strength and safe haven. He needed her to trust him, to sense he couldn't bear to hurt her in any way.

Caleb reached over to the bedside table, snatched the last of the condoms he'd brought and tore the packet open. In a matter of seconds he was ready and he grabbed her leg, drawing it over his hip. He entered her deliberately, inch by agonizing inch, and she quivered.

Chests heaving, they lay together in a tangled mess, staring at each other in the dusky darkness. When Syd averted her eyes, he coaxed her to meet his gaze once again.

"I hate the sadness in your eyes, baby," he whispered. "Let me take it away." He leaned forward to kiss her and she choked a sob against his lips.

He pulled his mouth from hers and gathered her in his arms, holding her as close to him as humanly possible. He closed his eyes and tried to control his own emotions as she cried softly.

"Shh, baby, it's okay. Shh," he murmured, resting his cheek on the top of her head, stroking her hair until she finally fell asleep in his arms.

Chapter Twenty

Syd woke with a start and freed herself from the tentacles of the bed sheets to flip over and read the clock.

Four o'clock in the morning.

Shit. She still had a million things to do before she left to go to Seattle, and there was no getting back to sleep now. Especially after the dream she'd been having.

She was dreaming of Caleb. Again. But this dream was different—it was so vivid, so real. She plopped back onto the mattress and groaned softly. She rolled onto her side, pulling the blankets up around her, and caught a scent.

Caleb's scent.

She wasn't dreaming.

"Oh my God," she whispered. CJ. He *was* here.

Syd sat up straight in bed and glanced around the room. But where was he? She turned toward the master bathroom, but the light was off and it appeared no one was in there.

She climbed out of bed and grabbed a thin robe from the en suite, throwing it over her shoulders and tying the belt in a knot as she scanned the room. His clothes were nowhere to be found.

Maybe her mind *was* playing tricks, and it really was a dream, after all. She laughed softly. She was beginning to confuse herself.

I'm losing my mind.

Still, part of her refused to believe she was slowly going crazy, and she drifted into the hallway. She peeked into the spare bedroom, when a thought suddenly struck her. Of course his clothes weren't in her room—he'd already been naked when he'd come up there with her.

A slow smile spread across her lips. It really *had* happened. She continued searching for him, moving to the stairs. She found an empty condom wrapper on the landing, along with one of Puff's toys. Where was the little bugger anyway? Normally the Pomeranian would follow her around like a fuzzy shadow. She moved down the stairs and padded to the back of the house. She peeked into the family room and found her clothes, along with Caleb's, scattered all over, exactly as they had left them.

Then she spotted him. He was in the kitchen, by the French doors that led into the back yard. He had pulled a cushioned dinette chair out and was straddling it, his arms laid across the back, chin resting on his forearms, looking out into the moonlit yard. Puff was curled into a little ball by his feet, snoring lightly.

"There's my rock star," she whispered.

Caleb turned to her and smiled affectionately. "No, darlin'. When the lights go down, I'm just an ordinary man."

Syd cocked her head to the side, taking him in. He had put his jeans on and nothing else. The moonlight played shadows of light and dark across his face and muscled back and made his blond hair almost glow. Seeing him sitting there like that, seemingly at such peace, evoked a million emotions. She walked over to him and planted a light kiss on his neck.

"Don't move." She scooted off and ran to the basement, carefully navigating the stairs in the dark before flicking on the overhead light. She rummaged through a few boxes, pulling items out and tossing them on the floor until she found exactly what she needed. She made her way upstairs and hauled her bounty into the kitchen, directly opposite Caleb.

"What's all this?" he asked as she set up the easel. He began to straighten up.

"No! No, no, don't move!" Syd squeaked, putting a large pad of drawing paper on the easel. "Go back to exactly the way you were."

"What are you doing, baby?"

She smiled at him. "I want to draw you. Now sit still."

He chuckled and rested his chin back on his forearms. "So, you're an artist too, huh?"

"I got it from my mom," she said softly. "She was... amazing."

"So are you," he whispered.

She smoothed the hair back off her face and gathered it into a haphazard bun at the base of her neck. "Back atcha, Mr. Jones," she said, winking at him. She turned on the light behind her and dimmed it to the point where she could still see what she was doing. "Okay, don't move and keep looking straight at me. I only need about"—she grabbed a pencil and tapped it against her lips—"half an hour or so. Maybe less. I can do the rest another time without my muse."

"Take your time, darlin'. I'm going to sit here and enjoy the view." He grinned suddenly. "It *would* make it much easier on me if you took your robe off, though."

"But then the focal point of the sketch would be much lower," she retorted, her eyes flicking to between his legs.

Caleb chuckled as she set to work.

Syd began outlining his face, starting with those gorgeous azure eyes, and from there moving to his shoulders and back. She lightly shaded with the pencil, only enough to point out where shadow and light fell.

"So do I get you all to myself today?" he asked out of the blue.

Syd frowned as she worked with the pencil, putting the finishing touches on her drawing. "I'm afraid not, CJ. I have to go to Seattle. My flight out is this afternoon."

"Shit, are you serious?"

She nodded. "Unfortunately." She put the pencil on the easel and got up to stretch. "Okay, stud. I'm done."

He stood, triggering Puff awake. "Lemme see," he said, taking a step toward Syd.

She grabbed the drawing and held it away from him. "No

peeking! This is just a sketch so I can remember what you look like. I want to put this on canvas and paint you. You'll see it when it's done. Not before." She stuck out her tongue at him and rushed the sketch pad back into the basement, where it would be safe from Caleb's prying eyes.

When she returned, she found Caleb on his haunches playing with a now fully alert and energized Puff. He was moving his hand in circles on the floor and she was chasing it, yipping excitedly. Syd leaned against the wall, watching them and smiling softly. *It's like a little family,* she thought. A little family she'd never have.

Puff seemed to sense her owner and froze mid-hop, staring up at Syd with her tongue hanging out of the side of her mouth, tail wagging at light speed.

"Looks like you made a new friend," she said as Caleb stood. She came up to him and wrapped her arms around his waist.

"It's not fair you have to leave so soon," he whispered, resting his cheek on top of her head. "We've barely had any time together. We just started this."

She stared for a moment into his deep blue eyes, butterflies in her stomach fluttering nervously. There was no letting him go. Not yet.

Don't do this, she thought to herself as she opened her mouth and uttered the words, "Come with me."

Chapter Twenty-One

Caleb let out a loud groan and stretched from head to toe. He had no idea how his whole body could feel as if it had been used and abused, muscles sore and aching, yet at the same time how he could be so incredibly relaxed and satiated. He curled his lips into a small smile and reached across to his left, only to find the bed sheets cool. He opened his eyes and surveyed the gloomy darkness. He was alone. Frowning, he wondered where Syd had wandered off to. A creak of a door sounded and a light shone in from the bathroom, illuminating the hotel room and forcing him to squint.

"Oh, crap," she whispered. "I didn't wake you up, did I? I was trying to be ninja-like." Syd walked to his side and bent to give him a light kiss on the cheek.

He shook his head. "No, you didn't wake me up, darlin'. What are you doing up so early?"

She snorted. "Early? Caleb, it's nearly eleven o'clock!"

"It is?" He turned to the little clock radio on the oak nightstand to his right.

"Yes, silly," she chuckled. She walked over to her suitcase, rifling through it for a moment before exclaiming, "A-ha!" She held up a silver pendant victoriously. "There you are."

She continued talking while she latched the chain around her neck. "I've got a lunch meeting at the restaurant. I should hopefully be back at around five p.m. And then we're all done here."

"And at that point, you're all mine, correct?" he asked, his grin devilish as he gazed up at her, a million naughty thoughts running through his mind.

She sat on the bed beside him and slung on her heels. She looked fantastic in a blush-pink blazer and a pair of white dress pants.

"Are you trying to give everyone at the restaurant a heart attack?"

She creased her brow. "What on earth are you talking about?"

"No blouse under the blazer. Every man you meet is going to have a hard-on."

"Jealous?"

"You make it hard for a man to let you out the door alone, that's all." He examined her from tip to toe, his gaze finally resting on hers. "God, woman, you have to stop looking so damn good all the time."

She chuckled and leaned over him, running her fingers through his tangled hair. "And you make it hard for this woman to leave to begin with," she countered, moving her hand down his neck, along his collarbone, and at last stopping on his chest.

He took her hand in his and brought her finger to his lips.

She frowned and sighed. "Are you sure you're okay hanging out while I work? I've hated abandoning you the past couple days."

"No, no, darlin'. It's okay. Gives me a chance to gather my strength again and do a little more writing. Truth be told, I'd have to say I couldn't imagine being anywhere else."

"Well, I'm certainly glad you're here." She kissed his nose, chin and lips.

Caleb took the opportunity Syd being so close presented, and pulled her into his arms.

"I don't want to go," she whined, her face buried in his neck. "I just wanna stay right here with you all day."

"Don't worry, Syd. Once we get back to Vancouver we'll have all the time in the world."

She straightened up and looked at him, a slight frown creasing her brow. "Yeah, about that."

Caleb's stomach immediately tightened. There was

something in her tone that raised about a hundred bright red flags. He hoisted himself up and leaned back against the headboard. He grabbed her hand and began massaging the palm with his thumb. "What about it?"

Syd didn't meet his eyes.

Caleb's heart jumped into his throat.

"Well," she began hesitantly, "when I get back to Vancouver, I've basically got week after week of meetings. I won't really be able to dedicate any time to you."

"Oh," he said softly, more hurt in his voice than he intended. "Well, I'm sure you don't have meetings every single day. You've got to have a break, right?"

She shook her head. "I'm sorry."

"But you'll be available on weekends. I can come up to see you then." He clenched his jaw. He sounded desperate. He hated that he sounded so desperate. He hated that he *felt* desperate. Going weeks without seeing her would be impossible. He'd barely survived a week as it was.

She latched onto a piece of long hair that had come loose from her haphazard bun and began twirling it around her index finger. She shook her head again. "There's so much stuff going on right now, CJ. On the weekends too. Commitments I've already made, a weekend with a friend, business dinners and such." She let the silken lock go and sighed. "I hate this, you've no idea, but I can't drop this stuff, no matter how much I want to spend time with you."

"Ah."

She can't make any time for me?

Shut up, Caleb.

She finally met his eyes. "I'm so sorry, Caleb. I wish there was a way."

He let out a puff of air and brought the back of her hand to his lips. "Don't worry, it's okay, Syd. You *did* have a life before I came into it. I can't expect you'll be available all the time." He smirked at her. "And I certainly can't expect my girlfriend to reorganize her life because of me."

Her olive eyes widened and she stared at him, lips slightly

parted. "Girlfriend?"

He grinned. "The position for girlfriend is not filled at the CJ Mattress headquarters. You'd be a perfect fit." When the shock didn't leave her features, he continued, "That is, if you want it." He smiled softly. "I just wanted you to know that I'm kinda hooked on you, Syd."

Tears flooded her eyes. "I'm... I'm kinda hooked on you, too, Caleb," she said, her voice hitching as she spoke the words. "I wasn't expecting you to say that."

Caleb breathed an internal sigh of relief. "Yeah, well, in a way, neither was I. I wasn't exactly expecting any of this at all, darlin'."

She leaned forward and brought her lips to his, kissing him deeply.

"You've got to go," he murmured against her lips.

Syd pulled away and grumbled. "Fine. Fine. I'm going." She stood and smoothed out her pants. "I'll see you soon?"

He answered softly, hoping she'd believe his words were true and genuine. "You can't get rid of me that easily. I'm not going anywhere."

* * * *

Caleb twisted on the sofa to check the nightstand clock. Sydney was going to be back at the hotel in about half an hour. He grabbed the television remote and flicked off the mindless show he been mildly entertaining himself with and stood, stretching his back.

He sauntered over to the dresser, grabbed his cell phone and hit his brother's speed dial.

"Hey, baby," Pat answered.

"Aw, you missed me," Caleb joked back.

"Haven't heard from you in a few days. I thought either things went well with Sydney, or you were drowning your sorrows behind that guitar of yours in a blues bar somewhere in Canada." At Caleb's silence, he continued. "So...which is it?"

"I guess this is where I thank you."

"Ah," Pat said exaggeratedly. "So when you get back to Miami you'll be all relaxed? You'll be able to focus on the album and not be all distracted thinking about her?"

Caleb chuffed. "Yes and no. After tonight, I have no idea when we'll get together again."

"Why? The badonk-a-donk wasn't as good as expected?"

"No, you dick. Her calendar is booked." He paused. "Apparently." *There it is again*, he thought, frustrated. Every time he replayed his earlier conversation with Syd in his mind, he kept telling himself that he got it, he understood. She couldn't, and shouldn't, shift her whole life around just for him, especially since they were still so new to this.

And yet the fact that she wouldn't make room for him for even one day made him curious as to what her game really was.

Chapter Twenty-Two

Syd rested the trashy romance novel she had been reading on her stomach and leaned against the pillow. She glanced at the clock and groaned — it was closing in on nine in the evening. Ever since she'd returned from Seattle a week ago, she'd been heading to bed as soon as she was done eating dinner. She hadn't been able to rest during the night, endlessly tossing and turning. She'd hoped the early nights would at least make up for it a bit, but so far they'd done nothing but allowed more time for her mind to wander, making things impossibly worse.

She needed a friend.

She picked up her phone and punched in Cara's number.

"Yo!"

"Hey, Cara."

"Syddie! Where are you, girlfriend? Come out and play!"

Syd strained to understand Cara over the throbbing music in the background. "Are you drunk?" she asked. "It's only nine!"

Cara snorted. "Meh. Nine shmine. I'm at the Roxy. Come. Meet me. Drink with me. And dance…" Cara's voice drifted off for a moment. "Well, hello there, hottie."

Syd had to laugh. "Found a good one to sink your teeth into, Car?"

"He's my kind of dangerous, Syddie. Yum. So you'll be here in half an hour?"

"You know me and clubs, Car. Oil and water."

"So what's up then? What can I do you for?"

"Oh, um, it's nothing. You're out and having fun — it can wait."

Cara huffed. "Right. It's nothing. Sure. Because you're one to call me out of the blue for absolutely no reason. Hang on a sec." The receiver rustled in Syd's ear, and a moment later Cara came back on. "Okay, kid. Talk to me."

"No, no, Cara. We'll talk tomorrow. It's okay, really."

"Syd, come on. Don't tell me I came all the way outside for nothing. Now speak."

She sighed, unsure what it was she wanted to tell Cara anyhow. "It... It's just..."

"It's Caleb, isn't it?"

"What? How did you know he came here?" Syd asked, panicked.

"He came to visit you? Holy crap, are you kidding me? I was just guessing it had something to do with him, but, oh my God!"

Syd groaned. "Yeah, he dropped by last week."

"And you didn't tell me?" Cara shrieked incredulously. "But... But you're my friend! My best friend! And... And he's Caleb Jones!"

"I know, I know. I'm sorry. I've been trying to figure it all out myself."

"But you didn't tell me! I could've helped you figure it out if you told me, or at the very least I could have drooled all over him," Cara continued. "So, what happened? Uch, I can't believe I'm out, tonight of all nights!"

Syd twirled a strand of hair around her forefinger. "Long story short, he showed up at my door on Saturday night."

"And?" Cara prompted.

"And it was great to see him." She paused, debating how much she should tell her friend. "And he stayed the night and then he came with me to Seattle," she blurted out, bringing one hand up to cover her face in embarrassment.

Silence.

"Cara?"

"Sorry, Syd. I needed a sec to pick my jaw up off the sidewalk."

"I know, believe me, I've done that a few times myself."

She took a deep breath and pulled the green comforter up around her waist.

"Is he still there?" Cara whispered conspiratorially.

Syd frowned. "No. I, uh, told him I was busy for, like, the next month."

"You did *what*? Why on earth would you do that, Syddie?"

"Remember Brett, Car? And how impulsive he is? He could pop by the house at any minute. I needed an excuse to keep him away. I mean, I really, *really*, enjoyed my time with Caleb, but... Cara, what I'm doing, it's not right, even if I *am* being forced into this bullshit with Brett." Syd closed her eyes tight against the impending tears. "I don't know how to fix this."

"Fix it..." Cara said.

"Yeah, I mean, CJ's a good guy, Cara."

"Fix it," she repeated, "You really like him, don't you?"

Her turn for silence.

"Aw, Syd."

"Christ, Cara, it's terrible lying to Caleb, but I feel like I can't let him go just yet. It's self-centered, and awful, and I'm a bitch, and I see that, but he makes me crazy happy."

"I don't know, Syd. You don't sound happy at the moment. You sound even more stressed out than usual, and that says a ton in and of itself, girl." Cara said, her voice bubbling with concern. "I'm all for you having some light in your life, sweetie, but are you sure this isn't going to do more damage than good in the long run?"

"I don't know anything anymore."

"Well, you've got to figure it out, and quick, before either Brett finds out or Caleb gets too hurt."

"I don't really have much of a choice, do I?" Syd asked, resigned.

"With the situation Brett's put you guys in... Look, hun, try not to think too much about it tonight. Get some sleep and we'll talk tomorrow and figure this all out. You gonna be okay?"

She smiled. "Yeah, Car. I'll be fine."

Sydney put the receiver back in its cradle and switched off the nightstand lamp, determined to get some rest and start the day with a fresh perspective in the morning.

* * * *

Syd's eyes popped open and she turned over onto her back. It was only four-thirty and this was the fourth time she'd woken up. Yet another night with pretty much zero sleep.

She stared at the dark ceiling, trying to figure out what was wrong with her. She used to sleep solidly through the night, but the past week she'd flipped and flopped all night, hardly able to keep still, hardly able to be at rest.

What's my problem?

My problem, she told herself for the umpteenth time, *is that I miss Caleb*. She missed talking to him and the sound of his voice. She missed seeing him smile, and those adorably perfect dimples of his. She missed the way his calloused fingers felt as they stroked her cheek right before he kissed her. She missed the way his blue eyes twinkled when he looked at her, and she missed the way he lov...

Oh hell no, I'm not *going there!*

She grabbed a pillow, put it over her face and screamed into it. Puff, startled by the sudden sound in the middle of the night, popped to her feet fully alert, barking her head off.

"Puff! Shush, come here, girl."

With Puff once again cuddled into a tight little ball beside her, Syd lay back and resumed staring at the ceiling, as if seeking out the answers she so desperately needed in the shadows that resided there.

What she was doing to Caleb was wrong, plain and simple. This was not how her mother had raised her, not what she had been taught. She was engaged and had no right to harbor any emotions for Caleb. Forget the circumstances that had brought her and Brett to this place.

Those were irrelevant at this point. The fact she was lying to Caleb about her involvement with another man, the fact that she was knowingly stringing him along, made her a bad, bad, person.

And now it looked as if CJ was developing feelings—real feelings—for her. She groaned and swiped at her face in frustration. After all, it wasn't as if *she* wasn't starting to care for him in a serious way. But he had called her his girlfriend, for God's sake. That was huge. And, idiot that she was, instead of telling him that being his girlfriend would be oh so wonderful, she should've nixed the idea altogether. She should have said that all she was aiming for was a wild tumble in the sheets, a few days of great sex and shits and giggles, and nothing more. It would've been better to hurt him up front, rather than drag it on as she was doing.

She had to give him up at some point, but she didn't have the strength to do it yet.

Which of course made her feel even worse, because she was stringing him along to suit *her* purposes. She wanted him around for as long as possible, and because she was being so bloody selfish, a man who she was growing to care about in a way dangerously close to *love* was going to get hurt.

She rolled over and switched on the bedside lamp. Puff whined and buried her head beneath the blankets at the sudden brightness. Syd sat up straight, dragging the pillow with her, and leaned against the headboard.

She glanced sideways at her cell phone sitting so innocently on the nightstand and put her hand on it. She sat there, staring at the device for a moment, taking deep breaths to try to settle her quivering nerves. She was about to do something she should have done from the get-go, something she was unable to bear doing in person—and barely had the strength to do even miles apart.

She held the phone to her chest, eyes closed tight, trying to dam in the flood of tears. She thought of her father, the risk to his wellbeing and his future with her and her brother. She thought of her mother, looking down on her disapprovingly for her behavior. She thought about Brett and Caleb, and how differently they made her feel.

Her heart heavy with remorse, she punched in the number and worked to find the strength she so desperately needed.

On the fifth ring, a groggy voice answered, "Hello?"

She bit her lip and took a deep breath. "Caleb, it's me, Syd."

Chapter Twenty-Three

Caleb sat up straight in bed and raked his long fingers through his knotted hair, sweeping it off his face and out of his eyes. "Syd?"

"Yeah."

He squinted against the sunlight streaming in through the thin slit between the drapes and hauled himself into a sitting position. He glanced at the clock — it was before eight, which meant it was only around five o'clock in Vancouver. "Is everything okay, Syd? What's wrong?"

He instantly began calculating how quickly he could get himself to Vancouver if she needed him.

Too long.

He heard her take a deep breath on the other end of the line. She hesitated. Something about her silence unsettled him. "Darlin', what is it? Talk to me. Please."

She let out a whoosh of air. "Everything's okay. I-I'm sorry I worried you. And I'm sorry I called, it's early over there."

He shook his head. "That's okay, baby, it's earlier where you are, so who am I to complain? Are you sure you're okay?"

She paused again. "Yeah," she finally said. "Yeah, I'm sure."

"Okay." He swung his legs out of bed and stood. He moved to the window and opened the drapes, enjoying the warmth of the early morning Miami sun on his skin. "So, you calling me at five in the morning was for what, exactly? What can I do for you?"

"It just...I... I don't think..." she stuttered.

He grinned. "A bit sleep deprived, are we?" he joked.

"Funny boy," she said, sighing sadly. "Caleb, I… I missed you, that's all."

He furrowed his brow. "You sure that's it, Syd?"

She gave a shaky laugh. "What? Me missing you isn't enough?"

He knew she'd be able to hear the smile in his voice. "That's plenty, baby. I miss you, too. It's killing me, this not being with you." He went out into the hallway and down the stairs into the kitchen. As he set some coffee to brew, he asked, "How's your girls' weekend with Cara going?"

"My what?"

"Girls' weekend? Cara?"

"Oh!" She tittered nervously. "Yeah, it's going great, thanks. It's been a while since we did this, and it's good to catch up."

"So what does she say about calling the boyfriend during a girlie weekend? Isn't it a faux pas or something?" he snickered.

She laughed softly. "Cara's still asleep in the other room and has no idea. I can't sleep, have barely been able to for days."

"You couldn't sleep, and you thought to call me? Which means I'm on your mind," he stated.

"Maybe."

"I like that," he said softly.

She sighed. "You're almost always on my mind, Mr. Jones."

His heart rate quickened and he had to focus intently on the coffee he was pouring, otherwise he was pretty sure the mug would overflow. "Well, guess what, Syd? I haven't been able to stop thinking about you for more than five minutes at a time, and even those five-minute stretches are painful."

"Yeah, eh? That's why you've called me so often this past week?"

"Hey now! You said you were busy and I was trying to

give you space," he defended. "Unless, of course, you want me to be the overbearing boyfriend."

"Mmm," she murmured. "Say that again."

He took a sip from his mug and moved to sit at the breakfast bar. "Which part?"

"The part about you being my boyfriend."

"I'm your boyfriend, darlin'."

"I really, really, really like it when you say that," she whispered.

He smiled and placed the mug on the white granite countertop. "Sydney," he said softly, loving the way her name played on his lips, "every time I think about you, I have to pinch myself in disbelief. Here's this amazing girl and she's chosen to be a part of *my* life."

"Caleb, I—"

"Syd, let me finish. I need to get this out. Please."

"All right," she answered quietly.

He stood and began to pace. "Look, it's been a long time since I've been in what I would call a real relationship. I get that relationships take time, and I realize that if anything is supposed to be between us, it *will* happen. But at the same time," he said, stopping mid-stride, "at the same time, Syd, as much as I keep telling myself to move slowly, to take things as they come, God you make it difficult."

"Caleb..."

"I'm not usually like this, you see. Usually I'm that typical macho man who's rough and tough and I know I'm a musician but that doesn't mean I have to be all soft and sensitive all the time."

"Caleb, listen, I..." she started again.

"You're still talking. Stop talking."

"Yes, sir."

"Syd, you have no idea how much I hate not being with you right now. It kills me, because more than anything I want to be lying beside you in that bed, with you in my arms, and that little dog of yours between us, just like it was that first night. Whatever it takes, I want us to work."

He held his breath waiting on her to say something. It was unlike him to open up this way, especially at such an early stage in the relationship. There was something about Syd that made him need to reassure her he wanted her as badly as she wanted him.

He hoped.

There was silence on the other end of the line.

"You can talk now."

"Oh, okay, I didn't want to get in trouble again," she giggled. "Look, give it a couple more weeks and then things should settle, Caleb. I promise."

He smiled. "All right. A couple more weeks I can handle, darlin'."

"Listen, I'm going to try to get a bit more shut-eye before Cara wakes up. I'll call you next weekend, okay?"

"Sounds great. Sweet dreams, babe."

He snapped the cell shut and placed it on the counter. He headed to the ornate French doors that led into the garden and stepped outside. He smiled and tipped his head back, breathing deeply.

I could get used to waking up to the sound of Syd's voice, he thought. What a great way to start the day.

What a terrible way to start the day, Syd thought miserably.

She groaned and pulled the blankets up over her. "I suck," she mumbled.

She was livid with herself. She had fully intended to end things with CJ, and yet the second she heard his voice, she turned into a gooey puddle of emotions. When he had said he missed having her in his arms, with Puff sharing in the love fest no less, she couldn't do it.

He was everything she wanted and needed, everything she'd dreamed of.

No matter how long she held onto him, though, eventually she'd have to hurt him.

And she didn't know if she could survive that.

Chapter Twenty-Four

It had been an entire week since Syd had last spoken to Caleb, yet somehow it felt like a solid year. She found herself missing him all the time and resorted to playing his band's CD in the car and at home, simply to feel closer to him.

She stood in front of the mirror, only half caring about her appearance as she buckled the maroon belt at her waist. She smoothed the front of the powder-blue dress and pulled her hair into a loose chignon at the base of her neck. She hooked her fingers into her matching maroon pumps, grabbed her white knee-length trench coat, and scooted down the stairs.

Syd slipped her feet into her shoes and walked briskly into the kitchen. She reached into the cupboard and pulled out a canister of dog food, scooping some out and filling Puff's bowl, the little dog following her every move with keen interest.

"Dinner is served," she announced, putting the bowl on the floor and scratching Puff quickly behind the ears.

The dog wagged her tail double time in thanks and dove into her bowl snout first.

Syd swung her coat around her shoulders and headed out into the mild spring weather. Buckling herself in behind the wheel and pulling out of her driveway, Syd mumbled and grumbled to herself, internally complaining about the night ahead before it even began.

She tried not to think about the fact she was headed over to Brett's parents' house for dinner with his family. According to dear Brett, his family was unaware of the unconventional arrangement he'd made with her family, and part of the 'deal' was that they had to keep up appearances, pretend they'd just gotten back together, no strings attached. She hated the lies and if she had her way she'd kick Brett in the shins and run away.

But there was no having her way in the foreseeable future. Her father's life was at stake, in the most literal of senses, so, for now, she had to go along with this shenanigan and actually pretend to be in love with the heathen.

"I should seriously have pursued an acting career," she said, reaching out to turn on the radio.

As soon as Caleb's voice filled the car, her battered nerves were soothed — which was not a good thing, considering she should be breaking up with him, not looking to him for comfort.

About twenty minutes later Syd pulled into the long curved driveway that led to the Hudsons' majestic house. She parked the car and got out, rolling her eyes at Brett, who was standing on the porch waiting for her, tapping his foot.

"You're late," he said curtly.

"Your mother told me to come at eight o'clock. It's only eight now. Relax."

"You should've been here a few minutes early to chat before dinner. Now there's no time for that. I should've picked you up on my way over — that would've been better."

"It's fine, Brett," Syd mumbled, impatient.

"Yes, well, when you're my wife I'll be in charge and things will be different." He placed his hand at the small of her back and led her into the grand foyer. He helped her with her coat and stepped away from her to hang it in the closet off to her left.

Syd moved to the ornate decorative mirror that adorned almost an entire foyer wall. She was adjusting the straps of her dress when she heard a sweet voice call out from behind her.

"Oh, I'm so glad you're here!" Brett's mother said.

Syd turned at the sound of the familiar voice and smiled. Mrs. Hudson walked toward Syd, her arms opened wide in invitation. She had the same piercing blue eyes as her son and her shoulder-length blonde hair was swept off her face, revealing flawless skin and a bright smile. She pulled Syd into her arms.

Syd hugged her back. "Mrs. Hudson. You look exactly the same as you did the last time I saw you!"

"You've somehow gotten even more beautiful, Sydney!" she said warmly, putting a hand on her shoulder. "And how many times must I remind you — please, call me Anna."

Syd nodded and smiled. "Anna."

"Mother, need I remind you her given name is Nikoleta?" Brett said.

Mrs. Hudson raised her eyebrows. "No, Brett. You needn't remind me. However, she prefers to go by Sydney. Everyone knows that."

Syd nodded in agreement. "Yeah, Brett, why do you keep calling me Nikoleta? Only my family calls me that."

"And I'm going to be your husband, which last time I checked *was* family," he replied curtly. "Besides, Nikoleta sounds more elegant than Sydney."

"Oh, dear." His mother let out an adorable snort. She reached for Syd's hand and led her into the elegantly appointed living room. "Are you sure you want to go through with this?" she whispered when Brett was out of earshot. She glanced at Sydney, her eyes having lost all their cheer. "The men in this family are rather difficult to deal with at times…"

Syd, momentarily taken aback by Anna's comment, was at a loss for words. "I…uh… I mean…"

"My dear," a deep voice boomed. "You look lovely."

"Mr. Hudson, hello, so good to see you." Syd smiled and shook his outstretched hand. She had never been able to figure out Brett's father — he was pleasant and friendly, but there was an odd lack of warmth and sincerity.

"I should go check on dinner," Anna said suddenly,

hurrying away.

His eyes following his wife, he asked, "I didn't interrupt anything, did I?"

"Not at all," Syd reassured. "We were catching up."

"Really? She said nothing else?"

Sydney shook her head.

"And where's my son?" he said, still staring down the hall after his wife.

"He was putting our coats... Oh there he is now," she commented, as Brett headed along the hall toward them.

"Brett, a word please." He put his hand on his son's shoulder and led him aside, tossing one last glance at Sydney. It might have been her imagination, but his brown eyes were much colder than ever before.

That was weird.

"Syd!" Brett's sister, Melanie, bounded over to Syd and pulled her into a bone-crushing hug.

"Hey, Mel. You're looking great," Syd exclaimed, struggling to free herself from Melanie's embrace and breathe again.

She and Brett's sister had always gotten along even though Mel had been a sweet eleven-year-old when they'd first met. They had remained in touch with each other casually, even after Syd's breakup with Brett years ago. Melanie was the female version of her brother – they had the same thick wavy blonde hair and fantastic smile. But that was where the similarities ended. While Melanie shared her brother's business savvy, she was a kinder, softer version of him. She genuinely wanted to help people and had a warm, empathetic nature about her, whereas it seemed Brett favored exploiting those in trouble and generally being a controlling assbutt.

Melanie pursed her lips and her gaze moved from Sydney, down the hall to where Brett and his father stood, and back again. "Syd," she said, taking her arm and pulling her into the study. "Let's talk a minute, shall we?"

"Oh, okay, sure." Syd furrowed her brow. This night had

gotten off to a very strange start and she was unsure of what to expect next.

She allowed herself to be led into the room and glanced around, always in awe of the grandeur of the Hudsons' home. The study was the quintessential masculine hideaway — the walls were paneled in a rich dark wood and lined with shelf after shelf of books. The desk and coffee table were stained ebony and the couches and chairs were upholstered in pale gold and deep red striped fabric.

"Hey," Melanie began, interrupting Syd's survey of the room. "I'm not sure what my brother's up to, but there is definitely something going on. He can be controlling and a bit of a jerk, and I'm positive given your history there's no way you'd suddenly be okay with his behavior and agree to marry him. Is he holding something over you? What does he have up his sleeve? We both see how controlling he can be…" she repeated. "I've always loved you, Syd, and I don't want you to get hurt."

Syd feigned shock. "What on earth are you suggesting, Melanie?"

She rolled her big brown eyes. "Oh please, Syd. I'm not stupid. Mom is happy Brett is finally getting married and Dad is happy that Brett finally had the balls to get you back. But I know better, Syd — especially when it comes to the two of you. You've always been his 'one that got away'."

"I have no idea what you're talking about."

"Something's up, Syd. I'm not quite sure what it is, and maybe you're able to fool everyone else, but you can't fool me. If you let me in on what's really going on, I can help you fix it. You deserve better than to be a woman in *this* family. It's not what it's cracked up to be," she said, a surprising hint of bitterness in her voice.

There were no words to describe how badly Syd wanted to confide in Melanie, how badly she wanted to tell her the truth. Telling her wouldn't help the situation one bit, though. In fact, it would piss Brett off so much he'd pull right out of the deal and Papa would be sent back to Greece.

"Melanie, I appreciate that you're looking out for me, I really do. But nothing is going on, I promise. Brett and I, well, we got back together, fell back in love. It was as simple as that."

"Dinner's ready," Brett said, coming up behind them and glaring at his sister suspiciously.

"I don't buy it," Melanie whispered, walking past her and out of the study.

Syd followed Brett into the dining room, biting her lip and praying he hadn't overheard their conversation. If he had, she was positive it would come back to bite her later on.

* * * *

The night thereafter was blessedly uneventful. Syd was surprised that she actually enjoyed spending time with Brett's family. They were a lively bunch, the table talk never ceasing. Brett was quiet for the better part of the night, seeming to focus more on what Syd was saying rather than bothering to say anything himself.

"I'm glad Brett has finally managed to get you to come around after all these years and agree to marry him," Brett's father said, helping Sydney on with her coat. "It took him long enough."

"Yes, well, it's done," Brett mumbled.

Syd's eyes slid from father to son and back again. There was a hidden undercurrent to their conversation that she couldn't quite decipher.

Anna, visibly uncomfortable, interjected. "Do come pay us a visit again soon, Sydney," she cooed.

"I'm sure we'll see each other very soon," Syd answered, trying to smile.

"You'll have to come visit us at the cottage during one long weekend this summer, if you can pull yourself away from the restaurants," his mother continued, moving with Sydney to the open front door. "I have a feeling my son will be keeping you to himself after the wedding, and we won't get to see much of you."

"Mother," Brett said, his voice low in warning.

"Your mother is right," Mr. Hudson spoke up. "It might take your wife a little time to adjust to the rules of the Hudson way of living."

Sydney, suddenly suffocated, needed to escape. "I should get going. Early morning and all."

"Syd, call me if you need to talk, okay?" Melanie called out after her as she walked through the front door.

Syd glanced over her shoulder to Melanie—she was nibbling on her lower lip and her eyes were filled with concern. Syd smiled and nodded in response and felt Brett's hand at the small of her back, guiding her toward her car. "Well, thanks for dinner, Brett. Goodnight." She leaned in to give him a kiss on the cheek.

"You can at least act like you love me," he grumbled. "You do know my father is watching us."

Syd's shoulders sank and she shook her head. "Look, Brett, I—"

He wrapped his arms around her and pulled her to him. "Would it kill you to love me?" he demanded, crushing her mouth with his.

Completely stunned and taken off guard, Syd just stood there, numbly allowing Brett to kiss her.

"Mmm," he murmured against her lips. "Now that's more like it. I keep forgetting how good you taste."

"Goodnight," Syd said quietly, pulling away from him and opening the door of her Escape.

She got in and started the engine, glancing up to find Brett smiling smugly before driving off the path and away from the house.

Chapter Twenty-Five

Sydney hadn't driven more than five minutes after leaving the Hudsons' before the tears that she'd been working so hard to keep at bay finally blurred her vision. She pulled over onto the shoulder of the road and flicked her hazards on. Resting her head on the steering wheel, she gripped it tightly and began to weep.

She was tired of the charade, tired of the lying. She didn't love Brett. Hell, she didn't even like him, even if she'd cared for him once upon a time. She was surprised she fooled so many people. When they were together she stood or sat as far away from him as humanly possible, without stirring suspicion. When he smiled at her, she frowned or forced a smile so fake it was impossible to believe there was an ounce of genuine warmth. When he touched her, she cringed. And when Brett's lips met hers, it was near impossible to hide her disgust. Was everyone really that blind?

It was funny, how even though she was technically engaged to Brett, she felt as if she was cheating on Caleb every time Brett kissed her.

Syd let out a scream and punched the steering wheel. She wasn't mad at her father or Theo. At this moment, she didn't even care much about Bacchus, who had put her father in this position to begin with. Past was past, and this should have stayed in the shadowy recesses of their lives. This was one hundred percent Brett's doing—and for that she would never forgive him. She beat the steering wheel again in a flurry of frustration, and, just as abruptly as the vehicular abuse had begun, it stopped. Syd reined in her emotions, and drew in a shuddery breath as she tried to control her angst and compose herself. She sat in the darkened car for nearly ten minutes, the only sound that of the humming engine.

"Stupid," she muttered angrily, reaching for her purse and pulling her cell out of it. "I shouldn't be doing this."

But I'm doing it anyways, because I'm a glutton for punishment and a bad, bad person.

She hit speed dial and impatiently drummed her fingers on the steering wheel, waiting for the call to connect.

"Hey, baby," Caleb said, answering on the first ring.

Her whole body uncoiled in an instant and Syd had no control over the smile that touched her lips at the sound of his voice. "Hey, yourself. How are you?"

"I was fine before you called, but now I'm fantastic," he answered softly. "So how was that business dinner you went to tonight?"

"Terrible," she sniffled.

"Did something happen?" he asked, his voice full of concern.

Part of her loved how he worried about her so much. The other part of her worried that she loved it so much. No matter which way she looked at it, she was screwed.

"No, no, it was just boring as hell. It went well enough, I guess. I'm beyond thrilled to finally be out of there." She paused and bit her lip, suddenly worried she was somehow bothering Caleb with her call. "You're not in the middle of anything, are you?"

"Me? No, not at all. I'm sitting here messing around with a guitar, as usual." She heard the smile in his voice. "I've always got time for you, Syd."

Her eyes stung with fresh tears, and she sighed.

"You sound tired, darlin', and sad," he whispered.

"No, I'm fine, I promise," she replied, making a conscious effort to sound brighter. She hesitated a moment then caved in and spilled out what was in her heart. "I really miss you, Caleb."

"I miss you too, baby. Do you want me to come visit for

a few days? I'm sure PJ can spare me for a bit and the trek would be worth it to make you smile."

Her heart leaped at the mere thought of being with him. She was touched in a way she didn't think possible at the fact that he would consider dropping everything simply to be with her, to make sure she was okay. But she knew there was still too much going on to make a visit from him work safely. "Aw, CJ, thank you, really. You have no idea how much I want to say yes, how badly I'd love to have you here. But I can't. I'm still so busy. I'm meeting my brother tomorrow for brunch, and I have a ton of meetings during the week."

There was silence on the other end of the line.

"I'm sorry, Caleb," she whispered, her shoulders slumping against the back of the driver's seat.

"No, no. It's okay. Uh, listen, darlin', is it okay if I call you back?" he asked, suddenly sounding distracted.

"Oh, yeah. Sure, CJ. I'm still on the road, but I'll be home in about twenty minutes."

"Something's come up I need to deal with. Might take a while. What time is it now over there?"

Syd glanced at the console. "It's closing in on eleven at night."

"Okay. I'll call you at around three-thirty. It'll be late, but this is urgent, and I still need to talk to you."

Syd frowned. "Is everything okay?" It sounded like he had gotten up and was moving around.

"Yes, baby, everything's perfect. I'll speak to you in a couple hours."

Syd snapped her cell shut after saying goodbye and sat in silence for a few moments, reviewing her conversation with him. She pulled back onto the road and made her way to her house, her mind spinning as fast as the wheels of her car. Was Caleb being truthful with her? A few moments before they disconnected, he said he had all the time in the world for her then suddenly he was so busy with something — whatever it may be — that he wouldn't be able to call her back for more than four hours?

Part of her briefly considered there was another woman in his life. He never did explicitly say that she was the only one, and with them being apart for a couple weeks now, it might explain things. After all, she *was* kind of cheating on him with Brett.

"No, you idiot, it's the other way around. I'm technically cheating on Brett, not Caleb," she grumbled as she unlocked her front door and stepped inside the darkened house.

Syd bent to greet Puff, who was balancing on her two back feet, paws up in the air, desperate for attention. She walked to the kitchen and opened the French doors leading to the back yard and the dog bounced her way outside. Syd grabbed a bottle of water from the fridge and sipped it slowly, trying to piece together her conversation with Caleb.

She rubbed her face, trying to fend off the weariness that was taking over, and opened the door to let Puff back in. "Bedtime, little girl."

She climbed the stairs, each step feeling like a hurdle. She began unzipping the dress even before she entered her room and slipped out of it, leaving it where it lay on the floor, too worn out to bother hanging it back up in the closet. She threw on an old, oversized T-shirt and climbed into bed, pulling the fluffy down comforter up around her. She switched on the bedside lamp, setting the room awash in a soft amber glow. There was no way she was going to get any sleep until she spoke with Caleb again.

She leaned back, one hand behind her head, the other she used to gently stoke Puff's fur.

She felt empty when CJ wasn't with her. She was teetering on the edge of falling deeply in love with him. She was terrified that if she spent any more time with him — talking to him, looking into his deep blue eyes, laughing at his jokes, running her fingers through his thick blond hair, enjoying his touch — that she would tip right over that edge and would never be able to let him go.

She had no right to love him—not when she was engaged to marry another man in less than a year—but she didn't think she could stop it. Her heart was acting independently of her mind.

She'd been lying in bed with the same thoughts running circles in her mind for hours when her cell rang. Syd glanced at the clock as she reached for her phone. It was twenty minutes past three.

"Right on time," she answered, smiling.

"A bit early, actually."

She snickered. "You want me to hang up so you can call back in ten minutes?"

"Absolutely not. I missed hearing your voice as it is. Don't make me wait another minute."

She smiled again. He always made her smile, despite the turmoil she was going through.

"Were you sleeping, darlin'?" Caleb asked.

"No, I couldn't sleep. I was just lying here, waiting for you."

"Well, I'm all yours now."

"Hmm," she murmured. "I like the sound of that. So what was the big emergency?"

"Just something I needed to attend to."

"Oh."

He laughed. "You know, Pat's been getting pretty pissed off at me lately."

"Really? Why?"

"I can't concentrate for shit when we were working on ideas for the album. I've been a train-wreck."

Syd frowned. "Something on your mind?"

"Yeah. You."

"Oh. And, um, what exactly have you been thinking about?" she asked, her face burning.

"How much I've missed hearing your laugh and how much I miss talking to you. Among other things."

"Other things, eh? What other things?"

"I'm not sure you could handle me going into the details

of that, darlin'," he answered, his voice husky.

She grinned and leaned back against the pillow, deciding to call him on his challenge. "Try me."

"Well, settle yourself baby," he said slowly, "because you're about to see yourself through my eyes."

Chapter Twenty-Six

Syd propped her pillow up against the headboard. Puff, huffed and jumped off the bed to find somewhere else to rest. A wistful smile touched Syd's lips and she closed her eyes.

"Ready when you are."

"Remember," he began. "You asked for this."

Syd bit her lip.

What the hell did I get myself into, now?

He drew in a long breath. "Well, darlin'…where should I start? Maybe I'll start by telling you how soft your lips are. How when I kiss you, our mouths just seem to fit together, like two pieces of an immensely pleasurable puzzle. Mmm, and your voice," he said. "How your voice gets all husky after I kiss you. It's almost a whisper, but there's enough edge there to tell me you want more, so much more. That you enjoy what I do to you, and how you feel it from top to bottom." He cleared his throat. "Shall I go on?"

"Um, there's more?"

She could practically *hear* him grin on the other end of the line. "Oh yeah, darlin'. I could go on for days about how much I love to kiss you, alone."

"Oh."

"You don't want me to stop, do you? I thought you said you were up for this."

"I am…I think."

He laughed softly.

She inhaled deeply and let the air out in an audible huff. "Okay, mister, you've got so much to say…go on," she taunted.

"Do you recall that first night together?"

Her breath caught in her throat. "Not exactly something I'd ever be able to forget, Mr. Jones," she answered, almost embarrassed at the admission.

"I remember how fucking turned on I got when you couldn't even bother to take your skirt off. You just lifted it over your hips and pushed me inside you. I remember touching you and thinking how incredibly supple you were. Your body's so smooth, baby, and when we made love, when my body glided over yours, it was like I was moving over satin."

Her heart began pounding as she, too, recalled that night of fiery passion on the couch…and on the stairs…and in her bedroom, in vivid detail. She shifted on the mattress and moaned softly.

"And your hair," he continued. "It always smells faintly of plums? I can never get that scent out of my mind."

"It's my shampoo," Syd said absently.

"I love how your hair whispers like silk around your shoulders and down your back," he went on. "I love combing my fingers through it and grabbing hold, using it to pull your head back so I can taste the skin of your neck, or using that grip to hold you tight when I'm fucking you extra hard. You remember how you like it when I do that, don't you, darlin'?"

Syd heard heavy panting and, embarrassed, quickly realized the labored breathing was her own.

Everything Caleb said made her visualize the action. It was as if he was inside her, touching her and tasting her with the sound of his voice, and her body hummed with desire.

"Still with me, baby?"

"Yeah, still here."

"I haven't been with you in too long, darlin'."

"Too long," she repeated, closing her eyes.

"You need me, don't you? You need to let go," he whispered, his voice caressing her.

Syd rocked on the bed and closed her legs tightly together. "God, I need you," she murmured.

"Are you in your bedroom?" he asked, his voice smoky and delicious.

"Uh-huh."

"Go stand in front of the mirror."

Her eyes flicked open. "What?"

"Do it, baby. Please."

"Oh. Uh, okay." Syd threw the comforter off and climbed out of bed. She moved against the footboard to stand in front of the dresser mirror, as instructed. Even in the dim amber glow coming from the bedside lamp, she could easily see that her face was flushed, and no wonder — this was pure sexual torture. He was right, she did need him, and bad.

"Tell me what you're wearing," he said softly.

Syd snickered. "Nothing but a ratty, old, oversized T-shirt with a cartoon duck on it. Holding what looks like a margarita." She heard him stifle a laugh. "And there's some sort of beach umbrella behind him. At least I think it's a *him*."

Caleb burst out laughing, a rich sound that was full of life and that made Syd miss him even more. "Yeah, darlin'. You corner the market on sexy in that get up."

She shrugged, giggling. "I thought so, too."

"Good. Now take it off."

Syd blinked in double-time. "What?"

He chuckled. "Take it off. I want you to see what I see."

She cleared her throat. "Uh, Caleb, I'm not really comfortable doing that."

"Why not? You've seen yourself naked before, haven't you?"

"Well, yeah, but this is different."

"How is it different? Don't tell me you've never stood in front of the mirror examining yourself, touching your body here and there..."

"It's weird, Caleb."

"Because you're on the phone with me?"

"Yes, CJ. You've already got me all hot and horny talking to me like this. I don't need to be taking my clothes off about now, not without you here to finish the job," she retorted, her voice a near whine.

"You're a big girl, Syd. You can take care of yourself."

"I can *what*?"

"You heard me, darlin'."

Her eyes widened at the innuendo. Take care of herself? Was he serious?

Sure, she'd pleasured herself before—it wasn't as if the idea was foreign. But with someone on the phone with her? Someone as incredibly sexy and desirable as Caleb Jones guiding her through it, when all she really wanted was him to be the one touching her and making her come?

It was something she'd never do. It was insane. It was embarrassing. It was…

It was incredibly erotic.

"Hang on," she said, putting the phone on the bed and whipping the shirt over her head, tossing it somewhere behind her. Uncharacteristically self-conscious, Syd didn't dare glance in the mirror as she brought her cell back to her ear.

"You're not looking at yourself, are you?" Caleb asked gently.

"No."

"Look at yourself, Sydney. See what I do. See how beautiful you are, baby. I want you to *understand* how beautiful you are to me."

She flicked her eyes up to her reflection.

"Look at how your skin almost glows? And your eyes, Syd. Jesus. Those got to me the very first time you glanced at me. Now go down… Look at your neck, how long and elegant it is. And the hollow of your throat, God, so kissable. You love it when I scrape my teeth on your collarbone."

She moved her hand to her throat, running her fingers lightly along its length to her collarbone. She dragged her nails lightly along the sensitive surface and goosebumps spread across her body.

"Your breasts, Syd. Those two beautiful, flawless mounds. They fit perfectly into my palms, just a handful. I love how their tips get so hard and turn a bright pink when you're aroused. Mmm, and how your body arches when I take one peak between my teeth, or I roll the tip between my fingers. Go on, baby, do you feel that? Do you see how turned on you get?"

"Caleb," she murmured, trailing her hand lower and cupping one heavy breast, lightly pinching the tip between her thumb and forefinger, making her tingle. God, he was affecting her more than she was willing to admit.

"Your slender waist, and your hips... How my hands fit right on them when I pull you against me. The way your body feels when it's pressed up against mine, Syd, it's somehow *right*. Then there's that soft stomach that I love running my tongue along." He paused, slightly breathless himself. "Syd, are you following along, touching yourself the way I wish I could right now?"

"Yes," she breathed, moving between her breasts to her abdomen. She swallowed hard. There was no controlling the need raging through her. She wanted him. She needed him.

She was, for lack of a better way to put it, horny as fuck.

"Don't stop, Syd," he whispered. "Please don't."

"I... I won't," she managed.

"Move your hand to that little triangle of black hair where your legs meet."

Her gaze trailed down her body in the mirror as he spoke and her hand soon followed the same path. She shifted uncomfortably against the footboard, her desire spinning nearly out of control. She closed her eyes, focusing only on the lilt of his voice as he spoke to her.

"How tender you are in there, Syd — one flick is all it takes to make you go weak. Fuck, how wet you get for me, baby, I love it. Go on, feel."

She moved her fingers between the folds of skin and

stroked gently, imagining it was Caleb's fingers instead of her own.

"Oh, and how you taste, darlin'. A tantalizing mix of musk and sex—and the way it lingers on my tongue. I'll always be thirsty for you."

"Jesus, CJ…" she stammered, barely able to stay upright any longer.

"Come on, darlin', taste. Know what it is that drives me crazy and makes me so damn hard," he said, his voice hoarse with desire.

She brought her hand to her mouth, hesitant. She darted out her tongue, tasting the wetness on her fingers, and she sighed.

"Move your fingers back down, inside, where it's warm and wet and tight," he growled.

She did as instructed.

"Now, in and out, Syd—slowly at first, then faster." He waited a moment before continuing. "Shit, can you feel it, Syd? Do you see how your whole body trembles? There's nothing at all like that sensation, when I fuck you and you finally find that release, when you clench around me. It's perfection. Vibration after vibration of ecstasy. There's nothing better than giving you that pleasure. Nothing better than hearing you shout my name."

She moaned in response.

"Christ, I want to fuck you so bad, baby."

That did it. She tipped her head back, focusing only on his silken words and her fingers pumping inside her. She closed her eyes tight, back arched slightly against the footboard as she continued working herself toward release, so close, so close, the world around her only a fuzzy reality. She moved her thumb to the swollen nub nestled between her slick folds and she began circling her clit at the same time, applying gentle pressure.

"God!" She threw her cell down and grabbed the edge of the bed for support as she finally let go in a shattering release of tension. Winded, she shuddered with the aftershock and sank to the floor, reaching for the phone.

"Syd?"

"Oh...oh God," she stammered. Syd opened her eyes again and tried to focus on the room around her. She brought her hand back to her side, almost embarrassed at how slick her fingers had become.

He chuckled. "All better, darlin'?"

"Mmm, better if you were here to clean up the mess you made," she breathed.

"Oh, I'd love to, believe me."

"I can't believe I did that." She stood on shaky knees and rounded the bed, collapsing onto it.

"I wish I was there right now. I'd be on my knees, licking you dry," he whispered.

She groaned. "Oh, Caleb, please, no more. I can't take it. But what about you, Mr. Jones? What can I do for you?" she asked, grinning up at the ceiling.

He laughed softly. "Oh, I can think of lots of things you can do for me, but my main goal tonight was taking care of *you*."

Syd giggled. "Oh, you took care of me all right."

"Good. Now get some sleep, darlin', and I'll call you tomorrow night, okay?"

"Mmm-hmm. Sounds fantastic. Goodnight, Caleb."

"Sweet dreams, baby."

She clicked the cell phone closed and reached out to place it on her nightstand. Utterly exhausted, she flopped back against the pillow and closed her eyes. She was astounded by what had happened — not only the fact that she'd brought herself to orgasm, but by how powerful it was. She'd never experienced anything like that in her entire life. The things Caleb said to her, how he thought of her... God, it was all she could do to control her heart from bursting — and her loins from melting all over again. She let out a soft laugh and moved to turn off the small lamp, more ready than ever to succumb to sleep.

The doorbell rang.

Syd popped upright into a sitting position, startled. "What the..."

The doorbell sounded again and Puff immediately started barking, the furry alarm system engaged.

Syd twisted to check the clock—it was nearly four in the morning. Who would be at her door at this hellish hour? She flicked on the light and stared out the open door to the hallway, waiting to see if the bell would ring again or if it was just her half-conscious imagination.

It sounded again, more urgently this time.

Worried now, she sprang to her feet and hustled into the bathroom. She grabbed a robe from behind the bathroom door and swung it on. The last time she'd seen her father he wasn't looking all that well. What if the stress of their situation was too great a burden and something had happened to him? What if the whole time she was on the phone with Caleb, Theo had been trying to reach her and she was too engrossed in her own selfish sexual needs to even have heard the beep for 'call waiting'? She knotted the belt and ran downstairs in the pitch black of deep night.

Reaching the foyer, she nearly tripped over Puff, who was bouncing in place at the front door, waking the whole neighborhood with her yips and yaps. Syd furtively peeked out the small window to check who was there.

"Oh my God," she whispered, her jaw dropping and her heart thundering in her ears.

She quickly unlocked the door and opened it wide, inviting the cool night air in to swirl around her bare legs. Rooted to the floor with shock, her mouth formed a delicate 'O' before she managed to get a single word out.

"Caleb."

Chapter Twenty-Seven

Caleb crossed the threshold, forcing Syd to back up a couple of steps. He closed the door behind him and turned to face Syd again, immediately dropping to his knees in front of her.

He could barely see her in the darkened foyer, but he didn't need to *see* her. He only needed to taste her.

He drew Syd closer to him and untied her robe, pulling the plush white panels away from her body. He slid his hands up her thighs and hooked them around her bottom, bringing her toward him and thrusting his tongue up and inside her. She gasped in shock and bucked forward, bracing herself with her palms flat against the front door.

Caleb tugged on her, drawing her lower to his face, and worked his tongue between the slick folds and deeper into her center.

She's soaking wet. His groin tightened in response.

He dug his fingers into her soft flesh and began lapping gently from back to front. He paused a moment to torture her by wiggling his tongue on her clit, enjoying how it made Syd's entire body quake.

"God, I missed you," he breathed against her, driving his tongue inside once more. He unhooked one of his hands from her and slid it up her abdomen and between her breasts, coming to rest on her throat, and with his thumb, he gently stroked the hollow.

Syd gripped the hand at her neck firmly, squeezing it and moaning softly, while she threaded the fingers of her other hand into his hair, gripping tight. Her hips rocked in time with his tongue and in moments she cried out, her whole body shuddering and contracting around him again and again.

When she was done, her knees gave out and Caleb quickly wrapped his arms around her and gently brought her to the ground beneath him. She stared at him, her green eyes cloudy in the dim light that filtered in from the street, and she smiled.

"Hi," she breathed, the word shaky.

"Hey, baby," he whispered back, using his hand to wipe the excess moisture from his chin. He leaned in and kissed her, lightly tugging on her lower lip with his teeth.

"What are you doing here?" she asked, gazing up at him in wonder.

"You said you needed me."

She shook her head. "I never said that. I said I missed you."

"You didn't say the words, Syd. But it was there in your voice. It's been there the past few weeks."

She sighed and grabbed him, reeling him in for another kiss. "How do you know me so well?"

"Because I'm the best boyfriend *ever*." Those weren't exactly the words he longed to say, but they would do. Hell, he had trouble admitting to himself he was falling hard, but saying the words to her was something different altogether. He needed to get his head on straight first.

A shadow of emotion crossed her features and she furrowed her brow. "That you are, CJ," she said slowly. "Please don't misinterpret, I *am* glad you're here, but how? How did you get here so fast?"

He nuzzled her chin while he spoke. "Do you remember last weekend, when you called me early in the morning to tell me you missed me?"

"Uh-huh." She tipped her head back, silently urging his mouth to move to her neck.

He was more than happy to accommodate.

"Well," he continued between nibbles, "I was so terrified that something was wrong, and I realized how it would take me somewhere around ten or eleven hours just to get to you. That was unacceptable."

She propped herself up on her elbows and pushed him away. "Unacceptable?" she repeated quietly.

He smiled softly. "Darlin', if something was wrong, if you needed me, I needed to get to you quicker than that. So I told PJ if he was looking for me I'd be at my place in California."

Her eyes widened. "You were in California?"

Caleb sat back on his knees and traced his fingertips lightly along her jaw, down her neck and between her breasts, finally resting on her abdomen. "Sydney," he whispered. "I'd do anything for you."

Her eyes shimmered and she sat up on her knees, her left thigh pressing the seemingly ever-present bulge between his legs. She grabbed and kissed him. "Anything?" she teased.

"Anything, darlin'."

"Then take me upstairs."

Caleb growled in the back of his throat and got to his feet, bringing her up with him and carrying her to the stairs. She looped her arms around his neck and began lavishing any skin she found with smooches while he carefully navigated the steps in the dark.

"Happy to see me?" he asked jokingly.

"More than you know," she answered, kissing his cheek between words for emphasis.

In her room, Caleb plopped Syd on her bed and sat beside her. There was a startled yelp followed by rustling blankets, and Puff popped out from under the comforter, an accusatory glare in her eyes. She huffed at Caleb and let loose a soft growl.

Sydney burst into a fit of giggles as Caleb tried to make amends with the nearly squashed Pomeranian.

"I'm sorry, Puff," he said reaching a hand out to scratch her behind the ears. She pulled away from him at first and he continued, "I promise I won't hurt you."

Black eyes never leaving his, she stretched her neck forward and warily sniffed his outstretched hand. Deciding he was acceptable, she took a couple of steps toward him, climbed onto his lap and curled into a ball, preparing to go back to sleep.

Caleb was grinning like an idiot, but gaining the defensive animal's approval actually meant a lot to him.

"Okay, Puffy, go downstairs. Mommy needs some alone time with CJ," she said, shrugging off the open robe.

Puff licked him, hopped off the bed and trotted out into the hall. Caleb stood and closed the door behind her. He turned back to Syd and smiled. "She likes me."

"So do I," Syd smirked, a mischievous glint in her eyes.

"Really?"

"Come here," she whispered, getting to her knees and crawling to the edge of the bed. She reached out and hooked her fingers into the waist of his jeans, pulling him against her. "Let me prove it."

He raised an eyebrow and ran his fingers through her hair. "Prove away, babe."

She met his eyes and ran her tongue across her lips.

Such a small thing, but it made him thirst for her.

She reached up and slowly began unbuttoning his white shirt. She pulled it out of his jeans and spread the shirt to either side of his torso. Her pale green eyes locked on his. She feathered her fingers down his chest, tracing the planes and ridges of muscle. She carefully peeled the shirt away from his body and raked her nails over his back, raising goosebumps.

"You know," she said, her voice soft as she unbuckled his belt. "There's been something" — she paused as she unzipped his jeans — "that I've been dying to do to you."

In one fluid motion, she tugged his pants and underwear to the ground and he sprang free. She took his length in her hand as she slid off the bed and sank to her knees in front of him.

In an instant Caleb figured out what was about to happen,

and he groaned, "Oh God."

"Finally," she breathed, wrapping her fingers around the base of his cock and taking him into her mouth.

It was as if every nerve, every cell, was charged.

She pulled away and took him back in again, this time slower, inch by agonizing inch. Her grip remaining firm, she pumped him steadily, swirling her tongue around the tip all the while. Caleb threaded his fingers into her silken black hair and held on, drawing in shallow breaths.

Syd moaned and the gentle vibrations of it all around his length made him shudder with delight. She continued her tender manipulation of him and he tossed his head back, closing his eyes tight, trying to fight the almost desperate urge to release, wanting to prolong the sensation. Caleb let go of her hair and reached down to caress her cheeks as she drew him deeper into her throat.

In the end, he lost the battle, and with her steadily moving her head and hand in time with each other, he let loose a guttural cry, spilling into her. She kept going, not breaking rhythm until his body stopped quaking above her.

She pulled away and sat back on her haunches. Syd gazed up at him and, smiling softly, licked her lips. "Delicious."

He drew in a long breath. "Sydney, you're pure evil."

She shrugged and grinned. "But you like me anyhow."

"Yes, darlin'. Yes, I do. You have no idea how much." He helped her to her feet and, once upright, he wrapped his arms around her middle and pulled her in to a hug.

She buried her head in his chest and sighed. "I missed you, Caleb. I really, really missed you."

"I'm here now, baby," he replied, moving her raven locks away from her neck and inhaling her scent. She slumped slightly in his arms. "You have plans tomorrow and lots going on during the week, I get that. I'm heading back to California late morning."

She squeezed him tighter and trembled in his arms.

"Darlin', are you crying?"

She sniffled. "I'm sorry."

He put one hand on the back of her head, pressing her into him. "Why are you crying, Syd?"

"Uch!" She pulled away and rubbed at her eyes with her palms. "No reason in particular, CJ. I'm really stressed out about work, and about my father, and just everything. Then there's the fact that because of everything going on in my life, I feel like I'm ignoring you, and because of that I'm going to lose you, or that I shouldn't even be with you because it's not fair to you," she rambled. "And then I wonder if you're going to get sick of me and —"

Caleb brought his mouth down hard upon hers. He kissed her roughly, desperately needing her to believe that there was no chance in hell he'd ever tire of her.

He cupped her cheek. "Syd," he murmured. "You're not going to lose me, and I'm certainly not going to get sick of you. It's actually quite the opposite. I can't get enough of you, darlin', and I'm not sure I ever will."

She gazed up at him, her olive eyes unreadable. She gently stroked his cheek. "I… I worry, I guess. You're just so damn perfect, CJ. It scares me. *You* scare me. *We* scare me."

Caleb sat on the bed, took her hand, and pulled her down to sit on his lap. He cradled her against him, running his fingers lightly up one satiny leg. "Listen, we'll work this out, Syd. You're busy — so am I — and it doesn't help that we live in different countries. But even if we can make it so that we visit each other one day every two weeks, I'll take it, so long as I get to talk to you every day, if only to say goodnight."

Uncertainty creased her brow. "Are you sure you're okay with that?"

He nodded and kissed her forehead. "I came tonight, even though I have to get back on a plane and leave you in a couple hours, didn't I? I'll take what I can get."

But was he really okay with it? What kind of relationship was he setting himself up for, only seeing the woman he was courting every so often?

"It might be a couple weeks till I can see you again," she

said, her voice filled with remorse.

He admitted that it stung, the thought of her being too busy for him, but he meant it when he said that he wanted to make it work. "That's okay, darlin'." His hand moved up her thigh to her hip. "We're together now. What do you say we make the most of the next few hours?"

"Mr. Jones, that's a brilliant idea."

He pulled her onto the mattress and reached over to turn off the light, the soft smile on her lips as he climbed atop her the last thing he saw before they were plunged into darkness.

Chapter Twenty-Eight

"Okay, sis, spill it. What's got you in such a great mood?" Theo asked, raising his eyebrows. He leaned back in his chair and drummed his fingers on the table, dark eyes sparkling as he waited impatiently for her answer.

Syd shrugged and popped a piece of French toast in her mouth, trying not to smirk.

"Syd, come on! You're not being fair!" he protested, crumpling up a napkin and throwing it at her.

"Not being fair about what?" her father said, walking toward the small white kitchen table. He set down his plate and sat with them. "What aren't you being fair about, Nikki?"

She took a sip of her orange juice and waved her hand in the air. "Nothing, Papa. Theo's wondering why I'm in a good mood. Like I've never been in a good mood before." She rolled her eyes and tossed the napkin back at her brother.

"Well, Theo has a point, Nikki," her father said, wagging his fork at her. "This whole situation has been stressful, but even so, you haven't been acting yourself lately."

"Yeah, well, when you figure out what 'acting like myself' means given said situation—you let me know." She pushed her plate away from her, appetite suddenly lost.

"So much for the good mood," Theo muttered, chomping on a piece of watermelon and chewing enthusiastically.

"Nikki, we talked about this already, I don't know what else to say anymore. What you're doing is hard, more than hard. It only goes to show how good your mother raised you, and what a big heart you have. But I told you before, you don't have to marry him. We can find another way. I can go back to Greece and defend myself. Mistakes of my past should not be the mistake of your future."

"Yeah," Theo growled, tossing the watermelon rind into the sink. "And when we go to Greece I'll show that Bacchus fucktard what it means to mess with my family."

"Theo!" Sydney and her father cried out in unison.

"Don't say such things, Theo! These are dangerous men!" their father yelled.

"You promised you'd stop with those thoughts!" Sydney chastised.

Taken aback by their strong reactions, Theo hung his head and muttered, "Sorry."

Their father turned his attention back to Sydney and he took her hand in his. "I won't be on this earth forever, Nikki. I don't want you to be unhappy because of all this. It's not worth it. I love you too much."

Overwhelmed, she tore her hand from her father's. "Papa, please. Not now," Syd begged, rubbing at her face. "I'm trying to be happy, I'm trying to be positive. Just leave me be."

Theo nodded toward her plate. "Hey, you done with that?"

She shoved it toward him. "Knock yourself out." She stood and made her way out of the French doors and into the garden, walking a few yards before turning out of sight of her father's prying eyes.

Alone with her thoughts, Syd tipped her head to the warmth of the sun. Caleb had left less than two hours ago and already she wanted to book a flight to California to be with him. They'd made love twice more during the night, finally collapsing into a contented sleep in each other's arms. When they'd woken up they'd sat on the bed and talked and joked and played with Puff, until finally he had to force himself to leave for the airport. He'd given her one last kiss and pressed his cheek to her forehead while hugging her tightly, then he was gone.

Gone.

And all I really want is for him to stay.

Sydney sighed sadly. She had been happy when she'd first gotten here, the high of being with Caleb still coursing through her. She'd wanted to share her happiness with her father and brother, but when they'd started questioning her on her 'good mood', reality had come crumbling all around her, crushing her lifted spirits.

Come next spring, she was going to be married. She was going to become Mrs. Brett Hudson.

"Gross," she muttered, sticking her tongue out in distaste.

"What's gross?"

Syd turned around to find Theo standing behind her, head cocked slightly to the side, a confused expression on his handsome face. She gave him a small smile. "Everything. Everything's gross."

He gasped, placing a hand over his heart. "Even the French toast? But I made it!" he cried in mock indignation.

"Anything you cook is fantastic. Life as a whole, on the other hand, is gross and sucky," Syd clarified.

He frowned at her.

She threw her hands up in the air. "Well, it's true!"

Theo came up behind her and wrapped his arms around her waist, pulling her in close to him. "Papa's really starting to get worried about you," he whispered. "I am, too."

She reached up held one of his hands, threading her fingers into his. "I'm okay, Theo. I promise."

He shook his head in a definitive no. "You're not. Your moods are all over the place. One minute happy, the next minute sad, the next angry. What's going on, Syd? Talk to me—and don't blame it on them female hormones."

Tears stung her eyes and she closed them tight, trying to rein in her emotions. One salty drop escaped, tracking a wet trail on her cheek and finally dropping off, onto his arm. He sighed and squeezed her tighter. "Let's get out of here for a bit, okay?"

Sydney nodded, allowing herself to be led around the

side of the house to Theo's car. She waited silently while he went inside to tell their father they were leaving for a while and to grab her purse. When he returned, she got in the passenger seat of his garnet-red convertible Camaro and buckled up. She could feel her father's eyes on her but she didn't turn around to wave goodbye. She didn't want him to see the pain she was sure was etched into her features.

Theo drove, unspeaking, for nearly half an hour. Syd was content to sit quietly beside him, enjoying the wind in her hair and on her skin. She closed her eyes and tipped her head to the sky. At times like this, she really thought everything was going to be okay. She was going to be happy. She was going to marry the man she loved.

Her eyes popped open as the realization hit her full on. *The man she loved.* Dear God. She'd fallen completely in love with Caleb.

Oh shit.

She was well aware she had strong feelings for him, but had always left it at that, never assigning an emotion to them. Now that she did, she wasn't sure how to control it—or herself—and her spirits spiraled into that dark place again.

"See, you just did it," Theo piped up suddenly.

"What, Theo? What did I just do?"

He parked the car and got out, moving around to the passenger side and opening her door. "You went from smiling to frowning, like that," he answered, snapping his fingers.

She grumbled a string of curses together and he laughed. "Why are we at the park, Theo?"

He grinned, the big smile crinkling the corners of his eyes. *He looks exactly like Papa when he smiles like that,* she thought.

"I figured we could sit and talk a bit. That okay?"

She nodded and he draped an arm over her shoulders as they headed toward the trail that looped around a small pond. They walked in silence for a few minutes, taking in the smell of fresh spring dahlias, tulips, hyacinths and marigolds that bordered both sides of the paved pathway. Finding a small patch of grass that provided them with some privacy, they sat as the ducks, swans and geese floated around in the water.

"What's going on with you, Nikki?" Theo asked gently, reverting to her birth name as he often did when he was worried about her.

She sighed and rested her head on his strong shoulder. "It's the whole Brett thing."

He shook his head. "No, it's not, because the *'whole Brett thing'* has been going on a long time. You've only been acting weird since you got back from Banff." He nudged her in the ribs with his elbow. "Well, weirder than you usually do, anyhow."

Squeezing her eyes shut she mentally weighed the pros and cons of telling Theo the truth. He wouldn't judge her. He would continue to be the strong shoulder she was now leaning on. He would help her through the inevitable heartbreak.

And he would of course ask her what in God's name possessed her to date a famous rock star anyhow.

Okay, fine, I won't tell him it's Caleb, but I have to get this off my chest.

She scratched her forehead and grimaced. "I, uh... I kind of met someone."

He sat up straighter. "What do you mean you kind of met someone?"

"A guy."

"Okay. We all meet people. No biggie. Right?" He pulled away and studied her. "Tell me it's no biggie."

She peeked up at him sheepishly. "It's a biggie."

"Oh, crap."

"I've seen him on and off since I went to Banff back in March."

"Double crap."

"And I might have stumbled and fallen in love with him along the way."

He groaned. "Crap to infinity."

She frowned. "Yeah, that."

He twisted his body to face her, and raked a hand through his wavy brown hair. "So, how'd you two meet? How in love are we talking here? Does he realize you're engaged to fuckwad?" He grinned. "And, perhaps most importantly, does he like Greek food?"

"Theo, this is serious," she said, slapping his arm.

"Agreed. Answer the questions."

She shook her head at her glass-half-full brother and tried to gauge how he'd react to her answers. "Let's see, we met when my car went sliding into his on an icy road. Can't say how in love I am—I only figured it out myself on the way over here. I've barely wrapped my head around the idea." She sighed. "He has no idea I'm engaged. And yes, he loves Greek food."

"Great! When do I get to meet him?"

"Theo!"

"All right, all right," he conceded, putting on his serious face. "Does he feel the same way about you?"

She let her shoulders slump and gnawed on her lower lip. "I think so. I mean, I don't know. He hasn't said anything yet."

"How have you guys been seeing each other with Brett around?"

"We probably see each other once every few weeks," she said sadly. "He lives in the States."

A light bulb switched on over his head and his eyes opened wide. "That's why you were in such a good mood this morning! You were with him!"

Her face flushed crimson.

His brown eyes widened further. "Oh, you bad, bad girl, you!"

Syd buried her face in her hands, mortified.

He gently pulled her hands away and dipped his head to look at her. "So, what are we going to do about this?" he asked, his voice gentle.

"I don't know."

"Well, good thing you've got your big brother around. Because *he* knows what to do." He reached out and pinched her cheek. "Dump Brett. Cancel the wedding. Go be with Mr. Dream Boy."

She gaped at him. "I can't! Papa…"

"We'll figure something out. You know we will. Papa won't hate you, no matter what you think. In fact, I think knowing how unhappy you are is doing more damage than anything. It breaks his heart to see his little girl so sad all the time."

"I can't do that, Theo. Papa—*family*—comes first."

He scowled. "I'd bet anything Brett would never even utter a word about this if you told him where to go."

"And if you're wrong?" she countered.

The question hung in the air between them, as they mutely watched a mallard dunk its head under the water and pop back up.

"It's been too long since you've been happy, Nikki," Theo whispered.

She glanced up at him, her eyes moist with emotion. "You, too. Ever since Mom died you and I have sucked in the relationship game, haven't we? It's like we haven't allowed ourselves the chance at that kind of happiness."

He refused to meet her eyes.

"Theo?"

"Yeah, we've sucked. Right."

She gave him a half-smile. "By the way, Cara still doesn't have a boyfriend," she whispered, squeezing his hand.

It was his turn to blush. "So?"

Sydney sighed. Her brother was the most confident, optimistic, outgoing person she knew — until she mentioned Cara's name. Then he turned into a shy pre-teen with a huge crush on the most popular girl in school. He'd had a thing for Cara for a long time. She wasn't sure how Cara felt about him, though, beyond the fact that she thought he was a great guy.

"Nothing, Theo. So, nothing. And I'm not calling things off with Brett. I won't do that to Papa. It's not worth the risk."

"Well, I'm not sure what to tell you then, Syd."

"Promise you'll be there for me, okay? I have to call things off with Caleb, and when I do I'm really going to need a shoulder or two to cry on."

He reached out and hugged her fiercely. "I'll be here for you, sis. Anytime, anyplace. You know that."

Hugging him back, she was no longer able to fight the tears she'd been battling all morning. "Thank you for not judging me, Theo."

He kissed her hair. "I need my annoying little sister happy, okay. Whatever happens, happens. Just be happy."

She nodded. "I will be. I promise."

But, without Caleb in her life, that was a promise she'd never be able to keep.

Chapter Twenty-Nine

"Hey, how's Sydney doing? You haven't gushed about her much the last couple weeks," Pat asked, getting up from the plush chair he'd been sitting in for the past six hours. He carefully leaned his guitar against the wall and reached his arms up in the air to stretch.

Caleb frowned. "Syd, yeah, she's great man. Thanks for asking."

Pat halted mid-stretch and tipped his head to study his brother. "What aren't you telling me?"

Caleb's gaze flicked up to meet PJ's for a brief second before returning to the staff paper on the coffee table in front of him. "What do you mean?"

"A few weeks ago" — Pat began, making his way to the small bar fridge in the corner of the cozy makeshift studio — "all you could do was talk about Syd. If I asked how she was doing, you'd go on and on about how amazing she is. Syd this, Syd that..." He pulled two bottles of water out of the fridge and made his way back to Caleb. "Now you barely say squat." He tossed his brother one of the bottles.

He sighed. He had been wondering when PJ would ask him about this. His mood had been doing nothing but going downhill at a runaway speed since the last time he saw Sydney — almost four fucking weeks ago, now. It was inevitable.

He twisted the cap off the bottle and took a good long swallow before answering. "I don't get what's going on with her. I realize we live in different countries, and I get that we won't be able to be with each other every day." He shook his head. "Hell, even if we lived in the same city we'd be lucky to see each other more than twice a week, if only because of our respective jobs." He stood and paced the small room.

"But what?"

Caleb ran a hand through his hair. "But... But everything!" He capped the water bottle and slammed it onto the table. "*But* I haven't seen her in nearly a month. *But* I'm lucky if I've spoken to her twice in the past two weeks, and when I do talk to her she's distant. *But* she's always so fucking busy with God knows what that I have no idea when I'll get to see her again. *But* I've fallen completely and totally in love with her and I got no clue as to how she fucking feels. That's what!"

Pat leaned back and crossed his arms over his chest, his lips pressed into a thin line. He seemed to be waiting patiently for his brother to continue.

Caleb paced the room, trying to figure out what to say next. They both were silent a few minutes before he spoke again. "You realize I left Miami to come stay here in Cali to be closer to her, right?"

PJ nodded. "I kind of figured as much, to be honest. It's not like we live in Alaska and you were seeking warmth. We live in Florida, for fuck's sake—the eastern equivalent of California. I don't mind working on the album here with you, but you know I like to be close to home. You get how I can be."

Caleb chuffed. He certainly *did* understand how his brother could be. The two had fought for hours over his refusal to come back to Miami to work on the album. While the duo were usually in sync on everything from lyrics to album artwork to what takeout to order, the one thing Pat always fought for was working at home, in Florida. A single dad, he hated not being close to his daughter Lilly, and he worked best when he was able to sleep in the comfort of his own bed and wake up rejuvenated and refreshed in the morning. Caleb would never usually fight so hard for something like this, especially knowing what it would mean to his brother, but he was insistent. Pat must've sensed something else was really going on, and caved.

"So you love her, huh?" he asked softly.

Caleb plunked into his seat and groaned. "Yeah, man. I do like you wouldn't believe."

"Have you told her?"

"No, not yet."

PJ sat across from him and rested his forearms on his knees, hands clasped together. "Why haven't you?"

"I'm not sure, really," Caleb answered, leaning back and staring at the ceiling. "I mean, it's a good thing, right? *I love her*. I'm dying to tell her, but part of me is terrified. After all the crap I went through with Meg, maybe part of me is scared of getting hurt again and making another mistake."

"You didn't make a mistake with Meg, bro. She's the one who cheated on you. She's the one to blame. You don't need to be scared of other relationships because of that lying bitch."

"I'm not. I only think of how everything went to shit the minute I told her I loved her. In the back of my mind I'm scared that the same thing will happen with Syd. I can't screw this one up, too."

"Sounds to me like she's the one screwing this up, not you," PJ mumbled.

"What?"

"Nothing," Pat answered, waving his hand in the air dismissively. "I don't want to battle it out with you."

Caleb sighed. "No, you're right. She *is* screwing it up." He rubbed at his eyes, weary. "It's just that I thought what we had, what we were building, was great. When I was with her she was happy—she even said she was worried she'd lose me, and now she's the one who's pulling away and I can't for the life of me figure out why."

"Don't take this the wrong way, bro, okay? But maybe she's not as into you are you are to her?"

"Excuse me?"

Pat shrugged and grimaced. "Well, look, just playing a

173

little devil's advocate here, but you're the one who chased her all the way to Vancouver, even though she said she didn't want to see you again after your time together in Banff. You're the one freaking out about this, picking up and staying here in California only to be closer to her. You're the one who goes out of his way to be with her." He paused and grimaced. "Maybe she's not interested in you, not for a relationship anyhow. Maybe you're fun for a tumble in the sheets, but she doesn't want anything else?"

"No. You're wrong. She's totally interested in me."

Pat raised his eyebrows. "Is that your ego talking?"

Caleb shook his head and leaned forward in his seat. "Listen, I see the way she looks at me, man, the same way Mom looked at Dad. It's in the way she touches me and says my name." He shook his head again. "No. She has feelings for me that go beyond casual sex, PJ. There's no way it's all in my head."

"Fine," Pat conceded. "So then why is she pulling away?"

"I don't know," Caleb answered miserably.

"Well, you better find out, man, because it's eating you alive." Pat got to his feet. "Speaking of eating, I'm going to go upstairs and order us some Chinese. Maybe you want to give a certain someone a quick call and figure out what's going on in that pretty little head of hers?" He patted him on the shoulder as he walked out the door and up the stairs to the main floor.

No, Caleb thought. *No, I don't want to call her. I've been the one calling her every other day for the past couple weeks.*

But he had to try to figure out what was wrong. Was it something he said or did that was making her withdraw from him?

He reached for his cell phone and punched in her number, tapping his foot impatiently while waiting for the call to connect.

"Hello?" a quiet voice answered.

"Syd?"

"Caleb? Oh, um, now's not a good time," she said quickly.

"Can I... Can I call you later?"

He frowned. She didn't sound herself. "Is everything okay, Syd?"

"Yeah, yeah. You caught me right in the middle of about ten things." She tittered.

"I just need a minute, babe. It's really important."

"Um, all right. What's up?"

"What's going on with us, darlin'. Did I do something to make you mad at me?"

He heard her sigh. "No, Caleb. You've been perfect."

His shoulders slumped. "Well, then what's wrong? I'm the one always calling you lately. I understand you're really busy with Christou's, but come on, we haven't seen each other in weeks. I know I'm acting like a needy little teenager, but you went from hot to cold in an instant, and I deserve to be told why."

"CJ, I really can't get into this right now."

"I understand that, Syd, but we agreed to try to make this work. It's been almost a month, and you can't manage to take even one day to see me." A crash sounded and he heard Puff whining. He sat up in his chair rod straight. "What was that?"

"Nothing. It was nothing. Look, CJ, really. I'm sorry but I have to go."

"I'm still waiting for you, baby! Don't make me wait all night!" a male voice shouted in the background.

"Syd, what's going on? Who's there with you?" he asked, his stomach in knots.

"I'm in Toronto next week. I'll call you then. Goodnight," she whispered, hanging up.

A few minutes later PJ returned to find Caleb slumped over in his chair, deep in thought, brow furrowed. "Did you call her?"

Caleb nodded.

"And?"

He shook his head and turned to face his brother. "Pat, I have no idea what the fuck to think anymore. She couldn't

175

wait to get me off the phone. And…" He shrugged, unable to say the words.

"What, man? Come on, tell me."

He glanced up at PJ, sure that the confusion in his mind was reflected in his eyes. "And there was a guy there with her. I heard the voice in the background. Some dude said that he was waiting for her, and didn't want her to make him wait all night." He clenched his fists. "He called her '*baby*'."

Pat blinked at him.

"That's not exactly a good sign, is it?"

"Maybe it was the television?" Pat suggested.

"Don't think so. Syd was practically whispering to me, like she was trying to hide the fact she was on the phone. Shit," he murmured. "She's seeing someone else, that's gotta be it."

"I'm not sure what to say here, CJ. Maybe… Just don't assume anything or assume the worst, okay? Next time you speak with her, ask her about it and try to get to the truth. But till then, don't torture yourself with what-ifs."

"She said she'd be in Toronto next week and that she'd call me." Caleb ran his fingers through his hair. "I'm not calling her again, Pat. If she wants to be with me, if she wants to talk, then she needs to make the next move. I won't chase her like this."

He nodded sadly at his brother.

"I'm done trying, PJ. Done."

Chapter Thirty

Syd put her cell on the bed beside her and blinked back the tears that burned her eyes. Of course Caleb would choose to call her right now, at the worst possible time ever. She pulled a shaking Puff into her lap and flinched when she heard another crash downstairs.

Come on, Theo. Come on.

"Nikki! Oh, Nikki! You can't hide up there forever, baby."

"I can try," she muttered, hand gliding over Puff's smooth fur, trying to soothe the frightened dog. Every so often she'd let out a little growl, but even that quickly faded away into a whimper.

For a moment, the only sound was the rain hammering down on the roof and the occasional rumble of thunder in the distance. Normally Syd loved thunderstorms, the steady drumming of the rain soothing her and lulling her to sleep. Not tonight. Tonight, each thunderclap foreshadowed the inevitable fight with Brett and each flash of lightning frazzled her nerves.

Syd froze when she heard footsteps in the hall outside her bedroom door. Thank God she'd locked it.

"Nikki." The doorknob jiggled. "Nikki, Nikki, Nikki. Come on, baby. Let me in."

"Go away, Brett," she answered, her tone stern. "You're drunk, so call a cab and go home already."

"Drunk I may be. Going home, though, that's not an option. Not till we talk," he slurred. He tried the doorknob again. "Damn it, Nikki, let me in!" Brett pounded on the door.

Syd put the quivering dog gently on the duvet. "Stay,

Puff. Don't move," she whispered. The dog's eyes were filled with worry, as if she was trying to convince her mama to stay in the sanctity of the bedroom and not to go down and face the big bad monster. She gave the pup a quick kiss on the forehead, hoping to calm both their nerves. She got up and headed to the door. "Brett, go back downstairs. When I hear you there I'll come out, but not before."

After a moment of silence, he finally agreed. "Fine. Hurry your pretty ass up."

His footsteps faded as he left her door and headed for the stairs. He must've lost his footing on the way—Syd heard him slam to the floor, a string of curses following.

She pulled her cell out of her pocket and called her brother again. As soon as he picked up she breathed a sigh of relief. "Theo, I'm going to go talk to him. When will you be here?"

"Less than ten minutes, Syd. Don't go down there, please," he begged. "What if he hurts you?"

"He won't. I've seen him drunk before—he doesn't get violent, only stupid," she assured him, half trying to convince herself.

"But you said he was breaking things downstairs. Just wait for me, please."

She shook her head. "Try to picture a five-year-old having a temper tantrum. That's Brett right now. I'll be fine, but hurry up."

She heard the motor rev higher. "Five minutes, maybe less. Be careful."

She disconnected and opened the bedroom door, tentatively taking a step into the hall. She cautiously made her way to the main floor, stopping a few steps short. Brett was leaning against the wall, arms crossed over his broad chest, tapping his foot impatiently.

"Well, it's about fucking time, Nikki."

She bit her lip, suddenly unsure about her decision to talk with him. There was something different about Drunk Brett this time—he looked wilder, more unpredictable...angrier.

Maybe Theo was right.

"What do you want, Brett?"

"To talk, baby." He narrowed his shiny blue eyes. "Why are you still standing on the stairs?"

"Well, you're drunk, and you broke God knows what. You can't blame me for being a bit wary of you, can you?"

He frowned. "I'm not going to hurt you, Nikki. You know I wouldn't damage my property."

Syd studied him. Maybe he wasn't angry—more than anything he appeared to be sulking. She nodded her head toward the living room. "Go and sit. We'll talk there," she conceded.

He snarled at her. "Who the hell do you think you are ordering me around? You don't get to do that. *I* tell *you* what to do!"

Syd gaped at him.

His gaze moved slowly up and down her body, growing more heated by the second. He nodded toward the living room. "I'll wait for you in there," he mumbled, and turned away.

I should have waited for Theo. He was right, I should have waited.

When Brett was out of sight, Syd quietly reached for the front door and unlocked it so Theo could come in as soon as he arrived. Once that was done, she went in to talk to Brett. The living room, once an open and airy space, was now stifling with Brett staring at her the way he was. He was sitting on the dark brown overstuffed sofa chair, so Syd took residence on the cream-colored couch opposite him, making sure the coffee table provided a bit of barrier between them.

"You wanted to talk. Talk."

He didn't meet her eyes. "Why do you act like I don't exist?"

She blinked at him.

"Nikki, we're getting married in less than a year. *Married.* Husband and wife. And you don't love me."

She sighed. "Brett, look I'm sorry. You have to understand

179

the circumstances surrounding our engagement aren't exactly that of a typical couple. We've been over this—you can't expect me to suddenly love you."

His head jerked up and he glared at her, eyes bright with liquor. "Why not? We've been engaged almost eight months already. Am I that bad a person that you can't love me again?"

"Brett, come on. You know I loved you more than anything in university." She frowned. "But you changed, became someone I didn't want to love, someone who was vengeful and egotistical and cruel. Someone who started treating me as if I was property instead of a person, and who thought they could control every single aspect of my life. That's the person you still are now. I'm sorry. Maybe in time—but I'm going to need more than eight months."

It's only until we can figure out this mess with Papa, she reminded herself. *Then I can divorce him.*

His face flushed and his hands balled into fists. "There's someone else, isn't there?"

Syd stared at him with wide eyes.

"There is, isn't there?" he ground out.

Yes. But not for much longer, unfortunately.

"No, Brett! Don't be ridiculous. There's a lot at stake here. I'd never mess it up just to have a fling. I'd never put my father through that. He's already being put through enough by you."

He stood and moved toward her, eyes narrowed. "Watch your tone, Nikoleta."

Syd frowned up at him and quickly turned her head away.

"Tell me then," he continued, "Why won't you love me?"

"I told you, Brett, I…"

"I don't mean emotional love right now," he roared. "I mean *physical* love. I have to prove to my father that you're *mine* now."

"What does your father have to do with this?" Syd asked, confused.

"Why won't you touch me? Or kiss me?"

She shimmied as far away from him on the sofa as possible, her back finally bumping into the armrest. "I... I need time," she stammered.

Theo!

Brett stepped around the coffee table and towered over her. "Well, guess what? You're out of time, Nikoleta," he growled, grabbing her shoulders and pushing her onto the sofa, making it easy to climb atop her. The suddenness and force of his movements made Syd's head snap back against the armrest, and she was momentarily dizzy with pain.

He clasped both her wrists with one large hand and straddled her. "I'm not waiting for you anymore."

"Brett, what the hell are you doing?" Syd yelled, turning her face away from the alcoholic stench of his breath.

"I'm taking what's mine."

His free hand slid up and underneath her thin pink T-shirt and shoved her bra out of the way. He roughly latched onto a breast, squeezing hard.

Syd gasped and sat there unmoving, frozen in shock.

His hand left her chest and slinked around her back and down to her ass, lifting her up and pressing her into his groin. "See? It's not too hard to love me," he spat out. He let go of her behind and tried to wiggle her sweatpants off her.

Another bolt of lightning lit up the room, and as a boom of thunder sounded, the promise of what was about to happen crashed around her, snapping Syd out of her stunned state and back to reality. She twisted beneath him, trying to free herself. "Get off me!" she screamed.

"Get the fuck off my sister!"

Theo stormed into the room and grabbed Brett's shoulders, flinging him off Syd as if he were nothing more than a ragdoll. Brett tumbled to the ground and quickly righted himself into an unsteady crouch.

Theo advanced on him. "I'd strongly suggest you get the hell out of here, Hudson," he roared. "And be quick about it before I do something *you'll* regret."

"Fuck you," Brett spat, getting to his feet. "That's *my* wife. I have the right to do whatever I want to her."

"Syddie!" Cara ran into the room and pulled Syd out of her semi-frozen state and off the couch.

What's Cara doing here?

"You fucking asshole." Theo pulled his fist back and punched Brett square in the jaw.

Brett stumbled back, but Theo didn't give him a chance to regain his balance. He grabbed the back of his shirt and roughly led him through the front door and into the rain. A moment later he returned, slamming the door shut behind him.

Theo ran back into the living room and pulled Syd away from Cara and into his arms. "Shit, Nikki. I told you to be careful," he whispered, hugging her.

"I... I..." Syd began to quake with tears.

"Aw, sweetie," Theo cooed, squeezing her tighter.

"What happened?" Cara asked softly.

Theo continued hugging her, rubbing her back and smoothing her hair off her face while she tried to compose herself. "When I came in, Brett was...forcing himself on her." His jaw clicked. "I should've killed the son of a bitch."

"Oh my God, Syd," Cara whispered, lowering herself onto the couch and taking one of Syd's trembling hands in hers.

"I'm okay. It's okay. It's over. He was drunk and upset."

"Stop making excuses for him," Theo ground out. "I don't care who he thinks he is, *no one* should ever do that, period."

She smiled softly and pulled away from Theo, trying to make light of the situation, because it was the only way she could deal with it. "It's not like he hasn't fondled me before."

"This isn't funny."

She nodded and frowned. "You're right, it's not. What he did — or was trying to do — was vile. I'm not making excuses for him, and I will *never* forget he did this." She sat next to Cara, whose face was still scrunched up with a mix of anger and worry. "I would never have thought him capable of anything like that."

"Yeah, well, did you even think he'd pull a stunt like he is now with Papa?" Theo asked.

Syd shook her head no. "I'm all right. I promise. And," she continued, turning to her brother, "I'll be more careful in the future."

"You better, little sis. And that piece of shit better watch his step."

She turned to Cara. "Now, what on earth are you doing here? I wasn't expecting you to come by."

"Theo called me for backup."

"You? Backup?" Syd snorted. "What were you going to do, throw a stiletto at him?"

"Hey, I pack a mean punch, missy," Cara defended. She squeezed Syd's hand, serious again. "Honey, you've told me time and again how you're against the idea, but really, please call things off with Brett. We can figure something out if he follows through on his promise to rat out your dad."

"No."

"I've tried telling her the same thing, Cara," Theo piped up, raking his wet chestnut hair off his forehead. "And, as much as I hate the whole idea of it, Syd is right." He turned to his sister. "I don't think Papa has told you yet, but I'm moving back in with him for a while. He's not doing so good."

"He finally admitted it?"

He nodded. "He's weak. Gets these sudden dizzy spells. I took him to the doctor and all she said was that he appeared to be in decent health, and it looks like stress is getting to him. He's not sleeping much, so that doesn't help. I feel better knowing I'm near him in case he needs me."

Syd reached up, took hold of her brother's hand and pulled him down to sit beside her. "Thank you for being there for him," she whispered. "I knew this situation was affecting him more than he let on."

"And you think if Brett really did have him extradited, that things would only get worse," Cara said, a statement more than a question.

"Yes. It's not worth the risk, not right now."

"Meanwhile, I've got some calls in to a few more contacts to maybe get a lead on how to deal with this situation in case the details of what happened in Greece surface," Theo added. "If we can figure out a way to avoid extradition, we're golden and Brett can go screw himself."

"But what about Caleb?" Cara asked. "What's going on with all that?"

"You know about that Caleb guy, too?"

Cara rolled her eyes at Theo. "Of course I do, I'm her best friend. She knows better than not to tell me she's dating an international rock star."

Theo choked on spit. "Excuse me? An international rock star?" He shifted widened eyes from Cara to Syd and back again. "Rock star?"

"Caleb Jones from Divine Intervention," Cara clarified.

"Caleb fucking Jones. Holy shit." He stated at his sister, still in apparent shock. "Why didn't you tell me?"

"It doesn't matter anymore." She sighed and sank into the couch. "No sense talking about the past."

Cara gaped at her. "Did you call things off with him?"

Syd frowned. "No. Not yet. But I haven't really been talking to him very much lately. I'm trying to distance myself from him so it's easier for both of us when I do finally let him go."

"But you love him!"

"You *love* him?" Cara gasped. "Why didn't you tell me you loved him?"

Theo laughed and stuck his tongue out at Cara. "See, there *are* some things the brother knows before the best friend."

"Now, children, try to behave," Syd said. "It doesn't matter who knows what first, it doesn't change the fact I have to figure out how to let Caleb go."

"Don't you dare," Cara warned. "Don't you dare give up

the first good thing you've had in years."

"I have to. I'm engaged."

"I hate this!" Theo let out a frustrated growl and popped up from the sofa. He pulled off his rain-soaked T-shirt and draped it over a chair, sat back down beside Syd and ran his fingers through his hair again, pushing the dripping wet waves off his forehead.

If there was one thing her mother had taught her, it was to not ever dwell on the bad in life. Sometimes the bad to reminded one to be appreciate the good when it happened. Everything happens for a reason, she would say, and the only way to get through a rough situation was to remain positive no matter how hard it may be. And so, after everything Syd had been through, she tried as hard as humanly possible to focus on the good, the happy, the promising. Lately there hadn't been too much of the good stuff to focus on, so when Cara glanced at her brother's lean frame with an interest she hadn't shown before, she latched onto the opportunity and smiled.

"Shall I leave you two alone?" she taunted, smirking.

"What? No!" they said in unison, each appearing as flustered as the other.

Syd snorted. "Guys, I'm fine, really. I promise. I swear. Scout's honor. You don't need to stay and babysit me."

"But what if Brett comes back?" Cara asked, nervous.

"He won't, and, God forbid, he does, I'll call the cops on him."

Theo nodded. "Okay. But you call me if you need anything at all, okay, sis?" He held up his sopping wet T-shirt between thumb and index finger, ever so dainty. "Uh, you don't still have any of my stuff here, do you, sis? I'd love a dry shirt."

Syd nodded. "In the guestroom there're some of your old college tees that you pawned off on me. Go grab one. Oh, and can you let Puff out of my room while you're up there?"

"Sure thing." He kissed the top of her head and sprang up the stairs.

Syd grinned when she noticed Cara shifting her eyes to follow Theo as he made his way. "Ahem."

Cara's head snapped toward Syd and she cleared her throat. "What?"

She shrugged. "Nothing. I just caught you looking."

Cara's face flushed. Cara's face *never* flushed. "I wasn't looking at anything," she retorted quietly.

Syd glanced up when she heard the thunder of little paws in the upstairs hall, followed by footsteps. "Uh-huh. We'll have to talk about this later."

"There's *nothing* to talk about, I swear..." Cara's voice drifted as Theo came back into view and her gaze wandered over him.

He froze, stunned. He scratched his head and swallowed hard. "Uh, yeah, so I'm going to take off now, Nikki. Call me if you need anything, okay?" He moved behind the sofa and wrapped his arms around her, hugging tightly. He wouldn't meet Cara's eyes. "Goodnight, Cara. Thanks for the support tonight. It, uh, it was good to see you."

"Yeah," she answered lightly. "Thanks for inviting me to the festivities. If you're *sure* you're okay to be alone, I'm going to head out, too."

Syd got up and walked her brother and best friend to the door. "Thanks for rescuing me, bro," she said affectionately, giving Theo another hug and kissing his cheek. She turned to Cara. "And you, I'll be fine. Thanks for giving me something else to think about."

Cara's eyes narrowed. "I did *not* give you anything to think about."

"Yeah, you did."

"What?" Theo asked, glancing from one woman to the other. "What? What?"

"Nothing," Cara said between clenched teeth. She sighed and pulled Syd in for a hug. "You're a royal pain in the ass, you realize that, Syddie?" she whispered.

"It's my specialty."

Cara pulled back, face full of concern. "Promise me you'll

keep trying to come up with ways to avoid marrying that dimwit so you can stay with Caleb?"

I think about it all the time.

She nodded. "I promise. Now go. Scram. I need my beauty sleep."

As she shut the door behind them, making triple sure it was securely locked, she made a kissy sound and Puff darted down the stairs. She knelt to pet the dog. "Want to keep Mommy company tonight?" She was answered with a frenzied burst of affectionate licks.

Chuckling, Syd made her way into the basement, Puff following closely behind. She grabbed hold of the easel and made the trip carrying the awkward piece back up the stairs.

"You know, the least you could do is offer to help," she grumbled to Puff, who was doing nothing but complicating the matter by stepping underfoot. After several trips, she was done setting up her easel and she sat on a kitchen stool, staring at the hand-drawn image of Caleb to her right, eyes blurring with tears. This was the first time she'd brought out the picture she had sketched of him that night she'd found him in her kitchen. She traced her fingers lightly along the outline of his face came back to her in vivid detail. In that moment, seeing him sitting in her kitchen in the moonlight, so at home and so at peace — it was then that she fell in love with him.

She sighed and began mixing paints on her palette.

Everything seemed right with Caleb. She had a blast talking with him, fighting with him, debating with him, joking with him. She loved the way he looked at her and how she felt when she was with him. She craved him, longed for him and ached for him when he wasn't around. It was easy to picture her future with him — a wedding, children, family vacations. He was truly everything she ever wanted.

And she had to let him go.

Chapter Thirty-One

After a long day on the streets of Toronto with a commercial real estate agent, Syd dragged herself into her room at the Grande Hotel and tossed her bag and purse onto the plush taupe sofa as she passed it. She moved to the makeshift kitchenette and pulled a bottle of water from the bar fridge, twisting the cap off and taking a long swallow. She wiggled out of her lightweight blazer, draped it over the gleaming black countertop of the small peninsula and made her way up the stairs to the second floor of her suite.

She eyed the phone on the bedside table and nibbled her lip. She had promised Caleb she would call him when she got to Toronto and she'd already been in the city for two days. There was no avoiding him forever and it was better to get the inevitable over with sooner rather than later. She'd purposely booked an extra two nights in the city so she could have some time for herself, without Brett, without interruption—time she needed to heal her heart.

Syd peeled off her sheer maroon blouse and black pencil skirt and, leaving on her thin gray camisole and panties, walked into the adjoining bathroom. She twisted the faucets by the tub and, while it filled, stripped the rest of her clothes off and left them on the tile floor. She dropped a bath bomb into the steaming water and carefully stepped into the oversized tub. Lying down at last, she leaned her head back and tried to relax as the water fizzed around her and her nose filled with the heady scent of lavender.

Over the past week she'd thought long and hard about what needed to happen in her life. There was a definite disconnect between what she *needed* and what was going to happen. She needed Caleb yet she had to marry Brett. She needed happiness yet she would have to live with sadness for a while. She needed Caleb all around her, touching her, kissing her, making love to her, but she was going to have to deal with being celibate for a while, because there was no way Brett was getting anywhere near her.

And after the stunt he'd pulled a few days ago…

She wasn't even close to forgiving him yet, not even a little. Although he'd sent dozens of bouquets of flowers and had called umpteen times apologizing, he didn't seem to get the point. Yes, he seemed genuinely apologetic for trying to force himself on her, but in the same breath he would say that he has every right to have that kind of affection from her, and that he shouldn't have had to force himself. Basically—he was throwing the blame for what happened back in her face.

Syd held her breath and closed her eyes, sliding down so she was completely submerged in the tub. She stayed that way till her lungs burned, part of her wishing she didn't ever have to come up for air, wishing she could stay beneath the cloudy water and not have to deal with the mess she called her life.

A few minutes later she stepped out of the tub and dried off with a plush ivory towel as the bathwater swirled and funneled down the drain.

She nodded and muttered, "Yup. That's my life… Right down the fucking drain."

She threw on her most comfortable oversized nightgown, grabbed a box of tissues and reached for the bedside phone. Taking a deep breath, she dialed Caleb's number.

He answered on the second ring.

"Hello?"

"Caleb, hi. It's Syd."

Silence.

"Caleb?"

"Yeah, I'm here. How's your business trip so far?"

"It's good. I have a couple more places to check out with

the real estate agent tomorrow, but I think I already picked out a spot for the restaurant."

"That's nice."

He was distant with her, too quiet. She'd wanted to start driving him away. That was why she didn't speak to him often or see him at all in weeks on end. But to hear it in his voice, to realize she'd succeeded, nearly broke her to pieces.

Syd heard the sound of children screaming and laughing. "Where are you?"

"I'm back in Miami, at PJ's house."

"Oh. I thought you were staying in California," she said quietly.

"I was when I thought I was in a relationship, but since I was apparently mistaken I came back home."

A tear slid along her cheek. "Caleb, I'm sorry. You know with everything going on, how incredibly busy I've been –"

"Right."

She let out a puff of air. "That's actually why I'm calling you."

"Really?" His voice was tight, as if he anticipated what she was going to say.

"Things... Things are difficult for me, Caleb. I'm busy with work, with my father. I barely have any time for me, let alone a relationship. Plus, we're in different countries, and it's impossible to get together."

"No it's not. All you need to do is make a little time for me, like I would for you," he whispered.

"I have no time to begin with, Caleb," she started.

"You had time for someone else last we spoke, Sydney."

"What?" *What on earth was he talking about?*

"Don't play dumb, Syd. I heard him in the background while we were on the phone. I get it, I'm too far, not worth your effort. That's fine."

Brett.

It was funny, because in a way she *was* breaking things off with him because of another man. It would be so simple to apologize and hang up the phone, to let it go and let it be.

But she couldn't. She wasn't able to let him believe she'd cheated on him in the short duration of their pseudo-relationship. Part of her was desperate to make sure he realized how much he meant to her. "Caleb, I'm not sure what you're thinking, but last time we spoke I had a friend over who was quite drunk."

"Sure."

"I'm serious! Damn it, Caleb, I don't have time for a relationship right now!"

"Uh-huh."

"We were just bad timing. There's too much going on in my life, Caleb. So much I can't even tell you about..." she stopped herself short of babbling on hysterically about the deal she'd made with Brett and the consequences to her family if she didn't follow through.

"Try talking to me, Sydney. *Make* me understand," he implored.

"I... I can't. I can't tell you."

He laughed, and it was a hollow, fake sound. "But I'm sure you made time to tell your *drunk friend*."

"Stop it! I didn't cheat on you. I couldn't—I could never do that to you and live with myself."

He sighed. "But you *could* easily break things off with me. *That* you could do to me, no problem."

She was openly crying now, her voice high-pitched, in near hysterics. "No, Caleb. It's not like that at all. It's killing me to do this, but I have to. It's not fair to you with the way things are." She groaned, aggravated. This was supposed to be a two-minute call—get him on the phone, say they were through, she was sorry and hang up.

"Why don't you let me be the judge of what's fair to me and what's not, Syd?"

"Because I care about you more than you can ever know, and I refuse to let you waste your time on me when I can't devote even a percent of my attention to you. This isn't our time, CJ, and you so deserve better than me. Just hang up the phone and forget about me. Find someone who can love you the way you should be loved, someone to love with all your heart and who you can be with forever."

"I thought I did find that person," he said quietly.

Syd felt as if she'd been stabbed. "So did I," she whispered back. "Goodbye, Caleb. I'm so sorry," she managed between sobs. She quickly put the receiver back in the cradle before he had a chance to say anything else.

It pained her to hear she had hurt him…but when he'd basically said he thought he could be with her forever, it had ripped her apart. She brought her legs to her chest and rested her head on her knees. Her body shook and convulsed as she wept, her heart aching.

I love him. I love him and I just let him go.

* * * *

Caleb stared at his cell phone, mouth slightly open and body rooted in shock.

"Dude?"

He was in sheer disbelief. She'd broken things off and hung up, just like that.

"Dude?"

Caleb turned around slowly. The look on his face must've said it all.

Pat put his arm around his shoulder. "Come on, let's take a walk. Lilly and her friends will be fine for a few minutes," he said softly, leading him through the doors that opened to the spacious back yard.

They walked in silence a few minutes before he spoke again. "CJ, what happened, man?"

"She… Syd, she broke up with me."

Pat pressed his lips together, waiting for his brother to continue.

"I… She… She said she didn't have time for a relationship."

"But you don't believe her," PJ stated knowingly.

"No, I don't. You make time for a relationship if it means anything at all to you. Saying you don't have time is a cop out." His hand started aching, and he realized he still had his fingers tightly clenched around his phone. "She said goodbye, I'm sorry and hung up. She told me that voice I heard was a drunk friend. She swore left and right she wasn't cheating and basically said that our relationship was bad timing in her life."

"Shit, Caleb," Pat said, rubbing his chin. "Something tells me you don't completely buy it, though."

Caleb sighed and slipped his phone into his pocket. "I don't know. If you'd heard her... Pat, she's either an amazing, top-notch actress, or she really *is* as devastated as I am that she broke things off. I mean, she was *sobbing*, man. Totally and completely crying so hard she couldn't catch her breath."

"That doesn't exactly sound like a person who was breaking things off with someone she doesn't care about – a lot."

An elfin girl, with a heart-shaped face and long wavy blonde hair, came running out of the house and crashed into Pat.

"Daddy, Daddy," she wailed, "Nessa isn't letting me play! It's my turn!"

"One sec," Pat said, winking at his brother. He walked Lilly back to the door and gave her a kiss on the top of her head. "Now, ladies," he called into house, "let's play fair and let everyone have a turn, all right?"

"Yes, Mr. Jones," a chorus of five overly dramatic nine-year-olds said at once.

"Look at you, handlin' the ladies," Caleb joked. "Do you think you can work that magic on Sydney, tell her to not give up on us, and maybe she'll comply with a simple 'Yes, Mr. Jones'?"

"If I thought there was a chance in hell of it working, I'd do it in a heartbeat for you, bro," Pat answered, his words sincere.

"I dunno, maybe you were right, Pat. I chased after her and followed her to Vancouver, even though she said she didn't want to see me again. I did this to myself."

"Or..."

"Or there's something going on in her life that she feels she can't tell me about, something that's making her break up with me, even though her voice says she doesn't want to do it."

PJ bent and ripped a blade of grass out of the ground, flipping it around in his fingers as he spoke. "Well, now what? What are you going to do?"

Caleb frowned. "She broke up with me, so we're supposed to be through, right? Then why do I feel like we have unfinished business? Why do I feel like we're not done?"

Chapter Thirty-Two

"So what do you think of this place? The high ceilings offer endless possibility, and amazingly enough the hardwood floors are in impeccable condition."

"Yeah, it's nice," Syd murmured.

The real estate agent, Mona, furrowed her brow. "Are you sure you're okay, Sydney? I mean, I asked you earlier, but you're really not yourself today."

Of course I'm not all right. I gave up the man of my dreams and I cried all night.

She nodded. "I didn't sleep very well, so I'm a bit low on energy."

Mona frowned and gave a slight nod, her dark eyes still reflecting worry.

Syd mustered a smile. "I'm fine, Mona. I promise." She waved her hand in the air. "And this place is lovely, but I've still got my heart set on that little place near Yonge and Bloor."

"But, Syd, that place is *half* the size of this one. Based on your budget you could more than afford this place. It's so spacious, there's enough room to even convert it to a banquet or party space!"

She nodded. "I know, Mona, but Christou's is not about grandeur. It's about a family atmosphere with a bit of class. A small, cozy venue is perfect, and the extra unspent budget will do wonders going toward getting the restaurant ready to open in record time."

Mona shrugged. "All right, if you insist. Would you like to go look at it again?"

Syd shook her head. "No, I'm good, thanks. If you could

send me all the info pertaining to the property via email so I can go over it with Theo and my dad when I get back home, I'd really appreciate it."

They parted ways and Syd headed back to the hotel, grateful she no longer had to force herself to socialize with another human. From this point on her companions would be her bed, pillow and tissues. Not to mention the three tubs of Ben & Jerry's she'd bought.

She let herself into her room and dumped her bag and purse on the ground. She put two cartons of ice cream in the freezer and took the third upstairs with her, grabbing a spoon along the way. She ripped the top off the container and dug out a huge chunk of the frozen treat, nibbling it before it melted. She continued eating mouthful after mouthful while she undressed and slipped into a pair of jeans and an old University of British Columbia T-shirt, finally glancing into the small tub and realizing she'd eaten nearly half already.

Syd put her hand to the side of her head. "Christ," she muttered. "That would account for the brain freeze."

She set the carton on the dresser and picked up the phone, deciding it was about time she got some real food into her system.

"Room service," a friendly voice answered.

"Hi there. I'd like to place an order."

"Yes, ma'am. What room are you in?"

"Three-oh-four," Syd answered, quickly flipping through the menu.

"And what can we get for you, Ms. Bennett?"

"Um, I'll have the cheeseburger with extra cheese and no onion please."

She heard the telltale click of nails on a keyboard. "Anything else?"

"Two orders of fries." Syd paused. "Oh, and a couple cans of whatever brand of cola you have, please."

"Yes, ma'am. Your food will arrive in roughly forty-five minutes. Please call us back if there's anything else you need."

"Thanks," Syd said, returning the phone to its cradle and resuming her pigging out on the Chunky Monkey. She settled back on the bed and turned the television to some soap opera she'd never seen before, staring at the colors flashing by on the screen as she shoveled the frozen dessert into her mouth.

"Oh, Cliff, but I love you so much!"

Syd's eyes instantly focused on the screen. The buxom blonde was clutching the tall, dark-haired man's arm, trying to convince him that they were destined to be together. He shook his head adamantly, telling her he was married, that what they had was nothing but a fling, a mistake.

Syd closed her eyes. A tear escaped and rolled down her cheek as she blindly reached for the remote to turn off the television. She didn't need any more reminders of her own heartache.

A knock sounded at the door, and Syd, still clutching the tub of ice cream, jumped out of bed and headed downstairs.

"Who is it?"

"Room service," an oddly accented high-pitched voice answered.

Syd stuck another spoonful of ice cream into her mouth and, the silverware still dangling from her lips, opened the door.

The spoon promptly fell to the ground.

"Caleb? What the hell are you doing here?" she asked, her voice strangled and somewhat panicked.

He nodded his head toward the cart of food in front of him. "It's not obvious? I'm bringing you your food." He pushed her out of the way with the little table on wheels and moved into the room. He turned and shut the door behind him, bending to pick up the spoon she had dropped.

He motioned for her to hand him the near empty tub of ice cream she had in a death grip, and she mutely complied. He peered into the carton and raised an eyebrow, grabbing a fresh spoon off the cart and digging in. He stared at Syd while he licked the spoon, his head cocked to the side.

"So," he said quietly.

She turned away from him and covered her face, shaking her head. She couldn't look at him. It hurt too much. "What are you doing here, CJ? You shouldn't be here. You're not supposed to be here."

His hands were on her shoulders, gently turning her to face him again. He pulled her hands away from her face and stroked her gently along the jaw. Her vision blurred and he trailed his thumb to swipe at the tears that fell.

"If you want to get rid of me you'll have to try harder than that, Syd. I don't care what you said—we're not over. We're connected, you and I, and I love you too damn much to give you up so easily," he whispered.

He loves me.

Her face crumbled and she collapsed against his chest, her body shaking as she cried. He wrapped his arms around her protectively, smoothing the hair off her face, rubbing her back, murmuring that everything was going to be okay.

Syd pushed away from him, sniffling and rubbing her nose. "No. No, CJ, you can't be here. I told you, it's over."

He hooked an arm behind her legs and carried her up to the bedroom. "Look," he said as he climbed the stairs. "Maybe I'm stupid, or a glutton for punishment. Maybe I'm delusional and irrational. Hell, maybe I'm just a silly lovesick pup. But," he said, depositing her on the bed in a flourish, "there are a couple things I do know."

He sat beside her and took her hand in his, tracing circles on the inside of her wrist. "First off, I know that, unequivocally, without a doubt, I love you. I'm also willing to bet everything I own that you love me too. And that if you didn't love me, then you wouldn't be sitting here, crying and letting me hold you." He leaned in close and brushed his lips on hers. "Letting me kiss you."

He kissed her then—lightly, tenderly, his lips barely putting pressure on hers.

She was powerless.

Damn him.

She wrapped her arms around his neck and drew him deeper into the kiss. Not separating herself from him, Syd got to her knees and scooted closer to Caleb, scissoring her thighs with his. She tangled her fingers in his blond hair, pressing him closer to her. She parted her lips and snaked her tongue out, teasing the seam of his mouth. Lips parted and tongues met, sliding sensuously along each other one second, eagerly thrusting against each other the next.

Syd moved her hands to the front of his baby-blue top and hooked her fingers onto the hem, pulling the thin fabric over his head. She scratched her nails lightly along his torso as she stared into his eyes.

He furrowed his brow. "Syd," he said, taking hold of her hands and bringing the fingertips to his lips. "Syd, baby, these last few weeks, why were you pushing me away? Why did you try to break up with me when it's so obvious it's not what your heart really wants?"

Syd examined their hands—his were so large they completely enveloped hers. She felt safe when she was with him.

She couldn't meet his steady gaze. "I... It can't work with us, Caleb. I told you—"

He put his finger to her lips. "If you're about to say you don't have time for me, if you're about to claim that the distance would make it near impossible, I simply don't buy it."

"But..." she began.

Caleb shook his head. "Sorry, darlin'. Those excuses aren't going to work. The second I left Vancouver you began pulling away, Syd. You never even gave us the chance we deserved. How can you expect me to let you go when we haven't even tried? There's something you're not telling me and I wish you would trust me enough to be honest about it."

Syd's shoulders slumped in resignation. Short of telling him she hated him, which she'd never be able to do with conviction, there was no way she was winning this battle.

She tipped herself forward and rested her head against his him, sighing. "Why did you have to come here? Why couldn't you just leave it alone?"

His body quivered with a silent chuckle. "I thought I already told you, darlin', but maybe you didn't hear me." He kissed the top of her head. "I love you, Sydney Bennett," he whispered into her hair. Caleb hooked a thumb under her chin and lifted her head so she'd have no choice but to look at him. "I love you."

A flood of emotions washed over Syd. She loved him too, but to verbalize it, to *tell* him her feelings—that was something she wasn't able to do. How could she, when she was only going to break his heart?

And yet here I am, she thought, *in his arms, giving in when I should be pushing away.*

"Come on, darlin', we need to get some real food into your system." He settled Syd into a sitting position at the top of the bed, fluffing a few pillows behind her back for support. He kissed her forehead and vanished down the stairs.

She couldn't help but smile. He truly was one of the good guys.

He came back upstairs, plate of food in one hand, two colas in the other. He rested the cans on the bedside table and popped a fry into his mouth. He winked at her and snatched another from the plate.

"So, you don't have a hot date tonight, do you?"

Syd took a huge bite out of the burger and wiped the crumbs from her lips as she shook her head.

Caleb grinned at her and winked. "You do now."

Chapter Thirty-Three

Syd held a fry in mid-air and gazed at him quizzically. "I have a hot date tonight, do I?" she asked. "And, pray tell, who's this supposed hot date with?"

Caleb sat there, grinning as he shrugged. "I dunno. It could be with a sexy guitarist who simply cannot get enough of you. Or perhaps it's with a regular, run-of-the-mill man who loves you and would do anything to make you smile. Or maybe," he continued, leaning over and kissing her, feather soft, "Maybe, you'll just have to wait and see."

She sucked a dab of ketchup off her middle finger. "Or, maybe it's the guitarist and regular run-of-the-mill dude who's the lucky one. Maybe *he'll* just have to wait and see."

He chuckled and got to his feet. "Either way, I have a feeling they'll both be in luck." He nodded toward her suitcase. "By any chance, did you bring a bathing suit along?"

Syd nodded.

"Perfect. I'll be right back. Save some fries for me."

She raised an eyebrow. "And if I don't?"

"Well, in that case I'll have to find something else to eat," Caleb teased, his gaze flicking between her legs and lingering there.

Her face flushed and her eyes darkened. "I'll make sure to finish them off then."

Caleb took two long strides over to Syd, threaded his fingers into her black mane and gripped the hair tightly, bringing her mouth to his. He kissed her fiercely, his lips marking her as his. When he pulled his mouth away he gazed at her, grinning, loving how whenever he kissed her like that she appeared somewhat dazed.

"I'll be right back," he whispered, dropping a final peck on her forehead and turning to go down the stairs, grabbing his tossed shirt along the way. He heard the telltale squeak of the mattress as she plopped back onto it, along with the frustrated groan that tumbled from her lips, and he chuckled.

In the elevator on the way to the reception desk on the ground floor to pick up the suitcase he'd stashed there, Caleb couldn't help but smile. He knew she loved him, knew that she really didn't want to break things off. He *knew* it. And he was damn glad he had taken the chance to track her down and confront her. He had somehow managed to convince her to give it another chance, and he was going to use the opportunity to try every trick in the book to romance her right off her feet and into his life for good.

* * * *

Syd leaned back in her seat, patting her full belly. "Oh my God, that was so good."

"It looked delicious, darlin'. Especially the way you were sucking every last bit of meat off those bones," Caleb said, wiggling his eyes.

Syd snorted. "You liked that, did you? Well maybe if you would stop being Mr. Mysterious about our plans for this evening, I could actually get to work on sucking a completely different kind of…bone."

He growled.

"Shall we?" she asked, getting to her feet. "Not that I have a clue as to what's next on the agenda, but I simply can't sit here anymore. I'm this close," she said, pinching her index finger and thumb together, "to ordering up another plate of that rack of lamb."

Caleb followed suit and took her offered hand, and they left Citrus Lounge, the hotel's restaurant. "Come on, baby.

How about we go for a little walk?"

"A walk," Syd said flatly. "You want to go for a walk. After the way you kissed me earlier, and after all the bone talk, you want to go for a *walk*?"

He smirked and tugged on her hand, leading her out of the hotel and onto the street. It was a gorgeous early summer night—a slight warm breeze ruffled the blond hair that sat at the collar of CJ's embroidered denim shirt, making Syd want to capture the moment on her easel once again.

He felt her staring at him, and turned his head to her, blue eyes soft in the streetlights. "What is it, Syd?"

"Nothing. Every so often I just get struck with how beautiful you are."

"You think I'm beautiful?" he asked, batting his eyelashes in an exaggerated manner.

"Well, yes."

"Not helping the male ego here, babe."

Syd rolled her eyes. "You'll get over it. Don't forget, I'm an artist. I see beauty in things you wouldn't. And right now, the soft light from the street lamps shining down on you, the shadows that light creates on your face, the gentle movement of your hair in the wind...the way you're looking at me at this exact moment... Beautiful."

He stopped walking and turned her to face him. Each hand gently cupping a side of her face, he brought his mouth to hers in a soft, barely there kiss. He pulled away and winked. "Well, you're kinda beautiful, too."

She feigned hurt. "Kinda?"

Caleb tossed his head back and laughed. "Yup. Kinda." He reached down and smacked her behind playfully.

Syd jumped and squealed in protest, trying her best to put on an air of anger as she shoved CJ away and failing miserably as she was unable to contain the giggle that escaped her lips. He grabbed her and wrapped his arm around her shoulders, holding her close to him for the next twenty minutes while they walked around the block at a leisurely pace, talking about everything and nothing, before heading back into the Grande.

As soon as they returned to Syd's hotel room, she yanked on his hand, pulling him up the stairs behind her and finally pushing him onto the bed. She straddled him and tipped her head to kiss him. He threaded his fingers into her hair and held her close to him, slowly tracing his tongue along the gentle curve of her lips, making Syd's insides clench and her heart flutter.

Then he flipped her off him and stood.

"What...the hell?" she asked breathlessly, frustrated beyond belief.

He grinned and moved toward his suitcase. "How 'bout that swim?"

"*Now?*"

"Of course now, baby. Why else would I have mentioned it?"

"Sure, baby," she mimicked between gritted teeth. "Why the hell not."

Syd mumbled and grumbled under her breath while digging in her suitcase for her bikini.

I can't believe he's making us go swimming now. What the hell!

She glanced up at him. He had taken off his shirt and his bare, chiseled chest just begged for her touch. He caught her checking him out and tried to appear indignant. "Can I help you?"

She raised her head high and turned toward the bathroom. "No. You cannot."

"Hey, Syd," Caleb's voice was soft behind her.

She turned around and took in the sight of him pulling his jeans off his narrow hips—she barely controlled the urge to lunge at him.

"You're not getting changed in here where I can admire the view?"

"You don't deserve to see the view quite yet," she said, turning back toward the bathroom's open door. She continued under her breath, "Making us go for a stupid walk and now stupid swimming. Uch."

Syd closed the door behind her and stripped out of her black dress pants and charcoal silk blouse, folding them neatly and placing them on the counter. She slipped the black halter bikini top over her head and clasped it at the back, then stepped into the matching bottom, adjusting the small wood buckle detail that accented the garment near her left hip. Syd reached for the bathrobe, tied the belt tightly around her, and stepped back out into the bedroom.

Caleb wasn't there.

A rose and a letter, however, *were* there, sitting ever so innocently on her mattress.

She unfolded the small piece of paper.

Meet me at the bar.

"You've got to be kidding me," she muttered, tugging at a corner of her robe. "I have to go to the bar dressed in *this*?"

Muttering a string of intelligible curses, Syd slipped her feet into a pair of flip-flops, grabbed her room key and made her way downstairs. Walking into the hotel restaurant and heading toward the bar, Syd ducked her head, trying to be as inconspicuous as possible in her bright white bathrobe. She noticed several patrons glancing her way, raising their eyebrows, and swore to make Caleb pay for this somehow.

"Fuck." CJ wasn't at the bar.

"Ms. Bennett?"

She whipped around at the sound of her name. "Yes."

The bartender smiled at her and handed her two drinks. "These are for you. Oh," he said, pausing and reaching underneath the counter, "these are, as well."

Syd sighed and accepted the drinks, rose and piece of paper, and moved to the end of the bar to read the note.

Meet me on the 17th floor. Don't forget the drinks.

"Of course I won't forget the drinks, you dink," she grumbled, shaking her head. She grabbed them, along with the rose, and headed back toward the elevator. She carefully used her pinky to stab at the button for the seventeenth floor.

Ding.

The doors slid open and Syd stepped out into the hallway. It was dark, save for a single fluorescent bulb, and a glass door that led outside was the only way to go. She took a step toward it when the door suddenly swung open, and there stood Caleb, yummy chest exposed, towel wrapped around his waist, smiling brightly.

Syd chomped down on her lower lip, intent on remaining irritated at him for his little games. She lifted her head high and breezed past him, out of the door and toward the pool…and stopped dead in her tracks.

Roses were scattered everywhere—petals floated serenely in the pool and restlessly in the Jacuzzi, stemmed roses were strewn almost carelessly across the patio floor, bouquets and votive candles adorned the few tables that occupied a small corner. The door clicked behind her and she turned to look at Caleb in astonishment.

"You… You did all *this*?" she asked, her eyes wide in wonder.

He beamed.

She glanced around again before turning back to him. "But why?"

Caleb beamed and came closer to her, sliding his arms around her. "Syd, darlin', I love you. There doesn't need to be a reason beyond that." He dipped his head and brushed his lips feather-soft on hers.

Her body immediately sank into his, all the frustration she had been experiencing a moment ago whisked away in the cool breeze that played around them on the rooftop.

He took the drinks from her and placed them on the table behind him. He untied her belt and drew the robe off her shoulders, draping it carefully over the back of a chair. He tilted his head to the side, smirking at her, and whistled long and low.

Syd's face flushed. "What?"

Caleb chuckled and shook his head. "Nothin', darlin'." He took the rose she was still gripping, snapped the stem and tucked the red bud behind her ear.

"Come on, baby," he said, his darkened eyes focused on her. "Let's go for a little swim."

Chapter Thirty-Four

It really was beautiful.

The city lights twinkled all around them and the soft glow from the votive candles shimmered on the water's surface. Caleb has managed to somehow reserve the entire rooftop pool area for them and the total privacy and quiet was exactly what she — they — needed. Caleb was completely relaxed in the Jacuzzi, one arm slung over the edge without a care, the other he smoothed up and down her leg, making her tingle.

"How do you do it?" she asked suddenly.

"How do I do what, baby?"

"How do you manage to make me feel so special?" She shrugged, suddenly embarrassed to have made the admission.

He pulled her onto his lap and slid his arms around her waist, bringing her flush to him. He nosed her hair out of the way and nuzzled at her neck. "Because," he began, his breath hot on her skin, "you *are* special. You're perfect, Syd, in every single way, and you're perfect for *me*."

She shifted restlessly on him, his mouth against her neck doing everything *but* relax her. She angled her head to grant him greater access and his lips eagerly took residence on the exposed flesh.

"You make me feel loved, Caleb. So damn loved, and needed…and so much more I can't even begin to put into words."

"I'll say it as many times as I have to till you believe me, Sydney. I love you." He kissed her neck. "I love you." He moved to her jaw line. "I love you."

He was getting hard underneath her and she giggled. "I'm literally feeling the love, CJ."

He laughed. "Can't help it. Not with you around." He lifted her up and repositioned her so that she was straddling him. He raised his hips and pressed into her center.

Syd moaned low and reached between her legs to massage his ever-growing cock beneath the water. She gave it a squeeze and he let out a small contented sound that did all kinds of things to her. Her sexual frustration bubbled to the surface and, needing to do more than grope CJ, Syd popped off his lap and got out of the Jacuzzi.

"Follow me," she whispered. She headed toward one rather discreet corner of the rooftop, grabbing their towels and bathrobes along the way. This little nook was perfect for what she was about to do — it was tucked away underneath a small overhang, protecting them from prying eyes. She spread the towels out on the ground and folded the robes up to act as a makeshift pillow. When she straightened up she turned to find Caleb standing behind her, water beaded on his tanned torso and a crooked smile on his delectable lips.

"Enjoying the view, Mr. Jones?" She hooked her thumbs into her bikini bottoms and shimmied them off her hips a couple of inches. "Anything I can do to make it more interesting?"

No more than two strides and he was at her side, drawing her into his embrace, his hands on her ass and his mouth on hers. She let him envelop her, everything going fuzzy for a moment, before she pulled away. She nodded toward the towels.

"Lie down," she instructed.

"Bossy little thing, aren't you?" he joked, settling to the ground and doing as he was told.

"Only when you've been teasing me constantly and I'm dying to get off," she quipped, instantly silencing his laughter.

"Jesus, Syd…"

She dropped to all fours beside him and kissed his chest, slapping him away when he went to cradle her head. "No touching."

"But..."

"*No* touching."

He nodded and rested his hands under his head, no doubt a move to prevent getting yelled at again.

She went back to kissing him, lips feathering across his bronzed skin, while using her hands to explore the already familiar planes of his muscled chest. "I missed you," she murmured, moving her lips up his neck and finally coming to rest on his mouth. She lingered there, tugging his lower lip, nibbling on it, before she swung a leg over and settled on him. He mumbled something incoherent and reached for her hips. She grabbed his wrists and held him still, rendering him immobile.

"I thought I told you to sit still, Mr. Jones."

"I'm so sorry, Ms. Bennett," he quipped. "You're incredibly sexy and my hands tend to wander of their own volition when I'm around you."

She grinned. "That's a good answer," she said, tucking his hands underneath his ass for safe-keeping. "But if you keep misbehaving, I can't do fun stuff like this." She shimmied a couple of inches and ground down on his crotch. "Or this," she added, reaching up to undo the ties on her bikini top and let the fabric fall to her waist, revealing her breasts.

"I will definitely behave," he choked out, eyes fixed on her chest.

"Well, in that case," she continued, unclasping the back of her top and tossing it to the patio floor, "I can take these off." She untied the bows at her hips and slid her bikini bottoms from between her legs. Caleb let out a low growl. He raised his hips and rocked, the bulge in his shorts sliding between the wet folds of skin.

"Oh! I... I thought...touching...not..." she stumbled, the sensation rendering her unable to string a sentence together.

He shook his head. "I'm not breaking any rules, baby.

I'm sitting on my hands and my shorts are between us. Technically, I'm not touching you." He winked and continued moving beneath her, each stroke hitting the tender nub that made sparks burst behind her eyelids.

"That... That's not fair," she whimpered, bracing herself with an arm on either side of his head, enabling her to bear down and him to increase the pressure on her clit. It didn't take long. "I... Oh God!" she cried out, every muscle tensing as the orgasm ripped through her. She landed in a heap on top of him, breathless.

Well, that plan backfired in the most amazing way.

"Can I touch you now?" he whispered into her hair.

She nodded against his shoulder.

He shifted and his hands were on her, smoothing the hair off her face, fingertips gliding along her spine. She sighed, fully content, and nuzzled into him. She loved the smell of his skin, the sensation of him... She loved everything about him. Syd lifted her head to glance at him—his eyes were closed, and a soft smile played at his lips. He looked totally relaxed, but between her legs she could feel he was anything but. She kissed him and whispered, "Your turn."

He winged an eyebrow. "Yeah, eh?"

She slid down his body, taking his swim trunks with her. She wrapped her fingers around his length and giggled. "Careful there, stud, you're starting to sound Canadian."

He was about to respond—with some witty retort, no doubt—but the words fell out in a mumble of incoherent sounds when she licked the tip of his cock. She circled the head with her tongue, stopping now and then to again lick from the base to the tip and back again. She gripped him tight and pumped up and down in time with her mouth, sucking hard until he cursed then she turned it to gentle and teasing.

"Stop, baby," he whispered. "Please stop."

She lifted off him in a second, worried she'd done something to hurt him. "Is something wrong? Are you okay? Is—"

He put a finger to her lips to shush her. "I need to be inside you," he growled. He kicked his shorts from around his ankles and twisted his body to fish around in one of the robe-slash-pillows. He brought out a small foil packet and shredded it open savagely.

"Assumed you were getting some nookie tonight, did you?"

"I was hopeful," he replied, rolling it on and grabbing her by the hips in two seconds flat. He carefully lowered her on top of him, then he was inside her, filling her up. She rolled her hips and leaned back on him, resting her hands back on his knees for support. Caleb gripped her with one hand while using the other to focus on her center, rubbing the tender nub steadily. She tipped her head toward the sky, briefly noticing the stars in the clear Toronto night before another climax tore through her and she saw stars of her own.

But he wasn't done with her yet.

She was still reeling from the orgasm and CJ didn't give her a moment to catch her breath. He sat up and wrapped his arms around her back, pulling her chest to his mouth and teasing the stiff peak of her nipple between his teeth. Syd hooked her ankles around his waist and gasped his name.

"Hang on to me." He latched onto her ass and less than gracefully wobbled to his feet, still buried deep inside her.

"What are you doing?" she mumbled, nibbling his neck.

He backed her up into a corner. "You're gonna need to brace yourself, darlin'."

She stretched her arms out to either side, gripping the rough brick surface as best she could and letting Caleb take her full weight. His fingers dug into the soft flesh of her ass and he withdrew from her a couple inches, just enough to make the force of him slamming back in glorious. Syd was slick with want for him and he glided in and out easily, over and over, until finally he let loose a guttural sound as he found his own release.

"I love you, Sydney," he whispered into her hair as she clung to him. "God, I love you."

"I love you too, Caleb." She rested her head on his shoulder and bit back tears. "No matter what happens, I need you to believe that. I love you."

Chapter Thirty-Five

She teetered precariously on her tippy toes, doing some sort of unbalanced—and most definitely uncoordinated—dance as she tried to get Caleb's attention. He ignored her at first, swinging a small duffel bag over his shoulder and grabbing his green hoodie. She slapped at him, twirled in circles, hopped on the spot before finally giving up and sitting on the floor, staring up at him with a somewhat pathetic, forlorn look in her eyes.

"I think someone's going to miss you," Syd said, smiling and nodding toward his feet.

Caleb grinned and sat on his haunches. "C'mere, sweetie," he whispered, and the once-dejected Puff popped up again and placed her paws on his knee, seeking some love and cuddles. "I'm going to miss you too, fuzzy bear. Almost as much as I'm going to miss your mama." She boinged up and down again, trying to get into his arms. CJ instantly dropped his belongings to scoop her up and let her get in some kisses.

"My God, you're such a total suck with her," Syd laughed. "It's kind of adorable."

He scowled at her over Puff's golden fur. "First, two weeks ago you say I'm beautiful. Now you say I'm adorable. You *do* realize I'm a manly man, right?"

She leaned in to him and kissed him solidly on the mouth. "Mmm, well, I guess you'll just have to show me how manly you are next time I see you."

"I can do that."

"Over and over again," she added. "I will need loads of data to come to a proper conclusion, after all."

"I'd be happy to assist in any and every way I can. For the sake of research, that is. Not that I'm a horn-dog or anything."

"No, of course you're not. You're simply *adorable*," she teased.

He gently put Puff back on the floor and she scampered away into the living room to attack a squeaky toy. CJ grabbed Syd by her waist and reeled her in for a long, hot, lingering kiss. "God," he whispered, pulling away reluctantly. "How am I gonna survive without you?"

"It's only five days," she murmured against his lips. "I've cleared my schedule so we'll have the whole weekend." They had planned on meeting in Portland for the weekend to get away from their responsibilities in Vancouver and California, if only for a couple of days.

"Five days is too long. I want to stay." He hugged her tightly.

"CJ, you've got to get to the airport. You've got to let me go," she laughed, trying to wiggle away from him.

He groaned in resignation and checked his watch. "Oh, shit!" He let her go, grabbed his stuff, planted at least a dozen kisses on her face and turned to the door. "Love you, baby," he called, running out to his car.

"Back atcha, Mr. Jones." She waved goodbye, closed the door behind her and sighed.

She sank to the floor in the foyer and made kissy sounds, summoning Puff, who came bounding over with a small stuffed carrot in her mouth. Syd was positive she had a big, dopey, love-induced grin on her face, and wasn't certain it was going to fade any time soon. She and Caleb had been spending as much time as humanly possible together since their declaration of love back in Toronto. Caleb had even returned to the house in California to make the distance between them more reasonable and, quite frankly, more bearable. Shocking was the fact that even though their desire was tangible, they weren't tumbling around in bed the whole time they were together. They talked, saw stupid movies, played with Puff in the back yard—they were getting to know each other on a much deeper level and it made her love him even more. At this point he pretty well knew everything about her.

Not everything. Shut up!

She tossed the carrot into the hall and as Puff shot off after it, the smile left her lips. Her mind and heart were at war on a near-constant basis these days. She was happier than she'd been in, well, ever, and it was thanks to Caleb Jones. Unless a miracle happened—which was unlikely—she would have to say goodbye to him in something like eight months, given she was marrying Brett in April. There was no way she could carry on with this charade once she was living under the same roof as Brett. She despised herself for what she was doing—Caleb didn't deserve the hurt that was surely coming his way, but still she couldn't bring herself to believe her time with him was coming to an end.

Things will work out. I'll be with Caleb in the end. I'll be happy.

Flat out denial.

* * * *

That night, Syd was humming away happily as she dabbed at the canvas, putting the finishing touches to her painting of CJ. She was excited about how well it had turned out and was excited to show him. A few minutes later she was done and she gently removed it from the easel, leaning it against a kitchen chair while she started on cleanup. She was in the midst of washing a few paint brushes in the kitchen sink when the doorbell sounded. Wiping her hands on a rag as she moved toward the foyer she called out, "Who is it?"

"It's me. Open up."

Brett.

"Oh shit," she mouthed. "Oh, um, one second... Be right there!"

She bolted into the kitchen and grabbed the painting of Caleb, searching frantically for somewhere to hide it.

Why did Brett always have to show up unannounced? She skidded into the dining room and determined there was enough space to hide it behind the decorative wall unit without damaging the art. A second later she was back at the front door with a wriggling and jiggling Puff under her arm.

"Hi!" she said, cheerily. He wrinkled his nose and walked inside.

He remained silent and focused his attention on hunting around her place. He was poking at everything, checking between cushions and peering under the couches.

"Did you lose something, Brett?"

He whirled around to face her. "Who is he?" he demanded.

"Who is who?"

His eyes flashed. "*Him*," he ground out. "The guy you've been seeing behind my back?"

Oh shit, oh shit, oh shit…

She pasted a calculated frown on her lips. "What on earth are you talking about?"

Brett pointed at her with his index finger. "*Something* is going with you, Nikoleta. I'm not stupid, you know."

Debatable.

"Of course you're not stupid, Brett. What in the world has got you in such a tizzy?"

"You're fucking someone behind my back and you're going to tell me who it is!" he yelled in her face.

Puff growled and started fighting to get out of Sydney's arms, little paws flailing about. "Please, Brett, there's no need to scream at me." She turned her back to him. "Let me put Puff upstairs before she tries to eat you, okay?"

On the way up, her mind went into overdrive.

Why does he think I'm seeing someone, let alone fucking someone?

No way would Cara or Theo have let it slip…so who?

I've been careful about not going out with Caleb, not locally anyhow — no one would have seen us.

Unless he has someone spying on me…

That bastard!

Suddenly livid, she headed back downstairs and straight to him. He backed away from her as she stalked toward him, and she guessed her face displayed the fury she was feeling.

"After everything that's gone on," she ground out, "how dare you accuse me of anything? Do you think I don't realize what's at stake here? Do you think I would jeopardize my family for a fucking fling?"

I am, though.

Stop it!

Brett regained his composure. "Don't try to twist this, Nikoleta," he sneered. "I'm not blind to the change that's happened with you over the last couple weeks, you know."

She blinked. "W-what change?"

It was his turn to make her back away, and he advanced on her with a horrific smirk on his face. "You go from being miserable all the time, from picking fights, and never being polite to me unless your hand is forced...to, to...whatever *that* was!" He waved at her. "When you first opened the door you were polite and full of smiles. You were like this the last time I stopped by, too. It's strange and feels like such an act. No one has an about-face with their personality like that. No one!"

She frowned up at him. "You did," she said quietly. "All those years ago."

He froze in stunned silence.

She slipped away from him and walked into the kitchen to continue cleaning her painting supplies, leaving him standing in the foyer. Her back was turned to him when he finally followed her. She glanced over her shoulder — his face was pale and drawn and his eyes were lowered, his lips tight.

"You okay?" she asked softly.

He twitched. "Fine." His voice was stony, cold. He looked up at her. "Things are going to change now, Nikoleta."

"Um, okay?"

"We're not waiting for spring to get married."

She thought she was going to throw up. "Wh-what do you mean?" she stammered. "You know I wanted a spring wedding."

"What *you* want has never mattered. What matters is I absolutely do not trust you."

She turned on her heel to face him. "I'm not doing anything I shouldn't, Brett! First you're mad because I'm not happy, then you're mad I'm trying not to fight with you all the time. I can't fucking win!" she yelled, throwing the paint brushes to the floor.

He shrugged. "But I *can* win. We're getting married the first weekend of September."

"What? But that's only two and a half months away!" *Caleb...*

"Exactly."

"There's too much to be done," she said, frantic. "There's not enough time!"

"I've taken care of everything. The invitations have already gone out."

"I hate you for this," she whispered. "How can you even live with yourself? If anyone found out..."

He guffawed. "Do you think they would believe the daughter of a wanted murderer? Or me?"

"Melanie would believe me."

He glared at her. "If Melanie were to find out, there would be hell to pay, Nikoleta." He stepped back toward the foyer and tossed one last comment over his shoulder before he left. "You better start looking for a dress, Nikki."

She stared at him, shock having set in.

He opened the door and turned back to her, his face contorted by the evil grin on his lips. "You're running out of time."

Chapter Thirty-Six

Avoiding Caleb was proving to be harder than she thought it would be. When she called him to cancel their weekend plans in Portland, citing a stomach flu, the first thing he did was offer to come to her place to take care of her. It took everything she had to convince him to stay put and let her get through the 'sickness' on her own.

The truth was she *was* sick to her stomach, but not from any strain of virus. It was, instead, because Brett was right— she *had* run out of time. Run out of time to be with Caleb, to love Caleb...

She had run out of time and now she had to hurt him.

It had been over two weeks since Brett had informed her he'd moved up the date of their wedding and had set it for September. She did her best to put on a cheerful front when she spoke to Caleb, and so far, it was working. She wasn't pleased her acting skills had gotten more refined over time. Lying like this, to the man she loved, was *not* a talent she wanted to hone. But he had been patient and understanding with her when she had explained she didn't have the time to see him right now given Christou's Toronto location was being readied at light speed and slated to open in August.

Syd was putting off the inevitable, stringing Caleb along and trying to keep her broken heart together with worn Band-Aids, knowing full well the cracks and wounds would never heal.

It was time.

She picked up the phone and dialed, gnawing on her thumbnail while she waited for the line to be answered.

"Hello?"

"Hey…Caleb," Syd said, working hard to sound upbeat.

"Hi, baby," he replied slowly, drawing out the latter word. "How's my love doing?"

"Incredibly busy, you know how it is."

"Yes, I do. I'm missing you, darlin'."

God, I miss you, too.

"About that," she began. "What are you doing this weekend?"

"Same as always when you're not in my arms, darlin'. I'm working on some new material with Pat." She practically heard his eyes widen. "Why, what's up? Are you free? Do you have some spare time? Can I see you?"

She had to smile. His excitement was palpable.

"I might be able to clear some meetings, but I be can't certain till the last minute. I wanted to make sure you were around in case I could swing it."

Stop procrastinating.

"Awesome, great! If you can make it, I'll make myself available, you can bet on that," he laughed. "Oh, hang on a sec, baby." His voice was muffled, the receiver either covered up or pressed against his shirt. She was able to make out a word here and there, but not much else. "Hey, sorry," he continued a moment later. "PJ and his daughter are here."

"Oh, nice. So yeah, I'll try to make it out this weekend, then," she said, suddenly uneasy.

"You okay, Syd?"

She flipped the switch and put the cheer back in her voice. "Mmm-hmm, totally fine. Listen, let me work on wrapping this stuff up. Hopefully I'll be able to visit soon."

"Hop to it, baby. Love you."

Her heart clenched. "I love you, too, Caleb. Always will."

She returned the phone to its cradle and sank back on the pillows on her bed. Puff was curled in a ball at her feet, snoring softly, totally at peace. Syd would have given anything for even a fraction of that peace. The reality of what she'd been doing with Caleb all these months weighed on her. This wasn't a game, these were real emotions — and the person she loved most was going to get hurt.

She was never going to survive the weekend.

* * * *

Syd waited nervously for the door to open. Her eyes were grainy, her head was pounding and she couldn't stand still. She had taken the redeye to California, eager to get to Caleb and get this over with once she had made up her mind to go. All she wanted to do was sleep for a couple hours to ensure coherent speech, talk to Caleb and break things off, and head home…and somehow endure it all.

A rustle of noise came from behind the heavy oak doors and a few misty shapes jostled behind the frosted-glass inserts. The door suddenly opened in a *whoosh* and a girl who had to be no older than eight stood in front of her, her blonde pigtails swinging and her brown eyes wide.

"Hi!" she chirped. "You must be Sydney! You're so pretty, much prettier than Uncle Caleb said you were." She threw her arms around Syd. "Do I call you Sydney? Or Syd? Oh, oh, or Auntie Syd? Can I call you that?"

Oh God.

"Okay, Lilly, hold on a sec, there's no auntie anything going to be happening right now." A man came up behind her and swung her into the air. He looked just like Caleb, except his hair was styled in a buzz cut and he was wiry as opposed to muscled.

"Daddy! Put me down!" She giggled.

Instead of doing as told, he flipped her over his shoulder and extended his free hand to Syd. "You must be Sydney." He grinned. He had the same sparkling smile as his brother.

Her tongue was stuck to the roof of her mouth, so she only nodded mutely. The last thing she'd expected — the last thing she wanted — was to meet Caleb's family. She was about to devastate him and if she bonded even a little with his brother or niece, it would only make what she had to do that much harder.

"Okay, out of the way, out of the way!" Caleb pushed his brother to the side and reached for Syd, pulling her into a warm embrace. "God, is it ever good to see you," he whispered into her hair. She nodded again. He drew back and held her at arm's length. "Hey, you okay, darlin'?"

"Yes," she croaked. She cleared her throat. "Yes, sorry, just tired. I took the redeye in."

He beamed and kissed the top of her head. "Well, now you're here and you can kick back for a while and let me take care of you." He led her into the house and elbowed his brother on the way into the living room. Lilly shot past him into another room, saying something about showing Sydney a crafts project she was working on.

"You've already met my brother PJ, which technically stands for Pat Jones, but more often than not it means Practical Joker. He's two years my senior, but certainly doesn't act it."

The comment netted a soft taupe and burgundy striped pillow hitting him square on the back of his head.

That did it. Syd burst out laughing at the stunned expression on Caleb's face as he whipped around to confront his brother, who was innocently batting his eyelashes and whistling an unknown tune.

"You really want to do this now?" Caleb asked.

Lilly burst into the room armed with two more cushions. "Pillow fight!" she yelled, launching them as she ran by.

Caleb grabbed Syd around the waist and hauled her onto the chocolate-brown plush sofa, taking cover from the cushion missiles. He shook his blond hair out of his eyes and winked at her. "You're gonna love my family."

I'm going to hell.

* * * *

Caleb pulled his brother to the side. "Okay, man, you've managed to stay for lunch *and* dinner. Now get the hell out of my house so I can have some alone time with my lady."

Pat thrust his hips forward and grunted.

He covered his face. "For fuck's sake, PJ!"

"Bow chicka bow wow," PJ said, laughing. "Lilly," he called, heading into the kitchen to where she was showing Syd how to make a boondoggle bracelet. "Get your stuff together, munchkin, we're heading out."

"Okay, Daddy," she said, moving to put away everything. "Sydney, you can keep the one we were working on so you can practice, and I'll finish mine the next time I see you."

Syd smiled softly and winked. "Yes, boss."

Pat leaned down and hugged Syd. "It was fantastic to finally meet you, Sydney. You're the best thing that's happened to my brother in a long, long time."

Her smile faltered. "Thanks, Pat. Really good to meet you and Lilly, too."

While Lilly cleaned up her mess and chattered away at Syd, Pat grabbed his brother's arm and pulled him out of earshot. "Is everything okay with you two?"

Caleb was shocked at the question, especially after the great day they'd all had. "Yeah, of course. Why wouldn't it be?"

PJ scrunched up his nose. "I dunno, bro, something's off with her. She's been pretty moody — like one minute she'll be laughing and enjoying herself, and the next she looks like she's fighting tears."

"I'm sure she's pretty tired."

Lilly and Syd came out of the kitchen and started toward them, and Pat continued quietly. "Just be careful, okay, Caleb. Something isn't sitting right."

Caleb nodded and patted his brother on the back. "Thanks for always keeping an eye on me, man, but I think we're okay."

We have to be.

Lilly gave Sydney a quick hug. "Maybe next time you visit I can call you Auntie Syd?"

And there was that expression Pat described — Syd

looked about ready to burst into tears as she hugged the girl goodbye.

When they'd left, Caleb pulled Syd into his arms and kissed her. "Have fun today, darlin'?"

"Loads," she answered, pressing her face into his shoulder. "I'm so tired, CJ."

"Come on, let's get you to bed."

Upstairs, in nothing but the amber glow of a nightstand light, Caleb studied Syd as she moved around his bedroom. She was absolutely acting strange now, stiff and robotic, as if she were only going through the motions. She seemed shy almost, ducking into the en suite to change as opposed to stripping to nothingness right there and giving him a show.

She's just tired.

She stepped out of the bathroom in an oversized Vancouver Canucks T-shirt and headed toward the bed. Caleb was waiting beneath the cobalt comforter wearing a pair of pajama pants, and relief was written all over her face. He had suspected, after the late-night flight and the busy day they'd had, the last thing Syd would have energy for was a little playtime, and by the tired sigh that left her lips as she crawled into bed he'd assumed correctly. She climbed under the blankets and into his waiting arms, snuggling close.

"Are you... Is it okay if we don't...ya know?" she stumbled.

"Of course, darlin'. We can do anything you want. You're here with me now. That's all I need." He kissed the top of her head. "God, I love you."

She wrapped one arm around his waist and moved closer to him. "Please, I... Let me hold you a while, Caleb," she murmured, body quaking.

Caleb furrowed his brow and smoothed a few strands of hair away from her face. He brushed his lips on her temple. "Are you okay, baby?"

She buried her face into his chest and started crying, the

tears she appeared to have been holding back all day set free in a torrent. He let her cry for a few minutes, unsure what to do. What set this off? What was going on?

"I'm sorry," she whispered suddenly. "Oh God, I'm so, so sorry."

An uneasy sensation settled in the pit of his stomach. "Sorry for what, darlin'?" When she didn't answer, he asked again, "Sydney, sorry for what?"

Her only response was a shake of her head and shortly thereafter the slow and steady breathing of sleep.

Caleb wasn't certain how much time had passed when he was startled awake. It wasn't that he'd heard a noise or felt something...it was more the absence of sound and movement that alarmed him. He turned his head toward the clock—it was five-thirty in the morning, just before sunrise. Caleb fumbled around to flick on the bedside lamp and squinted as the light hit his eyes.

He was alone in bed.

He glanced toward the en suite. The room was dark and quite obviously empty.

Where did she go?

He rolled off the mattress and rounded the bed, careful to avoid tripping over Syd's overnight bag.

Except it wasn't there.

It was as if he had been punched in the gut. Suddenly everything his brother had said came flooding back to him and all the signs he'd pretended to be blind to over the past few weeks assaulted him. Last night, though, with Syd sobbing and apologizing, but not saying what she was sorry for...

He rushed from the bedroom, nearly stumbling down the stairs head over ass, and slid into the living room. It was empty. The family room and office didn't yield him better results. He rushed into the kitchen and there he found her, standing at the counter.

"Syd?"

She folded the piece of paper she had been holding, placed

it on the black granite surface, and turned to face him. She looked terrible — her eyes were red-rimmed and filled with tears, her face sunken and drawn. Her lips were nothing more than a thin line. She quickly turned away from him and moved to the French doors to stare out into the back garden, watching the sun rise.

He stepped behind her and put his hands on her upper arms, rubbing gently up and down. "Syd, baby, please. Tell me what's wrong." Her body shook and Caleb wrapped his arms around her, hoping the gesture provided whatever comfort she needed.

"Stop. Please stop," she whispered, her voice weak as she pulled away from him.

"Did I do something to upset you, Syd?" he asked, utterly confused.

She turned to face him, her cheeks wet with tears, whatever pain she was feeling evident in her expression.

"Syd..." he began.

"I can't do this anymore, Caleb. I... We... I can't be with you. This has to stop."

He wasn't sure he had heard her right — the sound of his heart cracking in two was almost deafening. "What? Everything was fine yesterday. How can you suddenly say this now? You don't mean that, darlin'. I know you don't." He reached for her again, but she dodged his embrace.

"I do, Caleb. I... I mean it." She covered her face. "I'm so sorry. I didn't want it to happen like this."

He shook his head.

What in the name of fuck is going on?

"It doesn't need to happen at all," he tried reasoning. "Tell me what happened. Tell me what's making you say this?"

"I was hoping I wouldn't see you before I left," she said. She nodded toward the note on the counter. "That says everything I need to."

"I want to hear it from *you*, Syd. Not read a goddamn letter."

She went silent and swung her purse over her shoulder,

preparing to leave.

"No," he said, more to himself than to her. "This isn't happening." He moved around her and blocked her path out of the kitchen. "You can't just walk away, Syd. Not when I love you, and you love me."

She hung her head.

Caleb cupped her cheek and tipped her face up to his. He waited until she met his gaze. "I love you, Sydney Bennett." He leaned forward and kissed her softly, tenderly. "My heart is yours."

She trembled and fresh tears sprang to life. She yanked away from him. "No! We... This never should have happened to begin with. This time it's real—there's no going back." She stepped around him and headed toward the foyer, where her overnight bag sat waiting for her.

Frustrated, Caleb slammed a fist onto the wall. "You can't up and leave like this, Syd! Don't do this to me *again*. Stay. Talk to me. We can figure it out."

She shook her head no and opened the door, stepping out into the early morning light. "Goodbye, Caleb," she whispered.

"Syd, I'm begging you, darlin', don't do this," he yelled after her, stepping onto the walkway to follow her, numb to the pain of the pebbles and stones on his bare feet. "Stay for a few minutes and talk to me, damn it!"

She hurried to the rental car and got in before he could reach her. Without another look, she started the engine and backed down the driveway.

"Don't leave me," he whispered, shattered. "Stay."

Chapter Thirty-Seven

"Okay, Lilly's with a sitter and I'm here. Now tell me what the fuck is going on?" Pat said, pushing his way through the front door, a slightly irritated expression overtaking his usually soft features.

Caleb's shoulders were sagging, his head hung. "Syd's gone," he announced.

PJ stared at him. "Um, of course she's gone. You knew she was only staying the night." He sighed and slapped his brother on the back. "You're not gonna be a sucky baby every single time she goes home, are you? Because I'm pretty sure I'd lose my damn mind trying to console you twenty-four-seven."

Caleb stepped into the living room and sank into the couch. "No, man. She's *gone*." He picked up the black acoustic that was leaning against the arm and began absent-mindedly plucking away at the strings. Usually a guitar in his hands would help to soothe and calm him—not this time.

Pat blinked and stared at him. "Say what?"

"She left this morning. Said we're through."

"Oh shit. Oh crap, man, I'm so sorry I was being a jerk to you just now. What happened? Did you guys have a fight or something?" He sat beside his brother and rested his elbows on his knees.

Caleb turned to face him. "No. No fight. You were right, Pat. Something was off with her. I noticed it, too. Even after you left she was acting strange and withdrawn."

"The one time I wish I was wrong," PJ mumbled.

"When we went to bed she only wanted to hug me and then she started crying, saying she was sorry over and over again, but not telling me for what," Caleb continued. "And then this morning I woke up and she was nowhere in sight. I came to the kitchen and there she was, all packed up and ready to go." He sighed heavily. "I tried getting a reason out of her, begged her to stay, but all she would say was that we never should have happened and that everything would be explained in the letter, and she drove off."

"Letter? What letter?"

Caleb nodded toward the coffee table. On it sat the note Syd had left him, the ivory paper still folded.

PJ gestured with his hand. "And? What did it say?"

"I haven't read it. Does it even matter?" He shrugged. He leaned the guitar up against the sofa again, and rubbed at his face. He felt destroyed — on so many levels.

Pat plucked the letter off the table, opened it and smoothed it out, and offered it to his brother. "Read." Caleb shook his head no. "Read. Older brother's orders."

Caleb took the offered paper.

Caleb,

The last thing I ever wanted was to do this in a letter, but I guess I didn't have the courage to say it to your face. I never, ever, wanted to hurt you, and yet here I am, doing just that, and I am sorry. So incredibly sorry. What we had was special, and I will remember my time with you forever, but it never should have happened. I was selfish, and stupid, and because of that, the most amazing, kind and beautiful man – inside and out – is getting hurt. I know you want answers but I have none to offer. Suffice it to say there is too much going on in my life right now, and I cannot give you my heart. I know – I know you're going to think that excuse is utterly lame, but I swear, Caleb, it's the truth. There's so much bad happening in my world that I haven't been able to tell you about. Not because you wouldn't want to hear about it, but because I literally cannot share the details with you. And while leaving you seems like my choice, in truth, it is not. Please, Caleb, you have to forget about me. You have to let me go. Hate me if you must – Lord knows you have every right in

the world to. Go find the love and the happiness you deserve from
someone who can give all of herself to you — mind, body, heart and
soul. I'm so sorry for hurting you. Sydney

Caleb gave the note back to his brother when he was done
reading.
Can't focus.
PJ grabbed it and began to read.
Can't breathe.
"Oh man, Caleb…"
What details can't she share with me? Why?
Caleb twitched, and suddenly he let out a roar and the
guitar was in his hands. He smashed it against the coffee
table, again and again, until there was nothing left of it but
splinters and twisted wire.
Pat took the broken guitar from him and placed it aside.
"Dude. Caleb," he said, his voice gentle. "Come on, brother,
calm down."
Stunned, he turned to face Pat. "What the fuck is going
on?" he whispered. "What can't she tell me?" Pat shrugged.
"What did she mean it wasn't really her choice?"
PJ pulled him to sit on the sofa again. "I don't have those
answers, bro. I wish I did." He frowned. "One thing is for
sure — since the whole thing started with you two back in
Banff, she's never been able to make up her mind on where
she wanted things to go. She flipped and flopped like a fish
outta water…"
"She said she loved me, God damn it! She *loved* me!"
His brother nodded. "I know, but, dude, her letter — it
sounds like this time she means it when she says you two
are over. For your sake, I think you have to let her go."
Caleb shook his head. "No."
I can't.
"I know it's fresh, bro. I'm not saying it'll be easy. I'm
not saying it won't hurt, some days more than others. I'll
always be here for you — hell, I'll even buy you a dozen
more guitars to bust up if that's what helps you," PJ said,

trying to make light of what Caleb had done only a few moments ago. "You can't let this consume you. Take your time. Heal. But you *have* to go on living."

He looked up at his big brother, Pat surely seeing pain and sorrow reflected in his eyes. "But how?" he asked softly. "How can I go on living without my heart?"

* * * *

"Yes, Papa, I'm fine."

"No, I'm fighting a bit of a cold, so I'm low on energy."

"I promise that's all it is, Papa, I swear."

She sighed and threw her hands in the air. "No, I haven't been crying."

Syd paced the kitchen from one end to the other while on the phone. Puff sat there and stared at her accusingly for lying to her father. Of course she'd been crying. It had been a week since she'd left California—and Caleb—and all she'd been doing was crying. She tried to refocus on the conversation.

"Absolutely. Everything is being pulled together faster and easier than we ever could have imagined. Jenny's a great assistant and a great help. She's been sending me pictures and constant updates from Toronto."

"Yes, the grand opening next weekend is going to be great. Just fantastic."

"Yes, I found a wedding dress and Melanie is helping me get the rest of the details that I need to worry about sorted for the wedding."

As soon as Syd uttered the word 'wedding', Puff heaved and threw up bits of grass on the kitchen floor.

That's exactly how I feel, Puffy.

"No, I'm not crying right now. Papa, please stop worrying. You're going to make yourself sick."

She grabbed some paper towel and the disinfectant from under the sink and walked toward the moon-eyed pup.

"I know, Papa. Everything will be okay. Yes, I love you,

too. Goodnight."

She hit *end* on her cell and left it on the counter. She bent to clean up the mess, and gave the little dog a scratch behind the ears. "You are *not* a lawn mower, baby girl. Stop eating the grass and puking everywhere, okay?" Puff whined in response and nuzzled Syd's free hand as she cleaned the floor with the other.

When she was finished in the kitchen, she went to tidy up in the living room before Cara got there. She'd asked Cara earlier this morning if she could stay at her place for a while. Being alone in this house, with memories of Caleb flooding nearly every room—it was too difficult for her to deal with. She tormented herself daily with thoughts of running back to California and to Caleb's arms. She envisioned what their life would have been like together—moving into his house in Miami, getting married, starting a family of their own, growing closer to Pat and forming a real aunt-niece bond with Lilly...

She plopped onto the couch and picked Puff up to cuddle the pooch close. "I miss him, Puffy. I miss him so much."

"I'd bet anything he misses you, too, Syddie."

Syd's head snapped up at the words. "Cara, I didn't hear you come in."

Cara shrugged. "I'm all ninja-like, remember?" She sat beside her friend. "Are you ready to go?"

Instead of answering, Syd focused her gaze on the piano in the corner of the room. "I promised I'd play for him, you know?" she whispered. "So much for that."

"Yeah, that's probably a blessing," Cara snorted. "You don't exactly tickle the ivories, my dear—you pummel them to death."

A small smile crept across Syd's lips. "I'm passionate," she defended. Her smile instantly faded. "So is Caleb..."

"Okay, that's it, we've had enough!" Cara bounced to her feet and grabbed Syd's hands. "Let's get out of here. You need Caleb-free surroundings."

"This is all such a fucking mess."

"Yes, yes, it is." She hugged her. "Hey, come on, there's nothing we can do about it right now, honey. You have a grand opening to get ready for and we're gonna need to remind you how to smile for that. You have a wedding to get mind-numbingly drunk for. And we have more work to do on figuring out how the hell to get you out of this damn fiasco before Brett tries to make itty bitty Bretts with you."

They both shuddered.

Puff sneezed.

"Let's move!" Cara pointed toward the foyer. "Puffy, lead the way!"

As Cara buckled Puff into her seatbelt harness, Syd tossed the last of her bags into the backseat. "Cara?"

Cara's head popped up over the roof of the car to look at her. "Yo."

"I wish I'd never met Caleb," she said sadly.

"Oh, honey…"

"I wish I never went to Banff. I wish I had left my meeting a littler earlier and never crashed into him. I wish I'd never agreed to see him again." She felt the hot sting of tears. "I wish I didn't love him, Cara. I wish… I wish…"

Chapter Thirty-Eight

"Thanks a million for getting back to me so quickly." Caleb tucked the phone between chin and shoulder and folded a hunter-green dress shirt carefully before placing it in the overnight bag. He walked over to his dresser and opened the top drawer. "Yes, I understand the opening is tomorrow." He pulled out a few pairs of socks and boxers and tossed them into the bag, as well. "He was good with me dropping by and making an appearance? Excellent." He snagged a pair of pajama bottoms and a T-shirt from the next drawer down and threw them onto the bed as he passed by it on the way to his bathroom. "Absolutely. If you wouldn't mind texting me the address... Thank you, Jenny. You've been incredibly helpful. I can see why Christou's hired you to begin with. You must be a real asset to them."

He hit *end* then speed-dial, trying for the third time to get hold of his brother.

"Sexy bear," Pat answered.

"Oh, you make me blush," Caleb joked back.

Pat perked up. "You sound like you're in a bit of a better mood, bro. That's good, really good."

"Yeah. About that..."

"About what?"

"I'm heading to Toronto."

"You're *what*?"

He sat on the edge of the bathtub. "I'm going to Toronto, Pat. For Christou's grand opening. She's got to be there. I need to talk to her."

"You're on drugs. Or drunk. That's the only explanation I can come up with for this fucking crazy idea of yours."

Caleb sighed, exasperated. "PJ, you don't get it, man. I need to do this."

"Yeah, of course. You need to torture yourself and get sucked back in to whatever game she's playing. Makes perfect sense. I'll be right over to shred your passport."

"I'm not looking to get back together with her, Pat. You have no idea what all this has done to me. I can't go down that road again."

"I can see exactly what it's done to you, bro. Why do you think I'm trying to stop this insanity? I'm your big brother and it's my job to protect you. I can't let you do this to yourself."

Caleb examined himself in the mirror — he was unshaven, his blond hair hanging limp over his forehead. His face was drawn and his eyes had lost all spark of life.

I miss her.

"Look, Pat, I have no illusions about this. I don't expect to show up there and have her run into my arms, proclaiming her undying love for me." PJ grumbled something incoherent. "You want me to get over her, to get over this? I've been trying to do that for the past month and a half and I'm no better off than the day it happened. No, to get over her I need *closure*, man. I need to know *why*."

"She told you why in that long-winded letter," Pat huffed.

"Wrong. She basically told me that she couldn't tell me why. I need answers and the truth."

He groaned. "Dude, you're setting yourself up for more hurt."

He raked a hand through his hair. "I have to do this, Pat. Please, try to trust me on this, okay? I'll see her, get my answers and walk away. I'll be fine."

Will I?

Would he be able to see Sydney and let her walk away from him yet again?

* * * *

Strolling along Yonge Street in Toronto toward Christou's, Caleb was flooded with memories of his time in the city with Sydney earlier that summer – going for strolls, staying in bed for a full day, the rooftop pool…

Don't go there.

He hated to admit he was excited, and some tiny part of his heart harbored hope that she would come back to him. His world was so empty without her in it and he had to believe, deep down, hers was just as vacant. It had to be. Every fiber told him her love for him was true – well, everything except telling him they couldn't be together and leaving him floundering and wondering why.

Yeah, that's true love.

He found the address Jenny had provided him and stopped in front of the restaurant. The bright blue Christou's sign was lit and another sign adorned one of the big windows that faced the street, boasting the grand opening. He peered inside – the place was packed. There were a few tables tucked away for guests to sit at, but for this event the room was left open and people milled about and talked animatedly. He took a deep breath and stepped through the door.

He spotted Sydney almost immediately. She was stunning in a white and sea-blue halter dress that cinched at her waist and flared out elegantly to just above her knees. Her glossy black hair was pulled away from her face in a ponytail that was swept over her shoulder. And again – as always – he was struck by her beauty.

Go in, talk to her and leave, he reminded himself.

He had taken but one step in her direction when a small, frail-looking man came up to him and held out a hand as he introduced himself.

"Oh! Oh, you must be Caleb Jones!" he exclaimed. "Nikoleta is going to go crazy when she sees you," he laughed, pumping Caleb's hand enthusiastically and grinning from ear to ear.

"I am," CJ smiled. "You must be Mr. Christou?"

He waved away the formality. "Please, please, call me Stefanos. Jenny said a music star would be dropping by for the opening, and when she told me it was you... Well, I had to keep it a secret from my sweet baby girl." He winked. "She's a big fan of your band, Mr. Jones."

Caleb nodded, confused. Stefanos had to be Sydney's father, but she'd never mentioned a sister named Nikoleta. He shrugged it off and allowed himself to be led away from Syd toward the other side of the restaurant. He dodged a server coming around with a tray of appetizers that made his mouth water and was suddenly face to face with someone new.

"This is my son, Theo. He's the mastermind behind all the menu items, and the head chef at our Vancouver location. Theo, this is Caleb Jones."

Theo stared at him. "Ya, I recognize who he is, Papa," he answered quietly. "It's, um, nice to meet you..."

"Likewise."

Theo kept staring at him. Was it possible Syd had talked to her brother about him? It had to be. Theo was looking at him as if he'd seen a ghost.

"Ah, there's my Nikoleta! Nikki, come here for a minute with Brett. There's someone I want you to meet," Stefanos called. "Mr. Jones, I want you to meet my daughter Nikoleta and her fiancé, Brett."

Caleb turned around, a smile on his face, curious to see who this mystery sister of Sydney's was.

He couldn't breathe.

Nikoleta...Sydney...they were one and the same.

Unless she has a twin she's never mentioned?

Not with the way her face blanched at the sight of him. It was her.

For once in his life, Caleb was stunned speechless.

No. No, no, no, this can't be happening. He can't be here. Why is he here? He can't be here.

She stared at Theo, panicked and desperate for support,

and he immediately moved around Caleb to stand beside her. He rubbed her back gently, trying to calm her. She opened her mouth to speak to Caleb, but nothing came out.

"Oh, hey! You're from that band Nikoleta likes so much, right? Divine something or other?"

"Divine Intervention," Caleb answered, his voice tight.

"Yes, that's right," Brett dismissed the correction with a wave. "Well, my Nikoleta should be over-the-moon excited to see you, but it appears she's a bit star-struck at the moment. Say hello to Mr. Jones, my love," he ordered.

"Hello," she said, her voice cracking. Caleb's jaw clicked and his eyes narrowed.

The way he's looking at me…

"We're getting married the first Saturday of September," Brett continued, blissfully unaware of what was going on. "Perhaps you can come play a song for us at the reception, Mr. Jones. Perhaps by then my Nikoleta will have found her voice…and her manners," he chastised.

Caleb shook his head. "No worries at all." He turned to her father. "I can't stay for long, but I did want to drop by and wish you luck on this venture, Mr. Christou. I'm a fan of your chain and I'm positive this location will do quite well. I'll be sure to recommend it to my friends."

Papa smiled warmly and put a hand on his heart. "Thank you, Mr. Jones. That means so much to me."

Syd watched as Caleb shook Theo's and Brett's hands, saying goodbye. When it came to her, he simply nodded and walked away.

He can't even bear to touch me.

She turned to find him pushing through the crowd. Now that her father had made a fuss about him, people turned their attention away from the food and to him, and he nearly had to fight to get through the sea of people and out the door.

"Well, that was nice of him to stay for all of five minutes," Brett quipped, rolling his eyes.

"I… Excuse me, I'm not feeling very well." Syd elbowed

past Brett and walked as fast as her heels would allow to the small office at the back of the restaurant. She closed the door and sank to the ground, sobbing. A knock sounded at the door and she managed a weak, "Just a moment."

Theo poked his head into the room. "It's only me. Can I come in?"

"Oh, Theo," she whimpered, hanging her head.

He let himself in and locked the door. "Nikki, shit, I'm so sorry you had to go through that." He knelt beside her and stroked her hair, trying to calm her.

"Did you *see* the way he looked at me, Theo?" she asked, her voice rising suddenly. "He hates me! I don't even know why he came here, but he hates me!" she said, her voice becoming shrill.

Theo helped her to her feet and pulled her in for a hug. "Sis, please, please try to calm yourself."

She shook her head. "How can I calm down? I love him and I hurt him so much already breaking things off. You should have seen the look on his face when I drove away." She buried her face in his shoulder and trembled. "But tonight... Theo, when he found out I was engaged and marrying in two weeks..."

"I know," he whispered.

She yanked away, stricken with guilt and sick to her stomach. "He was crushed, Theo. *Crushed.* That knowledge took the hurt to a whole other level." Lightheaded, she lost her balance, and gripped Theo's arms for support.

"Nikki, please stop!"

She collapsed against him, weak. "He despises me, Theo. The man I love despises me. And I deserve every ounce of that hate for what I've done."

* * * *

He sat in the plane, waiting for the call to come from the tower giving the pilot the go ahead to depart. As soon as he had left the restaurant he'd headed back to his hotel, gathered his belongings in a hurry and grabbed a taxi to Pearson Airport. There he'd managed to secure a first-class ticket on the redeye back to Cali—he didn't care what time the flight was, or what the cost was, he needed to get out of Toronto and away from Sydney.

Was Sydney even her real name? They kept calling her Nikoleta...

Caleb was thankful that at this hour there was only one other person in first class, and that individual was more interested in the liquor offered to him than trying to make idle conversation. He wanted to be left alone to stew about the events earlier that night. He wanted to be angry with her. He wanted to hate her.

It was the only way to manage through the pain.

She was engaged. Engaged! When the hell had that happened? He thought back to Banff, and her reluctance to meet him again. Could she have been engaged even then? All this time she was a taken woman, and she had been gallivanting in and out of the bedroom with him! Her smug fucking fiancé had mentioned they were getting hitched in about two weeks. Nice of her to break it off with him before the wedding, at least.

He shook his head in disgust and clenched his fists.

All this time, she has been cheating on me.

Wrong, he thought suddenly. *She had been cheating with me.*

Why the hell hadn't she told him she was engaged back when they'd first met? Was this all some sort of game to her? The 'let's fuck a rock star before I get married' game? One last hurrah? Had she even meant it when she'd said she loved him?

Does it even matter?

His mind was going a mile a minute. He took a breath, working hard to settle his nerves before he jumped out of his seat and started screaming at the top of his lungs. He rubbed at his face, trying to get her image out of his mind. She had looked so stunned and nervous in the restaurant.

Obviously, she hadn't wanted her beloved to discover she'd been fucking another man and she must have been terrified he'd say something or make a scene.

She's probably laughing it up right now, he thought. How she'd made him fall for her and come all the way to Toronto to see her. Her friends are probably getting a really big kick out of the whole situation. She must be pretty damn proud of herself and be all puffed up like a goddamn peacock.

He felt used and stupid—so, so stupid.

He had come to Toronto hoping to talk to Syd and find closure, and that was most certainly what he had found tonight. He was done with her—done with her stories, done with her lies.

Forever done.

Chapter Thirty-Nine

With only one day left before the wedding, Syd had decided to come back home to prepare everything she needed for their faux wedding night. The time she'd spent at Cara's had helped immensely. While the very thought of Caleb put her through hell, at least now she was able to say his name without crumbling to her knees in a heap of depression. Still, she was grateful her friend would be hanging around for the night. Thoughts of Caleb could sneak up on her at any given time and Cara's shoulder might be needed at a moment's notice.

Cara was helping her pack a bag of items she'd need on the wedding day. "So, is Theo swinging by?" she asked, her voice even.

Syd grinned. "I got a text from him a little bit ago. He should he here any second. Why? Do you need a minute to pretty yourself up?"

Her friend's face went beet red. "What? No! Why would you say that?"

Syd giggled. It was so obvious her friend was crushing on Theo as much as he was on her.

"And what in God's name is *that*?"

"Don't you like it?" Syd asked, holding up an ugly, green and orange floral-patterned, floor-length flannel nightgown. Bound and determined to not let Brett touch her, she had bought the garment especially for their wedding night. She stuffed it into her overnight bag.

"Brett's gonna get all riled up seeing you wear that," Cara joked.

The doorbell rang, followed by urgent knocking. Puff

barked *Alert, alert!* and ran down the stairs, nearly tripping over her fluff in her haste to get to the foyer. Cara shot her friend a confused look and they both headed downstairs to see who it was.

As soon as she opened the door, Theo burst in, visibly upset. "You can't agree to this."

"What's wrong?" the girls asked simultaneously.

He shook his head. "This is wrong. You cannot let that prick make you do this."

Syd put her hand on her brother's shoulder. "Theo, we'll be okay, honey, I promise." The poor boy seemed as if he was about to blow a gasket.

He stalked into the living room and threw a piece of paper on the coffee table. "Read it, go on," he insisted. He cracked his neck from side to side. "I'm going to kill that pus-infested, back-stabbing son of a bitch!"

Confused, Syd picked it up and scanned it, Cara peering over her shoulder.

"Oh, hell no," Cara said, her tone matter-of-fact.

"He... He can't make me do this," Syd stammered. "How can he expect me — any of us — to be okay with this?"

"I don't know what he's thinking, but I am sick and tired of his bullshit!" Theo punched the wall in anger.

They all looked at the hole, their eyes following the flakes of drywall that swirled to the ground.

"Please don't beat up my house."

He ran a hand through his chestnut hair. "Sorry. First this bogus fucking wedding, and now this — I'm incredibly pissed off."

Cara took Theo's hand, trying to calm him. "We all are," she said softly.

"I'm calling Brett," Syd said, grabbing her phone and dialing his number.

He answered on the second ring. "Oh, isn't this a nice surprise. My bride to be, Nikoleta, calling *me* for a change."

"Who the hell do you think you are, Brett?"

"Excuse me?"

244

She waved Theo away, who was desperately trying to pluck the cell from her fingers. "I read the email you sent to my father, Brett. What makes you presume I'd ever agree to this? What gives you the right to even suggest it?

There was a moment of silence on the other end of the line, then Brett let loose a bitter laugh. "I think you're forgetting your place, Nikoleta. Effective tomorrow you're a Hudson woman, and that gives me the right to do any damn thing I want. If I say sneeze, you'll sneeze, and if I say you're quitting your job…you *are*."

"I won't."

"Yes, my love, you will. Two things will be happening immediately after the honeymoon—you'll be packing up and moving into my house, and you will hand in your resignation to your father. You'll be at home, with me, where I can keep tabs on you at all times."

Theo snatched the phone away from her. "You can't do this, you fucking piece of—"

"Theo!" Syd grabbed it back and shot him a glance. "That won't help anything, please."

"Get your brother on a leash," Brett warned.

"I won't quit the restaurant, Brett. This is my life we're talking about here, my passion. I love my job and what I do, and, damn it, I'm good at it. Just because I'm marrying you doesn't mean you get to have that level of control over me. I won't be your little trophy wife to be kept locked away until you want to show me off to your friends."

He snorted and dismissed her comment. "I'll deal with your hissy fit another time, Nikoleta. For now, you should focus on getting ready for the wedding. Tomorrow, you become my wife."

She put her phone onto the coffee table and glanced toward Theo and Cara, who were staring at her expectantly. "He hung up on me."

"That little…"

She took a deep breath. "I can't deal with this right now. He said he wouldn't force me to resign until after I've moved in with him. I need to get through tomorrow first. One crisis at a time."

Her brother stepped in front of her and put his hands on her shoulders. "Okay, Nikki, one thing at a time, and I'll do my best to contain my need to throttle his fucking neck."

"Hey, have you made any headway with that criminal lawyer you found?" she asked.

"Which one?" he said, rolling his eyes. "I've only spoken to a dozen of them over the past several months."

"The newest one...Simonson, or something?" Cara piped up.

"Oh, right! Yeah, no."

Syd twitched. "Come again?"

He sighed in frustration. "She's pretty much saying the exact same thing every *other* damn lawyer I've spoken to had said. I go through an identical same rigmarole — say I'm taking a college law class, and I'm doing a research paper, and told her in very vague detail about the 'hypothetical' situation." He threw his hands in the air. "Like everyone else, she said that if the person was charged with murder in another country, no matter how long ago it may have occurred, that person needs to be held accountable and go to trial. And that trial would need to happen *in* the country the illegal act took place in." He scowled. "Ergo...since the crime happened in Greece, Papa would have to go back to Greece for the trial."

"So there really is no real way out right now," Syd murmured.

"There's got to be something we're missing," Cara started.

"We need to dig something up on *him*!" Theo exclaimed, rubbing his hands together as he paced the room. "Yes, we'll find some sordid little detail from *his* past, and blackmail him back!"

"Theo, Brett may be a total jerk, but he's no criminal. We'd never get anything like this on him."

"Then we can offer him money."

She scrunched up her face. "Are you serious? Theo, he's

from one of the wealthiest families in the city. He would laugh in our faces."

"Well, fuck! You deserve to be happy, not marry that jackass."

She frowned and fingered the boondoggle bracelet around her wrist.

With the way I treated Caleb, and how I hurt him? I don't deserve to be happy at all.

"We need wine," Cara stated and glided toward the kitchen. "Hey, what's this?" she called from behind them. She came back into the living room holding the painting of Caleb that Sydney had hidden weeks ago.

"Wow," Theo breathed. "Nikki, this is amazing."

"What on earth are you talking about..." Syd's heart sank to the floor when she saw what was in Cara's hands. "I forgot about that," she whispered.

"Syddie, this is absolutely beautiful." She frowned, and glanced at her friend. "You can tell how much you love him when you look at this, honey. This whole situation – it isn't right."

Sydney shook her head and snatched away the painting. Tears threatened to spill and she quickly put the picture back in its hiding place, out of sight. "I don't want to look at that, Cara, not now. Maybe not ever again."

An awkward silence settled over the trio.

"Hey!" Theo piped up suddenly. "So I'm betting the wine idea Cara had might be a bad one, given the fact we're all emotional basket cases right now. How about I go out and grab us some coffees instead?" He nodded. "Yes? Yes. I'll be back in a few."

When he left, the girls flopped back onto the couch and stretched their legs out on the coffee table. Puff cuddled between them and Syd closed her eyes, trying to distract herself from the knowledge that this was her last night as a free woman.

After a few minutes of contemplative silence, Cara said, "I've never seen Theo act like this before."

"Like what?" Syd probed.

"All mad and angry and protective, like he's been almost every time the name Brett is mentioned."

Syd smiled. "It's because, even though he acts like a goof without a care in the world half the time, he's got a huge heart. Lots of love to give to the right person." She snuck a sideways glance at her best friend.

Cara was looking up at the ceiling. "You're right. He's usually busy cracking jokes and being a total sweetheart. But *this* Theo," she hesitated. "He's so different."

"Anything you want to admit to yet, Cara?" Syd teased.

At that, Cara popped off the couch so fast she startled poor Puff and headed toward the front door. "You okay if I take off? Theo's coming back so you'll be good for a bit, right? I'm going to go home and grab everything I need for a sleepover here tonight."

"Yeah, Car, we'll be fine so you can avoid the topic of Theo... Oh, I mean, go home and get your stuff," Syd joked. She got up and followed Cara into the foyer, right at the same time the front door opened and Theo appeared holding a tray with three coffees.

He blinked. "Um...you guys weren't, like, waiting for me right here the whole time, were you? Because that wouldn't be strange at all."

"That's precisely what we were doing. Waiting for our knight in shining caffeine to come back to the castle and save us."

He stuck out his tongue at his sister as he moved past her into the house.

"Actually, I'm going to take off for a bit, so your nutter of a sister is all yours." Cara reached for Syd and hugged her. "I'll be back later tonight to help you finish up, okay?"

"Do me a favor and call me before you come in case I fall asleep."

Cara nodded and advanced to Theo, brushing a light kiss at the corner of his mouth. "Bye," she whispered.

His face went a lovely shade of eggplant and he cleared

his throat. "Uh, Cara?"

She turned to face him.

"Coffee," was all he managed, holding the cup out to her. She smiled. "Thanks."

Syd closed the door behind her and sing-sang, "La de da!"

"What... What just happened?" Theo asked. He was adorably rooted to the floor, the tray of coffee balanced carefully in his hand and a completely perplexed expression on his handsome face.

"Why don't you tell me, stud?"

He blinked. His mouth worked, opening and closing, and yet not a single word came out.

Syd took the tray from her brother and hooked her free arm in his, pulling him with her to the living room to sit. "It appears you have an admirer."

That snapped him back to this planet. "What? No, no way. Not Cara. I've known her for years. She's never thought of me like that before, it's totally impossible. To her I'm only your dorky older brother." He started bouncing his left leg, the knee going up and down at a steady pace. "She was just being nice or something, you know, given the stress we're all under."

"Nice, my ass," Syd snorted. "Nice is a warm hug and a pat on the shoulder. She practically planted one on you."

Hi face got impossibly redder.

This is awesome! Finally, something good to think about!

"But why now, all of a sudden? I mean, nothing has changed. I'm still me."

"Not entirely true."

He glanced down at himself, his brown eyes moving left and right. He was starting to panic. "What do you mean? I haven't changed, have I? What'd I do? Oh God, did I do something stupid?"

Syd laughed and pulled a decorative pillow to her chest, hugging it as she spoke, thankful for the distraction from the impending wedding. "No, doofus. Till now Cara has only seen one side of you, the sweet, cuddly, funny side.

Cara's got this thing—this monster attraction—for bad boys. The way you've been handling Brett, and how fiercely protective you've been... She sees you in a different light, I guarantee it."

He frowned. "But I wouldn't want her attentions strictly because I shoved that walking pimple of a human around. I'm not usually like that at all."

"I highly doubt you have to worry about that. I'm pretty sure deep inside she's always liked 'Sweet Theo' too... and now that she's gotten a taste of 'Bad Boy Theo'...well, she's starting to *really* like the whole package." She laughed again. "I think she *likes* you."

"Nikki, come on, stop it," he whined, swatting at her.

She held the pillow up to block him. "No, seriously, Theo. I really do think she *like* likes you."

"Okay, new topic!" He stood and offered his hand to his sister. "Let's get back to work on strategizing how we can get you out of this sham of a marriage ASAP, so you can go back to being your usual happy self."

She took his hand and stood beside him. She willed herself to be strong and believe things would work out for the best. "Yes, Theo. Let's."

Chapter Forty

Caleb leaned back in his lounger, enjoying the heat of the Florida sun on his bare skin. He drew a sip of beer and carefully placed the bottle beside him on the deck. He raised his arms above his head and stretched, yawning as he did so. Given how much he'd had to drink the night before, he was stunned his head wasn't throbbing and his gut wasn't roiling and trying to revisit the past.

Since he'd returned from California nearly two weeks ago, Caleb had been battling bouts of either depression or anger more often than not. One minute he longed for Sydney and what could have been, and the next he was filled with hatred for her — and himself. It was like Meg all over again.

Last night he'd had a small get-together — nothing crazy, only a few old *intimate* friends. And by 'intimate friends' he meant he'd invited all the pretty ladies he'd fucked over the years. He had planned on having a *good* night, hoping that would at last knock all thoughts of Syd from his mind and his heart. PJ had been very vocal in his objection to the party, stating that he was still wounded by what had transpired with Syd, that he needed more time to heal and it was too much too fast — and so Caleb had told his brother in no uncertain terms to either come to the party or go to hell.

After all — he was Caleb Fucking Jones, the lead guitarist, co-founder and co-writer for Divine Intervention. His kind fucks till the sun comes up, they don't settle down with one woman, fall in love, start a family...

He shook the thought out of his head and drained the

bottle of beer.

Last night was exactly what he'd needed to remind him of the person he used to be and, he decided as he popped the cap off another brew, he liked it.

He jerked as cold water hit his legs. "Hey now, ladies," he warned the two blondes who were giggling by the edge of the pool. They were gorgeous and buxom and curvy and fun—and clearly still not entirely sober from last night's festivities. They were friends with one of his invited guests who had tagged along for the party, and for the life of him he couldn't remember their names.

"Come on in, Caleb," one whined.

"You're not playing with us," the other chimed in.

He lifted his head off the lounge chair and pulled his shades down his nose. He looked at them over the edge of his sunglasses and grinned. "Excuse me, but I clearly played with you *both* last night. Several times over." He winked and settled back.

One giggled and her counterpart made a soft mewling sound. "Yes, you did," they said at the same time.

Caleb rolled his eyes. Last night had been fun, sure. He had sent everyone else home and kept these two beauties on hand for the night for some bed-messing antics. What had made them interesting was that they had enjoyed playing with each other as much as they had liked playing with him—perhaps even more so—which had added an interesting dynamic to the evening.

He was back to his old self—making music and fucking for the hell of it.

Life was good.

Yeah, you keep telling yourself that, buddy.

"What the hell, Caleb?"

He groaned, and the girls squealed with delight. He didn't have the patience to even glance over his shoulder and deal with his brother's patent disapproving expression.

"Oh my God, it's Pat Jones!"

"PJ!"

They hauled their naked bouncy selves out of the pool and boinged their way over to his brother.

"Whoa, ladies, no, no touchy," Pat cried. "You're soaking wet and I'd prefer to stay dry."

"We'd prefer to stay *wet*," one of them purred.

Caleb groaned and covered his face—he was almost embarrassed for her.

"Uh, right. So, ladies…you really need to get going."

"What? Why?" came the synchronized moans.

"Because my brother isn't nearly as much fun as I am."

They giggled.

"Because," Pat said sternly, "I said it's time to go." He came around to Caleb's lounge chair and bent to pick up the clothes that were strewn beside it. He tossed the girls their towels and belongings. "Go. Now."

When they whined, he piped up. "Best do what my big brother says," he remarked, "Or else he might ground me."

The two scampered off toward the small pool house on the other side of the back yard.

PJ sat on the chair next to him and pulled out his cell to call the girls a cab, all the while shaking his head in disappointment and giving his brother the stink eye.

When he was off the phone he started in on him. "What the fuck are you doing, man?" he hissed.

Caleb laughed. "Um, whatever the fuck I want? Why?" He went to take a long draw of his beer, but was too slow in the process, and PJ snatched the bottle away from him.

"Because, man, this…" he said, sweeping his hand around. "This isn't *you* anymore."

Caleb sat up straight and brushed his blond hair off his forehead. "This wasn't me for a summer, PJ. One fucking summer. And for that summer I turned into a desperate, overly emotional suck. For a summer I lost all of me to someone who was never really mine to begin with. For a summer my heart was repeatedly broken. So no, *that* me is long dead. Fun, fucking Caleb is back and overdue for action."

"Yeah," Pat snorted. "I can see you're totally over Sydney."

Caleb's lips pressed into a tight line. "Don't ever mention that name again."

The scantily clad girls came out and around the pool toward Pat. They pouted at him, quite obviously hoping their expression would somehow convince him to let them stay a little longer. Instead of bending to their pouty will, he reached into his pocket and handed them some cash, eliciting shocked and horrified gasps.

"We're not those kind of girls!"

"Do you think we're hookers?"

Caleb snorted with laughter and Pat shook his head and held up his hands defensively. "No, that's not what I thought at all. This is to cover the cab fare home, that's all. I've already called a taxi for you and it should be waiting for you out front."

With a *harrumph* they turned their attention to Caleb, each giving him a lingering kiss goodbye. They wiggled their fingers at PJ in a demure wave as they walked toward the side gate then, finally, they were gone.

With his brother's attention focused on the ladies as they left, Caleb tried to snag back the beer that had been taken from him, but was too sluggish. Visibly annoyed now, Pat grabbed the bottle, walked to the grass and emptied it.

"We all understand precisely what this is really about, Caleb."

He shrugged.

"Sydney is getting married tomorrow."

Caleb turned away.

Pat sat again and sighed. "Dude, come on," he said, his voice gentle. "You've gotta come out with it, man. Ever since you found out what Syd has been up to, that she was engaged, you've completely shut yourself off from all of us. You totally refuse to talk to me about it. When mom asks me why you're sad all the time, what am I supposed to tell her? There are only so many excuses I can muster to cover your sorry ass and she gets more and more worried every day." He threw his hands in the air. "Even Lilly is worried about her Uncle Caleb, and Lord knows I'm right there with her."

Caleb pulled off his glasses and rubbed at his eyes. He looked at his brother, unshed tears blurring his vision. "I hate that I loved her so much, Pat, you know? I hate that I still do."

Pat nodded.

"When we were together, when she told me how she felt about me, it was so fucking authentic. I *believed* she loved me. I honestly thought that was it—she was the one I was going to be with for the rest of my life." He shook his head. "Never in a million years could I imagine that for the last six months she'd been playing me. Using me as what? Some kind of fuck toy before getting hitched?"

Pat frowned and placed a hand on his brother's shoulder. "You know I'm here for you, right? That we can talk, or you can vent or we can just kill some time watching a movie until the hurt starts to fade. Whenever you need me, bro, whatever you need."

"Whatever I need?" Caleb muttered, and let loose a small, pitiful laugh. "I need *her*."

* * * *

Her last day as a free and single woman went much too quickly... The hours seemed as if they were flying by, and suddenly Syd was lying in bed the night before her wedding, tossing and turning, unable to fall asleep. She stared at the ceiling and frowned. She was going to miss this house. She had managed to put off moving in with Brett until after their so-called honeymoon. Once that was behind them, they would figure out living arrangements and more than likely she would end up living with him. The very idea of being under the same roof as him day after day made her stomach roil.

She sighed and instinctively reached out to Puff for comfort, but she wasn't there.

That's odd, she thought. The little fur ball was almost always by her side at night.

Her attention turned to the open doorway when she heard the creak of a floorboard in the hallway outside her room. Cara had been sleeping in the guest bedroom — likely she had woken up and had to use the loo or something.

Except the shadowy shape that stood at her doorway was a heck of lot broader than Cara's lean frame.

She sat rod straight and was about to yell out to Cara when the figure stepped closer.

"Caleb," she breathed.

"Hush, darlin'," he whispered. "I saw Cara's car in the driveway — don't want to wake her up." He came into her room and shut the door behind him.

"What are you doing here?" she whispered back. "How did you...?"

He peeled off his black T-shirt and began unbuttoning his jeans. "I said hush. Details don't matter."

A hot flush creeped up her neck to her cheeks as he pulled his pants and boxers off in one fell swoop. "But... How... You should hate me," she started.

He shook his head and climbed into bed beside her. He drew the linen off her body and ran his hand under her shirt and up her abdomen. "None of that matters. I need you and I can't live without you, baby. I won't. I don't care if you're getting married — I know I'm the man your heart belongs to and I'll take you any way I can get you."

She shook her head. "Caleb, you can't mean that."

He climbed atop her and spread her legs with his knee. "I can, and I do. Nothing matters, Sydney, except being with you, inside you, loving you." And with that he gripped the collar of her nightshirt and tugged hard, tearing the thin fabric straight down the middle, exposing her breasts. "I need you, baby," he said, pushing her shorts to one side and rubbing his rock-hard cock along her slit. "Now."

She gasped when he entered her with one swift thrust, up and in and buried to the hilt.

"Oh my God," she moaned, much louder than intended.

"Shh," Caleb warned, placing a hand over her mouth. "Not a sound or I have to leave you. No one can find out I'm here, Sydney. No one."

"What's gotten into you?" she whispered, her voice muffled by his palm.

He removed his hand and leaned in to kiss her. The moment their lips met, fire burned through her. He demanded her compliance and her mouth opened to his, letting him in, sharing each other's breaths and passion. He grazed the sides of her neck with his fingertips and traced the curve of her shoulder, along her arms, and finally came to rest on her wrists. He pulled her arms over her head and he held her there, forcing her not to touch.

"Caleb," she breathed.

"Quiet," he commanded. His voice, though heavy with desire, was charged, and she obeyed without even a moment of hesitation.

He glided his free hand down her side and cupped her breast, instantly finding the nipple and rolling the hard nub between his fingers. Her back arched when he pinched harder, a reaction to the sublime pleasure of feeling him all over her once again.

"God, I missed you."

His response involved withdrawing from her, then slamming right back in.

"Syd," he whispered. "I'm not going to make love to you tonight, baby. I'm going to *fuck* you — hard. Right now."

She whimpered.

He slid his hands under her ass and lifted her hips so she was angled to him. He stroked her slowly at first, each easy glide of his cock making her shudder and bringing her a step closer to release.

"You're mine and no one else's, Sydney, do you understand that? Your heart stays with *me*."

"Yes."

"You'll never forget that, will you, Syd?"

"No, never."

"Come for me, baby," he said, his voice wrought with yearning. "I need you to show me how much you love me." He pulled out of her and crashed back in, harder and faster than before, as if he was desperate for her to experience the kind of pleasure he knew only he could provide.

Syd clutched at him, holding on as he pounded against her, the sound of skin on skin and his heavy breathing combining to push her over the edge. She closed her eyes tightly and spiraled into a series of tremors that caused a chain reaction of orgasms. She came with him moving inside her steadily, over and over again, until she could barely breathe and she had no choice but to let out the cry she'd been holding in since the moment he'd touched her…

"Syd, are you all right?"

Her eyes snapped open and her vision quickly adjusted to the darkened room.

Puff whined, annoyed at her sleep being disrupted.

Cara knocked on her closed bedroom door. "Syddie?"

Caleb wasn't there.

It was a dream. A goddamn fucking dream.

"Honey, is everything okay? Can I come in?"

She finally found her voice. "Just a dream, Car. Go back to bed."

"You sure?"

"I'm okay, I promise. Totally fine."

But that was probably the biggest lie she'd ever told, because she would never really be fine again.

Chapter Forty-One

"Nearly done," Ester, the petite hairstylist, said, securing the last of the small white crocuses in Syd's hair.

Syd adjusted her position on the stool and silently appraised her reflection. Her hair was styled in a partial updo, half pulled away from her face and secured by the three white flowers, while the rest cascaded down her back and around her shoulders in a mass of loose, ebony curls. Her makeup was done — the gold undertones of eyeshadow and bronzer making her look radiant and glowing with happiness.

But the downturned corners of her nude, glossed lips betrayed her. She was about to marry a man whose actions she despised. Although the bridal room was adorned with red roses and decorated in elegant, calming tones of creams and whites, Syd felt as if she was trapped in a dungeon.

"Yoo hoo," Melanie chimed, coming into the room and smiling broadly at Sydney. One look and instantly she realized something was wrong, her smile dissolving on her lips. "Ester, if you're done here, could I have a moment with the bride?" she asked.

Ester nodded and quietly left the room, closing the door behind her.

"You're gorgeous," she said.

Syd stood and turned to the full-length mirror. "Thanks," she replied half-heartedly. She toyed with the crystal embroidered sash at her waist, making sure it was sitting level.

Melanie came around her and fiddled with the sweeping trail of the chiffon dress, moving it out of the way so that

Syd wouldn't step on it. She stood in front of her and smoothed the sheer straps of the V-neck gown. "One thing is for sure, though. As stunning as you may look, you sure don't seem all that thrilled to be here. You look anything *but* happy." She tilted her head to the side and gazed at her future sister-in-law. "Are you sure everything is okay?"

She didn't answer and instead turned her attention to the ground in front of her.

Ages ago, when she and Brett had been dating, Syd had formed an easy friendship with the then eleven-year-old Melanie. Although there was a nine-year difference between the girls, they'd gotten along amazingly. These last few weeks, with the wedding coming up so fast and having so much to do, Melanie had been a great help to Syd, tag-teaming and assisting with crossing items off the to-do list. The two had become close again and Syd was certain she was trustworthy.

"Look," Melanie continued. "You must be sick of me asking the same question all the time, but I've got this intuition thing going on. I know, I just *know*, something isn't right here. Brett's my brother and I love him no matter what, but I can admit when he's being a jackass, and he has been treating you absolutely horribly lately and is bossing you around like there's no tomorrow. What gives?"

"I know," Syd whispered.

"Did you guys have a fight?"

"Not one that would be the cause of this," Syd said, rolling her eyes as she slumped back onto the stool.

"Well then, what is it?" When Syd's eyes filled with tears she ran to get a tissue. "No tears, no ruining your makeup!" she cried, handing one to her. She dragged a chair over and sat in front of Syd. "Please, whatever it is, you can tell me. I swear it won't leave this room."

She glanced up at Mel. There was genuine concern on the girl's face. Was it the smart thing to tell her about everything, especially after Brett's threat all those weeks ago? Likely not. She was so tired of all the lies, the façade she'd had to keep up—she was losing strength minute by minute.

I'm on a roll with bad decisions, so why the hell not?

"So, a friend of mine," she started tentatively. "Her dad isn't originally from Canada. Back home, many years ago, something happened and some very bad people made it look like he did something very bad, very illegal."

"How bad are we talking here? *Very* as in…?"

"Drug trafficking, and…" She hesitated. "And murder."

"Oh, Jesus."

"But her father, he one-hundred-percent did *not* do it. He was completely innocent. This person who set him up and pinned everything on him, he was pure evil, and jealous of her father. He was the one who planted the drugs and murdered my father's… I mean, my friend's father's wife."

Melanie stared, her expression unreadable.

Unsure if she should go on, but knowing that she had opened the can of worms and it was too late to cap it, she forged ahead. "This guy… He threatened to kill her father's son, too, if he didn't get up and disappear from the country. If he didn't leave, or tried to prove his innocence, he and his son were as good as dead." She shrugged. "So he did the only thing he could think of—he took his boy and ran."

"Syd, what the hell is this all about?" Melanie asked, her voice low.

"Now, flash forward twenty-some-odd years later," she continued. "He has a happy life and a new family. He and his son have been safe and things are going well, until another evil man, a horrible, vengeful, controlling man comes along and finds out about this secret from the past."

Melanie didn't even have to ask. "Brett."

Syd nodded and no longer pretended to be talking about a phantom 'friend'. "Brett has an insanely controlling nature, and you know how spoiled he is. I think he has *always* gotten what he wanted—except for me, because I refused to be with someone like that. So he used this new power over me and this knowledge to blackmail us, Mel. If we didn't do exactly what we were told, he would let the authorities know and Papa would be extradited to Greece to stand trial," Syd explained, her voice flat and weary.

"Son of a bitch."

"He didn't blackmail for money or a stake in the business or anything," Syd rambled on. "What he wanted was my hand in marriage and a chance to control every aspect of my life. That's the price we have to pay for his silence and to protect Papa. It's what prevents him from going back to Greece to stand trial for possession of drugs and the murder of his own wife."

"What about getting a lawyer or something?" Melanie asked. "I mean, there's got to be something that can be done to help him, right?"

"Forget that it would take every ounce of money my family has…"

"I could help, financially, Syd," Melanie interrupted.

"But we've spoken *hypothetically* to many lawyers, and he would still be extradited and in Greece until everything was all figured out in court over there."

"Okay, but that's fine then, right? I mean, at least everything would be out in the open and finally dealt with."

Syd shook her head. "No, you don't get it, Mel!" Her voice rose and she twisted her hands anxiously in her lap. "Papa isn't doing well. He won't admit it, but just look at him. He's looking sicker and sicker these days and Theo and I can tell he's getting weaker, worn out much quicker than usual. The change in his health started the second Brett came to us with this information." She stared off into space, her eyes filling with tears. "If anything about this gets out in the open, it will kill him, and if he's forced to go back to Greece to face trial…his health might be the least of our concerns."

Melanie blinked. "What do you mean?"

"Theo and I have been doing some careful digging of our own. Bacchus, the asshole who framed Papa over twenty years ago, he's now the head of the Greek mafia family my father was affiliated with. God knows what he did to get there, but he's in charge now. If he gets wind that my father is coming back home, for whatever the reason may be... you may as well put a great big target on his back. And ours." She told Melanie about the mysterious — and threatening — letter that had been sent to their father.

"Oh, Syd!" Melanie leaned across to hug her. "We can't let this happen, honey. I'll talk to Brett and —"

"No," Syd pulled back and shook her head emphatically. "No, you can't do that. I should never have told you any of this. I'm just...I'm so tired, Mel. Tired of lying and hurting. If Brett were to find out I told you, I'm not sure how he'd react."

"I'll talk to Mom and Dad, too, and they'll —"

There was a knock at the door. Melanie got up to open it and was greeted with a grim-looking Theo, his lips pressed into a thin line.

Their father stood behind him, a weak smile on his face. Sadness instead of joy was reflected in his eyes and he appeared so very tired and pale. "Ah, there's my beautiful girl," he said, going through the motions.

"Are... Are you okay, Mr. Christou?" Melanie asked.

Papa's eyes flicked from Melanie to Syd, and back again. The guilt was all over her face. "Of course I am," he answered tightly. "My daughter is getting married."

A tear rolled down Mel's cheek and she reached out to hug the frail man. "I'm so sorry, Mr. Christou. Please, if there is anything I can do to help — any way that I can — I will in a heartbeat." She turned to Syd. "Same goes for you, Sydney. Brett or no Brett, you've always been like a sister to me. If you change your mind, know that I'll have your back, one hundred percent."

She turned and left the bridal suite, lightly touching Theo's shoulder as she left.

Her father closed the door.

Now I'm in for it.

"You told her?"

"Papa, I—"

"I can't believe you told her! Brett's sister! So close to silencing him, and you tell her!" he yelled.

Theo put a hand on his father's shoulder. "Papa, please try to relax."

"No!" he roared. "I cannot! You are my children, my family. Telling Melanie… If Brett were to find out, if he were to tell anyone what he knew, you *will* be in danger." Raw fear was apparent in his eyes. "I cannot protect you," he whispered. "I'm too old, too weak. But after today, after the wedding, the threats from him will stop."

Her brother shook his head in disagreement. "No, they won't."

"Theo? What do you mean by this?"

Syd grimaced. "Damn it, Theo is right, Papa. Brett will hold this over us forever, and use it to maintain control."

"No, he will stop. He promised this would be the end of it," their father said, the tremor in his voice not fooling anyone—he didn't believe his own words. "He… He has to." Beads of sweat broke out across his brow and his face suddenly got impossibly paler. He lost his balance and reached out to the wall for support.

"Papa!" they cried out at the same time, both jumping to their father to offer support.

"I'm okay," he breathed. "Only a little tired." He glanced at his daughter and read the worry in her eyes. "I'm okay. I'm okay," he repeated and gently patted her hand to try to reassure her.

It didn't. Instead it only made her take notice of how much weight her father had lost in recent months. His health was failing and it was *her* job to be strong for him. She stepped away from him and straightened her back, holding her head high. "Papa, everything will be fine, I promise." She leaned in to give him a light kiss. "All you have to do is stay strong for me, okay?"

He nodded slowly, the sadness in his eyes palpable as he gazed at her.

"Now, shoo, both of you. I have to finish up, and don't have much time before I go out there."

Her father opened the door and shuffled out into the hallway. Theo reached out and hugged his sister tightly, then rested his forehead against hers. His eyes filled with remorse as he whispered a coarse, "Fuck," before turning and following his father, shutting the door behind him.

Alone in the room, Sydney studied her reflection in the mirror. She smoothed out her dress and took a deep breath.

"Let's do this."

Chapter Forty-Two

Picturing waterfalls, placid lakes and waves rolling onto sandy shores, Syd breathed deeply and steadily, trying to calm herself. The knock on the door that signaled it was time to take her vows would come any minute. Theo had come back to her room with Cara, the two offering to stay with her till the clock ticked to zero. She'd gently refused their offer, opting to spend these last moments alone, trying to settle her battered nerves.

She jolted when the bridal suite door opened unannounced and Brett waltzed in.

"What are you doing in here?" she demanded.

"I wanted to make sure my bride was ready to go. I don't want a single delay."

She shook her head in disgust and turned away from him.

"You could at least try to look happy," he said, his voice bitter.

She whipped around on the stool to face him again. "Do you even *hear* yourself, Brett?" He shrugged a response. "How can you possibly expect me to be happy?"

His narrowed eyes shot daggers at her. "You have no choice but to be happy. Don't forget you'll be my wife in less than an hour, Nikoleta. You better get used to that idea — and quick."

She took a shuddery breath and gazed up at him with tear-filled eyes. "I remember when we first met," she whispered. "I was immediately smitten with you. You were fun and spontaneous, and you cared about everything and everyone. And you were funny — God, you made me laugh. You were so sought after by all the campus girls, and the fact you chose to date *me* always blew my mind."

His blue eyes pierced her.

"Those first few months," she went on, "you were kind and gentle. You took the relationship one step at a time and had an absolutely easy-going attitude about it. You loved me, and I loved you, and that was enough. We wanted to discover where it led us."

"Nikoleta, where are you going with all this?" he asked, his impatience evident.

"Brett, what happened to you all those years ago? What changed you?"

"Nothing," he answered quickly, averting his gaze.

"No," she shook her head. "I don't believe it. You practically changed overnight."

"Leave it alone, Nikki," he warned.

"Why?" she shot back. "I'm marrying you, aren't I? I'm giving you what you want, Brett. You won. I have nothing to lose by asking you the simple question—what happened to you?"

"I don't need to hear this," he growled, and turned to leave the room.

Her voice soft, Syd asked, "What happened to the Brett I fell in love with?"

He froze, his back to her. "I'm right here."

"No, you're not. The Brett standing in front of me is cruel, manipulative and abusive. He's focused only on getting what he wants, without concern for how his actions may affect anyone else around him." She got up and walked toward him, her words growing more urgent, in a desperate, last-ditch attempt to reach the man he used to be. "He's not the same guy that who went out of his way to teach me how to ice skate. He's not the same guy who happily stepped outside his box and tried to cook dinner for me—and who laughed uproariously at the disastrous results. You're not the same guy who cared for me when I was sick."

He turned to face her. "Why are you saying all this, Nikki?"

She placed a gentle hand on his shoulder and rotated him to face himself in the full-length mirror. "Where did you go? Why are you hiding?"

"Stop it," he whispered.

"You keep saying you want me to love you again." She frowned. "I can't do that. I'm sorry, but I can't now and I never will. You used to want me to be happy but...look at what you're doing, Brett. I'm not happy! You're so bound and determined to control me, but the one thing you will never control is my heart."

"I don't want your heart like that," he sighed. "I want you to give it to me freely."

Syd couldn't contain the laugh that bubbled up and escaped her. "Seriously, Brett? You're threatening to extradite my father and have some seriously bad people on his back — for something he *didn't even do* over twenty years ago — and you want me to fall in love with you again? You worked your ass off to dig up this filth and then, smug as a bug, you instantly used that knowledge against my entire family just to get me to marry you so you can sink your controlling claws into my life again — and you expect me to offer you my heart?"

"I'm doing this for us," he snapped, stepping away from her.

She threw her hands in the air, frustrated. "You did it for *you*, Brett. You and only you. If you really wanted me back, you would never have needed to force it, or me. You'd have actually tried to change and rediscover the man you used to be." She shook her head. "What you want from me, you'll never have. I may be your wife according to the law, but you will *never* have my love."

"You'll learn to love me again," he roared. "I'll make you!"

There was a short knock at the door, and it opened, Melanie standing at the threshold with widened eyes. "I was going to let you know it was almost time," she started. "But then I heard yelling..."

"Everything's okay, Mel," Syd said.

She stepped in and closed the door behind her. "It most certainly is not! Brett—how could you do this?"

Oh shit.

"You know?" he asked rhetorically, his eyes flashed an accusatory glance at Sydney.

"Yes I know, and I'm disgusted, Brett. This is a new low, even for you."

"Go back and play in your bubble of naiveté and happiness, little one, and leave the big conversations to the adults," he said.

"Melanie, please don't," Syd begged. "You're only going to make things worse."

"How can you say that? He's minutes away from ruining both your lives, and you want me to be quiet?"

"Both?" he snorted incredulously. "I'm getting what I want, there are no issues on my end."

"Do you honestly believe you'll be happy in a loveless marriage, Brett?" his sister asked. "How will your wife feel when her father *dies* from all the stress this situation has put him under?"

"Oh God," Syd moaned, weakened by the thought of losing her father.

"You have no idea what you're talking about. He's perfectly fine."

"I'm telling Dad what you've done," she threatened.

He guffawed. "Oh, please do, although I don't think he'd find fault in this. After all, digging up leverage like I did—it was all *his* idea."

Melanie looked as if she'd been slapped in the face. "I... I'll tell Mom, then," she stammered.

"You do that," he sneered. "And when she mentions it to Dad, he'll tell her to get back into her little hamster ball of happiness as well. And she'll climb in and sit pretty, smiling like a good wife."

What the hell is going on here?

Syd sat quietly, glancing from Brett to Melanie and back

again, letting whatever this was play out.

"Why… How can you say that?"

He rolled his eyes. "Oh, sweet Melanie, how could you be blind as to what's been in front of you for decades?"

"What do you mean?" she asked, her voice thick with confusion.

"Do you think Mom is *really* that happy all the time?" He laughed bitterly. "She knows better than to be any other way. Just like *you'll* learn, Nikoleta."

"You don't mean that!" Melanie gasped.

"This is something Dad taught me long ago. It's the only way I know how to be anymore." Syd wasn't sure, but she thought there was a hint of sadness in his voice. "Like father, like son." He turned on his heel and walked out.

"Mel, what the fuck was that all about?" Syd asked, uneasy.

"It can't be true," she whispered. She turned to Syd, her eyes wide. "There… There was a time when I was younger," she began. "You and Brett were dating, and I remember Mom crying all the time. She was at the front door with a suitcase and Dad was screaming at her. I don't remember what they were saying—I was scared, and hiding on the stairs watching them." She paced as she spoke. "Brett pulled me away and brought me to my room right when Dad grabbed Mom's wrist and dragged her into the living room. I'm not sure… I think… I thought I heard Dad hit her," she said, tears flowing down her cheeks.

Overcome by the girl's obvious pain, Syd stood up and took her hands. "Oh, Mel."

"Brett told me if Mom was leaving we were leaving, too, and that I shouldn't worry—he'd find a way to take care of us all, even if it meant dropping out of school for a while. God, I was what, eleven or twelve at the time? I didn't understand what the hell was happening." She met Syd's eyes. Her face was ashen, the memories hitting her hard. "Brett told me to stay put, and he went downstairs and started yelling at Dad. I don't know…it sounded like a fight broke out downstairs. They were yelling at each other, and Dad was screaming 'you're my wife, you do what I say when I say' — or something to that effect."

Syd's heart broke for her.

"I know for sure, it was loud and clear, that Dad told Brett he was a pussy with you. He said he acted like a submissive little boy and he needed to get you under control and he would teach him how to do it. I can't remember how long the yelling and fighting continued on for, but it suddenly went dead quiet. I remember opening the door and trying to listen, but all I heard were hushed voices and Mom crying non-stop." She squeezed Syd's hands. "Then Brett came back upstairs, and he looked so battered. Broken, now that I think back on it — he was broken in so many ways, physically, mentally, emotionally. One eye was nearly swollen shut, his nose was cut, his knuckles bleeding. When he said he'd fallen down the stairs I was eager to believe the obvious lie. I didn't want to believe our own *father* had done that to him."

"My God," Sydney breathed.

"I asked if Mom was still leaving and he said no, that she was Father's property. Said she wasn't going anywhere and neither were we. Since then he hasn't been the same, Syd. That night Dad said or did something to him and that's why he changed and has become the way he has."

"That was when he changed," Syd murmured. "I didn't see him for a couple weeks at one point. He'd said he went on a family trip, but when he came back, he was totally different — short on patience, got pissed off if I dared have an opinion of my own. That's when he became controlling and verbally abusive... That's when it all started!"

"You're lucky you've only been dealing with the verbal abuse," Mel whispered. "Mom wasn't so lucky. There are still bruises here and there on her, even though she tries to hide them, and when I ask about it I get the old 'oh I must have bumped into something' excuse. I knew it was a lie, but I couldn't bring myself to believe the alternative. Denial is bliss, and all."

She shook her head as if to clear it and hugged Syd. "I'm sorry I was of no help today. I wish I knew what to say. I truly believe the real Brett is still in there somewhere. All these years, my father has never laid a hand on me or treated me poorly—and I have to believe my big brother is somehow protecting me. I always hoped I'd be able to reach him."

Syd gently smoothed a lock of hair away from Melanie's face. "You did plenty," she said, leading her to the door. "As they say, knowledge is power, right? Now go, get yourself together. I'll see you out there in a few minutes.

As soon as she was alone in the room again, she sat to steady her frayed nerves.

What a fuck of a day this has turned out to be.

But if anything, she got it now. She understood why Brett had changed and what had happened to him all those years ago. It didn't make it right, but knowledge was power and it might help her get through this, and at least it explained his actions, more or less.

One part of the conversation in particular stuck in her head, though—when Brett had said this was all his father's idea. That was why he had appeared so smug every time she'd seen him since the engagement. She could only imagine what was going through his sick mind.

She stared at herself in the mirror, reflecting.

First there was Caleb, the man she loved with all her heart. After seeing her at the opening in Toronto he was out of her life for good—how could he ever forgive her continuous white lies? There was no way he harbored even an ounce of love for her the moment he found out she was engaged. How he'd looked at her in those last few moments said it all. He hated her and she deserved no less. He was gone and she needed to adjust to that reality, and quick.

Then there was Brett. She despised him now, but she had loved him in her university years. Now that she understood his past better, did she have it in her to be more forgiving and empathetic and to try to *like* him again? Would her kindness bring the old Brett back? Or at the least, would it make their time together more bearable and perhaps give him cause to release his stranglehold on her?

Could she try?

Did she even want to?

* * * *

"Sorry!" Lilly cried triumphantly, moving her final peg to the home space on the board. She jumped off the floor and turned her back to Caleb and her father, and did a little butt wiggle victory dance.

"You keep winning, Lilly-pot! That's the third time now. I demand a rematch!"

Lilly jumped over to and plopped next to him. "How about we play a different game? At least that way the two of you will have *some* kind of a chance to beat me."

PJ took another slice of greasy pizza out of the box and bit into it. "Okay, pumpkin, but this time let Uncle Caleb pick the game."

She nodded and bounded off to grab the stack of games that sat on the kitchen table.

Caleb gave his brother a soft smile. "Thanks for this."

He nodded. "I figured since today was...you know...*the* day, a bit of a distraction might be good for you."

And what better way to keep his mind off the fact Syd was getting married today than to spend time with his brother and niece? She was a natural at keeping him entertained, and a full day of pizza-eating, board game-playing and movie-watching, was exactly what the doctor of broken hearts prescribed.

The last thing he wanted to do was picture Syd, looking as beautiful as ever, walking down the aisle to be wed to another man.

The doorbell ringing snapped him out of the darkness and he stood to answer it. Pat stood, too, and motioned for

Caleb to stay put.

"I've got it, man. You help Lilly pick out a new game."

He shrugged, and helped Lilly sort through the pile of boxes she'd brought into the room.

A moment later PJ was back, carrying a massive package. He had no idea what it was.

"What the heck did you order, bro?" Pat asked, maneuvering to set it on the sofa.

He shook his head. "Nothing."

He and Lilly joined his brother, and he examined the package, truly confused by it. The thing was massive—it had so be something like thirty by forty inches, and fairly thin.

"It looks like a picture," Lilly piped up.

"You're right, sweetie, it sure does." He bent closer to read the name of the sender. "C. Martins," he read. He turned to his brother. "Who the hell is C. Martins?"

"Damn if I know. See what it is."

Caleb tore through the brown packaging and the label that indicted the package was for urgent next-day delivery, and threw the paper to the floor, finally revealing the mystery object.

He couldn't breathe.

"Holy shit!" PJ cried, then instantly covered Lilly's ears. "You didn't hear that, sweetie."

She squealed and pointed. "It's *you*, Uncle Caleb!"

Perched on the sofa before him was the portrait Syd had sketched of him when he was in her kitchen their first night together. It was absolutely stunning—the detail, the use of light and shadow… It made his heart clench with sadness.

PJ nodded at the corner of the canvas. "There's a note."

Caleb carefully peeled it off and opened it, reading it aloud.

"Hi. We've never met, but I'm Cara, Syd's best friend. I found this at her place yesterday and thought you should have it. She can't even look at the painting without crying, so what's the use of her keeping it, right? Anyways, Caleb,

I hope you can see the love she has for you in each and every brush stroke. And she *does* love you, you know. More than anything. She's going through a very bad time at the moment and she's trapped—but I pray for her, and you, that one day soon she'll be free to love you again. And I pray just as hard that when that time comes, you'll at least give her an audience and let her explain. Hurting you was the one thing she never wanted to do, and the one thing she'll never stop punishing herself for. Please—try to think about it. Thanks, Cara. P.S. She has no idea I sent this to you. P.P.S. She'll probably kill me when she finds out, so—nice meeting you."

Pat frowned. "That's the second time we've heard something alluding to her not having a choice in not being able to be with you."

Caleb nodded. "I know. And the second time I've been told there's something really bad going on in her life right now."

"Is that why we haven't seen Sydney lately?" Lilly asked quietly, looking up at him with a frown on her lips.

"Yes, baby," Caleb said, kissing the top of her head. "We're not together anymore."

Her cherub face grew serious. "Do you miss her, Uncle Caleb?"

His shoulders sank. "I do, but it doesn't matter. She's marrying someone else today."

She tugged on his arm and pulled him down to her level. She looked him in the eye and asked, "But do you still love her?"

Not about to lie, he answered. "More than anything."

"Well, then you should go get her before it's too late!"

Pat put an arm around his little girl and smiled. "It's not that easy, pumpkin…"

"Why not? I know she loved Uncle Caleb, too! She loved him a whole lot. I could tell."

"How's that?" Caleb asked.

"She looked at you exactly the same way Grandma used

to look at Grandpa," she stated.

Pat and Caleb glanced at each other and, as their eyes met, a spark of hope lit up in Caleb's heart.

"She has a point," Pat whispered.

His gaze rested on the picture, saying nothing. Lilly was right. The one thing he had always said he wanted out of a relationship was lasting love, for someone he could love with every ounce of his being, and for someone to gaze at him with as much love and tenderness as his mother had their father.

That was exactly how he felt about Syd.

And she really did look at him like that.

He turned to his brother. "You're right. She does have a point," he murmured.

"Well then, what are you waiting for, bro? Go get her!"

Chapter Forty-Three

The Bridal March sounded and Sydney linked arms with each of the two handsome men flanking her. She'd requested both her father and brother walk her down the aisle — there was no one else she'd rather have by her side on this day. She glanced first at Theo, then her father. "I love you both so much," she whispered. "There's nothing I wouldn't do to keep you safe."

His voice no more than a strangled croak, her father said, "Nikoleta, you are my angel." He leaned in to kiss her cheek.

"I'll figure out a way to get you out of this," Theo promised, his voice raw.

The love that she had from these two wonderful men was all she needed to keep her strong, to keep her whole. With them, she could survive anything.

They stepped out and she caught a glimpse of Brett waiting for her. For a moment, her vision grew fuzzy, the guests on either side fading away, and in her mind's eye all she saw was Caleb. She pictured him standing at the altar waiting for her, smiling that silly goofball grin he got on his face when he told her he loved her, looking gorgeous as ever in his tux with his blond hair combed back off his face and his blue eyes radiating love. The fog cleared and reality crashed in around her — and she began to shake, sick to her stomach.

If only it was you, Caleb.

Theo, as if knowing what was going through her mind, squeezed her hand for added support. She smiled up at him and nodded in acknowledgement of the gesture.

They began their walk down the cream-colored aisle and Syd took in her surroundings. It was the first time she'd seen the venue, since Brett had taken care of the majority of the details himself. The ballroom at the hotel was stunning—ornately crafted walls and detailed cornices drew in one's attention and the crystal accents were simply breathtaking. She could envision many weddings taking place in such beautiful surroundings—just not *hers*.

Yet, here she was.

As they approached the altar, they passed Cara, whose face was a mix of sadness and pain. She took a deep breath and winked at her, trying to silently reassure her that everything would be okay.

When they reached Brett, her father and brother took their seats and she turned to face the man she was about to marry. He clasped her hand in his and whispered, "We will be fine," his voice hard.

The small, gray-haired officiant smiled warily at them, obviously sensing the tension in the air, and instructed them to face each other. "We are gathered here today..."

Syd tuned him out—she had no desire to listen to his musings on love, life and relationships.

She glanced around the room and spotted Melanie sitting with her parents. The poor girl looked as if she was about to heave. Mrs. Hudson had a smile pasted on her lips and, to anyone else, she must have appeared to be the thrilled mother of the groom. Now that Syd had an inkling of what really went on in the recesses of the woman's life, she could easily see that the smile was in fact a carefully placed mask. The sadness in her eyes betrayed that mask, though, and the cracks and imperfections were visible to Syd. It was as if she knew what Sydney had in store for her with Brett. Mr. Hudson had that self-satisfied smirk on his lips, exactly as he had the night she'd visited their house for dinner. It was as if he'd won the lottery or placed a bet on the winning horse.

Disgusting.

The officiant cleared his throat. "Sydney?"

She turned to stare at him.

"Sydney, do you take Brett to be your husband, to live together with him in the covenant of marriage?"

She glanced at Theo—he was trying so hard to be strong for her, but the expression on his face said it all. He was devastated by what was about to happen.

"Do you promise to love him, comfort him, honor and keep in him sickness and in health, forsaking all others to be faithful unto him as long as you both shall live?"

She turned to her father. His eyes were shiny with unshed tears and he appeared as miserable as she felt, the sadness and worry taking over his features.

Oh, Papa.

She dragged her eyes away from him and faced Brett. "I—"

"No! Stop! Stop this right now! Nikoleta, you cannot do this," her father cried. He rushed to the altar and placed a frail hand on her arm. "You mustn't."

She covered his hand with hers, trying to soothe him. "It's okay…"

He shook his head adamantly. "It is not. Whatever happens, let it. But I won't… I can't… I… I…"

His face went white and beads of sweat broke out across his brow. "Nikki," he rasped, his eyes wide with panic.

"Papa!"

He clutched his chest and went limp in her arms, crumpling to the floor.

* * * *

While Caleb bolted from room to room gathering items he needed for the trip, his brother called the small airstrip that stored Divine Intervention's private jet and ensured it would be ready to go as soon as Caleb arrived. Lilly rushed around with her uncle, taking things from his hands and stuffing them into the overnight duffel he'd tossed on the bed.

He stopped mid-stride, picked her up and gave her a huge kiss on her forehead. "Best niece ever," he whispered, hugging her tightly.

She beamed. "I know."

He was grabbing a few things from the bathroom when his brother literally slid into the room, making Lilly erupt into giggles.

"Okay, jet will be ready for you. What else do you need me to do?"

Caleb nodded toward the green notepad that sat on his dresser. "Somewhere in there is Jenny's number, from Christou's. Can you call her and find out where the wedding is taking place?"

"On it!" PJ snagged the small pad and whisked out of the room, his daughter following him.

Caleb zipped the black duffel bag and swung it over his shoulder. He grabbed his car keys, wallet and phone, and headed downstairs. Pat was still on the phone with Jenny.

"No, I understand that," he said. "Yes, I know it's a family event, but that's the thing, see? We're supposed to be there." He shot a glance at his brother and rolled his eyes. "Well, no, we don't have an invitation, Jenny. That's why we're calling *you*, honey." A pause. "That's exactly right, and Mr. Christou asked us to surprise his daughter at the reception and sing a song or two." Pat let his tongue hang out the side of his mouth and crossed his eyes — Lilly had to cover her mouth to muffle her laughter. "I would really appreciate it, honey. I do. Yuh huh…" He grabbed a pen and began scribbling furiously on a blank page in Caleb's notepad. "I got it. You, Jenny, are one amazing lady. I owe you."

He placed the handset back in the cradle and tore out the page he'd written on. "Now go," he said, giving it to his brother.

He took a deep breath and gave PJ a quick hug. "Here goes nothing."

"Uncle Caleb!" Lilly called as he stepped out the door.

"Do you have your passport?"

His eyes widened, realizing he hadn't taken it with him. "Canada. Different country. Got it. Right," he mumbled, rushing by them and heading toward his office. A moment later he was back and tucking it into his bag.

He smiled at PJ. "I swear, that kid of yours. What would I do without the two of you?"

"Crash and burn," Pat called out as Caleb sat behind the wheel. "Now go get your girl!"

That was exactly what he intended to do.

* * * *

It was a short five-minute commute to Vancouver General Hospital from the hotel. They'd been there, waiting for information about her father, for nearly an hour now, and panic was beginning to take root in Syd's heart. Every time a doctor or nurse came out, they looked at them expectantly, but they would tend to someone else in the waiting room instead. It was a surprisingly light night in the ER and the room was emptying quickly as each person was taken in.

Theo was quietly frantic, pacing the room so much it was a wonder he hadn't worn a dent in the tile. Syd, perched on a chair and wringing her fingers, watched her brother as he moved about. Surely he was expending enough nervous energy for the both of them. Melanie was sitting on one side, Cara on the other, both speaking in hushed tones, trying to calm and reassure her that her father would be perfectly fine.

Mr. and Mrs. Hudson were there too — the former tapping his foot impatiently, as if put out by having to be there, and the latter staring at her hands, her face unreadable.

Brett sat off to the side, away from everyone, his expression guilt-ridden. Every so often he'd glance her way, but other than that he was unmoving, and said not a word.

Good.

At long last a doctor came out and approached their small

group. "Mr. Christou's family?"

Syd jumped out of her chair, and Theo skidded to her side. "That's us," they said in unison. "We're his children," Syd explained.

He nodded and held out his hand in introduction. "I'm Dr. Eddleson, the attending physician for your father and—"

"How is he, Dr. Eddleson?" Theo interrupted.

"Your father suffered a minor heart attack. He'll be okay—"

"Oh, thank God!"

"But please realize he may not be as lucky next time. Has he been under any stress recently?"

Theo narrowed his eyes and Syd shot Brett a glance. He was standing on the outskirts of the small group, his head lowered, a frown plastered on his lips. "A tremendous amount of stress," she answered.

She could have sworn Mr. Hudson rolled his eyes.

The doctor nodded again and jotted something in the file he held. "He needs to be removed from that stressful environment immediately. His heart is weakened and the next attack, if one comes, might not be as kind to him." He closed the folder and smiled at them. "He's resting peacefully. You can go see him, if you like, but only for a minute."

"That would be great," she breathed.

He smiled softly. "I'm sorry this had to happen, let alone on your wedding day. Your father is going to need all the love and strength you can offer him when he wakes, so might I suggest you head home and change into something a little more comfortable?"

Cara came up behind Sydney. "I'll give you guys a lift."

"By the time you get back to the hospital we'll have moved your father out of the ER and to a private room— ask one of the nurses for his room number when you arrive. When he's moved, Dr. Sagnet will be taking care of him, but feel free to have someone page me should you have any questions in the interim."

"Thank you so much, Dr. Eddleson," Theo said, taking his hand again and shaking it.

The doctor squeezed Syd's shoulder reassuringly. "Your father will be fine, and soon enough he'll be able to celebrate your marriage with you. Follow me, I'll show you where your father is."

She pasted a smile on her face. "Thanks."

As they started down the hall, Brett suddenly touched Syd's arm. She turned to him, and he couldn't even meet her gaze. His head tucked, he whispered, "I'm...I'm so sorry this happened."

"It's too late to be sorry, Brett. It's too late for a lot of things," she responded, turning away from him and going to check on her father.

Chapter Forty-Four

Pat, the saint that he was, had had the foresight to have a car waiting for Caleb at the airport when he arrived in Vancouver. All he had to do after he disembarked was go through customs and security, snag the keys from the rental kiosk and hop in the car. Behind the wheel, he pulled out the address for the Rosewood Georgia Hotel and punched it into his GPS. He took one last look at the note from Cara, then put the car into drive.

I'm coming to get you, Syd.

It wasn't long before he arrived at the hotel. After parking in the underground lot, he walked as fast as possible to the elevators. When he reached the main floor, Caleb began the hunt for the Spanish Ballroom, where the reception was taking place. The ceremony had happened hours ago, but if he was able to get to her, convince her to talk to him, and if he could understand *why* she'd done what she'd done, and what was going on… maybe, just maybe, it wouldn't be too late for them.

He skidded to a stop in front of the room and opened the heavy doors, expecting to see a crowd of people milling about, dancing and chatting at tables…but the room was empty save for one female employee and a dozen scattered tables, white table cloths bunched into the center of each. He was stunned — it was only eight o'clock in Vancouver — there should have been at least a handful of drunken guests wobbling about on the dance floor.

He wove through the tables and tapped her on the shoulder. "Excuse me, I was wondering if you might be able to help me out?"

She turned to him, and a shock of recognition flashed in her brown eyes. "I, oh my God, you're, it's…"

He smiled warmly. "Hi."

"Caleb Jones!" she squeaked, quickly smoothing her hair and licking her lips.

"That's me," he grinned.

She straightened her back and thrust out her chest. "What can I do for you?" she asked, her voice dropping an octave or two. She batted her eyelashes and pouted.

He groaned internally. He did not have time for this.

"The Christou-Hudson wedding. Did the party end early or have they moved to another room or venue?"

Her face went pale and a small hand fluttered to her throat. "Oh… Oh dear, you're here for that. Didn't you hear?"

"Hear? Hear what?"

"Mr. Christou, the bride's father, suffered a heart attack in the middle of the ceremony!"

"What?" He frowned, picturing the vivacious, friendly older man.

"Yeah," she continued. "They didn't even get to say 'I do' or anything. They halted the ceremony and sent everyone home. He was rushed to the hospital."

"Do you know which hospital they took him too?"

"Vancouver General," she answered. "It's pretty close to the hotel."

He leaned in to give her a kiss on the cheek. "Thanks, darlin'."

He bolted from the room and headed to the parking lot, leaving the poor girl standing there, her face bright red and mouth hanging open. When he got back to his car he sat behind the wheel a moment before driving away. His emotions were running rampant and he wasn't sure how he *should* feel.

From his brief interaction with Syd's father, he'd seemed like a genuinely warm person and had taken an instant liking to him. Deep down, given the chance, he believed they would get along without a hitch. His heart broke for

Sydney and her brother for what they were going through.

At the same time…

She's not married.

His heart soared at the thought. It was as if the fates, however cruel to her father, had bestowed upon them another chance to talk and maybe—hopefully—figure things out.

But what should he do? Did he dare try to hunt her down at the hospital—if only to be a shoulder and show he still cared for her?

Or should he keep his distance given the new development?

* * * *

Not even a half-hour had passed since Cara had dropped Syd and Theo off at her house to change out of their wedding attire and into more sensible clothing. Cara had gunned it home to do the same, and would be back straightaway to bring them back to the hospital. Syd insisted she and Theo eat something to help keep up their strength, but once the food was plated and in front of them, neither could stomach it.

Theo was back at walking to and fro restlessly, clearly agitated and muttering a continuous stream of expletives and threats of all the horrible things he was going to do to Brett. Syd let her brother get the anger out of his system and sat quietly. Her mind was overwhelmed with all that had happened—telling Melanie the truth, her discussion with Brett, then Melanie recounting what had happened to them all those years ago…

The guilt-ridden expression on his face as they were leaving the hospital told her that somehow, somewhere, the old Brett was still inside. Could she reach him before it was too late for herself *or* her father? While Dr. Eddleson had said that Papa would be fine, thank God, he also said he should not be exposed to any more stress. And the situation with Brett was nothing *but* stress — it was unavoidable, and it felt like a death warrant had been signed.

She was scared.

They heard a car honk outside the house and they raced for the door, Syd grabbing her purse along the way. She locked the house behind her and followed her brother to Cara's car. As soon as Syd buckled into the front seat beside her friend, she took off like a bat out of hell along the road.

"How are you guys holding up?" she asked, clearly worried.

Theo grunted a response and Syd answered, "We're keeping it together." She reached back and held her hand out to Theo, who looked at her with the sad brown eyes of an abandoned puppy and took it in his own. He squeezed her fingers and drew in a deep breath. "We have to keep it together for Papa," she continued. "We have to concentrate on *him.*"

He nodded, clearly understanding the unspoken message of her words — let go of the hate for Brett right now and instead focus getting their father on his feet and back home.

They arrived at the hospital ten minutes later, thanks to Cara's manic driving, and ran inside to check on their father while she parked the car. Theo was waiting by the elevators while Syd asked the nurse which floor their father had been moved to. Theo stabbed at the elevator call button when his sister returned to his side, and once the steel doors slid open, she hit the button for the third floor and texted Cara to let her know where they were.

When they made their way down the hall to their father's room they passed the small waiting area for that floor. Melanie was sitting in one of the dusty-blue armchairs, still decked out in her formal gown. Syd put a hand on Theo's arm, halting him for a moment. She nodded toward Melanie and they both walked over to her.

Syd sat beside her. "Melanie," she asked, her voice soft. "What are you still doing here? Why didn't you go home with your parents and Brett to change?"

"I wanted someone to be here in case he woke up and was scared," she whispered, glancing at her hands.

"Oh, honey." Syd looped her arms around the girl and hugged her. "You didn't have to do that."

Melanie looked up at her and nodded emphatically. "Yes, yes I did. It's like this is partially my fault. If I'd figured out sooner what Brett was up to, maybe there was a chance I could have helped you bring him to his senses and we wouldn't be sitting here right now." She swiped at a tear. "I'm so sorry, Syd."

"No, no, Mel, this isn't your fault, not even one iota. Please don't blame yourself."

She murmured a weak 'okay' and stood. "I'll go get Dr. Sagnet for you, and then grab a cab home to change. I'll be back soon."

Theo stopped her before she could run off. "Thank you for staying," he said, his expression warm.

She smiled at him, then took off toward the elevators.

A moment later a short balding man waddled toward them. "Mr. Christou's kids?" he asked, his voice higher-pitched than Syd would have expected.

They nodded.

He pushed his small round spectacles up his nose and smiled warmly. "Your father is doing quite well. He's stable and resting comfortably. Don't be worried that he's still sleeping—the heart attack took a toll on him and his body needs the break. Go on and have a visit with him. I'll come talk to you in a little bit to go over a few details."

They thanked Dr. Sagnet and followed him down the hall and around the corner to their father's room. When they opened the door and walked in, Syd was overwhelmed and had to lean against the frame, suddenly weak. Theo put his arm around her waist and brought her to a chair beside their father's bed, then moved to stand on the opposite side. They took hold of their father's hands, and gazed across the bed at each other.

He seemed so frail lying there under the thin white

bedsheet. His skin was pallid and cool to the touch, and once again Syd was struck at how weak he'd gotten these past few months. How could they have turned a blind eye to all the signs their father's health was failing this much? Guilt enveloped her and she brought his hand to her lips, kissing it softly, while all the machines he was hooked up to whirred and beeped away.

"He's going to be fine," Theo stated, eyes focused on his father, unshed tears in his eyes.

"Please be okay, Papa," Syd whispered. "We need you."

Chapter Forty-Five

He had woken up half an hour later, with his children at his side, and, in true Papa fashion, was more concerned about them than he was about his own wellbeing. Dr. Sagnet was called in and was extremely pleased to see him awake and lucid. He provided them with information on when their father would likely be released and what regimen he'd need to follow once back at home. When they were done chatting, he ordered them out of the room, stating their father needed rest and slumber, and they reluctantly followed his direction.

When they came back to the small waiting area, everyone had returned—Mr. and Mrs. Hudson were sitting on one side, Cara and Melanie across from them, and Brett was off by himself once again, staring out of the window into the black night.

Mrs. Hudson beat everyone to the punch. "How is he doing?"

Syd took the lead in replying. "He was awake and coherent, and is trying to get as much rest as he can right now. If things keep going as they are, he should be able to come home in a couple days."

Theo plopped into the chair next to Cara and let out a long sigh of exhaustion. "The doc says that he'll need a couple months to recover fully."

Cara placed a hand on his knee. "That's good. Then he'll be back to normal?"

"Sort of," Syd answered, gnawing on her thumbnail. "Dr. Sagnet said that though he'll seem okay, and just a bit more tired than usual, that he needs to go slow and get into a very low-key routine. He needs to take it easy, rest a lot and reduce stress." She shot a glance at Brett, who had turned to listen, and he quickly averted his gaze. "He'll need to talk to a dietician and someone else to help him get into some kind of exercise regime so he can gain some strength back."

Mr. Hudson bounced out of his chair and clapped his hands together. "Ah, good, everything is going to be fine then, yes?" He smiled broadly. "If he'll be home in a few days, we can go ahead and rebook the wedding for next weekend."

"James!" Mrs. Hudson cried out.

He ignored his wife. "Of course, it won't be anything quite as lavish as what Brett had planned for today, but, as inconvenient as all this was, things happen. What's more important is that you become Brett's wife post-haste. Right, son?"

To Syd, those last two words had a menacing undertone, and came out with forced cheer. He nailed his son down with his sharp gaze.

Brett looked away and mumbled, "Yes, Father."

"Inconvenient?" Theo ground out and stood to face Mr. Hudson. "Inconvenient? I'm sorry my father being in a hospital bed has caused such a disruption in your fucking plans, Hudson! I—"

Once she recovered from the shock, Syd interrupted her brother's tirade. "That will *not* happen."

"Damn right it's not happening," Theo barked. "We're not jumping into anything before Papa is totally better and out of the woods."

"Theo's right," she agreed. "Our father just had a heart attack. A *heart attack*! How could you be so cruel to even suggest this?" She motioned to the room around them. "We're still in the hospital, for God's sake! What's wrong with you?"

"Brett," Mr. Hudson said tightly. "Manage your future wife."

Brett remained silent, staring at his feet.

"Manage her?" Theo said incredulously. "Are you fucking kidding me?"

Sydney frowned and kept her eyes on Brett.

Doesn't he see this is all so wrong?

"Please, Theo," Mr. Hudson laughed. His tone condescending, he went on. "Do you really believe these women don't need to be managed by us men? That they don't need a firm hand to keep them and their emotional outbursts in check?" He huffed. "Brett knows this, I've raised him like a real man."

"Dad, stop it!" Melanie whispered.

He sneered at Theo. "Your father obviously hasn't done the same for you. I see how you look at her," he said, nodding at Cara. "Completely pussy-whipped."

"Hey!" Cara cried out in indignation.

Theo's face went red and he took a step toward Brett's father, his fists clenched and ready to strike.

Syd turned his face toward hers and shook her head. "He's not worth it, Theo. Focus on Papa," she said, the words instantly calming him.

"Dad," Melanie whispered. "No, Dad, how can you say all this?" She started to sob. "Mom? Is… Is it true? All this time, all those bruises…?"

Her mother was devastated.

"These women," Mr. Hudson spat out the word. "They think as long as they spread their legs for you they can get away with anything, but no," he laughed. "Oh no, not with this man, not with Hudson men. My father taught me how to be a strong man and head of the household, how to keep my wife well-behaved and how not to bend to every feminine whim. Your mother knows her place and how to behave, and by God, Melanie, when the time comes for you to get married, you'll do the same, I'll make sure of it. I'll teach your husband, as I've taught Brett. And *you* will bend to *him*."

Mrs. Hudson jumped to her feet. "Enough!" That one word, though softly spoken, held such power and authority everyone immediately hushed and turned to face her. Her husband glared at her with potent animosity. Tears streaming her face, she repeated, "Enough."

"Mom," Melanie said, reaching out and holding her hand.

"For years—*years*—I've dealt with you because I was made to feel worthless, nothing more than a speck of dirt on the ground. I have been less your wife than I have your punching bag, James. But I stayed. I didn't want to believe you could be like that forever, and I stayed because I thought it was the only way to keep my family together and my children safe. I thought I had no choice."

"How dare you, Anna."

She looked toward her children, her gaze settling on her son's sad face. "When you said you would make sure Melanie would go through the same hell that I've been through with you... When I could at last open my eyes and see what you've done to my son, my baby boy, I finally had the strength I needed." Her face hardened. "I see everything now, and clearly. I am done with you, James. Done."

"What?" he spat at her. "You don't get to say—"

"Yes I do." With everything coming out in the open, she appeared to gain confidence from the silent support and encouragement all around her. She straightened her back and held her head high. "I want a divorce, James. As soon as we get home I'm packing my things and walking out of that door, and there's nothing you can do to stop me."

"You can stay with me, Mom," Melanie said, hugging her.

Syd, Theo and Cara stood there, glancing from one party to the next, none saying a word. How the day had gone so quickly from wedding to divorce astonished her.

Mr. Hudson appeared flabbergasted, and sputtered nonsensical words for a moment. "You'll do no such thing," he managed. "How dare you even speak to me like that?" He advanced on her, his hand raised.

Brett snapped out of his trance and jumped in between his mother and father, blocking him. "No!"

His father bared his teeth. "Move. Now."

He shook his head. "No. I'm not twenty-two anymore, Dad, and you can't bully and manipulate me. This time I don't have a twelve-year-old sister to protect. This time I'm not scared for Mom, and worried about what will happen to them if I left. I'm taking Mom's lead and getting out from under your thumb once and for all. This time I can, and *will*, stop you."

His father's brow furrowed and he retorted, "No, you won't. You don't have the balls to stand up to me, just like you didn't when you were younger. You'll see when you marry her," he said, nodding toward Sydney. "This is exactly the type of strength you will need."

"There won't be a wedding," he answered quietly, shooting her a quick glance.

"Oh my God," she whispered, clutching Theo's arm.

Could it finally be over?

He turned back to his father. "You've lost, Dad. Go home and lick your wounds."

Mr. Hudson visibly deflated. The bully at last put in his place, it was as if he wasn't sure how to handle being confronted and losing. His tail tucked, he retreated and tried to get the last word in. "You'll come running back to me, Anna, of course you will, and useless Melanie will tag along because it's all she knows how to do. And Brett— when you get married and your slut of a wife has you wrapped around her little finger, you'll *wish* you still had me around to help you control her!"

"You will *not* be missed," Brett said, his voice even. When his father had left, Brett turned to his mother. "Mom... Mom, I should have protected you. I should have been stronger."

Tears flowed freely and she cupped his cheek affectionately. "My beautiful boy is back," she murmured. "It was I who should have done the protecting."

Theo and Cara exchanged a glance. "What the fuck just happened?" he whispered to her.

"Something wonderful," was her reply.

Mrs. Hudson hugged her children tightly, the trio alternately crying and speaking in hushed tones. Brett gazed at Sydney over his mother's shoulder. "I'm so sorry, for everything."

She nodded.

His mother pulled away and looked from Syd to Brett and back again. "I don't understand, though. Why won't there be a wedding?"

"I'll explain everything later, Mom. Suffice it to say this was all Dad's idea, and we work much better as friends than we ever could hope to as husband and wife."

She sounded concerned. "Are you happy, though?" She touched his cheek and glanced at Sydney again.

"I am now, Mom."

"Oh, Brett!" Melanie cried, throwing her arms around her brother's neck. "I'm so proud of you!"

Theo and Cara pulled Syd in for a hug of their own.

"We're free," Theo whispered into her hair. "We're finally free."

Melanie snuck into their hug. "And I have my brother back."

"Looks like you do," Syd said, smiling.

Mrs. Hudson came up behind them. "Okay, break it up, it's my turn." She smiled and hugged Sydney in a warm embrace. "You will always be like a daughter to me, whether you marry Brett or not. If you ever need anything— *anything*—you come right to me, okay?"

Syd unable to hold back the tears, nodded in response. "Thank you, Mrs. Hudson. Are you going to be all right?"

She beamed. "I'm better than I've been in over thirty years, my dear. But...you and Brett..."

"I'll tell you everything once we get you out of that house, okay, Mom?" Brett wrapped an arm around her shoulder. "Just know that things are fine, and as cliché as it sounds, I guess everything happens for a reason. Now go get started packing."

She hooked her arm in Melanie's. "Don't be too long."

When they had gone, Brett stood rooted to the floor, awkwardly staring at Sydney.

Cara grabbed Theo's arm and dragged him away from them, toward the window. "Um, let's give them a little privacy."

"Did you really mean it, Brett?" she asked, her voice uncertain. "Are you calling all this off?"

"What I did," he started. "Everything I did was wrong. I was under his thumb, his influence for so long... What I was doing was horrible but Father pushed for it, encouraged it, and was proud of me for it. He trained me to believe that this was how a real relationship worked, even though deep down inside I knew it was wrong." He moved closer to her, and met her gaze with the saddest eyes she'd ever seen. "He told me we needed to... You know, have sex... To seal the deal. That was the night I drank myself silly and...and I attacked you."

He paused a moment, the expression on his face that of self-loathing. "It wasn't until Mom finally stood up for herself that I realized how messed up it all was. I admit I'll need help. I'll need to talk to someone, to undo the...the brainwashing, because I'm not sure what else to call it. I'll need someone to help me remember how to be who I was when we first met, and to be a better person." He reached out to hug her, then let his arms hang limply at his sides. "Please know how deeply sorry I am for all of this, Sydney. Every last bit—I treated you abhorrently and I'll never forgive myself for that."

She flung herself at him and hugged hard. "You called me Sydney," she whispered.

He laughed softly. "Yeah, I guess I did. I haven't done that since we dated." He pulled away to look at her. "I will never, ever be able to apologize enough, though. And the knowledge I have... It will go nowhere. Not now, not ever. I've made sure all paper and electronic files were destroyed, Sydney. Everything is gone, and I will make certain it never haunts you again. It's over."

She began crying again in earnest and held him tighter. "Thank you, Brett," she whispered, her eyes closed and rested her head on his shoulder.

When she opened her eyes again, she saw Caleb standing at the end of the black and white tiled corridor. His expression was stony and he shook his head in disgust as he turned to leave.

A fraction of a second later he had rounded the corner and was gone.

Chapter Forty-Six

Sydney pulled away from Brett. "No," she murmured.

He was plainly confused. "What's wrong?"

She shook her head and continued to stare down the now-empty hallway.

"Syddie?" Cara asked, coming up beside her.

"What is it?" Theo asked, concerned.

"Caleb," she managed to croak out. "I... I thought I saw..."

"Oh, shit!" Cara cried out, frantic. "I'll be right back." She bolted along the hall and out of sight.

"Who's Caleb?" Brett asked.

"Hey, Brett, man, we're all cool now, right?" Theo said, saving his sister from having to answer that question. "I mean, we're not *cool*, but we're better. We really need some alone time with our father and stuff, and shouldn't you be with your mom right now? If your dad is home when your mom and Mel get to the house..."

"You're right. I've got to get there in case they need backup." He turned back to Syd. "Hey, are you okay if I maybe call you tomorrow to check on your dad?" he asked hesitantly.

"Of course."

He frowned. "When your father is doing better, I'd love to sit and talk, the four of us, and explain everything."

"Sounds like a plan," Theo said, his voice full of forced cheer. "You better get going!"

Alone at last, he turned to his sister. "Okay, what's this about Caleb?"

"I thought he was standing right there, no more than ten

feet away, and then he was gone. I... I'm sure it was him."
She shook her head in dismay. "Just when things begin to
turn around for us, I start to go crazy seeing things," she
tittered.

"Hey now, come on, sis. This hasn't exactly been a normal
day in the life of. A lot of shit happened and you still need
to absorb everything that's gone on. Hell, I do, too. Try to
relax." He settled her into one of the chairs that dotted the
floor's waiting area. "Papa will be out of the hospital soon,
and we can go back to leading normal lives again — without
fear or limitations. Especially you."

"You're right," she agreed. "My mind... So much going
on... It had to have been my mind playing tricks on me."

* * * *

Unbelievable.

He crumpled Cara's letter into a ball and stuffed it into his
pocket as he stalked toward his car in the hospital parking
lot. When would he ever learn that anything involving
Sydney Bennett meant heartbreak for him? He never
should have allowed himself to get sucked back into her
little games. He dreaded telling Lilly the bad news — she'd
had such high hopes for this reunion.

So did I.

The first thing he was going to do when he got back home
was burn that goddamn painting.

"Wait!" he heard from behind him. "Caleb, wait!"

He glanced over his shoulder to find a pretty blonde
chasing him down.

"Oh, awesome, another fan found me," he muttered,
increasing his pace to a steady jog.

"For God's sake, man," she yelled. "I'm wearing heels
that I can barely walk in, let alone run in, and I can't catch
up to you. Have some pity!"

While that did make him chuckle, her plea in no way
slowed him down.

He heard the steady click-clack of her heels slow to a stop, and she called out, "Caleb Jones, you insufferable, stubborn man. You stop running from me this instant!"

He froze. "What the hell?" He turned to catch a glimpse of her. She was bent over, her hands on her knees, wheezing and trying to catch her breath.

She met his gaze. "Oh, thank God." She righted her position and raised her index finger, pointing at him. "I don't care who you think you are, or what bloody band you're in—even if it *is* my absolute favorite—you will stay put and you will listen to me for one fucking minute."

He smirked and, his curiosity piqued, took a couple steps toward this mystery woman. "What's your deal?" he shouted to her.

She started walking toward him again, much more slowly this time due to a slight limp. "I twisted my frigging ankle because of you," she said when they were in reasonable talking distance. She shook her head. "The things I do for a friend. I take it you got my note?"

"Your note?" he asked, puzzled. Then the lightbulb clicked on. "You're Cara?"

"Duh," she laughed.

The smile left his lips. "Yeah, listen, Cara. Thanks for trying and all, but there's absolutely nothing to talk about." He moved to turn away from her.

"Whoa! Whoa, whoa, whoa there, buddy! I did not just run after you like a mad woman in four-inch heels for nothing." She continued limping her way over to him. "There has been a lot—and, by a lot, I mean a shit-ton—of stuff going on with Syd for a year now. All hell broke loose today… Actually, it's more like all hell broke loose twenty minutes ago. If there was *ever* a good time for you to show up, it would be now."

His shoulders slumped in resignation. "I really do appreciate you trying to help smooth things over with me and Syd. Really, I do." The next words he spoke pained him to the core. "But Syd and I, we're finished, and there's no going back."

"Don't say that."

He faced her. "Cara, it's true. Look, I don't even know you, but I see how much Sydney loves you. I'm not so sure how happy she'd be with you trying to convince me to go in there and face her at the moment. She's with Brett. She chose Brett. She didn't choose me, and it is what it is. So please, just let me go home."

She hobbled closer to him and put her hands on his arm, giving a gentle squeeze. "No, but that's the thing, Caleb. It is *not* what you think it is. She loves you, Caleb."

"Bullshit," he said, anger and hurt bubbling up inside him. "She loves me so much, that's why she was cozied up to her fiancé in there, right? Because she loves me oh so much? Don't even try to sell me that line. I won't buy it anymore."

"She *does*," Cara interjected. "She does love you more than anything…but she couldn't do anything about it. Her hands were tied, I swear."

"And what the hell is that supposed to mean?"

"It means that with everything that went down tonight, she's ready to talk to you, and since you came all this way, maybe you could suck it up, buttercup, and *let* her try to explain. Even if you only give her a couple minutes," she pleaded.

"Shit," he muttered as he ran a hand through his hair. He was torn. He had no idea if he should bother going back inside to talk to Sydney. He anticipated the heartache he'd undoubtedly have to deal with—yet again—but at the same time, he owed it to himself to give her a chance to enlighten him as to what the *fuck* was going on. All along he'd said he wanted the truth, that he wanted answers and closure, and this was his opportunity to get just that.

He let out a little growl. "Fine, I'll give her five minutes, but that's it."

Cara squealed like a four-year-old on Christmas morning and threw her arms around Caleb's neck, hugging him hard. "Oh my gosh, you're as awesome as she always said you were. This is going to be great!"

"Yeah, don't get your hopes up, Cara. All I said was that I would listen to her." He took her arm and helped her stagger across the parking lot, back toward the hospital. "I can't even imagine how her fiancé would react to me being there."

She laughed, and to Caleb's ears it was the sound of pure, unfiltered joy. She beamed up at him. "Oh, you mean ex-fiancé." She winked, and led a stunned, slack-jawed Caleb into the building.

Chapter Forty-Seven

Syd sat in the waiting room chair her brother had settled her into, bouncing her leg up and down at a furious pace, her nerves getting the better of her. She glanced toward the hall that led to the elevators, anxiously waiting for Cara to come back. Then she turned her attention toward her father's room, waiting for Theo to come back. He had gone to check on Papa one last time for the night when a nurse came around and informed them visiting hours were coming to an end.

Worried that they would be told to leave right when Cara was returning, Theo had used his charms on the pretty nurse and asked her if they could stay a little bit longer, and she acquiesced. Her consent came with a firm deadline, though—they had fifteen minutes, and not a moment longer.

Syd looked down the hallways, looked down at her hands, looked out of the window—she was unable to sit still and she couldn't stand the waiting. If Cara had managed to find Caleb what on earth she would say to him—if he would even bother talking to her?

Part of her was still unconvinced she wasn't going bonkers and, in fact, hadn't seen him at all, and the more and more the clock ticked on silently, she was further convinced it was the latter. She'd probably sent her friend out on a wild goose chase, and she'd never let her live it down.

Theo was suddenly in front of her, and placed both hands on her knees to stop the incessant bouncing. Her eyes flicked up to meet his. "How's Papa?"

"Sound asleep. The nurse said she'd call us if there were

any problems, but he's strong and she doesn't anticipate any. We can come back and see him first thing in the morning."

Syd nodded. "Okay." She chewed on a fingernail, and her legs became active once again.

"Oh my God, please stop with the bouncing," Theo begged. "You're shaking the whole floor and it's driving me crazy."

"Yeah, sorry," she answered absently. She got out of the chair and began the pace the small room.

"Gah!" he cried out, standing in front of her and resting his hands on her shoulders. "Calm. Yourself." He gave her a little squeeze. "You must calm yourself."

"But I can't, Theo. I mean, what if he really *is* here, and Cara found him and he's coming back here right now? What if he doesn't want to hear what I have to say, or he doesn't care and he's mad at me and just wants to see me tormented as I try to make him understand?" Her green eyes went wide and she took a breath before continuing her steady rambling. "What if the only reason he's coming back is to give me shit for everything that happened and that I had to tell him, and oh my God, I don't think I could handle that, Theo. I mean, not that I don't deserve it but…"

Theo clamped a hand over her mouth, putting an end to her hyperactive chatter. He grinned and spun her around so she was facing Cara—and Caleb. Cara practically pranced alongside him as they walked the last few feet to the sitting area. She was positively bursting with excitement.

She limped over to Theo and latched onto his arm, leading him away. "Come on, come on, let's get out of here."

"You know, the way you keep dragging me around is going to give a boy a complex," he joked, following her. "Hey, what happened to you?"

"Nothing," she answered. "I twisted my ankle, no biggie. Let's *go!*"

Their conversation continued as they walked down the hall and around the corner, until the words finally faded, leaving Syd and Caleb in silence. He gazed at her—she had no idea if he hated her or was thrilled to see her. His expression was neutral. She couldn't move, couldn't speak—couldn't do anything except stare at the man she loved and try so hard not to collapse in a mess of incoherent sobs and garbled choking sounds in front of him.

He hadn't said a word, and she didn't know what to do. "So, I…uh…" she began.

"How's your dad?" he asked.

She gazed into his blue eyes, thankful she didn't have to delve into the difficult stuff right off the bat. "He's holding up," she answered, her voice hardly more than a whisper. "He, uh, he had a heart attack, but the doctor thinks he'll recover and be okay."

Caleb nodded. "That's good."

"It is." She hesitated. "Um, Caleb…"

"Why don't we sit?" he asked softly.

She nodded and followed his lead, sitting side by side. She had never been so nervous in her entire life.

"Why didn't you tell me you were engaged?" he asked, getting right to the point.

"Oh, God," she sobbed instantly, covering her face. "Oh, God, I'm so sorry, Caleb. You have no idea what all this has done to me."

"Yeah, I 'm pretty sure I *do*, actually," he retorted, his voice hard.

I deserved that.

He pulled her hands away from her face. "Syd, look at me." Only when she met his eyes did he continue. "I loved you, Syd. What happened…it hurt me like hell. I deserve some honest answers."

He loved me. Past tense.

"I'm not even sure where to start."

"How about from where it all began? And don't leave anything out."

She nodded and spoke in a whisper. "I've been engaged since September of last year." The tension was palpable now and she was unable to meet his gaze, instead focusing her attention on the tiled floor. If she looked into those eyes — the eyes that used to be filled with such love for her — she wasn't sure she'd be able to go on. "I... I never wanted to be engaged. I don't love Brett. I couldn't imagine a life with him. And... And then I met you, Caleb, and everything changed."

"Hang on, back up a little there, Syd. If you never wanted to marry him, why did you accept his proposal?" he asked. "What could possibly drive someone to marry a man they don't love...? And give up someone they profess *to* love? I know his family is rich as fuck, and you said yourself the restaurants weren't doing all that awesome. Were you with him for the money?" He tensed, and prayed it wasn't for that reason. Because if it was...was that why she said she loved him, too? Because of his bank account?

"What? Oh, God no! I'm not that shallow, how could you even suggest that?"

He frowned. "Well, you *were* fucking me while you were engaged to another man. What do you expect me to think?"

"I deserved that," she whispered.

No you don't.

God damn it all to hell. Here she was, trying to explain everything to him, and all he wanted to do was kiss her.

"It was never money-related or anything. I was blackmailed into it, Caleb. Brett dug up some information about my father, and if it got out he would have gotten in trouble and would have been sent back to Greece. My family," she murmured. "It would have been torn apart." She gazed up at him. "I couldn't lose another parent, Caleb. I couldn't lose anyone else. But in the end I lost someone anyhow. Someone I love very much."

He remained quiet, waiting for her to continue.

She took a deep, shuddery breath and got to her feet. "My father...the stress of all this has put him in the hospital. Do you really believe I *wanted* any of this to happen? I was a horrible, wretched person who lied time after time to the man I had fallen deeply and unequivocally in love with, all because I was happy and selfish and didn't want to give it up." She began to cry again. "Now my father is lying in the hospital, hooked up to God knows how many machines, and you're sitting there looking at me like you hate me, and everything has gone to shit."

"I'm not quite sure what happened, Syd," he said, getting up to stand in front of her. "Everything you're saying, it's so disjointed and I can't make heads or tails of it yet. But you have to believe one thing," he said, leaning closer to her and brushing his lips on hers. "I could *never* hate you."

She broke down in a torrent of tears and collapsed against him. "But you *should* hate me," she rasped. "What I did to you..."

"Was every bit as bad as what I was doing to myself," he interrupted. "Syd, you tried to push me away so many times I've lost count. Did I ever listen? No. I kept refusing to see that something was so evidently wrong." He wrapped his arms around her, rubbing her back in soft circles, trying to help her get hold of herself. "Was the way the situation was handled right? No, absolutely not. But fact of the matter is this—I'm here now, Syd, and I want to understand."

She peered up at him through tear-dotted lashes. "Why did you even come here, anyhow?" she asked, her voice soft.

He grinned. "I received a little package from your friend Cara."

Her green eyes widened in surprise. "What? What did she send you?"

He reached into his pocket and pulled out the letter. "This," he said, holding it up. "And your painting of me."

"She... You... The painting," she stammered, her face beet red. "I can't believe she sent that to you!" She took a step back and plucked the paper from of his hands. She smoothed it out and scanned it, her eyes welling up as read.

"Excuse me," the pretty little brunette nurse interrupted.

"I'm sorry, it looks like you're in the middle of something, but visiting hours were over nearly twenty minutes ago. You have to head out now."

Syd nodded and thanked the nurse for her for letting them stay as long as she had. Sydney picked up her purse and started walking down the hall with Caleb at her side.

When they reached the elevator he said, "So, I understand from Cara that Brett is now your ex-fiancé?

"You understand correctly. A *lot* has happened today." She sounded exhausted. "We can sit downstairs in the main lobby and I can explain it all to you."

He cupped her chin. "How about we find some place more comfortable to finish this conversation?"

She studied him for a moment.

God, she's beautiful.

"We can go back to my place."

Chapter Forty-Eight

The drive back to her house had been uncomfortable and tense. There were still too many of Caleb's questions she had left unanswered, and she couldn't expect — nor did she believe she deserved — any of the kindness he'd displayed toward her in the hospital until she explained everything. He pulled into her driveway and the awkward silence that plagued them in the car was carried with them inside her home.

They sat on her couch — she was tucked away in one corner, with her legs folded underneath her, and he was all the way at the other end, one leg bent so that he was turned to face her. Puff, as excitable as ever, didn't know who to give love to first. She bounded back and forth between them on the cushions, delivering licks and paw-slaps and getting in some scratches behind the ears whenever she could. Her energy depleted, the little gold and cream pup climbed onto Syd's lap and curled into a ball.

She latched on to the small dog, gently stroking her fur, trying to soothe and calm herself. She was so thankful Caleb had come and was willing to let her explain. She had a feeling her story would garner sympathy from him, that he would be able to understand the predicament she had been placed in. Would he be able to forgive her, though? Having to marry someone due to blackmail was one thing. But carrying on for all those months as she had — that was something else altogether.

She was scared.

"Let me try this again," she said, taking a deep breath and forcing herself to be courageous. "And let me start from the very, very beginning, over twenty years ago."

"Over twenty years ago?" Caleb repeated, undoubtedly confused. "You got engaged last year, didn't you? You were only a kid back then — had the marriage been arranged since your youth?"

She raised her hand, putting a halt to his questions. "Let me explain."

She started slowly, recounting the story she'd told Melanie earlier that morning. She explained what her father had been through, how he'd had to take his son and run to a foreign country with nothing except what they could manage to carry. She described her relationship with Brett when she was in university, that everything had changed in an instant, and how even all these years later he couldn't handle her leaving him.

Saying all this, all over again...it was much harder than she thought it would be. By now this story should be old hat, but Syd found herself fighting tears on more than one occasion.

Each time she glanced at Caleb, there was a different emotion on his face. First it was sympathy, then horror, then confusion...and when she got to Brett, his face screwed up in jealously, rage and disbelief.

She shrugged. "And then you came along," she whispered, averting her eyes and focusing on her hands. She continued to smooth Puff's fur. "You came along and quite literally my whole world was turned upside-down. When...when I was with you, it was like nothing bad could ever happen. The world was suddenly *right*. It was as if none of this bad stuff had happened. Papa was safe and healthy, my brother was happy, and I was loved."

She glanced up at him, tears escaping and trickling along her cheeks. "You were my Superman, Caleb. You were exactly what I wanted, and everything I needed, in a friend, lover and partner. Back in Banff you were my escape from reality and from Brett, and as hard as it was to let go, I had to. It wasn't right, and although at that point I didn't realize how strongly I felt for you, I didn't want to cause you any pain, and so I said goodbye." She laughed softly. "But that goodbye didn't last very long, did it? You tracked me down."

His face a mix of emotions, he interrupted. "And knowing that inevitably you'd hurt me, you went along with it anyhow."

She frowned. "I did."

"Why? Why would you do that?"

Sighing, she answered, "When I read the note you left for me in the box with my earring my heart went wild, Caleb. I didn't call you because I knew beyond hope there was something special blossoming between us and I was terrified of it. From the moment you showed up at my door, that was it, you had my heart. We turned into so much more than I ever could have dreamed, and your love was like a drug — a painkiller almost — and I couldn't give you up."

"You couldn't but you did try to warn me, time after time."

"Caleb..."

"I couldn't give you up, either, Syd. I didn't want to." He shook his head. "I won't lie. When I walked into the restaurant in Toronto, I went there to find you and get closure on us. I needed to turn the last page on our story and close the book for good. That's what I kept telling myself, but in truth I had no idea how I'd react. When your dad introduced me to Brett and his daughter Nikoleta — when you came out, I had no idea what to think anymore."

"Nikoleta is my first name. I've always gone by my middle name, Sydney," she explained in a murmur.

He closed his eyes. "I started to wonder just who this Sydney person was. Was that even your real name? Was *anything* you said true, or was it all a fanciful fabrication? Was I a fling before you settled down? My mind spun in seventeen directions, and I had to get out of there."

I hurt him so much.

"I was done with you at that point, Syd," he continued.

"I couldn't talk about you, think of you, let alone say your name. My God, I was such a mess that Pat and my mom worried about me, and Lilly was asking about you left, right and center, wondering why you weren't around to make me feel better."

A sob caught in her throat. "I'm so sorry, Caleb."

"I'm not saying this to make you sad, Sydney. I'm trying to make you understand how much I loved you. What a wreck I was without you. If I was your Superman, you were my hero, too."

She played with Puff's fur, focused on her steady breathing and tiny little snores.

I will not break down again.

"And then a painting came along," he said, his tone gentle.

She met his gaze, his blue eyes alight with a fire she hadn't seen since he'd arrived. Hope sparked in her heart.

"The second I saw that canvas and read Cara's note, I had no choice in the matter. I had to fight for you. If you loved me the way Cara said you did, I had to come here and at least talk with you, at least try. I needed you to tell me if what we had was *real*."

"I still don't know if I should be livid with her for sending it to you, or grab her in a bone-crushing hug," Syd laughed shakily.

He grinned. "She already informed me that you were going to kill her."

"I have to admit, I kind of want to. But depending on what happens tonight, I might just suffocate her with undying affection instead."

Silence.

"Syd," he started slowly. "What ended up happening with Brett today? You managed to break things off? Will everything be all right with your father?"

"Actually, the break was mutual."

He blinked, completely taken aback. "What do you mean *mutual*? How could it be mutual after everything he's done? Why would he even consider putting an end to this when he had you right where he wanted you?

She nudged the sleeping dog, and Puff awoke with a startle, letting out a little bark of annoyance. Syd stood. "Can I get you a beer? We're going to need a drink for this part of the story." He nodded and she headed to the kitchen. "So here's where the story gets even more screwed up," she stated, rummaging around in the fridge.

"How is that even possible?" he muttered.

She came back into the living room with two opened bottles and handed one to him as she moved past. "Oh, it is, believe me." She took a long swig of the amber fluid before diving into the Hudsons' story. She told him everything she'd learned about Brett's father, what had made him change when they were together, and how his father was a big part of Brett blackmailing them. "In the end," she finished, "I guess seeing his mom finally having the strength to stand up for herself lent him the courage he needed to do the same. He confronted his father, and suddenly the wedding was off."

"And so you hugging him the way you were, earlier. That was about what exactly?" he asked, his voice tight.

"That was me thanking him for putting an end to this madness, and him apologizing to me over and over and over again."

"How does the word sorry even fit for a situation like this? There's not enough sorry in the whole goddamn world to make up for what he did," Caleb started getting angry.

"Believe me, sorry doesn't work all that well, not yet. Right now, I'm simply grateful for the fact this nightmare is over, and feeling blessed that Papa will be okay, given it could have been a hell of a lot worse." She sighed and placed her bottle on the coffee table. "You have to understand, Caleb, Brett was a really great guy before his dad sank his claws into him and twisted his mind. You actually would have really liked him."

He grunted in response.

She chuckled. "No, really. In a lot of ways you remind

me of how he used to be." She shrugged. "If he can manage to find his way back to his old self... I don't know. I might have it in me to fully accept his apology. I might not. I don't know." She shook her head. "All I know, CJ, is that we have come to a somewhat uneasy peace, and this war is over. I'm finally free of all the bullshit that has consumed my life for the past year. I am, at last, able to do as I please, without worrying about consequences or extradition or my father's failing health."

Tears flooded her eyes, and she bit her lip before continuing. "I can finally, freely, be with the person I want to be with most of all, Caleb. The person I would give anything to spend the rest of my life with."

He studied her as she spoke, his gaze unwavering.

"The question is, after everything I did, and everything I put you through, could you find it in your heart to give me — give us — another chance?"

She reached out and took his hand in hers. "I...I've missed you so much, Caleb, and I don't want our story to end. I'm terrified that now this is all out in the open and you have your explanation, you're going to leave, and I don't want you to go."

He remained silent, stoic.

"Stay, Caleb. Please...stay."

Epilogue

"The answer is still no."

"How on earth can it still be no?"

"I'm guess I'm just one stubborn son of a bitch." He grinned.

Syd flashed a smile back his way. "Funny that, so am I. And," she continued, sliding beneath the covers and kissing his hip, "I'm more than happy to continue working on convincing you to say yes." She ran her tongue from one side to the other and back again, stopping right below his navel.

He sucked in a shuddery breath. "Naw, baby, it takes more than a mere three hours to do that."

She popped her head out from under the covers and winked at him. "Well then, I'd best get to work, Mr. Jones."

"Please do," he rasped, grabbing a corner of the blanket and tossing it to the side, revealing them both.

She bit her lip and gazed up at him beneath hooded eyelids. She slid her arms up his torso and hooked onto his shoulders, using them as leverage to pull her body along his. She purred as her nipples glided across his chest, making the tender nubs instantly hard. She skimmed her tongue along his jaw line, pausing to bite his chin lightly, and gazed down on him.

He made a guttural sound and grabbed a fistful of her hair, bringing her mouth hard on his, kissing her deeply. "I don't think I'll ever get enough of you, baby," Caleb murmured.

"Prove it."

"With pleasure." He reached behind her and cupped her

rear, lifting her and bringing her to his lips. She gripped the headboard and leaned over him, now able to support herself, and freeing his hands for more important things. He slipped his fingers between the swollen folds of her sex and spread them apart, exposing the bundle of nerves that provided so much pleasure. He flicked his tongue on it, ever so lightly.

Her entire body quaked.

He did it again, harder this time, then drew it between his lips to gently suck on it. He knew exactly what to do to drive her crazy and he did it well. He moved his tongue lower and dipped inside, tasting her. He circled her core with his tongue while using his thumb to fiddle with her clit, sending jolts through her.

"God, Caleb, please don't tease."

He thrust his tongue inside her and increased the pressure and pace of his thumb. She tossed her head back and cried out, grinding down on him, needing more pressure. It only took a moment for Syd to spiral out of control, the orgasm hitting her hard. Caleb dug his fingers into her ass and continued drinking her in, as if parched.

Her arms weak, she let go of the headboard and crashed onto him. She rested her head on his shoulder, trying to catch her breath.

"Was that enough proof?" he whispered into her hair.

She turned her face to his and kissed him, relishing the taste of her juices on his lips. "Never," she answered, and tugged on his lower lip with her teeth.

"Fantastic answer, Ms. Bennett." He reached out and blindly felt around his nightstand till he found the small foil pack he was searching for. In seconds, he was ready for her, and he latched on to her waist, raising her and bringing her down onto his cock.

Syd moaned, the sensation of him moving inside her the way he did overwhelming her senses. "God damn, that feels amazing."

His blue eyes flared bright with desire. "I'm all yours,

baby."

Syd rocked back and forth, moaning each time her clit was engaged. Her hands flat on his chest, she lifted off him and watched him slide back inside. The urge to be filled to the hilt with his shaft was unbearable and she ground into him. He thrust up as she bore down, leaving her in a state of cathartic bliss. She wanted to tell him to go harder, but when she opened her mouth all that came out was a string of unintelligible noises. It was too good — when Caleb was inside her, it was heaven.

She gazed down at him, wanting to commit every detail to memory. His bronze skin was dotted with sweat — evidence that he was working as hard as she was — and the Florida sun shining in through the wooden slats of the blinds drew lines of gold along his body. His face, screwed up with passion as he pounded into her, was as beautiful to her as it had been the first time she had met him on that icy road.

There was Caleb, there was only Caleb, and there would only ever *be* Caleb for her.

Her love for him washing over her in a rush of raw emotion, Syd clenched around him and she came, screaming his name as the waves crashed into her.

"Fuck!" he yelled, pulsing inside Syd as he reached climax along with her.

Spent, Caleb gently rolled her off him, and pulled her into his embrace. He cuddled her close, brushed his lips on her dampened forehead, and traced his fingers, featherlight, along her spine. He brought her left hand to his lips and kissed the back of it. He held it up into the light and smiled.

The midday sun glinted and glittered off the diamond. She tipped her head to kiss his chin. "It's pretty, isn't it?"

"It's perfect, and so are you, almost-Mrs. Jones," he answered, a huge grin on his face. He played with her slender fingers while they spoke, twining his into hers, drawing a fingertip along her palm, then holding it to his cheek. He nuzzled into it. "So much has happened in the last six months."

"Mm-hmm," she agreed. "And now in a week I become Mrs. Caleb Jones. Crazy, eh?"

"Very."

"And pretty damn amazing."

"You don't miss home?" he asked, his voice soft.

"A bit," she admitted. "But I like it here, too, CJ."

He laughed. "Lord knows you certainly adjusted to Florida real quick."

"Well, living with an incredibly sexy man certainly makes it easier," she giggled.

"And, of course, let's not forget the copious amounts of mind-blowing sex whenever we're together."

She smiled at the thought. They weren't able to see each other as often as they'd like, even though they were living in the same house. Pat and Caleb had begun work recording Divine Intervention's new album, and that kept him busy at the studio. Syd was occupied herself with opening Miami's very own Christou's. However, when they were together, they most *certainly* made the most of it.

"Yes, the sex," she sighed. "That is a definite perk. I've never been in such great shape before."

"Well, you're gonna need to be in top form if I agree to this. You'll be doing nothing but running around."

She popped her head up. "Does that mean I managed to change your mind?" she asked eagerly.

He sighed. "I don't know, Syd. Are you really sure about this? It's a big step for us, and you want this so soon after the wedding…"

"Please," she begged. "I've wanted this for as long as I can remember, and the timing is perfect. The restaurants are picking up, and I don't need to be onsite all the time, so I travel only seldomly. Plus, I have an assistant now, so that helps free up loads of time."

He shrugged. "But think about all the pee and poop and clean-up, and the whining, and possibly waking at all hours of the night." He combed his blond hair off his face. He maneuvered himself into a sitting position and leaned against the headboard. "It's a ton of work."

"I promise you it won't be that bad," she replied, following suit and sitting cross-legged. She pulled the blankets over her chest.

No way am I letting the boobs distract him from this conversation. "Please, please, please!"

"Let's ask Puff," he suggested. CJ whistled and a thunder of paws sounded down the hall. The little dog clambered up the small stairs they'd placed by the bed and she landed on his chest rather gracelessly, making them both burst into a fit of giggles. "Puff," Caleb said, his expression serious. "Would you like to be a big sister?"

She stared at him, her black eyes unwavering, and her tongue lolling out of the side of her mouth. Her tail swished from side to side.

"Would you like a little brother or sister?" he asked again.

"Brother!" Syd commented. "Definitely a brother." She scratched her best pup behind the ears. "What do you say, Puffykins?"

She barked three times.

Caleb kissed the top of Syd's head. "Well, the master has spoken."

"Really?"

He nodded and smirked. "I get to name him, though."

She frowned. "Should I be concerned?"

"Nope, I already have a great name in mind."

"Which is?"

"Electro."

"What! You can't name him after a super-villain!"

"Aw, come on, Syd. It's the perfect name for a Pomeranian, don't you think?"

She burst out laughing. "I'm not sold on the name, buddy."

He suddenly leaned in to kiss her. "You can name him whatever you want, darlin'," he whispered, brushing his lips softly on hers again. "Whatever you want, so long as you stay with me forever, Syd. Just stay."

More books from
Totally Bound Publishing

Book one in the Secrets of Stone series

Once upon a time, there was a girl who dressed up and went to a big party at the palace. When she was there, she met a prince. They danced and fell in love…

Part of the What's her Secret? collection

Invisible. A ghost. No one sees her. No one knows her. Until him.

Two hearts, both broken… Two lives ready to be lived.

Book one in the Single in Seattle series

Finding the perfect cup of coffee in Seattle is easy. Finding a guy, not so much — unless that guy finds you…in the most unexpected way.

About the Author

Madison Night

Madison Night has fiddled with the written word for years — be it in song, story, or poem. A high school creative writing class piqued her interest in storytelling, and she's been writing ever since.

Madison's works have always included a romantic element, but recently she's found her niche in the world of hot, steamy, sensual erotic romance. Some have called her stories romantic mysteries, others call them real life sex on a page, and still others call them everything in between. To her, though, writing was simply a chance to pour heart and soul into words, bringing life to the not-so-innocent thoughts in her head, and getting the heart pumping a wee bit faster in the process.

A devoted mother of one human child and two fuzzy puppy children, Madison currently resides in Toronto, Ontario. In her spare time she sings and writes music, dabbles with interior decorating, and has a blast chasing her son around the house.

Madison Night loves to hear from readers. You can find contact information, website details and an author profile page at https://www.totallybound.com/

Home of Erotic Romance